Where the Heart Lands

Indie Artist Press | Brackettville, Texas

Where the Heart Lands

Marjorie Jones

Where the Heart Lands
A novel by Marjorie Jones
First Paperback Edition
ISBN: 978-1-62522-114-8
Copyright © 2016, 2017 Marjorie Jones
All Rights Reserved
December 2017

PUBLISHER INFO:
Indie Artist Press
Brackettville, Texas
www.indieartistpress.com

Printed in the United States of America

Look for these titles by Marjorie Jones

The Jewel and the Sword (Medallion Press)
My Lady's Will (Champagne Books)
The Lighthorseman (Medallion Press)
The Flyer (Medallion Press)
Hope (Indie Artist Press)
Dance in My Heart (Indie Artist Press)
Loving the Heartland (Indie Artist Press)

Writing as Starla Childs

Dawn of Love (Champagne Books)
Dawn of Redemption (Champagne Books)
Firelight (Indie Artist Press)

*If you enjoy reading Lacey and Brandy's story,
Where the Heart Lands, please consider leaving a
review on your favorite venue.*

For Anna

PROLOGUE

Everything was black. Her breath came in ragged, hurried gasps filled with the taste of gasoline and the scent of rust and toxins. Sirens sliced the throbbing silence with a distant shrill. Lacey forced her eyes open. A shaft of light illuminated crackled shards of glass interspersed with gravel and tiny pieces of sharply-broken plastic. Grey plastic.

The dashboard.

The laser-like beam of light shifted slowly, crawling across the roadway to reflect off a larger piece of glass partially obscured with blood. Lacey frowned. Where had the blood come from? She lifted her head and pain materialized from the blackness. Her head seemed as though it would split apart as she tried to move any part of her body, just to test what might still be there. What might be missing.

Toes worked. And her left calf, although she couldn't move her right one. She could feel it though, caught beneath something heavy.

Her stomach clenched, and the blackness threatened to overtake her. She was trapped.

The sirens were closer.

"Lacey? Can you hear me? We're gonna get you out. Just hang tight, alright? Stay with me."

The voice was familiar, but she couldn't quite place where she'd heard it before. Or when. Cracking one eye open, she couldn't see anything except broken road and blood. There was more now, pooling beneath her face. One of her eyes had begun to swell closed and it stung if she tried to open it. The voice was behind her. She couldn't turn around.

"Get the Jaws," the voice continued. "We're going to have to cut her out."

"Has anyone called her sister?" Another voice. Familiar. Beyond her grasp. A woman.

Kendra was going to be so pissed about the truck. She'd had this truck since before their Mom and Dad died. It was Dad's truck first, and he had given it to Kennie for her eighteenth birthday. Kennie loved this truck.

"Okay, Lacey…" The first voice was back. Why did people always use names when something was wrong? He'd called her by her name every time he'd spoken to her since the rescuers arrived. It was unnerving.

Annoying.

A face flashed in her memory. "Mike? Is that you?"

"Sure is, Little Bit. We're going to start cutting you out. You just lie still and we'll have you out of there in no time."

"No! No! Gas leaking. Sparks!" Her mouth filled with the bitter, metallic taste of blood and she spat the fluid out with a cough.

"It's okay. There won't be any sparks. You're going to get out of there. I promise."

A hand touched her shoulder. It was warm; heavy. She wanted to turn around, but she couldn't move. She could barely breathe. Mike squeezed his fingers and she winced. Everything... everything hurt.

An air pump churned nearby. A moment later the truck began to rock slightly. Not much, but enough to change the pressure on her leg. She screamed. Her mouth filled with blood again. She gagged and then spit it out, refusing to scream again. Gritting her teeth, she squeezed her good eye closed.

After what seemed like an eternity, the sunlight broke through the tangled mass of metal and broken glass to warm her face. The sky was red. The air was red. Something hard slid down her back and someone wrapped her neck and head in a huge, molded plastic brace.

She was on her back.

She was on a stretcher.

Mike hovered over her, his fireman's helmet casting a narrow shadow over his ruddy cheeks. He hadn't shaved that morning and a slight stubble accentuated his jawline. "How you doin'? You holding on for me, Lacey?"

Stop calling me by my name! Am I going to die?

"Not if I have anything to do with it, you're not.

She hadn't realized she'd spoken aloud.

"We're taking you to Mountain Vista. You remember Doc Carlson? Well, she's there waiting for you. She'll fix you right up." He raised his jaw and looked at someone or something above her head. "Did anyone get a hold of Kennie Williams, yet?"

"Not yet. We called the ranch and that lady from Las Vegas was there. She said she'd find Kendra and they'd meet us at the hospital."

Michelle. Her best friend. The woman her sister was falling in love with. At least Michelle would be there for Kendra. And her brothers. And her new sister-in-law. Oh, and the baby. Brad and Lenise had only been married yesterday and in a few months, they were going to have a beautiful baby. If it's a girl, maybe they'll name her Lacey...

"Knock it off, Lacey. You've got to keep fighting. If Brad and Lenise name their baby after you, it'll be because you're going to be the best damn aunt in the history of spoiled kids, right?"

Lacey nodded, although her head couldn't move inside the plastic. "Okay, Mike. Stop saying my name."

The stretcher locked into place and the door of the ambulance slammed shut. A woman she didn't recognize covered most of Lacey's face with a huge piece of gauze. The man on the other side of the compartment grabbed her upper arm with a grip so tight she thought her eyes would bulge. As the pressure released, he said, "One-forty over ninety-seven. Pulse is steady at ninety-two."

"Pulse-Ox is a little low."

The woman pulled a plastic mask from a rack fastened to the wall above Lacey's head and slipped it over Lacey's mouth and nose. It felt odd and useless as it pressed against the gauze. She was out of the wreck, but still trapped. Still couldn't move. She pulled against the straps holding her to the board. She kicked against the covering they'd wrapped her in.

"Easy does it, Lacey," the woman cooed. "We'll be there in just a few minutes, but you need to lie still. We don't know what might be wrong inside, yet. Just lie still and we'll get you there as quick as we can."

The man squeezed her arm again. "Her pressure is rising."

The woman clicked the speaker on her shoulder and spoke into the mic. "Let's step it up."

Sirens rang out, cutting through the afternoon like a neon knife.

At the hospital, the portico ceiling shifted and swayed as they pushed her into the bright white of the emergency room. Two women rushed past her, their bubble-gum pink scrubs out of place against the bright white.

"They're waiting for her in radiology. We've got her from here."

A moment later, after a couple of sharp turns that set Lacey's stomach on its side, they stationed her beneath the huge X-ray machine. "We'll be right outside. Don't be afraid."

The nurses left. A young man with a buzz cut leaned over her. "We're going to take some pictures and make sure nothing is missing. Don't worry. It won't hurt."

The room echoed with a chill silence. The technician moved the camera around the gurney, lowering the side bars for a couple of them and then returning them to their normal position. Did he think she might fall off? She couldn't move if she'd tried. She had tried. She couldn't move.

Her throat closed around a sob that she was afraid to

release. Instead, she held her breath and forced back the tears. Williams women didn't cry. They persevered. When the world took away everything they'd ever wanted, they gutted through on sheer determination and pride. That's what Williams women did.

They didn't cry.

"All set. See? That wasn't so bad was it?" The technician frowned. Then he was gone and light flooded into the room. "She's ready." His voice sounded hushed as it came from the light. "She's pretty upset, obviously. She's crying."

Williams women don't cry.

One of the pink nurses pushed her back to the emergency department, finally stopping beneath a shining silver light in a small room. On one side, a huge window looked out onto the nurses' work station.

Lacey had been in this room before. When she was eleven years old her horse had thrown her. She'd collided with the corral fencing and Kendra had rushed her to the ER in case she'd had a concussion. She hadn't, but she'd been in this room because of a possible head injury. It was the trauma room.

She was in her local hospital in the trauma room because... Because... why?

"Hi there," a gentle voice spoke from above.

Lacey focused with one eye on the face leaning over her. Silky red hair. Bright blue eyes. A warm smile. A crease in her brow.

"Can you tell me your name?"

Of course she could. She nodded as much as the straps around her head and the neck brace would allow.

"Try not to move your head, sweetheart. I'm Doctor Carlson. What's your name?"

She knew it. She knew her name… didn't she? The word hovered on the edge of her reality, covered in a red mist.

"Lacey!" she yelled through the plastic mask, as more people in scrubs filled the tiny space.

"Good, good. Okay, we're going to move you to the bed now. It might hurt a little, so be brave for me, okay?"

She nodded again.

"On three. One, two, THREE!"

Every person in the room heaved as one and she gently floated into the air before coming down on a much larger stretcher. A bed. When she landed, pain ripped through every muscle, every tendon and every joint in her body. Somehow, there was a measure of relief in that. As far as she could tell, all her parts were where she'd left them.

Those brief seconds of calm evaporated into the red mist and everyone moved at once. A heavy sense of urgency quaked the air.

"Let's do something about that pain, shall we?" Doctor Carlson had always been kind to her. When Lacey's parents had died, she'd been there for Kendra and helped her learn everything she'd needed to know about taking care of little kids. "We'll get you off that board just as soon as we get those pictures back. It won't be long."

"We just heard back from her sister. She'll be here in about fifteen minutes."

"Fifteen minutes from the Heartland? She must have installed wings on that old truck of hers."

"Lacey was in the truck," Mike, the EMT, replied. "Mac's

bringing them in a cruiser. You hear that, Lacey? Your sister is coming, complete with lights and sirens, just for you."

Kendra had never really had her own life. As soon as it had started, she'd had to come home and be a mom instead of a sister. It wasn't fair. Life wasn't fair.

At least she'd have Michelle.

Something sharp poked her arm near her elbow.

"Let's do eight milligrams of Morphine with a Thorazine back." Dr. Carlson stood beside Lacey's head and wrote something on a clip board before handing it to the nurse. "Any word on the x-rays?"

"They're already on their way, Doctor."

Then everyone was gone. The room was empty and dark. She'd never really been afraid of the dark before. Someone had replaced the bandage over her face and covered all of one eye and most of the other with new wrappings. Was that why it seemed darker?

An alarm sounded nearby; a high-pitched tone that lasted only a few seconds. The subtle buzz of machinery took over the silence until it sounded like a train engine.

The nurse came back and injected something into her IV line. It burned into her vein like a red-hot poker for a second before warmth traveled up her arm. She closed her eye. She tried to inhale a deep breath but the straps on the board still held her hostage.

It was dark behind her eyes. The world shifted and a blanket of calm descended.

At least Kendra would have Michelle. And Brad would have the baby.

CHAPTER ONE

"File Two. This is Lacey Williams, staff reporter for KLVN, All That and More, continuing an interview with Clark County Detective Jethro Martin." Lacey glanced at her digital recorder to make sure it was still working before she returned her gaze to the craggy, weathered features of the veteran law enforcement officer on the opposite side of the desk. "Sorry about that, Detective. Where were we? Oh, yes... So, who was the last person to see Cynthia Kincaid alive?"

Frowning in her direction, the etched lines around his mouth deepening, Jethro Martin sat back in his over-sized office chair and rested large palms on the deteriorating faux leather arm rests.

"You know I'm not gonna answer that question, Ms. Williams. Why do you keep askin' it?"

"Probably for the same reason you ask the same question a hundred times in an interrogation. Maybe you'll let something slip." Lacey smiled in that way she'd developed to set her interview subjects at ease. Sometimes it worked. Sometimes it didn't.

Today, it didn't. From what she'd been able to learn about the detective, he was a hard nut to crack, so she wasn't altogether surprised.

"I will tell you that we have a suspect in mind. We are taking the woman's disappearance seriously and we're investigating. That's what we do around here. But we aren't going to tip our hand quite so cavalierly. Besides, we don't even know if the missing woman is dead. She could be holed up in a casino somewhere losin' her husband's retirement."

"She doesn't have a husband, Detective. You know full well she's married to Brandy Kincaid. Is that who you're refusing to name as a suspect? Her wife?"

"Nice try, little girl." Half of Jethro's mouth turned upward in a wry grin. "Are we near done here, sweetheart? I do have several cases that need my attention."

"Almost. I just want to show you something." Lacey dug through her notes and pulled one sheet of paper free. She placed the paper on the desk in front of the Detective's beefy belly and pointed at the woman in the center of a black-and-white photo. "This is a still taken from the security video at the Touchdown Club and Casino. It was taken last Thursday morning, about 3 a.m., and it shows the couple fighting near Casino Pit Three, on the second floor. Brandy Kincaid is the tall brunette. Her wife, Cynthia, the missing woman, is the shorter one with lighter hair. The other people in this photo overheard the entire exchange. Several of them have told me that they came forward to your office to report that Brandy Kincaid threatened to kill her wife that night. Nobody has seen Cynthia Kincaid since that surveillance video was taken, nearly a week ago."

The Sheriff's keen gaze didn't so much as skim the photograph, as though he were avoiding it deliberately. Or maybe he'd seen it before. Instead, he rested his elbows on the desk and intertwined his thick fingers so he had to look around them to focus on Lacey. "Do you have a question for me, Ms. Williams?"

"Of course I do. Are you looking at Brandy Kincaid for the disappearance of her wife?"

"No comment."

"But you're not going to deny it, right?"

"Where did you get that photograph?"

"Tut, tut, Detective. I have my sources, which I have no obligation to share with you. Let's just say it's authentic, and I think you've known about it all along."

He placed his hands flat on the desk and pushed himself back again. His cell phone, resting on the corner of his desk, sounded with an old Ozzy Osbourne classic, Crazy Train. He lifted his right hand to quiet Lacey while he answered the phone with the other. "Martin. Go ahead."

Listening intently to overhear the other side of the call proved fruitless. The Detective's expression on the other hand revealed the call was obviously of profound importance. His brow narrowed before his gaze lifted to the ceiling and he pushed out a hard, full breath between tightened lips. "Is the scene secure?"

What scene?

"And have you notified the coroner?"

Somebody is dead.

"Don't let anybody in until I get there. I'm on my way."

Detective Martin stood and replaced his cell phone into its holder. "I'm afraid we're done here, Ms. Williams."

"What's going on? Somebody found a body?"

"As a matter of fact, yes. You'll hear about it on the scanner in a few minutes anyway, so I suppose I'm not revealin' any state secrets. Goddammit." He sighed as he pulled an automatic pistol from the top drawer of his desk and tucked it into the shoulder holster strapped beneath his suit jacket. "If you want a scoop, Ms. Williams, follow me to Mission Hills."

"Mission Hills? Those mansions off Tropicana?"

"The very same mansions. We're goin' to the Kincaid house. Deputies just served a search warrant and found the missing woman in her bedroom. It's now officially a murder investigation."

"Hot damn," Lacey announced, then thought better of it. "Sorry. No offense."

"No offense taken, although I'm not sure why. A woman is dead, Ms. Williams."

Lacey gathered her things and followed the detective out of his office. She hurried to her car, dumped her recorder, her purse, and her notebook on the passenger seat and then turned the engine.

A murder investigation.

And not just any murder. The murder of the filthy rich socialite wife of one of the most prominent people in Las Vegas.

This could be just the ticket to bump Addison Parker's show high enough in the ratings to get national attention. She'd definitely be getting at least some air time on NPR national. If Lacey played her cards right, as the field reporter for the daily morning news show, she could ride those coattails all the way to one of the major commercial networks. ABC. NBC. The sky was the limit, really. She had no intention of sticking around Las Vegas for the rest of her life.

This story? Yeah, this story had legs in the form of money, power and sex. And not just sex. Gay sex. Lesbian sex.

A niggle of something she didn't like crawled up Lacey's spine. She frowned as she slowly turned her car through the parking lot to watch for the detective. Was she really that shallow? Did the fact that Brandy Kincaid was a lesbian, married to a woman, make the story that much more interesting? Her stomach lurched at the thought. Her professional side stomped her feet and screamed, "Yes! Why, yes it does."

She sighed.

"Too bad," she whispered to no one.

Pulling her car into line behind the detective's nondescript sedan, Lacey tried not to tailgate. He certainly wasn't in a huge hurry to get to the scene based on his perfect adherence to all known traffic laws. Still, she followed as patiently as she could through the Las Vegas traffic. There was no better way to get closer to the action than to follow the lead cop onto the street and pass all the other news crews which would undoubtedly descend before she got there.

Twenty-five minutes later, they arrived at the gates of one of the most private and prestigious addresses in

Las Vegas. Dozens of elaborate homes, all priced in the millions, sat behind the guarded gates of Mission Hills' only entrance. Several of Las Vegas' finest stood in a grouping near the guard shack door.

A rather excited private security officer stood with them, his face beaming with all the attention. His job probably consisted of little more than vetting deliveries, so having the entire Las Vegas police force on his doorstep had to be just a little thrilling. Outside the gates, a collection of news vans, some with satellite equipment on top, parked haphazardly in the wide, arched driveway.

The security guard immediately waved the detective's car through. Lacey bit her lip, expecting either the guard or one of the officers to stop her before she passed through the opened iron gate. They didn't and the excitement in her belly grew exponentially.

The wide streets led to house after house of immense proportions. The fact the homes were set closer to the road than she would have imagined spoke to the intense property value of real estate in the city. Most were in the Spanish style, with arches, red tiled roofs and stucco exteriors in a mixture of muted, desert colors that ranged from off-white to sage. Huge palm trees decorated manicured front lawns. Some of those lawns were lush green carpets that matched the sprawling golf course behind the houses while others were sculpted, xeriscape masterpieces full of rock art and elaborate water features.

Neighbors stood anxiously on their front porches. One neighbor in particular, an older woman with short, obviously dyed black hair, wrung her hands and seemed more-than-a-little distraught.

She drove by at least ten homes before she came upon five or six cruisers and a CSI van parked at an odd angle in the driveway of what must be the Kincaid house. The desert sun beat down on the street with ferocious candor and the light reflected off the windshields. After climbing out of her car, parked directly behind Detective Martin's sedan, Lacey lifted a hand to shade her eyes while she turned on her digital recorder and tucked it into her pocket. The detective hurried into the house, his head bent in conversation with two officers who'd met him at his car.

In the distance, a horn sounded with frantic and urgent bursts. A moment later, a bright red Range Rover powered into view and screeched to a halt. Instantly, Brandy Kincaid's lanky form dove from behind the wheel and raced toward the house. When she reached the front door, she collided with an officer who refused to let her pass.

"Get out of my way! That's my house, damn it! That's my wife in there!" With apparently all the strength she could muster, she fought against the weight of his chest and arms. She was tall, but she wasn't a large woman and he easily held her back. Eventually, her size played to her advantage. She slipped free of his grasp and disappeared inside.

"Hey, who are you?"

Lacey turned around at the sound of a deep, demanding voice. A robust woman wearing plain clothes marched in her direction. From the glittering gold of her modest earrings and the cut of her expensive suit, she ranked somewhere on the high side of the officials on the scene.

"Are you supposed to be here?" she asked with a concerned scowl embedded in her handsome, chiseled features.

"Well, hi there." Lacey canted her head to one side and smiled.

"Who are you and what are you doing here?" the woman repeated.

"I'm Lacey Williams with All That and More, KLVN, Las Vegas." She picked up the press credential that hung from the lanyard around her neck with one hand and extended her right hand. "I'm with Detective Martin. And you are Detective...?"

"Assistant District Attorney, Sal Crenshaw." Ignoring her offer to shake hands, the attorney pulled an ID wallet from the inside pocket of her suit jacket and flashed her ID.

"You're not supposed to be back here," she continued as she shoved the wallet back into her pocket. "You're going to need to leave."

"Oh, I don't think so, Counselor. The private security firm let me pass and just because there's a crime scene here doesn't mean I have to wait behind the gate. If you want to bring that guard up here, I'll be happy to talk to him about the appropriate use of private property and the First Amendment."

"You're going to lecture me about the Constitution? That's rich, lady."

"Like I said, I'm a reporter. Chances are, I know more about the First Amendment than you think."

"Don't get in the way, and stay behind the tape."

"Of course. I wouldn't dream of becoming a nuisance." Lacey turned her attention back to the massive, double entry doors that led to the mansion's interior.

Within a few minutes of entering the house, Brandy Kincaid reemerged. Her face pale, she stumbled down the front walk. The same officer who had been trying to keep her outside now offered his assistance to help her remain standing. He succeeded long enough for her to reach the corner of the three-car garage and then she fell backward to lean against the stucco wall. Slowly, she slid down the rough surface, her eyes closed, and her face raised to the sun. When her bottom hit the designer cement of her driveway, her head fell forward onto her forearms, propped on her raised knees.

Her shoulders trembled. Her head turned from side-to-side as though she were asking the universe to take it back. After a few minutes, she raised her face and stared forward with unseeing eyes. Unseeing dry eyes.

Lacey retrieved her phone from the center console of her car and made a call.

After three rings, her sister-in-law answered. "Well, hey, Lacey. What's up?"

"You have got to get me an interview with Brandy Kincaid."

It had to be a mistake.

God, her chest hurt. Brandy Kincaid could barely breathe and the suffocating heat of the Las Vegas desert didn't help. She squinted against the afternoon sun, ignoring the tightness in her lungs and the sluggish quicksand that had replaced the muscles in her legs.

She sat against the iron-hot wall of her wife's house, unable to feel anything but the heat. She didn't know what she'd expected to find inside those walls, but she hadn't been prepared. Not by a long shot.

The house was trashed. It looked like nobody had washed a dish in weeks. In the living room, most of the sofa cushions were strewn on the floor and the big screen TV that Brandy had mounted over the marble, mostly unused, fireplace had been knocked free of its support structure. It hung limply to one side while distorted lines flashed in a random display that had reminded her of lightning.

Brandy hadn't been inside the house in more than three months. She'd elected to live at her home outside the city limits. The small ranch house that she'd called home before Cyndi had come barreling into her life like sex-in-a-saddle wasn't as luxurious as the city house, but Brandy had never really needed luxury.

But Cynthia did. Cynthia had.

It had been great in the beginning; all about intimacy, yearning, great sex, and learning how to love. The first few months had been an erotic escape into worlds of emotion and connection that bound two people together. She'd bought this house for Cyndi when Cyndi had complained about the drive into town from the ranch. Brandy would have been happy with a crash pad, something cozy where they could sleep over when they needed to, but Cyndi was nothing if not flamboyant. That was part of what had drawn Brandy to her like a moth to a flame. Cyndi was bright. Exciting. A real Rhinestone Cowgirl. Exceedingly attractive and only moderately selfish.

When had it changed? When had the love they'd taken such care to nurture turned into a swirling pool of disgust and loathing? And if that were true, why in God's name did the thought of losing her fill Brandy's entire body with wet cement?

Cynthia was dead.

It wasn't a mistake.

And it was only a matter of time before the cops turned their attention on her. Hell, she was pretty sure they already had. But now that Cynthia's blood-covered body had turned up in her own house of all places, there was very little to keep their suspicions off her.

Nobody knew that Brandy didn't live here anymore. And they always looked to the spouse first.

The fact that she and Cynthia were three months into a nasty divorce certainly wasn't going to help. With the edge of that thought embedded squarely between her shoulder blades like a knife, she regained her feet and headed in the direction of her SUV. The same officer who had tried to keep her from entering what was still her house approached with a long, determined stride.

"Where are you going?"

Brandy stopped and faced him. "Excuse me?"

"Where are--"

"That's none of your business."

"You need to stick around for a minute. Detective Martin is going to have some questions for you."

"Am I under arrest?"

The cop rolled back on his heels slightly and his thick hand rested on his service weapon. "No, no, of course not. He'll just want to clear up a few things, that's all."

Brandy stared at the man's hand on his gun. Was he trying to intimidate her? She stamped down the beginnings of fear and moved her gaze to the deputy's face. "Then I'm leaving now. He knows how to reach me."

"Listen, Mrs. Kincaid, we understand you must be upset by all this, and--"

"I'm leaving, and there isn't a damn thing you can do about it." She turned in the direction of her truck and noticed a small woman leaning on the fender of a black, midsize sedan, studying her. It didn't look like a police car, and she didn't look like a cop.

Blonde shoulder length hair had been cut in a style that cascaded evenly in gentle waves over one side of her face. Her bright blue eyes pierced the heavy air and seemed to notice everything at once. She looked vaguely familiar, but Brandy couldn't place where she might have seen her before.

Those eyes...

A slight breeze lifted the hair away from her cheek for a few seconds, revealing a thin scar that ran from the corner of her left eye to her chin. She raised a digital recorder toward full, pink lips and spoke into the mic.

A reporter.

Of course.

Brandy's stomach roiled, nausea growing with each passing, scorching second. She marched to her SUV, which was still running in the middle of the street. She climbed into the cab, rotated the vehicle with a tight, three-point turn and sped out of her old neighborhood.

After she reached the tall iron gates, it took her a full five minutes to get through the swarm of reporters.

"When was the last time you saw your wife?"

"Was your wife murdered?"

"Do you know who did this?"

"Did you murder your wife?"

When she finally managed to maneuver through the throng, thinking that she probably should have just run their asses over, she drove another ten minutes in the direction of her casino near the resort strip. Finally, unable to focus on the winding roads of Las Vegas' off-strip underbelly, she pulled into an almost-empty parking lot in front of an adult novelty shop. She picked up her cell phone and selected a number from the contact list. It was a number she hadn't called in a while, but one that she needed now more than she had any other time in her life.

"Hey, Brandy," the voice answered after only a single ring. "I thought I'd be hearing from you."

"Yeah?"

"I got a call from my sister-in-law. It's already hit social media. I'm so sorry about Cynthia. Are you okay?"

"Yeah, I'm fine." She lied. No way the woman on the other end of the line believed her, either. "Who's your sister-in-law?"

"She's a reporter. You'll be the lead on the five o'clock news."

"Michelle, this is going a bit beyond casino PR, but I think I'm going to need some spin control on this whole thing. And in case you were wondering... I didn't kill my wife."

Lacey joined a crowd of reporters jostling for position as Detective Martin raised his hands to quiet the crowd. They stood just outside the main gate of the wealthy suburb where the rich were duly separated from the unwashed masses. She'd been raised to appreciate hard work and struggle. If she broke one of her toys, she and her sister would fix it. If she had to buy a replacement, she had to earn the cash by doing extra chores around the ranch. When she was a teenager and she'd wanted a car, she'd had to earn that money, too. Nothing came without a price. Nothing came easy. Kendra, the sister who had raised her after their parents' deaths, had always told her that anything worthwhile was worth working for.

It was only a few years ago that Lacey had learned Kendra had millions of dollars tucked away, the proceeds of a lawsuit she'd been required to file as a condition of being awarded sole custody of four young kids when she was only twenty herself. Kendra could have replaced every single broken toy and purchased Lacey a car for every day of the week. At first, Lacey had been upset about having been brought up in such a rustic environment; no amenities to speak of. No Internet. No video gaming consoles. When she moved to Las Vegas right after graduation, before she'd learned about the money, she'd discovered that she hadn't been as deprived as she thought. At no point during her upbringing had she ever worried about the lights turning on when she flipped a switch. At no time before living on her own had she opened the freezer to find no food.

And now, having come into her inheritance, she could spend her share of the family fortune without fear of a rousing case of Affluenza. She didn't need diamonds, or cars, or furs. She didn't need to live in a huge house behind an iron gate that kept everyone, and everything classified as "other" away.

Apparently, Brandy and Cynthia Kincaid were a different kind of people.

Detective Martin approached the group of reporters carrying a clipboard in one hand while adjusting his cowboy hat with the other. Planting his feet firmly in grass that seemed too green to be real, he cleared his throat. "Alright, listen up. I'm only going to say this once. I don't know any more than you do and I'm not gonna answer any questions until I have somethin' to say."

"Jethro! Who found the body?" Kevin Conrad, a reporter from one of the local television network affiliates, shouted from the front of the pack, his microphone extended at arm's length as a hot breeze lifted the ridge of his perfectly coiffed hair.

"What did I just say, Kevin?"

"You must know that much. C'mon! Throw us a bone. We're going live in three minutes!"

"Was it Mrs. Kincaid? I mean, the other Mrs. Kincaid? We just saw her driving away. Why isn't she being questioned?"

Lacey couldn't be sure who'd posed that last query, but the snide attitude about the couple's same-gender marriage rubbed her the wrong way.

Lacey shouted, "Is Brandy Kincaid a suspect?"

"I don't know, Lacey. Perhaps you can solve this crime in the next fifteen minutes and save the rest of us a pile of work. Any additional questions should be directed to the Undersheriff's office."

"A lot of good that'll do us," Kevin commented under his breath.

Detective Martin turned with military precision and punctuated the end of the impromptu press conference with a word that would never make it on the air.

"Well, that was uncalled-for," Kevin chided as he made his way to the sidewalk where a dozen techs had set up a row of cameras, all pointed in the direction of the mansions beyond the gate.

Lacey pulled her cell phone out of her pocket and pressed the speed-dial image for her station. A second later her producer, Jane Smith, answered.

"They found Cynthia Kincaid's body. I need a live feed to the news desk."

"Holy shit!" Jane responded. The phone rattled like she'd dropped it before she came back on the line. "Gimme one sec to patch you in."

The line went silent for a moment before the current broadcast, a local business news program that catered to investors, filled her earpiece.

"...and we'll be taking you live to the scene with Lacey Williams of All That and More. Lacey, can you hear me?"

"I hear you, Jim. I'm standing on the sidewalk about fifty yards from the front door of a large, Spanish-style mansion in Mission Hills, a normally quiet neighborhood just west of Las Vegas Boulevard. Moments ago, the Las Vegas Metropolitan Police learned the whereabouts of 36-year-old Cynthia Kincaid who has been missing for nearly a week. The wife of prominent casino mogul Brandy Kincaid is no longer a missing person. Her remains were found in her own home after deputies served a search warrant on these premises roughly one-hour ago."

"Do we know why they were serving a search warrant?"

"We don't, and we can only speculate that it had something to do with the missing person's report the dead woman's parents filed just about forty-eight hours ago."

"Have the police said how she was killed, Lacey?"

"At the moment, we have no more information to give you. We don't know the condition of the body, or how she died, or even if there is any indication that foul play was involved. I can tell you this, Jim: I was sitting with Detective Jethro Martin of the Clark County Sheriff's Department when he received the call and he said that the missing person case had just become a murder investigation. That doesn't bode well for what his deputies found inside this enormous home in Las Vegas. I was inside the private gates when Brandy Kincaid arrived at the scene, visibly shaken and naturally upset by the news. She has left the scene now and nobody, including the detective, knows her whereabouts at this time."

Once she disconnected from her call to the station, she moved closer to the gate. Kevin was still on the air, standing three feet in front of a large camera poised on a black and silver tripod. She listened to his commentary and grinned when she heard him imply that he didn't know if there was a murder victim inside the home or if Cynthia Kincaid had died of natural causes. He paused, listening to the feed from the studio that came in through a nearly-invisible earpiece. It wasn't as easy as it looked; holding a conversation in front of a video camera knowing that your audience could see you, but you couldn't see them. It took talent to be engaging in a one-sided visual medium. For Lacey, reporting through her voice only, it was different. She didn't have to pretend to be looking directly into the eyes of someone she couldn't see and had never met. She'd done it before, of course. And she'd been good at it.

A twinge of regret stole through her spine. She straightened her posture to chase it away.

Kevin replied to whatever question he'd been asked by immediately intimating that, since Cynthia had been found in her own home, and Brandy Kincaid had obviously not allowed the police access prior to obtaining a search warrant, things didn't look good for the local millionaire.

All eyes were turning on Brandy Kincaid.

When he wrapped his broadcast, he handed his mic to his cameraman. Then he joined Lacey on the edge of an expansive lawn that separated the entrance of Mission Hills from the main thoroughfare. "Jesus, those are big houses."

"Yup. I think she paid something like eight million for her place a couple of years ago. She bought it after she got married."

"Who did?"

"Brandy Kincaid."

"You know her?"

"No. I mean, not really. My sister-in-law did some work for her a while back. I know of her; same as you. And her wife was missing. I've done a bit of research. Didn't they teach you that in broadcasting school?"

Kevin smirked. "Anyone ever tell you you're a smartass?"

"Only since I learned to talk."

"So, your sister-in-law? That's Michelle Loving, right?"

"Michelle Loving *Williams*, thanks to the Supreme Court of the United States."

"Right. She married your sister. And Brandy Kincaid is a client of hers?"

"On and off. Michelle helped to launch the Touchdown Club and Casino."

Truthfully, Michelle had talked about Brandy many times over the last couple of years. Brandy had given Michelle her first big account when she'd opened her own PR firm, and when Lacey and her brothers had received their inheritance, several million dollars each, talk had naturally turned to managing, and spending, the money. Michelle had suggested that Lacey get with Brandy for advice. It surprised her that she even remembered the conversation she'd had with Michelle last year about how careful Lacey would need to be with the money in order to make it last. That's when Michelle had mentioned the cost of these homes in particular, and how one of her clients owned one. "I don't know her personally, though."

"Ha. One degree of separation and I smell an exclusive brewing in that gorgeous little mind of yours. When are you going to give up on the radio thing and come work at the TV station with me. We'd make one helluva powerful anchor desk."

"Right. The last time I checked, you were just as roving a reporter as I am."

"Not for long, Lacey-cakes. Not for long."

A sly smile formed on Lacey's lips. He was right about that.

CHAPTER TWO

Brandy couldn't sleep. No matter how many times she twisted and turned on the soft leather of the old sofa in her office, she couldn't erase the image of Cynthia's body lying in the middle of their bedroom. Cynthia's bedroom, she corrected herself.

Had her wife come home and interrupted a burglary? Where had she been all this time? She hadn't been at the Mission Hills house, that was for sure. Brandy's mother-in-law had a key and had checked the house several times over the past week. She'd asked Brandy to go with her, but Brandy had avoided the house for so long, it would have felt like she was invading Cynthia's private space. She'd declined, but now wished she hadn't. Maybe Marion hadn't set the alarms properly when she'd left. What if that was how the burglar, if there had been a burglar, had gotten in? She couldn't blame Marion. The only electronic device she knew how to operate had spinning images that promised, and rarely delivered, a jackpot.

She threw the fleece blanket off her bare legs and sat up, rubbing away what little sleep had formed from her eyes.

Scrubbing one hand through her hair, she stood and paced to a window made of one-way glass that looked out over the entire casino. It was after three on a Saturday morning, and while the casino never closed, it did slow down considerably in the wee hours, even on the weekends. It was the price of building her casino off the main resort strip.

The nightclubs were still rocking, full of tourists and locals. Surprisingly, there weren't many bars in Las Vegas that catered to the LGBT crowd. Maybe it was the distant thump of the bass, like distant thunder, but she doubted it. The DJ was a pro, pushing out just the right number of beats per minute to get the dancers good and thirsty. She'd change it up when the bartenders gave her the signal they were ready for another drinking frenzy. But she was used to that. She'd been listening to it for two years.

A group of six or seven men appeared in the huge, tilted mirror over the main entrance. The massive glass spanned the entire width of the building and gave her a bird's eye view of the entire casino floor. It was old school. She could bring up any security camera she liked on her desktop computer, but she liked her mirrors better. She could watch for trouble, but she could also relish the enjoyment her guests were having just a floor below. These particular guys had been at the gay club on the first floor.

The clubs weren't exclusive, and patrons often moved from one side to the other, but one was targeted at gay men and the other designed for lesbians, generally. As the young men made their way from the nightclub to the street, they laughed like nothing was wrong. Like they'd been having a really great time. Like Cynthia hadn't just died. They left the casino and climbed into a waiting cab at the stand in front of her valet parking station, jockeying for position in the minivan as it pulled away from the curb.

The cleaning crews inside the casino were busy polishing the tile floors, vacuuming the bright red-and-black patterned carpets of the various gambling pits, and polishing the strategically placed brass bars that served as subtle hints to the patrons for where to go to lose their money. A few gamblers, the die-hards chasing their losses, sat throughout the massive hall. Two white-haired men sat at a Blackjack table, and a group of three gray-haired ladies laughed around a slot machine.

Then Brandy saw her in the far corner of the mirror, sitting at a Blackjack table. There was no mistaking the woman's posture or the color of the thinning hair, which bordered somewhere between an Arizona sunset and a ripe Florida orange.

Brandy pulled her jeans back on and threw a light sweater over her sleeveless T-shirt before she tucked her feet into a pair of sandals and headed downstairs. On the main level, she waved to a few of the overnight staff, but didn't stop to talk.

"Marion, what are you doing here?"

The older woman jumped slightly on her stool before she turned to face Brandy. Too much blue eye makeup and cheeks covered in unblended rouge gave her pale, wrinkled complexion a clownish look. Coupled with the unnatural color of her hair, she barely looked human much of the time. Some of her mascara had smeared from the corner of one eye.

"Brandy, honey. I just couldn't sleep, you know. I had to get my mind off of things for a little while. What are you doing here? I didn't think you'd be working tonight, of all nights."

Of all nights? But it's okay for her to gamble? Brandy shook her head slowly. "I'm not working."

"Then what are you doing here? You're not looking for me, are you? Frank didn't send you, did he?" Her eyes widened, and her bottom lip trembled slightly.

"No, but I imagine that if he wakes up, he's not going to be happy you're not at the house." The house was another one of Cynthia's ideas. Her parents lived in Oregon, but they came to Las Vegas so often, she wanted them to have a place of their own to stay. At least, that had been her excuse. Truthfully, Brandy suspected that she didn't want her aging parents underfoot while she and her entourage used and abused every substance known to man. "Come on. I'll drive you back."

"Oh, no, not yet. I'm down about three grand. Give me a little while and I'll get right back on top. I don't suppose you could manage a little marker, could you?"

"Your daughter's body was found today. She was murdered. You do understand that, don't you?"

Her mother-in-law's age-misted eyes filled with sparkling tears that accentuated her fragile appearance. She pursed her lips before turning back to the table and nodding to the dealer to do his job.

Brandy placed her hand on the grid-iron themed felt

between her mother-in-law and her employee. "No more, Jacob. She's done. And you're not to allow her to gamble here anymore. You got that?"

"Yes, Mrs. K. Whatever you say."

"Oh fine," Marion grumbled. "I suppose you think you're so much better than me, don't you? You own a casino; so doesn't that make you the biggest gambler of them all? Self-righteous. That's what you are."

"I'll take you home."

"I don't want to go home. I want a drink first. It'll help me sleep." She slid off the barstool. If she weren't so old, she would have marched in the direction of the main bar. As it was, she waddled, holding her leather handbag against her side as though it were made of gold.

Brandy followed, unwilling to leave her alone anywhere there may present a possibility to gamble. She had a small point, of course. Brandy really had no right to judge people who gambled. She'd earned a great deal of money in the two years since she'd expanded into the casino business in addition to her night clubs. Still, she wasn't the one gambling. The house always won eventually. And gambling to have a good time and gambling away the family homestead were too different things. Marion very rarely won and with the odds stacked against her anyway, she was far better off sticking to penny slots.

Not that it mattered much. It wasn't her money she was losing; it was Brandy's. Brandy had no doubt that a large portion of the monthly allowance plus the extra money she'd given to her wife routinely went to pay for her mother's habit.

After she ordered a drink, Marion sat at a small football-shaped table near the edge of the first slot machine bank. The machines, lighted with images of professional football cheerleaders, flashed with colored lights and the artificial sound of coins hitting metal trays. Marion dropped a handful of football-shaped cheques onto the lacquered black table-top and frowned.

Brandy sat down across from her. "How much did you lose tonight?"

After a humbling silence, Marion replied, "I told you. Three thousand dollars."

"That was at that table, since you got here. How much all together?"

Shifting in her chair and clutching her bag, she refused to answer. Brandy repeated the question.

Finally, she said, "Almost ten. I started with ten and that's what I have left." She nodded at the stack of plastic on the table. "I was up almost fifteen thousand a couple of hours ago. If I could just play for a while longer..."

Less than two hundred dollars in Touchdown tokens sat in a small heap.

"You have to stop this, Marion. I never told Cynthia how she could spend her money, but she's gone. And I'm not going to finance your addiction. You need to get help."

"I do not have a gambling problem. Why do people keep saying that? I'm a grown woman and if I want to gamble, I'm going to gamble. In case you haven't noticed, it's legal here."

Brandy sighed. "Of course it is. So is drinking and some people just can't. You... just can't gamble."

"Humbug. I can do whatever I like. Besides, I don't

have much choice, do I?"

"Of course you do. Everyone has a choice, Mom."

"I suppose you know that better than anyone, don't you? All superior like you are. So much better than everyone else."

"I'm sorry. I'm sorry you're hurting, but I'm not going to finance this anymore. I'll make sure that you and Frank can keep your house, the one here and the one in Oregon, and that you have enough to live on, but the money train just left the station. You're going to have to deal with that."

Stricken to the point that all remaining natural color left her cheeks, Marion wrung her hands over the handle of her purse. "Take me home, then. If you're not going to help, you might as well just take me back home."

Saturday morning was Lacey's time to regroup from the week. She usually spent a few hours on her computer working on the stories she'd been assigned, wrapping up her interview notes, and making plans for the upcoming week. This morning, she'd finalized an interview with the Executive Director of the local Chamber of Commerce, replied to several requests on her HARO account, and was just about to create a new profile folder for Brandy Kincaid when her phone vibrated. She turned the screen to face her and smiled as her sister-in-law's image lit up the device.

"Well?"

"Good morning, Bright Eyes."

"Good morning. Right. So, what did she say? Did you talk to her?"

"We're here and thought you'd like to have brunch."

"You're here? In Vegas?" Lacey spun around in her office chair and rested her elbows on her knees. "Awesome. When did you get in?"

"About four this morning, actually. There was a terrible accident near Beaver and we were stuck for a couple of hours."

Lacey's heart leaped into her throat. "Are you guys okay? I mean, you weren't in the accident, were you?"

"No, no. We just got stuck in traffic. I-15 was a parking lot for a minute. But we're fine."

"You're sure?"

"Lacey, we didn't even see it happen. We were miles behind the wreck and perfectly safe."

Lacey took a deep breath and forced herself to release it in a slow, steady stream. "Okay."

"So, are you busy?"

"Not really. Did you talk to Brandy Kincaid?"

"That's kind of why we're in town. I did talk to her not long after you called, and we need to talk first."

First? Did that mean that Brandy had agreed to an interview?

"Can you come up?" Michelle asked.

"Yeah, sure. Let me throw on some sweats and I'll be right there."

After she disconnected the call, she hurried into her bedroom at the other end of the three-bedroom condo she'd purchased with her inheritance. She found a pair of black sweats, slipped on the BYU sweatshirt she'd picked up at a thrift store back home just to tick off her sister and her black suede sneakers. Grabbed her keys from the hook by the front door as she hurried past, she headed for her sister's place.

Michelle and Kendra lived in Utah most of the time. They ran the family cattle operation and lived in the same house in which Kendra had raised Lacey, her twin brother Casey, and their brothers Brent and Brad. But since Michelle's business was in Vegas, they kept a condo in the same building as Lacey. She owned a three bedroom with a view of the resort swimming pool. Kendra and Michelle had opted for a four-bedroom penthouse with a three-hundred-sixty-degree view of the city, so the boys would have a free place to stay whenever they were in town.

The elevator dinged open to reveal a crowd of about fifteen passengers wedged in like Vienna sausages. Even without the multiplied reflections in the horrible mirrors that lined every interior wall, it was too full for her taste. She waved it off and waited for the next one. Crowds had never really bothered her before, but since the accident, she'd been more careful. Her sister – who had raised her from the time she was about five years old – called her a hermit. She wasn't a hermit. She just liked her privacy, that's all.

The next elevator only had one passenger. She waved it off as well and was rewarded with a third, empty option a moment later. She stepped in, selected her sister's floor and turned her attention to the carpeting. A few seconds passed, and the doors rang open again. She hurried out of the car. The door to Kendra and Michelle's place was only a few steps away. When she reached it, it was already open.

"Anybody home?" They were probably in the kitchen. When Michelle invited someone over for brunch, she meant she would be doing all the cooking. Strange, considering that until she'd met and married Kendra two years ago, her idea of making dinner involved calling a restaurant for a reservation. Since their marriage and her move out of the city, she'd begun stretching her comfort zone a bit. She had taken to being a housewife like a fish to water, concentrating her attentions on making a home for her new family. They'd even taken in two foster children and were in the process of adopting them. Five-year-old identical twin girls whose father was missing-in-action and mother was far more attached to her meth pipe than her children.

"We're in here!" Kendra's deep voice traveled through the space with the same commanding tone Lacey had grown up with.

"Smells great," Lacey announced as she entered the spacious kitchen and gave her sister a quick squeeze around the shoulders. Then she plopped herself onto a bar stool. "Bacon?"

"In the oven, of course," Michelle answered, leaning over the bar to plant a quick kiss on Lacey's forehead. "And how are you today?"

"Can't complain. Working hard, but a girl's got to eat, right? Where are Trina and Lyssa?"

"They stayed with Brent. He'd promised to take them swimming at the spring today and we didn't want to make a liar out of him. We're only here for a day, anyway."

"I'm guessing you're not here by coincidence."

"Nope. Brandy called me about twenty minutes after

you did."

Kendra said, "There I was, happy as a new foal in a patch of sweet grass, cleaning out Bethany's stall when Michelle comes out and tells me to pack a bag. Next thing I know, we're on a Vegas vacation."

"You're on vacation, honey. I'm working, remember?"

Lacey smiled. These two were so perfect for each other. It was amazing how well they got along, even if their initial relationship had been stressed. After months of heartache, during which their younger brother, Brad, and his wife were killed, and Lacey had been run off the road and nearly killed, Michelle and Kendra had found absolute, perfect, life-time love. It was hard to believe that such a thing existed, but there it was... right in front of her every time the girls came to Vegas. Tangible. Real.

They'd been married for a few months now and as far as anyone could see, the honeymoon was far from over.

"So, tell me everything you know about the Kincaid thing," Michelle demanded with the same tone of voice she might use to ask for directions to the bathroom.

"There isn't much to know. What did she tell you?"

Michelle pulled the last of the bacon out of the oven and laid the strips on a paper towel to dry.

"I can't really say. She's my client, Lacey. I know you want an interview, and as her publicist, I am the right person to call for that sort of thing. But we've got a small ethics issue here, don't we?"

Lacey frowned. "What do you mean?"

"That I'm privy to confidential information. I mean, it's not confidential like with a lawyer or anything, but my clients trust me to keep their business private. I can't just feed you information that we don't want made public."

"That's why I want an interview! So she can go public with her side of things. They... we... the press is going to eat her alive!"

Kendra chuckled. "Listen to you, all worried about poor Brandy Kincaid. You want the scoop. Be honest about it."

"Of course, I do. But with Michelle there, it could be a controlled scoop. More like... you know... a few tablespoons worth of really good information that could—"

"Bolster your ratings?" Kendra interrupted.

"No. I was going to say that it could get the court of public opinion on her side. People love this kind of stuff. It's like reality TV only it's actual reality. They're going to make decisions based on what we tell them. You don't want them all coming to the worst possible conclusions, do you, Michelle?"

Michelle's chest rose slightly as she inhaled a deep breath and released it in a heavy sigh. "You're probably right. I haven't asked her about it yet. But you have to tell me what you know first."

"Okay. I'll bite. Five days ago, the parents of one Cynthia Kincaid filed a missing person's report. Initially, the authorities didn't want to accept the report because, after talking to the missing woman's wife, Brandy, they learned that she has a habit of taking off for as long as a week at a time. By they, I mean Detective Jethro Martin, who got the case in the luck of the draw, basically.

"The parents, however, were rather insistent, so he put

out a BOLO and added her to the missing person's index. In short, they would be alerted if she got pulled over for speeding in Wisconsin, or something."

The timer dinged. Michelle stood and pulled a quiche out of the oven. The steam rose in cloudy waves and the spicy aroma filled the kitchen. "Go on."

"A couple days later, day before yesterday, they found Cynthia's car at McCarren, but there was no record of her having flown anywhere. So, they started to take things a bit more seriously. Yesterday afternoon, they served a search warrant on the Kincaid house and found Cynthia's body in the bedroom."

"Why did they get a search warrant?" Kendra popped a piece of bacon into her mouth.

"I imagine it had something to do with the fact that Brandy wasn't really cooperating." Lacey frowned. Why wasn't Brandy cooperating?

"Ah, those deductive reasoning skills. No wonder you're such a crackpot investigative reporter!" Kendra continued to chew on her bacon as her mouth turned into a wide, genuine grin.

Michelle frowned as she sliced the quiche into pie-shaped servings. "Cooperate with what? The cops didn't take the report seriously right? I mean, if they had, wouldn't they have found her car at the airport right away? If Brandy told them that her wife liked to take off, that's the first place they should have looked for her car. Then, suddenly, they need a warrant? It doesn't add up."

"I completely agree. Which is why I want that interview."

Michelle shot her a glare through the steam.

Lacey's mouth watered as she ignored Michelle's censure and waited for her breakfast. She leaned back on the stool to give Michelle room to set down an earthenware dinner plate brimming with quiche, bacon, hash browns, and two slices of toast. "Your turn. Why did Brandy call you? She should have called her attorney, if you ask me. It's not looking really good for her right now. I have security footage and eye-witness testimony that Brandy threatened to kill Cynthia if she didn't stop doing something. Not sure what the something is... was... but I'm going to find out."

Michelle and Kendra froze. After a surreptitious glance between the two older women, Michelle finished serving herself and sat down.

Lacey glanced first at Michelle, then Kendra, and then finally leveled a glare back at Michelle. "What's going on?"

"Nothing. Well, not really. It's just we hadn't heard about that part yet."

"Not many people have. I asked the detective about it yesterday, but then he got the call about finding the body and he never answered me. I'm pretty sure they have the same footage and stills."

Michelle ate in silence for a few moments, her brows drawn together as she studiously chewed her food. Finally, she put down her fork and lifted the bright blue linen napkin to wipe the corners of her mouth. "I know one thing for sure. Brandy isn't capable of murder. I've known her for years and no matter how pissed off she was at Cynthia, she would never kill her. Wouldn't even lift a hand to her, actually. I have serious doubts that she would even threaten her.

There has to be more to it than that." She paused, leveling her deep blue eyes on Lacey. "I'm meeting with her at the Touchdown in about an hour. If I ask you to come along, you have to promise that anything you hear won't be on the record. But you know me and my business. I spin. It's my job. Having an ally in the press can only help matters at this point."

Lacey could barely breathe but did her best to hide her excitement behind her own napkin. "You mean, off the record, like entirely off the record?"

"I mean, like you're not even there. This is an introduction, not an interview. Full stop."

"And if she agrees to an interview later,"—Lacey narrowed her gaze—"I've got exclusive access?"

"Yes, but you can't sensationalize the story. Hell, it isn't a story. It's the real life of a very dear friend of mine. This entire thing has the potential of becoming a national story; it's got all the elements that make people like Nancy Grace go absolutely spin crazy. There are going to be enough local reporters turning it into a dime-store melodrama. I need someone who will take things another direction. When it's all over, Brandy is still going to have businesses to run and a life to live."

"I won't lie," Lacey retorted, straightening her back and placing her palms on the counter at either side of her plate.

"I wouldn't dream of asking you to. What I'm asking is that you report the facts with no extra negative spin just because we're talking about sex, lies, and murder here."

"Like I said, I won't lie. But I won't dramatize and I won't spin it into a guilty-until-proven-innocent farce. I'm a reporter."

"There's no such thing these days. All reporters are commentators now. Everyone is a pundit. I need someone in our corner."

"And if she is guilty? If I go with the she's-a-really-great-person angle and it turns out she did something to her wife? My career would be on the line, Mike." Lacey used the old nickname for her sister-in-law, in part to punctuate the subtle use of family connections going on.

"Come with me to meet her. Judge her character for yourself, up close, and then let me know what you think you can do. Just promise that this meeting is off the record."

Exclusive access to the most newsworthy person in Las Vegas, maybe even the entire country, could only help Lacey's career. Michelle knew that as much as Lacey did. The fact that they were family, of course, meant that Michelle was willing to trust Lacey more than she would some other reporter. She probably wouldn't even think of using a member of the press to help in spin control were it not for the fact they were sisters-by-marriage. Of course, the fact they had been friends for much longer than that helped, too.

"Alright. You've got a deal. Today, I'll just meet with her. And I won't use anything I learn from this meeting until I can corroborate it through outside sources."

Michelle's lips turned into a lopsided grin that usually meant she'd received exactly what she wanted. "If that's the best you can do, then fine. Deal."

An hour later, Lacey and Michelle climbed a wide, curving staircase to the second floor of the Touchdown Club and Casino. They landed in the loft, almost precisely where that video of Brandy threatening her wife had been taken. Turning slightly to get her bearings, she found the eye-in-the-sky camera that had most likely shot the pictures and resisted the temptation to wink.

Lacey had only been to the Touchdown once before – when she'd picked up the copy of the surveillance video from her source in the casino security office. She'd heard good things about the club, which opened only two years earlier. But it was after the accident and her social life had been nonexistent since then. Before the accident, she would have been all over the newest club on the strip.

That was then. This was now.

The casino, themed after a sports bar that had swallowed a glamour girl, had a huge goal post towering over the entrance to the nightclubs as though it held up the loft, and a bar in the center looked like an open-air clubhouse. Card tables covered in lawn-green felt and a gridiron pattern dotted the perimeter. Flashing, electronic slot machines filled the interior in neat rows. Lacey preferred the old one-arm bandits that actually required the gambler to pull the lever. There was something historical about it that reminded her of a Vegas she'd never known.

At the top of the stairs, Michelle turned to the right and led Lacey past the banks of five-dollar slot machines and onto a narrow catwalk leading to a single door. One side of the walkway opened to reveal most of the casino floor. The other side of the catwalk was made of a large mirror that spanned the entire length of the twenty-foot stretch from floor to ceiling. Lacey kept her gaze locked on Michelle's back until they reached the door. A gold plate with PRIVATE etched into the surface was the only indication that it didn't lead to a broom closet. Michelle knocked.

"Come on in, Michelle. It's open."

Michelle opened the door and ushered Lacey inside.

The other side of the door revealed a large office filled with over-sized, antique furniture. It looked nothing like the main spaces of the casino, which were garish and loud, as casinos were in general. By stark contrast, the owner's private office reminded Lacey of an English drawing room or a rich man's study. Dark wood furniture and hardwood floors created an atmosphere of understated elegance, like an oasis of class in a classless world. One entire wall was a window that overlooked the casino – the interior of a one-way glass that formed the mirror on the catwalk. This room belonged to a woman who liked to keep her eye on things that belonged to her.

Brandy stepped from a separate room and strode toward them on long, shapely legs encased in the same worn Levis she'd been wearing the day before. She wasn't wearing a shirt other than a wife-beater style tank-top in a salmon hue that complimented her olive complexion and short, dark hair. The top accentuated her small breasts, free from any type of bra or support. Most of the times Lacey had seen Brandy, which wasn't many and always from a distance, she'd come across as entirely androgynous.

Not today.

Lacey hadn't given any thought to the woman beneath the headlines, but seeing her like this made her think of frightening, lurid thoughts like intimacy and trust. And sex. The unbidden, final thought sent tingles to parts of her body she'd nearly forgotten she had.

From the small, red towel Brandy used to dry her hands, Lacey concluded the other room was a private bathroom. Brandy finished drying her hands and tossed the towel gently on the back of a winged chair. "Are you ever a sight for sore eyes," Brandy said to Michelle as she wrapped her in a warm, familiar hug. "I'm really sorry to drag you away from the ranch."

"Don't worry about it, Bran. I just wish I were here under different circumstances. I'm so sorry to hear about Cynthia."

"Thanks, 'Chell. I appreciate that."

"I was surprised that you were here, though. Why aren't you staying at your place?"

Lacey nearly choked. What a thing to say! Maybe she wasn't staying there because her wife was just murdered in their bedroom?

"I drove out last night, but the press had already staked the place out. I got about a half mile from the main gate and turned right back around. Vultures."

The two women separated before Lacey had a chance to feel any more awkward. They both turned their attention on her and suddenly she felt even more awkward. Brandy's smile faltered, but didn't vanish completely. She canted her head to one side and asked, "Don't I know you from somewhere?"

Michelle waved a hand and said, "This is my sister-in-law, Lacey Williams. Lacey, I'd like you to meet my very dear friend, Brandy Kincaid."

"It's nice to meet you, Lacey." Brandy indicated they should sit. "I swear, you look really familiar to me."

"I used to cocktail at the MGM Grand. Maybe you saw me there? But I think it's probably because I was standing in front of your house yesterday afternoon."

CHAPTER THREE

"She's a reporter, Michelle! You brought a reporter to my office?"

Brandy had trusted Michelle with many things in the time they'd known each other. She was one of the best public relations people in the business and had helped her launch both of her nightclubs and the casino. If she wanted a good public front on this thing, Michelle was the one to do it. Why would she bring a reporter to their first meeting about the murder of her wife? "Christ, what were you thinking?" She wiped her palms, already beginning to sweat, on her jeans. She turned her back on the two women and placed her hands on her hips.

"It's okay. Trust me," Michelle stated as she settled onto the leather sofa. "I'm going to ask you some pretty awful questions, Bran, and, well, I don't want you to take it personally. I brought Lacey along because she'll be asking questions too, from another perspective. She doesn't know you like I do, so let's just say that she'll be acting as the general public so we'll have an idea about what the infamous they might be thinking."

Brandy turned back around and glared at Michelle while pointing in Lacey's general direction. "She's not the public. She's a reporter. You get that? They make their living off the carnage of everything around them. No offense," she added to Lacey, standing behind the same chair where Brandy had tossed her towel.

Lacey hiked her purse higher onto a slender shoulder encased in an oversized BYU sweatshirt. "Reporters are the mouthpiece of the people. We speak for them and we ask the questions they would ask if they could. We're not vultures."

"That's debatable." Brandy was being mean. She knew she was being mean, but she didn't care. She'd been blindsided by the idea that anything she said to Michelle today would be plastered all over the Internet, TV and radio by dinner time. This was exactly what she'd been trying to avoid.

"Brandy, calm down. Sit down, for heaven's sake. Have I ever steered you wrong? Have I?"

Brandy hesitated. "No."

"Then trust me on this. Nothing we talk about today will be on the record. Nothing. Think of Lacey as a... a... a media consultant. I hired her to give us insight into what to expect from the press. That's all."

"Did you pay her?"

"What? Well, no. She's my sister-in-law."

Lacey cleared her throat before rounding the overstuffed arm chair and sitting delicately on the edge. The momentum caused strands of her hair to shift just enough to reveal the scar on her cheek. She immediately tilted her head in such a way that her hair covered it again.

"I think what Brandy is saying is that if you don't pay me, we don't have a legally binding relationship. My fee for the afternoon is one dollar. And it's only for this afternoon. After that, I'm firing myself."

Michelle dug through her purse until she pulled out a fifty. "It's all I have."

Lacey leaned forward over the coffee table and plucked the bill from her sister-in-law's outstretched fingers. "Thanks for the tip."

Brandy couldn't help the beginnings of a laugh from forming in her diaphragm. She squelched it, but not the smile that formed on her lips against her will. She sat in an overstuffed chair that was the exact twin of the one Lacey occupied. "Okay. Okay. You win. What do you need to know to keep me from going down with the ship here?"

"Let's start with what the police have told you. Have they let you know a probable cause of death, yet?" Lacey asked.

Brandy tried to focus her attention on Michelle, but it proved difficult with the small, curvy blonde sitting so close. So close that Brandy could inhale the scent of fresh soap and some kind of floral perfume. She sat with a posture that seemed at once poised to respond and timid, while her expression remained fairly bland. Her face was beautiful in a girl-next-door kind of way and her body, hidden as it was behind athletic gear too big for her, oozed sex appeal. If she were trying to hide that essence behind an old track suit, she'd failed epically.

"You're on that news show, right? The one that covers pretty much anything and everything?"

"All That and More. Yeah, that's mine. Well, kind of. I

mean, it's Addison's show, but I'm the field reporter to her anchor chair."

"You're really good. I guess I'm a fan, actually."

"Thanks. Now, have you heard anything regarding the cause of death?"

A knot formed in Brandy's belly as Lacey's gaze turned from meek and invisible to almost predatory. Lacey licked her lips and the knot turned into a fire ball. "Nothing; not a single word."

"Why did the authorities have to get a search warrant for your home? Why didn't you allow them in when they asked?"

"First, they didn't ask. The one detective, something Martin, called me once to ask about Cynthia's whereabouts. That was when her folks filed the missing person's report, and that was it. I never heard from them again until I got a call that they'd found her body. But even if they had asked me, I couldn't have given consent. I didn't live there anymore."

One of Lacey's perfectly shaped eyebrows arched. "Go on."

"I moved out three months ago when I filed for divorce. Cyndi has… had… exclusive use and occupancy of the 'marital residence' for the time being, and probably would have wound up with it once the divorce was final, too. I didn't want it. Still don't. I live on my ranch outside of Pahrump."

"So, they never once asked you to let them in to look for your wife?"

"Nope. Hell, I heard about them finding her car at the airport on the news. From you, actually. The cops never told me a damn thing."

"Why do you suppose that is?" Michelle asked.

She shrugged. "Maybe because I didn't believe anything was wrong and I told them so. God, how could I have been so wrong about that?"

Michelle continued. "Some people would ask why you weren't more worried about your wife, even though you were separated. You've said that she takes off pretty routinely; does that mean she never even called in to let you know she was alright?"

"There was a time that she would." Brandy peered at Michelle and then turned her attention back to Lacey. The media consultant. If she thought of Lacey as a reporter, she'd just get upset all over again. She took a deep breath, willing the air to nourish her lungs and feed her blood. It didn't work well, but she found the energy to continue. "But I wasn't in love with my wife. And I'm pretty damn sure she wasn't in love with me. She had no reason to report to me anymore, not that she ever did."

There. Done.

Move on.

"Well, that might cause a bit of a snare for you, don't you think?" Lacey quipped. "What made you hate your wife?"

"Seriously? I didn't say I hated her."

"I'm just playing devil's advocate here. That's what the reporters are going to ask you. You have to be prepared for it."

Brandy squinted, trying to see past the professional façade that surrounded Michelle's sister-in-law. Her eyes held a hint of mystery and a crap-ton of I'm-capable-of-kicking-your-ass. But there was something else; something fragile and needy that appealed to the protector inside Brandy.

Lacey canted her head. "Did you ever love her?"

"Cyndi? There was a time when I loved her very much, and for the record, I don't think I could ever really hate anyone. I didn't love her anymore because we discovered, too late, that we weren't looking for the same things. I wanted peace and family. She wanted shopping and more shopping. I wanted to live in a grounded world and she wanted to swing from the chandeliers. We were just different."

"And that made you fall out of love? Was she a librarian or something when you met?"

"No, but she did present herself a little differently. She was a barrel racer. Who's more grounded than that? She loved the land, she loved horses, she loved competition. She was everything I'd ever wanted in a woman and I fell. Hard. Over time, though, she got more and more wild. She stopped competing when she realized she wasn't going anywhere in her career. She wasn't winning; never had, actually. And she wasn't willing to try any more, even though she'd only been doing it professionally for less than a year. I saw our marriage as a signal that it was time to settle down. She didn't see it as much of anything, apparently, and found my money a great excuse to party her ass off."

"What else was going on? I'm not buying the whole we-grew-apart spiel. And if I don't buy it, neither will CNN."

"Lacey," Michelle gasped. "What a thing to say!"

"I'm doing my job, Mike."

"It's okay." Brandy stood and headed for the bar. It was past two on a Saturday, which meant she would break no unwritten rules of decorum by fixing herself a large glass of scotch. As she moved, she tried to ignore the two sets of eyes that were searing into her back. When she'd shot down a finger's worth of alcohol, she poured a second glass, two fingers this time, and took one additional sip. "This is going to get really ugly, isn't it?" she asked the bottom of her glass.

"It could," Michelle replied, her voice soft and matter-of-fact.

"I told you, a couple of years ago, that Cynthia was cheating on me, right? That I couldn't divorce her because of the damn pre-nup we signed which promised her half of everything if I filed for a divorce? If she filed for anything other than my infidelity, she'd get nothing. But if I filed, she'd get half even if she slept with my best friend on the craps table during a tournament."

"Yes, I remember that. I remember thinking you were an idiot to sign it."

That hurt, but Michelle was right. She had been an idiot to sign it. She'd been played for a fool the entire time, if she were going to be completely honest with herself. "We figured it would make up for the fact that we weren't legally married in Nevada, or pretty much anywhere outside of Massachusetts. We decided to go to Canada for the ceremony and she was worried that being married in a foreign country would cause too many problems if we split up. Well, it turns out she was cheating, not only with other women, but men, too. I couldn't take it anymore. I was doing pretty much anything I could to make her life miserable so she'd file for divorce. It didn't work, though.

She stepped up her time away from home, spending weeks in California and Mexico. Europe. Finally, I gave in. I wound up filing myself. I packed up and moved back to the Rocking T."

"You still financed her, though," Michelle pointed out.

"Yeah. I did." Brandy downed the rest of her scotch and poured a final, single finger. "I had court-ordered support, but I never really cut her off. I just felt like I had a bit more control."

"So, basically, you have no motive to want your wife dead except for the fact you were going to lose half of your rather immense fortune to a woman who was sleeping with anything that walks upright," Lacey stated flatly.

"Well, when you put it that way…" Brandy finally returned to her seat and the fabric all-but burned the back of her legs. She immediately stood and paced in the open space covered with the rug she had purchased in Turkey five summers earlier. From the corner of her eye, she caught the wall safe behind her desk hanging open an inch or so. The damn thing was like the rest of her life; falling apart. She closed it and fell into the leather creases of the swivel chair behind her desk. "What's your point?"

"And there's the fact that you refused to file a missing person's report. Her folks had to take care of that."

"Yeah. Her folks."

"You don't like them?"

"Let's just say they weren't really upset that we were splitting up."

Michelle shifted in her seat and brought out her notebook. "First things first. You need to make sure that when you're around other people, you act and sound like a woman who has just lost her wife should act and sound. If anyone asks how you feel about the loss of your wife, you may feel compelled to bite back at them with something off the cuff, but you won't do that. No, you'll find more flowery and precious ways to express your grief than a porcupine has quills and you'll mean every word of it." She rested the notebook on her knees. "You loved her once upon a time. And, as far as the rest of the world is concerned, you still loved her until the day she died."

"Are you sure?" Lacey asked. "I mean, if we look at it from a logical point of view, the fact that she wasn't in love with her wife gives the jealous-rage motive a lot less bite, doesn't it?"

"But it emphasizes the money angle. When you filed for divorce, your pre-nup became a part of the public record."

"Yes, and the paperwork itself asks that the agreement be set aside based on a few ideas my divorce attorney dreamed up. I don't really understand all of it. But basically, she's claiming that because Cynthia never intended to live up to the idea of a monogamous marriage, the agreement was fraudulent. She's also got something in there about our marriage being legal in the States now and that normal divorce precedents should apply. You know, how we weren't married very long, and she shouldn't be entitled to alimony or whatever. But you're right. I may have been jealous early on, when I first found out about her little hobbies, but at the end? Not so much. I simply didn't care enough for it to hurt anymore. I don't... didn't hate her. I just wasn't head-over-heels in love anymore. And I didn't think she should walk away with half my assets."

Lacey stood and walked to the one-way glass. She seemed to be taking in the vastness of the surroundings. Today was Saturday and the casino was packed with tourists from all over the world, mostly gay and lesbian couples and singles who had read about The Touchdown Club in gay-friendly tourism guides. There were also locals who preferred to gamble off the main resort strip. Millions of dollars were changing hands just one story below. That made for a hell of a lot of assets to share.

"Had Cynthia been served with the divorce complaint?"

"Yes. We have had one hearing where the judge said she could live in the house exclusively until the whole thing was settled. That's the only movement there was, though."

"We're getting off track a little bit," Michelle interrupted. "The important thing is that you didn't hate her. Which means in public, you grieve. You miss her. It's a tragedy. She had so much to live for." Michelle's voice was adamant, forceful and confident. Brandy had spent a great deal of money on this woman's advice over the years and even when her own life had been crumbling, the advice had always been sound.

"I can do that," Brandy answered, her resolve growing like steel beams in her bones. "But if someone asks me if I loved her when she died, I won't lie."

Lacey avoided her reflection in the glass and studied the casino floor in the massive mirrors placed above the main entrance doors. They tilted at a strategic angle that allowed someone in the office to see not only the parts of the floor visible to the naked eye, but also the spaces located below the office loft. From her vantage point, she watched as a group of tourists left the casino and entered the lesbian nightclub directly beneath her.

When she sensed movement behind her, she caught Michelle's nearly-transparent reflection on the office side of the glass moving to stand behind Brandy's chair. "No one is asking you to lie." Leaning from the back of the chair, Michelle wrapped Brandy in a gentle hug.

Lying might not be a bad idea, from the way things were looking. But no, she wouldn't want Brandy to lie, either. She'd only get caught.

Michelle continued, her voice hopeful and determined. "We'll help you get through this in one piece. Starting right now. I brought Lacey so we can set up an exclusive interview. She'll put together a list of questions and we'll go over them together."

Turning to face the interior of the office, Lacey said, "Right. But there are conditions. Neither of you will see or hear the final piece until it's aired. I'm nobody's flunkie." She folded her arms.

Brandy sucked in a breath that raised her small breasts slightly, wrapping her arms around Michelle's where they still held her, as though she were guarding her very existence. "I'm trusting you here, Lacey. I'm trusting that you're not going to take my statements out of context and that you'll actually hear me."

"I will. I am very good at my job."

"I don't doubt that. I just can't be exactly certain what your job is yet. But I trust Michelle, and Michelle trusts you, so... I guess I'm in."

Michelle gave Brandy one final squeeze before she poured herself a drink and sat back on the sofa.

Lacey shook her head when Michelle silently offered her a drink and turned her attention to Brandy. "Let's start at the beginning. When did you come to the conclusion that your wife may have been in some sort of peril or distress?"

Brandy's deep brown eyes focused on Lacey with an intensity that seemed to exude the odd combination of warmth and compassion with outright panic, resentment and derision. When she answered, she did so without looking away, but focusing more deeply. "When I walked into her house yesterday and saw her body for myself on the bedroom floor." When she finished speaking, she finally lowered her eyes, turning her head to look out the window.

Heat pooled in Lacey's gut when she looked at the torn, suddenly worn features of Brandy's expression. She looked to be somewhere in her early thirties. Surprisingly, Lacey's research had revealed Brandy was closer to forty-five than twenty-five. But at that moment, the air around her seemed to age her infinitely. She was strong. She'd made herself a force to be reckoned with on the Vegas strip and had done it all on her own, starting with nothing. Had she nearly lost it all to one voracious and voluptuous gold-digger? Lacey cleared her throat and forced herself to disregard her compassion.

"Your wife's parents filed a missing person's report

when you basically refused to. Obviously, they thought there was a problem. Any idea why they would think that?"

Brandy shrugged. "They didn't know her like I did, I'd imagine. To them, she was their sweet little girl. Princess Cynthia. They were in town — they live in Bend, Oregon — and happened to notice she wasn't around. They came here looking for her, and I told them she'd turn up eventually. They hadn't told her they were coming, so I figured she'd probably just gone off somewhere with her jet-set friends." Finally, Brandy turned her attention back from the window and leveled her gaze on Lacey's face. The attention manifested nervous knots in Lacey's belly.

"And I didn't refuse to file a report. I just didn't see the need for one," Brandy continued. "I knew her better than anyone else. I knew that she'd take off from time to time, so a couple of days wasn't a big deal."

"When was the last time you saw your wife alive, Brandy?"

Brandy's brows dipped slightly and she was silent for a few seconds before she answered. "Here. In this office, or more precisely, on the casino floor just outside the door."

"What happened?"

Stiffening in her chair, Brandy pushed herself back a couple of inches and folded her arms. "What's that supposed to mean?"

"Brandy, you haven't done anything wrong," Michelle interjected. "You can't see every question as an accusation. You're not defending yourself; you're letting the general public get to know you better, that's all. This will make pretty good practice for talking to the cops, too, actually. Only, I won't be there. Your attorney will."

"Michelle is right, you know. I'm only asking the same questions that every other reporter is going to shout at you starting now. Only they don't care how you answer. They'll turn it to their advantage and make you look like the worst possible spouse since Scott Peterson. So just answer calmly, or if you don't want to answer, say so."

"Alright. Fine. Let's just get this over with." The air around Brandy's squared shoulders bristled, sending shocks that reached out and touched Lacey as surely as fingers. It was easy to see how broken she could be—how broken she should be—but she stood strong, with her defenses firmly in place.

"Remember, this is more like a rehearsal. Nothing is on the record, yet. Now, what happened the last time you saw your wife?" Michelle finished her drink and set the old-fashioned glass and melting ice on the coffee table.

"We met here in my office to go over some financials. I walked her out to the casino floor and she left. I don't know where she went. She might have gone home for all I know. But it was pretty early, only about ten or so, so I'm thinking she may have met friends somewhere. She was dressed up like she was going to the fucking Oscars or something."

Michelle interjected, "Remember to answer only those questions you're asked, okay? Talking too much can give the opposition—sorry Lace—more ammunition."

"There wasn't an argument?"

"Why would there be an argument?"

Leveling a narrowed gaze on Michelle before focusing on her subject's suddenly sheltered expression, Lacey continued, "I have information that indicates your last meeting with your wife wasn't a pleasant one. There is video footage my station has obtained that shows you arguing vehemently with your estranged wife, based on body language, of course, since there is no audio. That said, several patrons have stated on the record, and told the investigating officer, Detective Martin, that they heard you threaten your wife."

Brandy levitated out of her chair and circled the desk, suddenly appearing so much larger than her nearly six-foot frame. Lacey leaped to her feet and escaped the confines of the tight, narrow space between the chair and the desk. Michelle immediately positioned herself between Brandy and Lacey.

"What the hell are you talking about?" Brandy's intense gaze sent icy daggers at Lacey, each one a frozen reminder of the fragile human condition. "Where did you get a video?" She threw her hands in the air. "Nevermind. That's a stupid question, right? You got it from one my own guys in Security, right?"

Ignoring the rising panic in her blood, Lacey straightened her posture. "From one of your security officers, yes."

"Oh, so, yeah, I can really believe that you're on my side. Who was it? Who gave you that recording?" She swiped one trembling hand through her short-cropped hair until it rested on the back of her neck. As she turned slightly away, her other hand found her hip. "Whoever he is, he is so fired..."

"I'm not on your side. I'm not on any side. I am reporting a series of events and I don't take sides! I'm not a commentator. I'm not a pundit for the falsely accused. I'm a reporter. I am doing my job. Right now, that job is to prepare you for what you're going to be dealing with for the next few months."

"You're just like the others," Brandy spat, glaring at Lacey as though she were a monster. "Your job sucks." Brandy placed both of her hands on those narrow, wonderfully androgynous hips encased in stone-washed denim and moved to the window. She looked over the casino floor below and slowly shook her head as she pinched the bridge of her nose.

A part of Lacey wanted to leave. Brandy had scared her; had made her think of the many ways in which one human being could harm another. Reminded her of all the reasons she had to not trust anyone. Another part of her watched this woman who stood so stoically against the world and Lacey couldn't bring herself to believe that she was guilty. There was something about her that exuded innocence. Lacey took a tentative step forward, prepared to run if the need should arise. "Listen, if I have the video, then by this time tomorrow, chances are pretty good everyone else will have it. I certainly didn't pay for it, but someone else will offer that guard money. He'll take it, I'm sure. I'm giving you a chance to explain it publicly before the rest of the world can form their own opinions."

Michelle guided Brandy to the sofa. "Did you fight with Cyndi before she went missing, Bran? This is really important information. I need you to be completely honest with me if we're going to get out in front of this thing."

Brandy glanced over her entire office, from the door, to

the desk, to Michelle and finally to the surface of the coffee table. She seemed to stare absently at the neatly arranged trade magazines and an old edition of The Advocate with Ellen DeGeneres on the cover in a white tuxedo. Finally, she shook her head. "I didn't threaten her."

"What did you say, then?" Michelle asked.

Lacey suddenly felt like she didn't belong in the room. Every professional bone in her body told her that she should use every word and gesture for her coverage of the story. Every compassionate bone in her body screamed she shouldn't use any of it.

Brandy was hurting. She had been taken for a ride for the past several years and probably had no idea when it had even started. All because she'd fallen in love with the wrong woman.

"She wanted more money. A lot of money, actually. Until the divorce was finalized, I still controlled one hundred percent of the assets. She had access, through me, to all of it, of course. I paid her a monthly amount— court ordered support. A very generous allowance, but it wasn't really enough for her. The judge ordered me to pay forty thousand dollars a month. It wasn't enough for her. When we were first married, in one week, she spent more than eighty-thousand dollars on clothes, jewelry and restaurants for herself and a dozen or so of her closest friends. It was completely nuts. Out of control."

Michelle released a slow whistle. "I doubt I could spend that much if I tried."

"And it's not like she had to clear what she spent it on. I wasn't asking for receipts, for Christ's sake. Neither was the judge. But it wasn't enough for her and she was constantly asking for more. Usually, I'd give it to her. A few thousand here; a few thousand there. But it was worse than that. This time, she wanted a half million dollars."

"Jesus! For what?" Michelle asked, her eyes wide.

"She wouldn't say," Brandy replied, shrugging. "Naturally, I refused. She got angry and stormed out of the office on her goddamned five-inch designer heels. I followed her, grabbed her to keep her from leaving so upset. I was trying to get her to tell me what she needed the money for, but she said that wasn't any of my business. She said I had the money, like it was lying around in the goddamn broken safe or something, and that she was just as entitled to it as I was. I was frustrated."

The weight of a lifetime seemed to be attached to each syllable falling from Brandy's lips. She'd appeared so strong and confident until this moment. Now, she looked like a little girl, lost in a world she didn't understand, as though her very existence plotted against her. "What did you say to her?" Lacey prompted.

Brandy looked at Lacey with something in her eyes that seemed to say she was sorry and appreciative at the same time. Finally, she swallowed and turned her attention back to the nothingness in front of her. "I did not threaten her. What I said was, 'The only way I'm coming out of this with a dime to my name is if one of us doesn't live through it.' But I was talking about me."

The words hung in the heavy air for several quiet ticks of a very slow clock. Michelle was the first to break the spell. "Okay, that's not good, but it's not horrible, either. It's not exactly a death threat, is it?" She looked at Lacey. "They misunderstood her sarcasm, that's all. It's not a threat."

"It's close," Lacey quipped.

Brandy fell onto the sofa, sitting with her elbows on her knees and her face buried in her hands. She began to hyperventilate. Michelle knelt in front of her. "Just look at me, Bran. You're going to be okay. Everything will be fine, you'll see."

"I hated her. I really fucking hated her," Brandy growled. "Maybe I did want her dead. Maybe I—"

"Don't ever say that where a reporter can hear you. Do you understand me?" Lacey fell to one knee, so Brandy could see her face. "Never say anything even remotely close to that in front of the press."

"What about you?"

"We're off the record."

The walls of Brandy's office had never felt quite so tight before. It wasn't a huge room compared to some of her counterparts' spaces in other, larger casinos. She didn't need a lot of space for the work she did here. She didn't even have a secretary. But now it seemed like a cage, narrow and dark.

The brightest thing in the room was Lacey. She peered up at Brandy with her eyes narrowed with determination. Brandy could lose herself in those eyes and as a chill ran over her flesh, she suspected she might immediately drown in those cool, blue depths. "Thank you," she whispered. "I know that must be difficult for you."

Lacey offered a wan smile. "Listen, you and I are going

to do an exclusive, don't get me wrong. But we're going to do it properly, with predetermined questions your publicist will approve, and I won't have any concerns about breaking any invisible boundaries when I go live with it. I don't like this. I'm not going to lie about that. But Michelle trusts you, so I guess I'll need to trust you to."

Brandy grinned as Lacey tossed her own words back at her. She was a beautiful woman, there was no question about that. As a general rule, Brandy didn't trust beautiful women anymore. But, she was Michelle's family, and Michelle had never done anything that hadn't been in Brandy's best interest. And there was something about Lacey's eyes that made her want to believe in her. Made her want to trust her, no matter how difficult it was. Brandy's entire life was on the line. Her businesses, her home, everything. Did she actually have a choice in the matter?

Not really.

"Deal." Brandy released a deep sigh, refreshing her lungs with air she'd somehow forgotten to breathe for the past twenty minutes or so. "So, what's next?"

Michelle positioned herself in the arm chair and left Lacey to sit next to Brandy on the sofa. "We keep prepping you, so this doesn't happen when you're cornered in the grocery store by some asshat who doesn't know you like we do. I need to know everything about Cynthia. Assuming this wasn't some random act of violence, do you have any idea who might have wanted to kill her? To hurt her in any way?"

"You mean, besides me?" She ran both hands through her hair and settled them on the steel cords in the back of her neck. "Oh, gee wiz, I don't know," she crooned.

"Perhaps one of her lovers? Or her official boyfriend?"

Lacey gasped. "An actual boyfriend? Seriously?"

"Oh, so there was something you hadn't discovered yet? Good to know," Brandy replied.

"Yeah, no. I hadn't come across that little tidbit. She had a boyfriend. Wait... is that in the divorce complaint?"

Brandy tilted her head and narrowed her eyes. "No. I went with a standard irreconcilable differences approach to try to keep millions of dollars out of her shiny little purse strings." Brandy tried to bite back her sarcasm, but somehow, she simply couldn't. She sighed. "I'm sorry. Yes. It's in the complaint."

Michelle pursed her lips and leaned forward in her chair, and then asked, "How long have you known about it?"

"A couple of months before I filed, I guess. It wasn't hard to figure out once I finally admitted something was really wrong; that we weren't just not getting along. I guess she either forgot, or it never occurred to her, that I got bank statements and credit card bills. And that I actually read them.

"She'd started buying men's clothing and cologne and things like that. I assumed, initially, that she'd met a woman like me and would explain all of the masculine purchases. I mean, I'm not exactly into diamonds and furs. It made sense."

Nobody had ever accused Brandy of being too girly, and it had taken years for her to learn that she didn't have to wear makeup and skirts to be a real woman. She was proud of who she had become; a confident woman of means surviving in a man's world. But apparently, that hadn't made her man enough for Cynthia.

"How did you discover differently?" Lacey's voice drew

her back to the moment and she shifted her full attention in the younger woman's direction.

"I... I followed her."

Michelle groaned. Lacey shook her head slowly, her hair falling in wavy strands to almost obliterate her scar.

"I know, I know. It doesn't look good. Now I'm a stalker, right? I hired a local PI to follow her around for a while. But honestly, I couldn't tell you now if I was following my wife or following my money." Her palms began to sweat again, and she dried them on the thighs of her jeans. Leaning forward, she placed her forehead into her palms and stared at the floor. "I'm so screwed."

"No. No, we can spin this. You were concerned that she was being led astray by someone after her money," Michelle stated.

"My money."

"You really do need a lot of work," Lacey insisted. "Don't say that in an interview. You were married. The money belonged to both of you."

"I was a jealous, practically-jilted wife. And I was learning to hate her more with every passing minute. I. Am. Screwed."

"I'm going to want to talk to the boyfriend. Do you know where we can find him?" Almost like some wind had shifted, Brandy inhaled a scent of woman and lilacs. Lacey had leaned forward and glanced into the little tent Brandy had created around her face. The scent settled in her stomach and sent ripples through her blood until it reached between her legs and set up camp.

Brandy swallowed. Hard. Where the hell had that come from?

"Do you have an address?" Lacey continued to push. "A name? Anything."

"Uh, yeah. Yeah, in fact I was on my way back from trying to find him when I got the call about Cynthia. He lives on a boat at the marina on Lake Mead. He's kind of a bum, really. Until yesterday, I don't think that boat left the slip once the whole time I'd been checking up on them, so it's like he just can't afford to live anywhere else. Last month, Cynthia paid up the slip fees for six months."

"When you talked to him, did he say that Cyndi had been there at all since she'd gone missing?"

"No. He didn't say anything, actually. He wasn't home. Like I said, it was the first time I know of that the boat wasn't in the slip. He must have taken it out on the lake."

"I'll drive out tomorrow and see if he's around," Lacey offered. "Again, I want to talk to him before anyone else figures out about this. Is there anyone else that might have had a problem with her?"

"No. Nobody. She was the life of the party. Everyone loved her."

Brandy fought a battle in her chest. Part of her already missed Cynthia. They'd been married for six years and they hadn't always been miserable. There had been some pretty amazing times while they were dating and the first few months after they'd raced up to Canada to elope had been like a fairy tale, minus the prince. They'd traveled and explored an entire world of romance Brandy hadn't known existed. It wasn't until they got back to Vegas that everything changed. Cynthia had started overspending and surrounding herself with dozens of hangers-on who were more interested in spending Brandy's money than they were in her wife's well-being. Before long, Brandy had agreed to purchase the house in Mission Hills and all but abandoned the ranch house, just to be close to her wife and make her happy. Ultimately, her sacrifices hadn't mattered. Cynthia was still complaining when she wasn't partying and partying when she wasn't complaining. About everything.

Two years ago, Brandy had had enough. She'd started trying to figure out how to get divorced without losing millions of dollars in the process. Yesterday, her wife's body on the bedroom floor solved all of that.

Brandy had wanted her out of her life. And now, she was.

She closed her eyes and swallowed against the lump in her throat.

"Uh oh." Lacey leaped off the sofa and headed for the door.

"What is it?" Michelle asked.

A rough banging on the office door followed. Brandy got to her feet just as Lacey reached the door and opened it. Detective Martin loomed on the other side with several uniformed officers in a half-circle behind him.

"Good afternoon, Detective. Did you find out anything?" Lacey stood in the doorway as though she were deliberately blocking the entrance. Brandy couldn't help but feel just a little as though the pint-sized woman was trying to protect her.

Still, Brandy's stomach knotted. Were they here to arrest her? Had they learned something new about what happened to Cynthia? Did she want to know if they had?

"If you don't mind, I'd like a word with Mrs. Kincaid."

"You got a warrant?" Lacey asked in a voice Brandy

hadn't heard her use before. Tough. Determined.

"Well, no. We aren't here to arrest anybody," he chuckled. "I was just hoping that we could go down to my office and have a talk, that's all."

"But you don't have a warrant. Not even a search warrant?" Lacey stood her ground. "I don't believe she has anything to say at this time. She'll be happy to hear any information you have about the cause of death, though. Is the coroner's report completed yet?"

Jethro Martin pushed his wide-brimmed, black Stetson back an inch or so on his forehead and then placed both hands on his hips. "Now, Lacey, this isn't an interview. For crying out loud, it's only been one day. That report won't come back for a least a week, and you know it. And the lab work is gonna take even longer."

"Then why do you want to talk to Brandy? She has no information to give you that you don't already know."

"Is that so? You her lawyer now? I thought you were just in this for the story."

"No, I'm not her attorney, obviously. If you don't have a warrant, you'll need to leave. And all contact with Mrs. Kincaid should go through her actual attorney. She'll provide you with that information within forty-eight hours." Lacey shut the door on the detective's open-mouthed, bewildered expression as though she were the supreme commander of the Allied forces and the detective had a tiny mustache.

"Was that really the smartest thing?" Brandy asked. "Shouldn't I at least go talk to them? You know... somehow cooperate in the investigation?"

"No," Lacey replied, leaning her backside on the closed door. "You don't actually have to cooperate when he will use everything you say against you. Not yet. Not to mention the leaks. Half my information comes from 'sources close to the Sheriff' or 'unnamed officials' in the department. If we want to keep certain information away from the press, we have to keep it away from cops. Call your attorney and bring him up to speed. I'll go with you if you'd like me to. But do not give an interview to the police."

Michelle added, "From a PR standpoint, we should probably make at least a cursory show of cooperation. The court of public opinion tends to swing to guilty when it looks like you're hiding something."

"You know all those TV docu-drama shows? The one's that highlight actual cases? What's the one thing all those shows have in common?" Lacey's question was met with silence. "Every single one of them has footage, shot from the ceiling of an interrogation room, where the accused was cooperating with the cops, without an attorney, so they wouldn't look like they have something to hide."

"But I don't have anything to hide!" Brandy insisted.

"They don't care about that. The cops, I mean. They will twist and turn every single word that comes out of your mouth and use it to put one more nail in your coffin. You cannot trust the cops. Ever."

"Why not? What do they have to gain from doing that?"

"It's their job. Have you ever actually listened to the Miranda rights? 'Anything you say can and will be used against you in a court of law.' There is nothing ambiguous about that.

"Fact. You didn't love your wife. Fact. You fought with and threatened your wife before she went missing. Fact. Your wife is dead. Do you really think they need to know anything more than that? It doesn't matter if you did it or not, they are already convinced you killed Cynthia and they will spend all of their energy proving that conclusion. They aren't even interested in looking at other possibilities right now."

"And the court of public opinion you talked about? What about them?" Brandy asked.

"That's what I'm here for. To tell the real story in a way that the public can understand, and to spin it in your favor."

Michelle nodded. "Right, but when they do ask for a formal interview, with an attorney, I think we should do it."

Brandy folded her arms and pulled in a deep breath that did nothing to quell the see-saw of confusion that poured from one side of her brain to the other. Michelle had taken pretty darn good care of her reputation for years, but the little reporter made some damn good points, too. What if she had gone to the station and answered questions? What if they had turned her words around and got her to admit how much she really did loathe that woman she'd married. It hadn't taken Lacey long to do it.

She cringed on the inside, sucking her bottom lip between her teeth to stifle what might have been an actual moan. That woman, her wife, was dead. Brutally murdered in a bloody massacre in her own bedroom. Just a few minutes ago, she'd been thinking about the good ol' days. The days when she had actually loved Cynthia.

But now?

How did she feel about everything right now, this minute? Deep down, in that small place where Cynthia had meant love and a future, raising children and growing old together... how did Brandy actually feel about the loss?

Nothing. That emptiness festered. And it hurt. And despite the loss and bitterness, or maybe because of it, she was going to have to fight for her own life.

CHAPTER FOUR

"Alright. I'll take your advice on this, Lacey, for now." Brandy pulled a pillow from behind the sofa and tossed it into place against the rolled leather armrest. "Listen, I don't think I can do this anymore today. If it's alright with you ladies, I'd like to get some rest."

"Have you been sleeping here?" Michelle picked up her purse and wrapped the strap over her shoulder.

"I do sometimes, when I'm too tired to drive. Last night, I came back here when I couldn't get through the mob at home."

"That's silly. Come stay at the condo with me and Kendra. We have plenty of room. And the press is going to stake out the casino, too, more than likely."

"Thanks, but I'm used to it. It's not a big deal."

"Actually, it is kind of a big deal," Michelle continued. "You can kiss your privacy good-bye. You need to be somewhere safe."

"I'll get a suite at the Rio, then."

"That's the last thing I'd advise, personally," Lacey said. "All those employees willing to sell information; from what you ordered for breakfast to how many towels you use. Or worse... who visits you in the wee hours of the morning."

Brandy's full lips twisted into a sardonic half-grin while her eyes held a note of self-deprecation. "I don't think we'd have to worry about that," she huffed.

A spark ignited someplace deep in Lacey's center at the thought that Brandy wouldn't have any late-night guests. She shifted slightly as she replied, "They'd make something up, then." She swallowed, shifting in place again. The temperature in the room seemed to rise suddenly and she wanted nothing more than to leave.

"Come on. Let's go back to my place and you can get some real rest."

Dark eyes narrowed just a fraction and Brandy huffed. "You live in a hotel, Michelle. What's the difference?"

"We're in the residential side of the building; all condos, individually owned. Private entrances from the garage and our own concierge. We even have an HOA that prevents short-term rentals or overnight lodging. No press, no Lookie-Lous. At least not hanging out in the halls, for sure. Come on. Grab your stuff. You're coming home with me."

An hour later, Lacey hugged the back wall of the mirrored elevator, her shallow breaths echoing in her ears as she stared at the floor. When the chime announced their arrival on Michelle's floor, she was the first one off. Instantly, the air seemed lighter. It even tasted better.

The claustrophobia had begun about six months after the accident. She'd been sitting in the cemetery in Utah, at the foot of Brad's grave, the first time she'd had a full-fledged panic attack. She had actually believed she was going to die. Brent, her eldest brother, had thrown her in the truck and raced her to the emergency room.

Not a heart attack.

In therapy, she'd realized that it had been brought on by the image of her younger brother's body confined to the casket. Alone in the dark. The effect had been doubled by the fact that his pregnant wife lay in the next grave. That had brought up the whole confined spaces issue.

Lacey had been trapped inside the wreckage of Kendra's pickup truck for nearly an hour after she'd been run off the state highway near the ranch—surrounded by mangled steel, shards of sharpened fiberglass from the dashboard and the scent of fresh blood. Conscious the entire time, she'd struggled to keep her panic at bay. She'd succeeded then. But ever since that day in the graveyard it seemed that panic found its way in at the slightest provocation. Of course, she knew that nobody else was going to harm her; nobody else had a reason to.

She knew, in her logical mind, that an elevator was innocuous. Harmless. Still, trapped inside a tiny space with no escape should something, anything, go wrong, made her heart race and her chest hurt. The mirrors didn't help.

She'd already undergone five surgeries to minimize, as much as was possible, the horrifying effects of the gruesome facial laceration she'd received. The first time she'd looked in a mirror after the accident, she'd been appalled at the grotesque image. The doctors told her that the brutal scar would fade, that the redness and swelling would go away in time, and that plastic surgery would work wonders. And it had. But every time she looked in a mirror, she saw that first reflection of an oozing, jagged gash that ran from her temple to the tip of her chin. They'd rebuilt her eye lid, and she'd kept her eye, which was a plus, certainly. But they hadn't been able to repair the way she saw herself.

Damaged.

Worse, she was covered in scars that were even more horrible on her arms and legs. The five surgeries on her face didn't include the medically necessary repairs to her broken bones and the most recent, life-saving procedure which left its indelible mark on her chest.

"Are you okay?" Kendra's voice seemed to come from far away, sifting through the gravel inside Lacey's head.

She shook away the haunting images and realized that she was sitting on the sofa in her sister's condo. She'd even pulled the throw blanket off the back to hug against her chest. She didn't remember coming inside.

Clearing her throat and forcing herself to sit up, she croaked, "Sure, Sis. I'm just tired, that's all."

How long had she been sitting like a frozen lump? She scanned the great room with its vaulted ceilings and open floor plan that included a gourmet kitchen. Suddenly, she missed the ranch with its antiquated furniture and home-spun charm.

Unbidden, an image of Brandy leaning against the wide, white railing of the corral in front of the Heartland's immense barn flicked through her mind like an old, home movie. She was smiling; something Lacey hadn't see her do since they'd met. She wore a straw cowboy hat and snug jeans. One booted foot rested on the bottom rail as she laughed.

Heat poured through her blood.

"You sure?"

"What?"

"Are you sure you're okay?" Kendra frowned.

"Yeah. Of course. I'm fine."

Michelle stood in the kitchen next to Kendra while they chopped fresh vegetables and Michelle sipped dark red Merlot from a crystal, long-stemmed glass. Kendra popped the top of a bottle of Coors Light and handed it to Brandy. Sitting on an elegant stool on the living room side of the kitchen bar, Brandy rested her cheek in the palm of one hand and dipped a tree of broccoli into a small bowl of ranch salad dressing before taking the offered drink.

The handsome, older woman glanced at Lacey briefly and then suddenly returned her attention to the kitchen. She took a long pull from the beer, swallowed and said, "I think I'm going to take a shower, if that's okay with you, before dinner?"

"Of course, it is. You know where to find everything, right?"

"Yup. Your tour was perfectly thorough."

"Make yourself at home. You may be here a while." Michelle popped a baby carrot into her mouth and crunched.

"Let's hope it's not too long."

Kendra swigged her beer, swallowed quickly and asked, "Who's taking care of things out at your place? Do you need me to head out there and do anything?"

"That's sweet of you, Ken, but my foreman has everything under control. It's not quite the spread you've got. Just a few saddle horses. Nothing fancy. I inherited the foreman from the previous owners. He's been there for years. He's fine." Her lanky figure slid off the stool and meandered across the living room. Pausing in front of the coffee table, she tilted her head slightly. "Lacey? I just wanted to say that I'm grateful, you know? For everything you're doing and for using your position to help me out."

Lacey's throat closed slightly. She swallowed against the lump. Brandy was a millionaire, maybe even a billionaire. She had the power to quite literally vanish if she wanted to. A couple of Internet bank transfers before the Feds got wise, and she could set herself up in a nice little hacienda in a non-extradition country in a matter of hours. Was she so arrogant to think she could beat the wrap, or was the fact she was staying to fight some kind of indication of her innocence?

Lacey had trusted people before, and those people had hurt her. Some had done so deliberately and deserved whatever punishment they got, but others had done so without meaning to. Her parents had died. Her brother had died. A man she'd looked up to her entire life had been involved in an attempt on her very life. Everyone was a risk. Everyone she knew, everyone she met, had the ability to destroy her.

She blinked away the encroaching panic and forced herself to smile. Well, she forced the corners of her lips upward. She probably couldn't call it a smile. "You're welcome, Brandy. Anything I can do to help."

After Brandy nodded and disappeared into the hall,

Lacey tossed the blanket away and threw her head back onto the cushions behind her neck. She was, quite literally, losing her mind. Her whole body reacted in ways she couldn't explain when Brandy looked at her.

Kendra moved from behind the kitchen bar and settled into the sofa next to her, pulling her to snuggle against her shoulder. "Baby girl, are you sure you're alright? Have you kept your therapy appointments? I don't mind saying that I'm a little worried."

"I told you, I'm fine." Lacey pulled herself back to an upright position against the arm of the sofa. "It's been a long week, tracking down leads about Cynthia's disappearance and stuff."

"I'll take that as a no."

"About what?"

"Therapy." Kendra pointed her motherly x-ray vision directly at her. Kendra had used that same look when Lacey was fourteen and had skipped the high school football game to hang out with friends at the old rock in the foothills where they'd go to party most of the night.

"I've been busy."

"Make an appointment. Do I even want to know if you're taking your meds?"

"I take them when I need them. I don't like how they make me feel, Kendra. All light-headed and discombobulated."

"One Xanax in the morning is not going to turn you into a space cadet. Or, if you're that worried about it, take them at night instead."

"I take them when I need them." Lacey searched the

floor around the couch, having forgotten she put her purse down at all much less where she'd placed it. She found it next to the end table. She deliberately opened the latch, delved inside and withdrew the small, orange prescription bottle. She tried twice, unsuccessfully, to twist off the child-safe lid before it opened. When it finally did, she pulled out one small tablet and popped it into her mouth, swallowing without a drink. "There. Happy? I took my chill pill."

Kendra pushed herself up, stood and glared at her wife. Lacey followed the direction of her sister's gaze to find Michelle glaring directly at Lacey. "What?" Lacey demanded.

"You're not taking care of yourself, Lace. We're both worried. And it's not just us. The boys are worried too. Did you know that Casey wants to actually move here? To move in with you?"

"Oh hell, no. Nobody is coming here to babysit me. I am fine."

Casey had been trying to protect Lacey since they were in the womb together twenty-six years ago. He had it in his head that because he was a man, and eleven minutes older, that he had some chivalrous duty to make sure she never got hurt. When he found the man who had run her off the road two years ago, he'd done things that would make most people cringe. He'd been trained in the military and worked in divisions that didn't necessarily exist when it came time for subpoenas and Senate Oversight Committee hearings.

There was no way she was going to have some combatant with a hero complex hanging out in the spare bedroom.

"You're not fine. Nobody expects you to be," Michelle cooed. "We just want you to be happy and that's going to take time, and attention. You have to take the steps to heal, baby."

Happy? They wanted her to be happy? "I'm happy. Just back off, all right?"

Brandy stood in the long hallway that separated the bedrooms from the main living areas, just beyond the view of the occupants in the other room. She hated that awkward feeling that always came from overhearing a conversation that was meant to be private. Still, she found herself frozen in place, afraid that if she moved they would know she was there.

"We're not convinced, honey. Saying you're happy and being happy are two entirely different things."

"Any fool knows that," Lacey spat. "You'll just have to take my word for it, I guess." The sofa creaked slightly as someone, probably Lacey, stood.

"You don't have to do this, you know. The work thing. You don't need the money. You can take off all the time you need and get well."

"I'm not unwell."

"That's not what I meant, and you know it." Kendra's voice grew firm and there was a certain level of authority in the tone.

After a brief pause, Lacey asked, in a voice that was far less confrontational, "Why are you both so worried about me? I am a big girl and I know how to take care of myself. I love my work. I don't do it for the money. I'm not going to give that up just because I have a few bad days every now and then. If anything, my job keeps me sane. I can only imagine what things would be like if I had nothing to do all day but dwell on the shit storm."

"They've set a trial date," Michelle whispered. "Mac's going on trial next week. Kendra and I have to go back tomorrow so we can meet with the county attorney on Monday morning."

The silence that followed seemed to stretch for a lifetime. Finally, Lacey answered, "And you're scared because you think I'm not strong enough to testify. Is that it?" Lacey's voice cracked, sending a shiver down Brandy's spine. The tough reporter with the ideals and the solid-steel strength was gone. In her place, a little girl stood alone against the world.

Brandy closed her eyes and leaned against the wall, her hands tucked behind her bottom. Something in her belly reached out to that little girl, wanting to comfort and reassure. Wanting to pull her into a safe place where she couldn't get hurt.

At one time Michelle had been a business contact, but over time that had changed into friendship. But, they hadn't been close enough for Brandy to get all the details surrounding the problems she'd uncovered in Utah. Or maybe she'd just been too busy with her own issues at the time. She'd seen bits and pieces on the news – something about a long-standing family feud that had turned into murder. The local sheriff had been indicted on conspiracy charges, among other things.

"Do they know when I'll have to go back?" Lacey asked, her voice stronger but still shaken.

"Not yet. You'll be officially served once you are back home, but the county attorney will want to see you before court. You'll have to come home for a while to meet with him."

"A day. I'll have to go back for a day. Maybe two. That's all."

Michelle heaved a forlorn sigh. "Whatever you say."

Lacey passed within sight of where Brandy stood, but she didn't turn her head as she made her way to the front door. After she left, Brandy released her breath and headed back in the direction of the guest bedroom. She'd wanted to ask about borrowing some shampoo, but she couldn't bring herself to reveal that she'd overheard any of that incredibly personal and tense conversation. Instead, she borrowed the shampoo anyway and went back to her assigned space.

Poor Lacey. What had happened to her that her family was so concerned about her mental condition? What had happened to her physically to leave that scar on her face? Not that it detracted from her looks at all. She was an incredibly beautiful girl, with winsome expressions that put a person at ease but could also turn all-business; and tough enough to make a grown man shake in his boots.

She was a little shorter than the women Brandy generally found attractive. Cynthia had been nearly as tall as Brandy's five-foot-nine-inch frame. Her wife had been built like a fashion model, but Lacey was more curvaceous with a body that screamed, "I'm a wonderland. Come explore me."

Brandy had wanted to explore her from the moment

Lacey had walked into the office this afternoon. She had been almost unable to speak, and she certainly had trouble concentrating on the mock interview. She'd been afraid that if she stared too long into Lacey's eyes, she'd forget just about every question the little blonde posed.

Even when she'd lost her temper, Brandy had felt that mysterious, gentle tingle running through her blood.

When she finished her shower, she dressed in a set of borrowed sweats. Her own clothing, hastily packed before they'd left the Touchdown, had already found their way into Michelle's washing machine. The pants were a little short, but not by much, and the sweatshirt fit just fine if she hiked the sleeves up a little to hide the fact they didn't quite reach her wrists. By the time she returned to the great room, dinner was ready, and Michelle was placing the finishing touches on the dining room table.

"Just in time," Michelle quipped as she set a platter of broiled asparagus next to a heaping pile of mashed potatoes. Gilding edged the serving dishes. China dishes, real silverware and crystal glasses sparkled beneath the overhead chandelier.

"Wow. You really didn't have to do this just for me," Brandy offered, taking her seat at the table.

"We didn't." Kendra pulled a linen napkin out of a silver ring and spread it on her lap. "That is, we do this every chance we get. This is just dinner for us."

Michelle smiled at her wife and nodded. "We don't always have the time, but we do what we can to make meal time special. It's a time set aside to catch up with the family every day. Everyone is so busy, sometimes there's barely enough time for microwave popcorn. But especially with the girls, who haven't exactly had a steady and nurturing home life up to this point, it's important to have a routine as much as possible."

It was Kendra's turn to smile and the grin lit up her weather-worn features. "Of course, I can only imagine what Uncle Brent is making them for dinner tonight. Chocolate cake? Rice Crispy Treats? It's a crap shoot."

"He's probably burning inch-thick T-bones for them, forgetting that they would probably prefer mac and cheese with sliced hot dogs."

"Well, thanks just the same," Brandy chuckled.

She glanced under her lashes at her hosts. Theirs was the kind of love that Brandy had hoped for her entire life. She thought she'd found it with Cynthia. She'd believed in it so much that she hadn't thought twice about proving it with that damned prenuptial agreement that gave away half her amassed fortune. They'd run off to Canada, where they could legally marry, without Brandy so much as calling her mother. She'd been completely swept away by the possibility of living happily ever after, as though such a thing really existed.

In the years since, she'd learned differently. She hadn't given much thought to what she might do now, or what she'd planned to do once she'd been freed from the marriage. The idea of dating again had never entered her mind.

That is, until Lacey had stepped into the picture. For the first time in more than two years, Brandy felt those little pleasurable stirrings in her belly and lower. She'd been through enough to know she could never again mistake those fuzzy little strokes of heat for love. She'd fallen for that once and once was enough. Not to mention, Lacey was a determined and fortifying force with a promising career in the news corps. No matter what she said, Brandy's story could launch her career. So, how much of her willingness to help was because Michelle was her sister-in-law, and how much of it was based solely on the fact that she was getting exclusive contact with the story of the decade?

"You're in good hands," Kendra said around a mouthful of braised beef.

"What's that?" Brandy asked, cutting her meat with an exceptionally sharp steak knife before dipping it in steak sauce. She didn't really need the knife. The meat was perfect and melted in her mouth.

"Lacey. She's a fantastic reporter. She'll treat you square. I raised her, so I know she can be a little stubborn, but in this line of work, that's a good thing, right?"

"I suppose."

"And I know she'll do her very best on your story. This thing could really make her career, so like I said, you're in good hands."

The story of the decade. Careers made. Careers lost. All over her life and the death of a woman she once thought she loved. Dread muted the taste of the steak, turning it to ash on her tongue. No matter how many deep-seated stirrings appeared in her belly, Lacey wasn't an option. She'd already given one determined woman with an agenda her heart.

She wasn't going to let that happen again.

Lacey hurried into the safety of her private space. For the first time, she was thankful Kendra had insisted that she buy her own condo and not live full time in Kendra's like she'd wanted. The compromise had been to buy in the same building, of course. She'd insisted on coming back to Las Vegas after the accident – after her brother's funeral – but as time had passed, she'd felt more and more like she needed to be with her family. She'd traveled back and forth between her old, tiny apartment and the ranch until she'd been spending more time in Utah than Vegas. Kendra and Michelle had all but kicked her out, finally convincing her to buy this condo because of the added security features. She'd hated the idea. She didn't want to be alone.

Now, she was thrilled to be able to get away. To become invisible.

After three or four deliberate steps into the interior, she backtracked to slam the deadbolt into place and move the safety bar over the small brass knob. She leaned her head against the cool metal and inhaled a breath meant to calm. It didn't work, and she pushed away from the door, wrapping her arms around her torso in a tight hug.

Everything is going to be fine.

They can't hurt you anymore.

Once in the living room, she paced from one side of the wide room to the other. She avoided the ottoman from memory, her eyes closed against the visions in her mind. Broken glass. Blood-stained asphalt. Two caskets. An empty cradle.

A sob escaped her chest and she stopped pacing long enough to rummage through her bag again. She pulled two pills from the medicine bottle this time and swallowed them. One stuck in her throat, swollen with unreleased cries, and she careened to the wet bar by the sliding glass doors. She opened a bottle of Jack Daniels. Drank directly from the spout. It burned, either forcing the pill down or dissolving it. She didn't care which. Gasping, she set the bottle down and allowed her exhausted frame to slide down the glass doors to the floor.

The force of her panic peaked and her entire body shook painfully. She abandoned any pretense of control and allowed the agony to consume her, silently begging for the world to stop turning for just a few minutes. She needed to rest. For just a few minutes.

Slipping to one side, she curled into a tight ball. When she cracked open an eyelid to stare blindly at the ceiling, the shadows had shifted.

Night had fallen over the strip. From her vantage point, she stared at the beam of light erupting from the top of the Luxor Hotel, like a beacon in a sky so full of nothing that the stars had abandoned it.

Everything was going to be okay. Everything had to be okay. Her cell phone chirped and she pulled it from her pocket. Sitting up, she frowned as she read the display. She'd missed four calls.

She flicked the screen, clearing her throat. "Yeah,

Michelle. What's up?" Her body ached as she stood and continued to stare out at the abandoned sky.

"Are you feeling better?"

"Sure, I'm fine. Is something wrong?"

"No, not really. We... I was just checking up on you. I guess you took a nap. I was almost worried. But then, I figured you might just be angry with me still."

"I'm sorry about earlier," Lacey sighed. "Really. I think I'm just nervous about testifying. I mean, I've known Mac since I was a little girl. My whole life. I still can't believe he was involved in that whole mess."

"Money is a powerful motivator."

"I suppose."

"I know you don't want to relive what happened to you. I mean, who would, really? But you know how important it is, and you're strong. Stronger than I think you realize, and we'll all be there for you. Just don't hold anything in; let it all out and please, please, talk to someone."

Kendra and Michelle had always believed her to be stronger than she really was. That's why they had kicked her out; so, she could stand on her own like she had. Before. Those days were gone for the most part. Any fool could see that. Why couldn't they? "I will. I'll make an appointment tomorrow."

"Promise?"

"Sure. Listen, I've got another call coming in," she lied. "My producer. I have to take it."

"Okay, honey. I'll let you go. We're heading back to Utah tonight, but we'll see you in a couple of weeks."

"Right. Bye."

Lacey disconnected the call and tossed her phone onto the far end of the sectional while sliding to sit. Almost immediately, she stood again and went into her bedroom. She took a shower, avoiding the mirror out of habit. When she finished, she toweled herself dry and pulled on a floor-length terry robe. She pulled a brush through her wet hair and then laid on her empty double bed.

There was a time when she'd wished for someone to share the bed with her. There had been a point in her life when she couldn't wait to be half of one of those power couples who would take the world by storm. Maybe another reporter, so she'd understand the demands of her job. Or maybe a homemaker type, a lesbian Martha Stewart who would take pride in turning their home into a showplace and raising their children to be honorable, decent human beings.

Had that been too much to ask?

She pulled herself up and took slow steps to the far corner of her room. She untied the sash of her bathrobe and allowed the thick fabric to fall away from her shoulders. When it pooled in a mass around her feet, she reached forward to remove the sheet covering a full-length mirror. She hesitated, inhaling deeply, and then continued. The sheet drifted to the floor, revealing a monstrous image that still shocked her every time she saw it.

CHAPTER FIVE

Sitting at her kitchen table, Lacey shuffled through her news feeds and looked for any information about Brandy Kincaid that might have broken overnight. She was behind schedule. Last night had been a total wash out, thanks to her little breakdown, and she'd spent a fitful night in and out of sleep, nightmares, and a distinct inability to close her eyes. Every news outlet had some kind of story about Brandy, but most of them were fluff pieces about her business ventures and how filthy rich she was.

A couple of them presented her as a one-percenter who lived a life of luxury based on her ownership of a casino and a couple of large nightclubs. Most of them painted her as a down-to-earth, self-made woman of power and influence. The pastor of a local church played up the gay-angle and asked his reader whether they'd expected anything else from a declared and proud sinner.

None were terribly flattering. The real Brandy seemed to be somewhere in between. Sure, she owned a mansion, but she also had no problem sleeping on the couch in her office if she needed to. She wasn't a jet-setter and most of the time, when her name appeared in the news, it had to do with some charity project she'd fully funded or a gift she'd made to the local hospital or veteran's group. At least, until now.

One thing was perfectly clear. Lacey had to conduct the interview and get the story out as soon as possible. She called Michelle to let her know that she'd work with Brandy that afternoon and put something together for All That and More this week. She still needed to run the spot by her producer, but she couldn't imagine her or Addison having a problem with it. After she dressed, she left her condo to drive out to Lake Mead and look for the boyfriend.

The hallway, as usual, was empty. There were only three other units on her floor and two of them were unsold. She pressed the Down button by the elevator and bit her bottom lip. She was tempted to take the stairs. They frightened her as much as the elevator, but at least she wasn't trapped. There were escapes on each landing, right? Unfortunately, the lingering aches in her hips from the physical trauma of the accident made the descent of fourteen flights nearly impossible.

By the time she'd reached her car, she'd managed to stave off two minor panic attacks. It was going to be a good day. It was Sunday and the city streets were relatively quiet given the early hour. When her phone rang, she waited until it connected to the Bluetooth in her dash before answering. "This is Lacey."

"Good morning. I hope it's okay that I called you this early. Michelle gave me your number before they left last night. It's Brandy."

"Morning. Yeah, I'm already on the road, actually."

"Good. So, I was just wondering when we were planning to get the interview over with? I don't mind telling you I'm a little nervous about this, but I was looking online this morning–"

"Don't. I mean, I would highly suggest that you not read anything about yourself in the feeds. My particular segment of the population at the moment is going straight for the jugular. If it bleeds, it leads."

"I don't know. It's kind of hard to miss. But it's not just the reports. It's the comments, too. One guy actually said I was guilty just because I'm a lesbian and can't be trusted."

"Just one

"It'll get way worse than that before it's over. Don't read them. It's too tempting to respond, and that's the worst thing you could do."

"It'll be hard."

"Try. Anything you put online will land straight in the hands of the prosecutor as evidence. Do you want to meet at your office or at the Condo? About three? I've sent the questions off to Michelle, but I didn't have your email address, so she'll forward them to you. That way you can go over them together. It's best to write out your answers and practice them aloud, so you get used to what you're going to say ahead of time. Once the recorder is on, everything is fair game. There won't be any second takes."

There was a pause on the line. If it hadn't been for the long, slow breath sounds, Lacey might have thought she'd dropped the call. Finally, Brandy answered, "Three is fine. And I just checked and I got the email from Michelle already. I have a couple of things to get done this morning, but I can meet you here."

"Where is here?" Lacey chuckled.

"Oh, right. I'm still at Michelle's place."

"Sounds good. I'll see you then!" Lacey touched the button on her steering wheel to disconnect the call.

A few minutes later she cruised onto the highway and headed for Lake Mead.

It seemed a little strange that while under surveillance for months, the boyfriend's boat never once left the marina, and then, the very week that Cynthia Kincaid is murdered, he'd decided to go sailing. It was most likely a coincidence, of course, as most things were, but the part of her that made her question everything found it... odd.

When she reached the marina, she pulled into the public access parking lot. From her laptop case, she retrieved the file Brandy had given her before they'd left the office the day before.

John Miller. Forty-eight years old; originally from Texas. Disavowed son of a small time, but very wealthy, oil producer. He wasn't bad looking from the file photo, which had been taken less than a month earlier. There were a couple of other photographs of the two of them together, embracing on the deck of a thirty-foot luxury yacht that had seen better days. The watermark of the Fairchild agency spanned the bottom of each image with the date and time each picture had been captured. She scanned several report pages until she found the one she'd seen earlier with Miller's exact address.

Slip twenty-five.

Lacey turned on her voice recorder and slid it into her

pocket before she climbed out of the car and headed in the direction of the boat slips. If Miller had been raised in affluence, it's possible that he enjoyed having a seemingly endless supply of cash in the form of a wealthy married woman at his beck and call.

Twenty-one. Twenty-three.

She stopped in front of an empty slip.

Twenty-five. She frowned.

What were the odds that he was sailing two visits in a row when he hadn't left the dock in months? Had he left for good? Why would he do that if Cynthia had just paid for six months' worth of slip fees?

A young woman peered from the cabin doorway of a small houseboat moored in the next slip. Slowly, almost as though she were painfully shy, she stepped further into view. She still hid slightly behind the louvered door. A short black pin-up style bob kissed her high cheek bones. The exotic slant of her eyes, sans make-up, and her dark, naturally tan skin tone spoke of Asian heritage. Her rather skimpy, bright green bikini barely covered... well, anything. Her arms and part of one leg displayed colorful, high-quality ink. A dragon clawed its way up her thigh and tribal lines swirled up both arms from her wrists to her shoulders. One upper arm revealed a skull in the Dia de los Muertos style and the opposite wrist revealed a black leather band, covered with square, silver studs. Lacey put on her best I'm-not-going-to-bite-you smile and asked, "Have you seen John lately?"

"Who're you?" The woman's guarded expression darkened.

"Just an old friend."

"He's not home. Obviously."

"Do you know if he moved off the lake, by any chance? Maybe a change of scenery?"

"No."

"You don't know, or you know he hasn't moved off the water?"

"Both. I don't know anything." She turned sharply to go back inside.

"Wait!" Lacey stepped closer to the woman's craft, a pontoon houseboat that reminded her of a floating tenement. "I just need to find John. There's been a problem with a mutual friend. He'll want to know about it. I promise."

"You mean Cyndi getting shot, right?"

Lacey nodded. "She's been missing for a little while. They found her body yesterday." She paused, searching the girl's reaction for any kind of acknowledgment. Her expression grew even more closed, if that were humanly possible. "You knew her?"

She didn't answer for what seemed like far too long. Finally, she shook her head. "No. I didn't know her. John did, though."

"By any chance, have you seen her around lately?"

The girl shook her head again, closing the door slightly as though she were hiding from the world and didn't like the interruption. "What's your name?"

Another long pause. "Marcia."

"Hi Marcia. I'm Lacey. Has John come back at all, for supplies or anything?"

"No. I live here, and we play cards on Fridays. He was always nice to me, too. He's a nice guy, but he missed two card nights. He hasn't been back at all."

"Right. Well, thanks. I guess I'll catch up with him later."

On her way back to the car, Lacey stopped into the small shop where tourists could purchase souvenirs and rent boats. There were two boys working the counter. She showed them each a photo of Cynthia and a photo of John.

"Yeah, she comes around all the time."

The other boy peered over his co-worker's shoulder. "Hey, isn't that the lady on the news? She's dead, dude."

"Seriously?"

"Yeah. My mom called into that number on TV a couple of days ago to tell the cops she'd been here, but nobody ever came to check it out." He shrugged. "She left with John Miller, that big-ass boat in Slip Twenty-Five, like over a week ago. He hasn't been back since."

A spark of lightning erupted in Lacey's blood. "You're sure? You're absolutely positive that she was on Miller's boat when he left the marina?"

"Well, yeah. I mean, she came in here, bought some groceries and a book, and they left that day."

"Did she say anything? Did she seem upset at all?"

He shrugged again. "You'd have to ask my Mom. I wasn't here. That's just what she told me. She went back east a couple of days ago to visit my aunt."

"I'd love to chat with her. Can I call her?"

One side of the boy's mouth raised in a quirky smirk. "Now, I can't be giving out my mom's number. She'd kill me."

"How about I leave you my number and then you can call her and tell her someone is finally following up on her sighting report?" It wasn't the whole truth, but neither the kids or the mom really needed to know that.

"Sure. I can do that."

Lacey left her card with the boys and then hurried back to her car and turned off her voice recorder. Miller wasn't gone again; he'd never come back. And Cynthia might have been on his boat when he left.

She pointed her car back to Las Vegas, determined to do as much investigating as she could before she met with Brandy later that afternoon. She'd mentioned she'd had errands to run. If Lacey hurried, she could tag along on the down low.

Ninety minutes later, Lacey sat in her car in the parking garage of her building. She wasn't in her normal parking space, but sat idling not far from her sister's assigned spaces. Each condo was allowed two spaces and guests were expected to park in the main area. Brandy's Range Rover was parked in one of Kendra and Michelle's spaces because they never used both.

She focused her attention on the local news event of the year. Of the decade. Maybe even the century. If Brandy had anything to do with her wife's disappearance and murder, Lacey would be the one to break the story. It could propel her career forward like nothing else had been able to.

She shouldn't really care one way or the other, but the news that Cynthia had been on Miller's boat, and that Miller hadn't come back into the dock, gave her another avenue of possibility. She shouldn't care, but a part of her jumped with glee that Brandy might be innocent. She told herself it was because she could break that story, too.

Neither of those scenarios could remove her scars or replace her dreams of a career on television news, but it could solidify her position as a national radio personality, and that was as good as it would ever get for someone like her.

After the accident, she'd withdrawn her application for an internship at the local television affiliate, even though they'd already offered her a spot. Even though they'd said they would wait for her to heal. It was an off-camera job as intern producer, but Lacey had had only one goal – her own news program.

Every decision she'd made until that point had been strategically planned to reach that singular end. She'd start with the internship, and eventually, maybe in a year or two, land a field reporter slot with on-air reporting. After a while, a weekend anchor position would open up and she'd begin to make a name for herself. From there, she'd apply for an overseas desk with one of the networks. After a few years reporting on Ebola outbreaks or wars in forgotten corners of Africa or refugee crises in the Middle East, she'd sit on the Washington desk and cover the White House. She'd had it all planned out, her road to the New York desk of a major network; her own show.

Christiane Amanpour had cleared the way for women in the media trenches. With the out-and-proud success of pioneers like Rachel Maddow and Anderson Cooper, she didn't have to worry about the fact she was a lesbian getting in the way. But she did have to worry about the camera, and the fact that the camera doesn't like hideously scarred people unless they were the subject of the story. Nobody wanted to watch Quasimodo delivering the news.

She'd been sitting, tapping the steering wheel, for a little more than an hour when Brandy emerged from the elevator and headed for her truck. She wore blue jeans and a loose top. No purse, but she dug into her front pocket and pulled out her keys. There was something truly sexy about her, the way she moved so effortlessly with no pretension or expectation.

Lacey had spent several years schlepping drinks at a casino where how she moved – how sexy she moved – often had a direct correlation to her income. She knew what it meant to sell an attitude through a walk, and Brandy didn't do that. She was one hundred percent authentic. No make-up. No jewelry except a wedding ring and small, stud earrings. Just a hint of scent that reminded Lacey of illicit, sinful things. It wasn't perfume or cologne. It was her.

The very center of Lacey's body tingled, and she shifted in her seat.

Enough.

Brandy was her focus; her story. Thinking about her as a woman was the last thing she needed to do and, due to circumstances well outside her control, a total waste of time and energy.

A moment later, the Range Rover roared to life and pulled out of the parking space. Lacey waited just long enough for the vehicle to turn onto the ramp before she followed.

The city streets were crowded now. Tourists were heading to the airport and jumping onto I-15 to head back to Utah, Arizona or California after a weekend in the world's most profane adult playground. Once they left the resort area, heading into the locals-only part of the city, traffic thinned, and Lacey held back a little further.

Brandy pulled into the parking lot of a funeral home, choosing a spot close to the door. She didn't get out of the truck right away and Lacey passed the lot to slide her car into a stall in the convenience store across the street. A few minutes later, Brandy got out of the truck and met an older couple as they climbed out of a Lincoln Town Car. The woman was short with unnaturally red hair pulled into a bun at the base of her skull. She wore a polyester pant suit in a horrible mauve color; the kind where the shirt is sewn into a vest to look like two pieces when it was only one. She wasn't an overly large woman, but she wasn't thin, either. The man was taller, with a shock of white hair and bushy eyebrows. He was built well for an older man, indicating a lifetime of keeping himself in shape. Dressed in jeans, a plaid, western-style button-down and boots, he carried a black felt cowboy hat and looked very much like a cowboy stuck in a world of flashing neon.

Brandy shook the man's hand as he put on his hat. The three of them entered the funeral home together as the older woman dabbed her eyes with a handkerchief.

They were obviously parents; but whose? Her gut told her they were Cynthia's folks; the ones who filed the missing person's report. It surprised her that they would meet Brandy at the funeral home. Wouldn't they blame her for not acting more quickly? If Brandy weren't involved in the actual murder, could she have prevented it if she'd filed a missing person's report the day her wife had vanished?

Michelle was convinced her friend was innocent. The only feelings Lacey got when she was with Brandy had nothing to do with fear for her life. But she'd trusted people before who had turned out to be downright evil, so she was hardly the best judge of character. Hell, the only reason she'd settled in Las Vegas was because she'd followed her boyfriend from Utah on the promise of a spectacular life far away from what she'd considered a boring and lackluster existence on the family ranch.

Her sister had done an excellent job raising her younger siblings after their parents had been killed in a plane crash, but Lacey hadn't been able to see it then. She'd wanted more. She'd wanted excitement and a fast lifestyle. She'd already earned the title of Miss Randall County when she was seventeen, so obviously she would take a city like Las Vegas by storm.

What she'd gotten in Las Vegas in those early months had been more than one black eye, a few split lips, and abandoned on the strip like one of those little paper cards that advertised sex-for-sale.

But she'd pulled herself up, with Michelle's help, and over the following five years she'd put herself through college and come out on top. Well, almost. The accident, which hadn't really been an accident, had almost stopped her. If she didn't get a grip soon, it could still keep her from realizing her full potential. She refused to let that happen.

Glancing at her bag, she considered taking her medication. She felt fine at the moment, but ideally she was supposed to take the Xanax once each day, regardless, to keep the panic attacks at bay. She fingered the buckle on the leather purse.

No. She was fine. For now.

Refocusing her attention on the funeral home, she watched patiently for the small family to resurface. She hated funeral homes. When she and Kendra had planned her brother's funeral, she'd been a puddle of goo most of the time. That was before the panic attacks had started, but she' been only a couple of weeks post-op and still confined to a wheelchair for any trips outside of the house. So, she'd sat there, listening to the funeral director, who had buried her parents all those years earlier, talk about the best lining for the interior of the casket, the best materials to use and how heavy they were so they could choose appropriate pall-bearers. Lenise, her brother's wife, had been murdered the same day, so Lenise's mother was there too. She'd insisted on a pale pink casket for her daughter, so that it would match her daughter's wedding dress. Of course, she would be buried in it, her mother had insisted. It was the nicest thing she owned. Lenise's father, the County Sheriff, had no input at all. He'd been sitting in his own jail house awaiting an arraignment for charges that included the conspiracy that had resulted in his own daughter's death. And Lacey's scars.

The driver's seat of the car seemed to harden beneath

her and she shifted, packing up the dark thoughts and shoving them into one of the many compartments in her mind made for such things.

What was Brandy insisting on, inside the funeral director's office, right now? Something in red, perhaps, to point out the fact that her wife had been a harlot? Lacey frowned. It wasn't exactly nice to think ill of the dead, but it escaped her how someone lucky enough to find a woman like Brandy could be so stupid and callous as to throw it all away?

If she were married to Brandy, she'd be more than careful to guard it, and her, from anything bad in the world. She'd take every step necessary to protect their love from the evil outside influences.

The gilded doors of the funeral home opened, and Brandy exited. The older couple trailed behind with the man practically carrying his wife. Lacey's heart broke just a little at the obvious pain the couple shared, and the man's willingness to hold her up through it all. Brandy settled the older couple into their car and headed toward her truck, her head bent, and her shoulders rolled like a woman carrying the entire planet between her shoulder blades. When she reached the driver's side door, she paused and then glanced around the parking lot, finally settling her gaze directly on Lacey.

Crap.

Lacey threw her car into reverse and checked behind her. A huge four-by-four pickup filled the entire rear-view mirror, blocking her retreat as Brandy headed in her direction. Heat rose from the soles of her feet, traveling up her trembling legs and binding her gut into a concrete mass. Her palms grew moist and she struggled to hold onto the steering wheel, checking the rear-view again. Willing the truck to move.

Just move, god damn it!

Trapped.

She closed her eyes and tried unsuccessfully to calm her breathing. Her heart beat a throbbing cadence in her ears and her stomach turned over.

Everything is going to be okay.

Someone knocked on the glass of her driver's side window. Someone was yelling at her. Someone angry.

Lacey covered her ears.

Everything is going to be okay.

"Lacey, open the door! Are you alright?" Brandy slapped the glass. "Open the fucking door!"

Brandy's voice. Slicing the fog.

Angry? No. Not really. Panic. A hint of compassion?

Lacey forced her breaths to slow and removed her hands from her ears. She glanced out the window and Brandy stood there, staring into the car with a crease in her brow and concern in the depths of deep, brown eyes that seemed to go on forever. Her mouth hung open just a fraction before she said, just loud enough to sound through the glass, "Open the door, Lacey. You're scaring me."

Lacey swallowed hard as she pulled on the door release. It didn't open and she realized she was stomping on the brake because she was still in reverse. She placed the car in park and the door locks clicked. Brandy threw open the door and immediately fell to one knee in the opening.

"God, Lacey, are you okay? What the hell just happened?"

"It's... it's nothing, really. I'm fine. I was just... just grabbing a cup of coffee before coming over to your place. Kendra's place, I mean."

"There's a coffee shop in the lobby of the building. Several in fact."

"I know, but I really like the caramel iced coffee here."

"At 7-11? Seriously? I mean, it's good an all, but a twenty-minute drive out of the way?" Brandy's voice oozed her skepticism in a way that almost made Lacey laugh at herself. "Right across the street from where I happened to be planning Cyndi's funeral?"

Lacey glanced down, her eyes falling on Brandy's knee encased in faded denim. When she looked up she sighed. "Not a very good cover, huh?"

"Were you following me?"

Lacey found herself in foreign territory. Not only had she never been made by a subject before, she had never been investigating someone with whom she had any type of relationship for a story so vitally important. Should she try to lie, or...

"Why would you do that?" Brandy laughed, derision dripping from the sound, and reclined to sit on her ankle. "I know you have to be impartial to some extent, but do you really think I'm capable of... of what they are going to accuse me of?" She regained her feet and turned away, running both hands through her short, dark hair.

"I'm just doing my job," Lacey replied, climbing out of her car and relishing the freedom of air on her flesh. "I'm a reporter, and I don't do you any good if I can't defend my position independently of what you tell me. So, yeah, I was following you. For your own good."

Brandy turned back and leveled a disbelieving glare at Lacey. "I need someone on my side, Lacey. You're just like the rest of the vultures, looking to score with a big-time story that can make you a name. I'm not a fool."

"You know what? Maybe you're right!" The heat in Lacey's blood changed from panic to fury. "I am a professional. Do I think about my career? Of course, I do. Everyone does. You do it too, right? Worried more about how your wife was blowing your money than you were about what was wrong with your marriage. Maybe you should look at yourself for a change, instead of looking at me like I'm some kind of mon... monster!"

"I never said you were a monster. I never said--"

"You're the monster. For all I know, you did kill your wife and you're just using your relationship with my family to cover your ass. In the meantime, my integrity is on the line, and I'll do anything I have to to keep from coming out of this with anything less than a stellar reputation. You got that?"

Brandy rushed forward and wrapped her hands around Lacey's arms in a tight, forceful grip. Her mouth instantly consumed Lacey's in a hard kiss, pressing her lips tightly to Lacey's while her tongue demanded entrance. Lacey complied, her body growing hot and taut before melting into Brandy's body of its own accord. The kiss grew deeper as it grew hotter. Brandy's grasp on her arms gentled as Lacey's grasp on reality dissolved into the pavement.

A moment later, Brandy pulled away, her breath ragged. When she spoke, her voice was choppy and hoarse. "I'm not a murderer."

Steadying herself as the doors slipped open, Lacey bit her bottom lip and forced herself to step inside the empty elevator. She pressed the indicator for the penthouse and closed her eyes. A moment later, the doors opened, she released her breath, and fled.

Poised in front of Kendra and Michelle's front door, she lifted her finger to the keypad. She stopped. Normally, she'd use her key code to enter the penthouse condo without a second thought. But it was now, at least temporarily, Brandy's space.

After Brandy had kissed her, Lacey had jumped back into her car, unable to leave the parking lot quickly enough. Thankfully, the truck that had been blocking her earlier escape had vanished and she was able to back away undeterred. She'd left Brandy standing there, looking angry as her long, slender fingers curled into fists.

Lacey closed her eyes against that image. Brandy hadn't done anything wrong. She may not have known it before, but she'd wanted Brandy to kiss her. She'd never felt more cared for, more precious, than she had when she'd looked into those limpid brown eyes, filled with fear and concern, wanting to help ease Lacey's pain. She'd felt suddenly safe.

Cherished.

The kiss had been the result of that moment and the anxiety of the moment that had followed. Lacey cringed. She'd overreacted a little when Brandy had called her spade a spade. She was a reporter and her job was to get to the bottom of things; to tell the truth and if the truth was ugly, so be it. But she wasn't a vulture. That comment had made her angry enough to lash out, and she'd forgotten her panic for a moment.

Turning around to lean her back against the wall beside the door, she stared at the handle. The brushed brass latch and electronic key slot with its blinking red light was like the Hoover dam, standing in the way of a torrent of emotions that might come flooding in the very moment she looked at Brandy. Emotions that she couldn't afford even in a trickle, much less a torrent.

She had to do her job. She needed to stay impartial. She was a professional. She had to maintain her distance and do this job right or all of her hard work, the reputation for fairness she'd worked so hard to establish, would disappear.

Pulling on her deepest reserves, she knocked on the door.

Brandy answered so quickly, it seemed like she might have been waiting just on the other side. "I was worried you wouldn't show up." She slid the door open all the way and moved aside to let Lacey enter.

"Why wouldn't I?" Lacey knew the answer. She didn't know why she'd asked the question.

"Listen, about earlier... I'm sorry. I shouldn't have done that."

"Don't worry about it. Forget it. We've got business to take care of, so let's just do this, okay?"

"Fine."

"We'll use the dining room. Make yourself comfortable. It could take a while. Michelle will get a copy of the recording. I was going to have her sit in on Skype, but one of the girls is sick so she had to run her to the urgent care."

"So, it's not going to be live or anything?"

Lacey poured herself a cup of coffee and sat at the table across from Brandy. "God, no. I'll record the whole thing, but I won't use all of it in that format. I'll narrate most of it, and just use the best snippets so folks can hear some answers directly from you." Brandy's complexion paled slightly. "Don't worry. I'll make you look good."

"Alright. I'm putting myself into your capable hands," Brandy quipped. Her face suffused with color. She stood and crossed to the large windows overlooking the strip.

"What are you worried about, specifically?"

"I don't know. I can't help but think about all those interviews you hear on TV and on the radio where things are taken out of context."

"I'm not going to lie to you. That does happen. But it won't happen with me."

"I'd really like to see the final before it goes on the air."

"So would Michelle, but that isn't going to happen, either. The last thing you want is someone finding out that you 'approved' the message. It will remove all credibility and the whole thing will have been for nothing."

Pulling her recorder out of her bag, Lacey pressed the switch and set it on the dining room table. Then she retrieved the notes she'd made earlier. "Come. Sit down and let's get started. You'll feel more comfortable once you realize I'm not going to bite."

As soon as the words left her mouth, she wanted to pull them back. Biting and Brandy were two things that should never be in the same thought. It conjured images of naked bodies in dim lighting with soft music playing seductively in the background. She swallowed hard against the image and cleared her throat.

After an hour, the interview was complete and Lacey turned off the machine. "I think I have enough here to put something together that will really help."

Brandy had calmed considerably, as though talking out her relationship with her wife and the events that had led up to the day of her wife's death reinforced her level of confidence. Still, there was something she wasn't sharing. Lacey couldn't quite put her finger on it, but something was missing.

Brandy pushed out a long, slow breath and the hint of a grin turned up one side of her full lips. "That was... excruciating."

"I know. I'm sorry you have to go through this."

Brandy wiped a hand over her face, stood and moved into the kitchen. "So, how long have you been a reporter? I mean, I listen to you on the radio. Sometimes, when I'm in the car or whatever." She pulled a cold beer from the refrigerator and popped it open with an audible hiss.

"I've been on the air about a year or so. I graduated from UNLV two years ago, a little late, and took some time off before I started my internship."

"Did you take time off before you went to school, too?"

"Only a year. I graduated from college later because of the accident. I missed a couple of finals and had to finish a course I got an Incomplete in. It's a long story." Lacey walked slowly to the sliding glass doors. She peered over the city as the late afternoon sun radiated in a cloudless desert sky, offering no respite to the baking tourists who crowded the strip.

"I heard bits and pieces. All that stuff that happened back on your ranch in Utah? I was working with Michelle on the launch for the second club and the casino. It put quite a kink in my time line," Brandy chuckled, "but Michelle is really good at what she does and it all worked out. I had other things on my mind at the time, too, so it wasn't a big deal."

Brandy joined Lacey, slid open the sliding glass door and stepped onto the terrace. She leaned against the railing and crossed her arms over her small breasts, the long-neck bottle of beer dangling from the slender fingers of one hand.

Lacey tried not to watch her, but it was difficult, and her gaze kept falling back onto the lean form of her lanky build. "Other things? I would think that a business-minded woman like yourself would keep her focus on the bottom line. You're like the lesbian Donald Trump. You're successful to the point that distractions wouldn't seem like an option."

"Really? You're going to go there?" Brandy laughed, shaking her head slightly before turning her attention to the view. After a moment, she said, "It was Cynthia.

It was just about that time that I realized she was more interested in sex and money than she was about who she had sex with or whose money she spent."

"I see."

"Don't get me wrong. I mean, I love my work, but it's not the end-all, be-all of my existence. I love my downtime, too."

"What do you do for fun?"

"I like to skydive. I like to climb. Anything that gets the juices flowing. And I love to ride. Horse or Harley, doesn't matter which."

Lacey grinned, sparing a glance at Brandy in time to catch another wave of blush that stained her cheeks. "You don't say?"

"Well, I mean, adrenaline. I get a little high on life, I guess. I think better hanging off the side of a mountain or straddling something than I do sitting at a desk."

Lacey's cheeks burned at the sudden image of Brandy straddling her. She pushed the thought away.

Brandy glanced over her shoulder and paused, canting her head slightly forward. "You have a dirty mind, don't you?" She swung her body around and leaned against the railing again.

Dear God, had she read her mind?

Lacey laughed nervously. "I've heard that before, yes."

"What about you? Do you get out much?"

That was a loaded question. Lacey's throat closed, and she swallowed against the blockage by taking another sip of coffee for cover. She'd used to. Before the accident, she was always on the move. She'd go dancing with friends, or hang out with the guys in the racing club at the speedway just outside of town. She once drove a stock car at over three-hundred miles per hour and the power had been incredibly exhilarating. Now, she was terrified every time she changed lanes going the speed limit on I-15. She still enjoyed horseback riding, but that was about as adventurous as she got these days. "Not as much as I used to," she finally replied, as she joined Brandy at the railing and focused her attention on the rooftops of the resort strip a few miles away.

"What happened?"

"I just have different priorities, that's all. The accident changed how I see the world."

"The accident. That's not the first time you've mentioned that, you know. What accident?"

Silence fell over the terrace in one of those awkward blankets. The kind that smother everything, but most of all the easy banter that had replaced the thickness in the air from the interview.

Lacey took a step back and sipped her coffee. Finally, she spoke. "So, I'll have a report ready to go in the next couple of hours and Addison has slated it for tomorrow morning on All That and More. The station will likely re-run some of it throughout the day, too. If you miss the show, there's a rebroadcast every evening at eight."

"Okay." Brandy didn't move away from the railing, but Lacey could feel the intense scrutiny of her gaze without actually looking at her.

"Are you staying here, in the building, for a while?" Lacey's heart fluttered. "Just because, you know, it'll be convenient for any follow ups."

"Yeah. Your sister and Michelle have offered their place for as long as I need it. I'm thinking a day or two. Until things settle down at the ranch." She blew out a heavy breath and turned to grip the railing. "Or I get arrested. God, I still can't believe this is happening."

"There's nothing wrong with admitting that it hurts, you know. Maybe you and Cynthia didn't have the best marriage in the world, but she was your wife. It's okay to grieve for her. Or admit that you're scared." Lacey sensed more than saw Brandy turn her attention back to the scenery.

"It's crazy, isn't it? One minute I get so angry about what she did to me that I swear, I'm happy she's gone. The next, I'm a weepy mess because I loved her so much, it physically hurts. All I can think about is what she must have gone through. What kind of torture was she put through for four days? What did they do to her? What if she was...?"

The anguish in Brandy's voice was like a rope, a lasso that fell securely over Lacey's shoulders and dragged her in. Unable to move, she wrapped Brandy in a hug that consisted of only a gaze. "You don't know that. Don't worry about things you don't know."

"I'm going to jail. I know that much."

"Maybe. For a little while, until you can bail out. If there is one thing I know about the so-called justice system in this country, it's that people with money can get out of jail. Not for free, but they can get out."

Brandy gritted her teeth and her head lowered, squaring her broad shoulders before she leaned on her elbows with her hands clenched into each other to form a single, trembling fist. Her body shook twice and then froze.

Lacey placed a gentle hand on Brandy's shoulder and a shock of something like electricity tingled through her fingers, racing up her arm to land square in her heart. She pulled her fingers back and sucked in a breath. Had Brandy felt it too?

Shaking off the notion, she replaced her hand and squeezed her fingers. "I have a mantra. Sometimes it helps. Sometimes it doesn't. Everything is going to be okay."

Brandy released a weepy laugh, stood and wiped her eyes. "Did you come up with that one all by yourself?"

Lacey smiled and nodded. "I sure did! Creative, huh?"

Brandy's mind swirled with so many emotions she wasn't entirely certain where the real world stopped, and her desire began. When they'd kissed, and just now, when Lacey had touched her, her whole body sang with want and need. She couldn't remember the last time anyone had made her feel like that. Maybe no-one ever had.

Standing, emotionally naked and soul-bared in front of this woman made her tremble, but at least she felt alive. She craved another moment of that contact.

"Not even a little creative," she choked, "but thanks."

A slight breeze caught the tendrils of Lacey's hair and lifted them away from her cheek. The scar reached from her temple to her chin, crossing over the corner of her eye just enough to change the shape slightly. It didn't detract one bit from the beauty she'd been born with. At this point, it was little more than a silver trace, although it had probably been much worse.

Whatever had happened, whatever the accident was, Lacey didn't like to talk about it. Had it something to do with what had happened at the ranch? At the time, Brandy had been too preoccupied with the casino launch and starting a new business – and dealing with a cheating, gold-digger of a wife – to pay much attention to everything Michelle had told her. But now, seeing Lacey up close and getting to know her, the pain she must have endured seemed more real. Brandy felt selfish and undeserving.

Lacey pulled her hair back into place. Rather than tucking it behind her ear like many women would have done to keep it from flying about, she folded one arm across her body and rested her other elbow on it, leaving her fingers entwined in the strands to cover the scar.

Brandy's fingers itched to pull her hand away, to reveal her entire face in all its beauty as her complexion reflected the amber of late afternoon. Her eyes danced in the light, even as their expression grew suddenly more closed.

"Don't look at me like that," Lacey whispered, her voice catching on the final words.

"Like what?"

"Like… that. Like the way you're looking at me."

"Can't help it. You're beautiful right now. I appreciate beautiful things." She shrugged as though she stated an obvious fact when really, she was probably more astounded those words had fallen from her lips than Lacey. If the look of disbelief that floated into those sparkling blue eyes was any indication, Lacey was pretty damn surprised.

She opened her mouth to say something, but no words followed.

The temptation to brush those tightly held strands aside grew too strong, propelling Brandy's hand gently forward. Lacey's eyes followed her movements, widening like some wild thing, too frightened or timid to move away from perceived danger. "It's okay, Lacey. I'm not going to hurt you."

"Please," she whispered. "Please, don't…"

"Don't what?" Brandy asked, her fingers finally entwining in the silky strands as Lacey's defenses lowered ever so slightly.

Lacey's fell away to land over her chest as though she stilled her own heart.

Brandy's lips itched to press against Lacey's. "Don't hurt you, or don't touch you? Because I think I have to touch you." She cupped Lacey's cheek.

Closing her eyes, Lacey's face curled into Brandy's palm so tenderly that Brandy thought she may have imagined it. If it weren't for the tangible warmth that flowed out of that gesture, she might have.

As quickly as the defenses had fallen, they returned. Like bricks falling into place in an impassible, impenetrable wall, the barricade appeared. Thick. Immovable.

Lacey turned and lunged back into the condo, leaving the door open behind her. She threw her recorder into her bag and headed for the door. "I have to finish the interview."

Brandy followed her, for the first time in her life grateful for her long legs and longer strides. She caught Lacey before she reached the door, grabbed her shoulder gently and spun her around. "Stop running away from me. Christ. What are you so afraid of?"

"I'm not... I'm not afraid."

The tremble in her chin called her liar, but at least she didn't pull away. No, she stood her ground like a wild tiger, her energy pacing and measuring every threat.

"I'm not going to hurt you, you know. I'm beginning to think you don't believe me about this whole thing."

The look in Lacey's eyes moved from terrified to wistful. Compassion? Was that what Brandy saw running through those blue orbs that searched for someplace safe to land?

"Oh, Brandy, no. No! That's not it at all. I'm just... it's just that... My job. You know, I have to be completely impartial and if you... I mean, if we – if we started something here? Well, the press would find out and we'd both suffer for it."

"And that's the only reason you don't want me to kiss you? Because of your job? Because I'm the subject and you're the reporter and it would be unethical."

"And dangerous. For you. It would be dangerous for you."

Brandy pursed her lips for a moment and finally forced herself to drop her hand. "Okay. You win. But it's not always going to be like this. I'm going to beat this and when I do? I have every intention of finding out what your next excuse is going to be."

CHAPTER SIX

Sitting at her worn desk in the confines of a warehouse-like office space at KLVN, Lacey finished the final version of her interview with Brandy and saved the file. After she loaded it to the station's secure cloud, she glanced at the clock hanging above the computer in her cubicle. It was coming on two a.m. In a little more than six hours, Addison would take the anchor desk for the live Monday morning edition of All That and More. Lacey's story was the lead. They'd been running teasers since yesterday evening, as soon as the station manager had given the okay to the raw recording. The teaser included a tremendous quote from Brandy about how easy it is to fall in love with the wrong person and how she had thought she'd found true love in Cynthia. Hopefully, that would be enough to get people to tune in. Everyone loved a good romance, particularly if it ended in murder and mayhem.

The phone on her desk rang and she picked it up before tucking it into the crook of her neck. "Lacey Williams."

"You got an exclusive? What did I tell you, Lacey-cakes?" Kevin had a hint of laughter in his voice, but she couldn't ignore the professional jealousy hanging out in the background.

"Oh, you know me, Kevin. I'm just that good."

"I guess so. What are you doing at the office this time of night?"

"Working, of course. Aren't you?"

"Ah, hell no. Birthday party for one of the interns. Just left LAX and I happened to catch the ad for tomorrow's show in the cab. So, what do I need to do to get in on this? Lunch? Dinner? Backrubs for a month? You name it."

"You're drunk, aren't you." Lacey grinned. The great, always-in-control Kevin Conrad drunk-dialing on a Sunday night. Who would have thought?

"Not really. Just a little. Yeah. Probably am. So, what do I need to do? Tell me and I'll do it."

"I'm not her handler. I just lucked into an exclusive. What do you want me to do? Put her up on the auction block?"

"Don't get all high and mighty, Lace. You know damn well if the networks come calling, she's going to the highest bidder." He hiccupped.

"Not a chance. She doesn't need the money and she doesn't want the exposure."

"We're talking network TV, here, kid. This could be the real deal for you."

That was never going to happen. Lacey knew that. Why did Kevin think she even had a sliver of a chance? It was cruel of him to say so and he had no idea. Maybe, if he were sober, he wouldn't have said it. Or maybe he would have. She ignored the tightness in her throat and forced a smile. "Listen, I've got some things to wrap up here, but be sure to listen in this morning. Eight, sharp."

"Wait, that's not really why I'm calling. I was wondering..."

The line fell silent. Finally, Lacey asked, "Yes? You were wondering, what?"

"Are you busy tonight? I mean, you'll probably want to celebrate your big story, right? I have tickets to the... to the Cirque show at the Luxor. I won 'em, actually, tonight at the club. And I thought you might like to come along? I mean, with me. Come for me. With me. Come with me?"

"Oh, Kevin, um--"

"You're busy, of course. I don't know what I was thinking. Of course you are."

"Well, no, not exactly. I have to be completely blunt here, so there's no misunderstanding. Are you asking me on a date? Like a pick-me-up-at-my-place, bring-me-flowers, date?"

"Yeah. I probably blew it with the whole auction block thing, huh?"

"Not at all. It's just, I'm gay, Kevin. I date women, not men."

Silence filled the distance for more than a moment until Lacey asked, "Are you still there?"

"Yeah, yeah. I'm still here. I'm just... are you sure? I mean, you're so pretty!"

"Really? Okay, listen, I've got work--"

"Don't hang up; don't hang up. I'm sorry. I just had no idea. Am I the only one who didn't know that?"

"I don't wear a sign or anything, but it's not a secret either. I guess I don't think about it much." Because the real truth was that she didn't date at all. She hadn't seen anyone socially in so long it seemed like forever. Like another lifetime.

It was another lifetime. Her former lifetime.

She had dated in college, and she'd dated plenty in high school, but since the accident, the thought hadn't crossed her mind. It wasn't a question of why, but why would she.

"Lacey, you there?"

"Yes," she answered, her voice purposefully short and professional. "Listen. I'm really tired and I need to wrap up here so I can go home. If Brandy Kincaid indicates that she would like to entertain additional interviews, I'll let you know."

When she hung up the phone, her hand lingered on the handset for a moment before she placed her fingers on her cheek and traced the scar from below her eye to her chin. This was the reason she didn't go out. This was the reason she'd hidden herself away behind the anonymity of a radio mic and avoided public appearances. She didn't open supermarkets or night clubs. She didn't hang out in coffee houses and flirt with the public the way Addison did. Addison was the face of the show. She was the one plastered all over the sides of city buses and tiny billboards on top of half the taxis in Las Vegas.

And Lacey was fine with that. She was a reporter; she didn't need to be famous, right? Not anymore.

She closed her eyes, bringing in a conscious calm before she focused her attention on her work. Clicking on the icon on her desktop, she opened her daily schedule to check for any appointments. A reminder dinged on her screen and she suddenly recalled setting it from her phone over the weekend.

It was a reminder to call the coroner's office first thing in the morning.

"Do me a favor, Marko?"

"Yeah, Boss. Anything."

It was four-thirty in the morning. Brandy had barely slept a wink all night. One minute, she was filled with heat from images of a naked Lacey laying in the bed beside her, around her. Beneath her. Her smooth, silken flesh highlighted by the glow of a single candle. The next, she'd shiver as flashes of a cold cell made of concrete and steel trapped her in a void of loneliness and deprivation. Finally, she'd climbed out of the guest-room bed and reached for her phone.

Marko, her ranch foreman, had answered the land line on the first ring. She could picture him in the kitchen, scrambling three eggs and covering them with salsa and cheese before wrapping them in one of his mother's homemade tortillas. The Bungay's had been with her since she'd bought the ranch fifteen years earlier. In fact, they'd come with it, having worked for the previous owners.

"I need to come home for a while. Can you saddle Zeus for me and bring her to the western gate? I know it's a long ride, but I can't think of any other way onto the property without having to wade through the press." Zeus was her twelve-year-old buckskin mare, named for the lightning-bolt-shaped markings on her forehead.

"No problem. What time?"

"I'm leaving now. I'll be there in an hour."

By the time she got to the old mining road that led to

the backside of her property, the sun had cast a glowing outline over the distant mountains. When she and Marko reached the barn near her house, the sun had set a course past hot and directly to scorching.

"Oh, *mija*. You been gone too long. We missed you too much." Juanita Bungay, the cook and housekeeper on the Rocking T for the past thirty-six years, hurried down the front steps of the house with her arms wide. She was a hugger; always had been as Brandy had learned on the first day.

Admittedly, Brandy could use one of Juanita's hugs at that moment and allowed the older woman to pull her into a motherly embrace. "I missed you, too."

"You are hungry, yes? I can make you breakfast." Juanita turned on her heel and marched back up the steps.

It didn't really matter if Brandy were hungry, which she wasn't. The food would come, regardless.

"How long have I been gone?" she asked Marko who approached her after stripping the mounts and placing them in the corral behind the barn.

"It's only been about three days, I think. You were here Friday morning."

"God, it seems like ages longer than that."

"A lot has happened, Boss."

"Hey, what time is it?"

Marko pulled a cell phone from the front pocket of his Wrangler shirt and glanced at the screen. "Not quite eight. Why?"

"I'm going to be on the radio in a minute."

"If you had to do anything over again, Brandy, what would it be? If you could change anything."

"Anything? I'd bring Cynthia back. I'd make sure she was safe. But if I had to do anything over again, you know, given what's happening now? I wouldn't have fought with her that last night that I saw her. I would have... well, I just wouldn't have argued with her. I'd want our last meeting to be kinder."

"I spent several hours with Brandy Kincaid, talking about her late wife and speculating about what might have happened to her. Despite everything that may happen to Brandy, her concern lies with finding out, for as much as that may be possible, what happened to Cynthia and bringing the guilty to justice.

"This is Lacey Williams, All That and More, KLVN Radio, Las Vegas."

Sitting in the lobby waiting room of a small law office, Sally Crenshaw checked the time on her iWatch and touched the surface to turn off the radio. She pulled the earpiece away from her ear and tucked it into her jacket. When the technology had first come out... God, was it nearly twenty years ago? ...she had worn the Bluetooth receiver all the time. It hadn't taken long to realize she'd looked like an idiot and restricted herself to using it when she actually needed to.

The radio interview had been enlightening to a certain degree. As the lead prosecutor in the case against Brandy Kincaid, she felt more than a little torn. She was a damn good prosecutor and had been for twenty-two years. She'd seen it all. Robbery. Rape. Murder. She had the skills needed to build a case and put Kincaid away for life.

A young man, Chandra Miles' secretary, called to her from behind a huge desk littered with court files and thickly-bound documents. "Ms. Miles will see you now."

A moment later, Sally Crenshaw sauntered into Chandra Miles' office and tossed her briefcase on the visitor's chair. "We've decided to convene a grand jury."

"Hello to you, too, Sal." Chandra peered at her over the rims of her narrow reading glasses. The bright white of the frames contrasted nicely with the rich tones of her skin. Miniature, corkscrew curls bounced ever so slightly as she spoke. The counselor gently removed the glasses and leaned back in her chair. "How are you?"

Sally tried to smile, suspecting that she failed. "Sorry. Good morning, Chandra. How are you this fine morning?"

"Crappy, and yourself?" She replaced the glasses and glanced at her computer screen. "I take it you're talking about Brandy Kincaid? Isn't it a bit early for that?"

"I just left a meeting with the DA where I was ordered to convene a grand jury to indict the first lesbian in Nevada to be charged with the murder of her legally-wedded wife. I personally get to set the LGBT rights movement back about three decades. If you ask me, there isn't a right time for that, early or otherwise."

"That's one way to look at it. I don't have the luxury of worrying about the movement right now. I have a client who is being accused of murder. That's what I prefer to focus on. And I say, it's too early for your office to move forward."

"What can I say? Jethro Martin's detective skills are just that good." Sal scoffed and finally moved her bag to sit. She crossed her legs and brushed her fingers across a spot of dirt that had attached to her loafers. "Truthfully, we've got a dead woman with an estranged wife and the body was found in her own home. Brandy Kincaid had motive and opportunity. The DA doesn't want to wait. Says Kincaid is a flight risk. He sent me over here as a courtesy to let you know we're coming."

The color on Chandra's high cheeks deepened and she final turned her full attention on Sal. "The coroner's report isn't even back yet!" Her eyes bore holes in the air between them; green lasers flecked with specks of gold.

"The woman's head was practically blown off. I have a feeling we already know the COD." Sal swallowed against a rise in her body temperature that happened every time she shared a courtroom, a cab or even air with Chandra Miles. Those eyes set against her dark complexion... It made her crazy. Every time.

"What other evidence do you have, other than the fact that somebody, that somebody as of now unknown, killed Cynthia Kincaid? Do you have anything that places my client at the scene?"

"We're not ready to divulge that information."

Chandra rolled her eyes and brushed an errant curl off

her forehead with the tips of her neatly-manicured fingers. "That means no. This is a witch hunt, Sal, and you know it."

"I can't say anything more than I already have. And technically, you're not even her attorney on the criminal matter. You're her divorce lawyer."

"Yeah, well, I don't abandon my friends. You can consider this my official appearance. I'll file with the clerk just as soon as you file the formal information."

"We'll do that if we get the indictment with the grand jury this afternoon."

"Fine."

Sal stood and grabbed her briefcase from the other chair. "Are you playing in the four-man scramble this weekend at the Mission Hills Club?"

Chandra smiled, all of the opposing counsel armor stripped away with a single grin. "I am. What's your handicap?"

"I have the faintest idea. I just know I come in under par most of the time."

"Who are you playing with?"

"A few guys from the office. You?"

"The girls from the legal office over at the Pride Center. Should be fun."

"Then maybe I'll see you this weekend?"

Chandra smiled, revealing a mischievous glint in her eyes. "I'll bet you will."

Brandy woke just as the sun was setting. The orange

glow on her bedroom wall was a dead giveaway that she'd finally slept for more than a few, shaky minutes at a time. Her entire body thrummed and, for the first time in a very long time, she didn't feel entirely hopeless.

Lacey.

She'd dreamt about Lacey again. Her mouth curved into a sly grin. Oh, man, had she ever dreamt about Lacey. Pushing the covers aside, she threw on clean jeans and a new shirt and then made her way downstairs.

The dining room was full of ranch hands filling their plates from the long buffet set against one wall. Juanita prattled around like a mother hen, making sure each of the boys had enough to eat and asking incessantly if they would like something else. Marko was the first to spot Brandy.

"Hey, Boss-Lady! Welcome back to the living."

"Thanks."

Juanita hurried to escort her to the chair at the head of the table. "So, a woman call for you. A couple of times, all day. I say to her you are sleeping, but she keep calling anyway."

Had Lacey been looking for her? Her heartbeat shuffled and heat crawled over her flesh. No longer interested in joining the boys for dinner, she asked, "Did she leave a name?"

"Chandra. She say she is your lawyer. Why you have a woman lawyer? You should have a man lawyer. They are better." Juanita shook her head as though having a woman for a lawyer was just about the most tragic thing in the world.

"Ignore Mama," Marko called around a drumstick. "She crazy. And old. She kinda missed the whole woman's movement."

"You hush, mijo," Juanita replied with a wave of her hand. "Chandra is a fine lawyer, I promise."

Making her way into the kitchen, Brandy grabbed a soft taco from the buffet. She'd missed being home. She still felt like she'd been gone for weeks instead of days. Once alone in the kitchen, she called Chandra back.

"Where the hell are you? I went by the condo and you weren't there. I've been trying to call you all day."

"So, clearly, you figured out where I am."

"You can't just vanish on me like that, Bran. I've been getting calls from the press all day. You gave an interview without talking to me? Are you insane? I've been on the phone with your publicist and she's freaking out."

"She arranged for the interview!" Brandy's stomach summersaulted, and she tossed the taco into the trash by the pantry door.

It was pretty doubtful she was freaking out, anyway. Michelle never freaked out. Ever.

"And that reporter you're working with? She's been looking for you, too."

"Lacey?" Brandy suddenly straightened her posture. "She's been looking for me?"

"Yes! Everyone has been looking for you."

Lacey was the only one that mattered. "I'm sorry. I had to get some rest, Chandra. I'm exhausted. Before today, I don't think I've slept more than an hour straight in a week."

Chandra sighed and then released a quiet groan. "Fine. Did you get rested up? Because it's about to the hit the fan."

CHAPTER SEVEN

"What the hell did you do?" Brandy asked, cradling her cell phone with her shoulder as she pulled away from the bank parking lot. She'd stopped by to withdraw some cash for Chandra, who was officially taking her criminal case instead of the now obsolete divorce, only to discover that her personal bank accounts had been frozen. The only access to cash she had was the petty cash at the casino. With the stringent oversight of the Nevada State Gaming Commission, she couldn't exactly use it for her mortgage payments. Or to pay her lawyer.

Not that she had any choice, now. That cash was her only option.

"I don't know what you're talking about, Mrs. Kincaid. You care to elaborate?"

"Don't play coy with me, Detective. You took my money! You froze my bank accounts."

"Well, my, my... Now, let me see. I don't believe I have that kind of authority. Perhaps you need to speak with the prosecutor's office. They might be concerned that someone with your resources could try to leave the country rather than face murder charges. If you'd come in when we stopped by your office the other day and answered our questions, well... maybe there wouldn't be a problem now."

"I have nothing to say to you." She disconnected the call as she turned onto Tropicana Boulevard and headed toward the Touchdown. "That son of a bitch," she muttered to herself.

She had about three thousand dollars in petty cash in the safe in her office. Her casino manager replaced it weekly, swapping out a new envelope of cash with the receipts for what had been spent. Usually, those receipts came in the form of an IOU from Brandy, herself, as she handed the cash over to her wife. It had never been a problem in the past because she'd simply cut a check back in for what she'd spent. With frozen accounts, she couldn't do that.

Still, she'd grab the existing cash and move it to Michelle's condo, just in case the detective decided to serve a warrant on the business. Of course, they would sooner or later. This was really happening. They actually believed that she was guilty of murdering her own wife.

Fumbling with her cell phone, she scanned her recent calls until an image of Michelle flashed on the screen. She touched the image and waited for the call to connect. "Answer, damn it..."

"Hi Brandy. Are you okay?"

"No, I'm not, actually. They froze my assets. I have no money, no way to buy food or pay the mortgage on that damn house."

"I know. I talked to Chandra."

"I'm on my way to the office to check on the business accounts. If they froze those, the gaming commission is going to shut me down. I won't be able to make payroll. What the hell am I going to do? Sit around and let my people starve while they decide whether to charge me or not?"

"No, honey. I don't think you understand. If they've frozen your assets, it means they've already indicted. You're being charged with murder."

The street in front of her swayed as the bottom of the world fell out. Brandy's heart landed in the back of her throat. "Then why haven't I been arrested?"

"I'm sure it's only a matter of time. Very little time. Where are you right now?"

"I'm just pulling into the casino parking garage. I have some cash in my office I wanted to pick up."

"No. You need to get somewhere safe, like now, and get ahold of Chandra."

"I need money, Michelle. It's not a pretty fact of life, but it is a fact."

"Okay, just be careful and try not to linger anywhere. Get it and then go back to our place. You can't go back to the ranch. They'll look to serve you with an arrest warrant there. But they won't find you at my place. It can buy some time so we can get with Chandra and figure out what to do. Go straight there. No stops. You hear me?"

"Yeah. No stops. Crap."

"What?"

"Jethro Martin is waiting by the main entrance. I just

got off the phone with him. He didn't say anything about being at my casino."

"Why would he? He's looking to bring you in, most likely." Michelle paused and Brandy imagined the gears in her head spinning out of control. "Okay, has he seen you?"

"I don't think so."

"Do you have another way in?"

"Yeah. I never go in the front. I have a private entrance underground."

"Get in and get out. And don't get seen. When you turn yourself in, it'll be on your terms, with your attorney. And call me when you get out of there. Christ, I'm gonna be worried sick the whole time. Hang up. I want you thinking only about what you're doing."

Brandy pulled underground and disconnected the call. She made a full turn of the parking garage before she parked in an unmarked stall several feet away from her reserved space, just in case someone was watching it. Of course, her bright red Range Rover was probably a dead giveaway, she realized, almost laughing at herself. If the situation weren't so serious – perilous – she might have. Nobody seemed to be around, but she took a few minutes to steel herself against the knots forming in her gut before she got out of the truck and all-but ran to the elevator. She pressed the button, and then changed her mind. The stairs would be faster. It was only four flights.

When she reached her office, she unlocked the door and shut it quickly behind her. She leaned against it, her heart beating wildly. Through the one-way glass, she searched for any sign that the Detective had seen her enter. She could just make out the silhouette of his hulking figure outside the brass-framed entry doors. He didn't seem to be anxious. It was like he was waiting for nothing in particular; just hanging out. He was talking with George, the head valet. One of them said something funny, apparently, as they both burst into silent laughter.

Get the money. Get out.

She hurried to the safe behind her desk. For the first time, she was thankful it was broken, refusing to latch consistently. It hung open about an inch or so and she pulled it open the rest of the way. Removing the manila envelope in which she kept her emergency cash, she judged the weight of it. Peering inside, she confirmed that it was just as she'd left it that night.

The night Cynthia had come first asking, then begging for, and then demanding more money. There was usually about fifteen thousand dollars in this envelope, but now there should be only about three thousand. She'd given the rest to Cynthia and ultimately refused to give her more.

What if she'd agreed to give her the half-million she'd wanted? Would she still be alive? Would she have gone straight home and been safe? Would she have gone to her lover's boat and been safe? Had she done either of those things and not been safe?

The not-knowing what had happened to her wife was the worst part of the whole thing. She wasn't in love with Cynthia anymore, but that didn't mean she'd want her to suffer.

She shook off the thought, but not the guilt that came with it.

Tucking the envelope under her arm, she closed the safe, jiggling the handle to encourage it to latch. It did, and she left her office the same way she'd come in. Quietly. Talking to no one.

Down the stairs.

Back into her truck.

Start the engine.

She turned it back off immediately. It would be clear to anyone with a brain; she'd gotten lucky on the way in. Biting her lip, she squeezed the steering wheel and forced herself to think. She was driving a bright red Range Rover with personalized plates. She was, in effect, the proverbial sore thumb.

Instead of backing her truck out of the stall, she climbed from behind the wheel, grabbed the pink University of Utah ball cap she'd purchased four years earlier when she and Cynthia had gone skiing at Snowbird from the center console and slapped it on to cover her hair. Then she put on her Roy Orbison sunglasses, which she seldom wore despite the bright desert sunlight, and tucked the envelope into the waistband of her jeans. Her leather motorcycle jacket was in the back seat. She grabbed it and slammed the truck door, wincing at the reverberating echo in the confines of the otherwise quiet garage.

Shucking on her jacket, she hustled out of the garage to the cab stand, her shoulders hunched and her head down. She had to wait for three cabs to load passengers and leave before she climbed into the back of the fourth cab.

"Where to?" the driver asked.

She gave him the address of Michelle's building and when he pulled away from the curb she peered over her shoulder to the Touchdown's front doors.

The detective was still laughing.

"Hey. Come on in." Brandy turned immediately and stalked back into the living area.

"Jesus. Are you okay?" Lacey followed Brandy and caught a whiff of rich, leathery scent. Aside from being in a near panic, or hell, maybe it was a full-blown panic, she looked much better than the last time she'd seen her. The dark circles under her eyes, which Lacey hadn't really noticed with nothing to compare them to, were gone. She wore a fresh pair of jeans and a bright purple, sleeveless T-shirt. And motorcycle boots. When they reached the living room, Lacey found a heavy, black leather jacket draped over the back of the sofa. She could picture Brandy easily on the back of a Harley Davidson – leathers, dark glasses and the roar of the engine carrying them both across the blacktop.

"I just got back a little while ago. Pretty sure I'm officially on the run."

Lacey listened to everything that had happened to Brandy that morning, from having her assets frozen to sneaking around like a wanted fugitive. She made a call to her media contact at the courthouse and confirmed Brandy's statement. "That was really fast," she said, disconnecting the call. "And you're right. There's been a warrant issued for your arrest, about two hours ago."

"How can this be happening? I didn't do anything wrong, I swear," Brandy panted, her breath coming in short, quick gasps.

"You need to sit down and calm down. Come on; sit here. You're going to hyperventilate." Lacey guided her to the sofa and placed her in the center of the soft cushions. If there was anything she knew about panic, it was that hyperventilating could be as bad as not breathing at all. She went to the bar and fixed Brandy a rather stiff scotch with very little soda. "Drink this. Slowly."

She considered giving Brandy one of the Xanax tablets in her purse, but she might have to take some kind of drug test when she turned herself in. And there was no doubt that she would, at some point, turn herself in. The last thing she needed was prescription medication, for which she had no prescription, floating around in her blood stream.

Brandy was terrified. That much was obvious, and Lacey could easily relate to the panic that must be building in the very fiber of her bones. Fear. Angst. Confusion.

The inability to breathe.

The sensation that the boundaries of the known universe were closing in.

Lacey sat silently on the sofa next to Brandy, placing one hand on Brandy's back as she stroked slowly in a large circle. The contact was warm and seemed to sooth Brandy and at the same time it made Lacey's insides tremble. Finally, after several moments during which Brandy got a grip on her own emotions, she took a final, cleansing breath. "I called my attorney and she'll be here soon. I'm not about to poke my head out the door until then. God, I really hate this!"

"I know. Me too."

"Thank you."

"For what?"

"For being here. For being sane when I'm crazy."

"No problem. I know all about crazy, in case you couldn't tell."

Brandy smiled. She had such an amazing smile! Lacey wanted to trace the curve of her lips with her tongue. The thought made her mouth water as though she sat next to a perfect filet Mignon instead of a living, breathing human. She swallowed against the temptation.

"I don't think I want you to be my reporter anymore."

"Excuse me?" Lacey canted her head to get a better look at Brandy's expression. She was serious, based on the set of her jaw and the furrow in her strong brow.

"I need a friend more than I need a reporter, or a media consultant, or whatever this is."

Lacey knew exactly what Brandy meant. She should be angry about it. She wasn't Brandy's reporter. She wasn't her media consultant.

But she wasn't angry. Not really. No matter how little sense it made, she didn't want to be Brandy's reporter anymore, either.

Against her better judgment; against every reasonable thought in what was left of her brain, Lacey leaned forward. With one shaking finger on Brandy's chin, she pulled until

Brandy faced her. Brandy's lips parted, and her breath grew distinctly not rhythmic.

Lacey only wanted. Nothing made sense anymore. Nothing mattered except tasting Brandy's lips. When her lips made contact, the earth shifted beneath her. Vertigo. Hapless, wonderful, excruciating vertigo overwhelmed her and they both cascaded back onto the sofa.

The kiss deepened. Lacey was in control for the first time in longer than she could recall, demanding and taking, giving and pleasuring like she'd never done before. She wanted to be inside Brandy and she wanted Brandy inside of her. Their bodies melded like liquid metal until she could no longer tell where she began or ended.

Brandy shifted her weight, gaining the upper hand until Lacey was on her back. The weight seemed weightless and heavy at the same time. Fire singed her soul and warmed her heart as Brandy moved her attention away from Lacey's mouth and found her neck. Lacey, suddenly consumed by that same dancing flame, exposed her neck more, needing to feel the human connection that only came from passion uncontrolled.

She felt drunk. Like she could touch the moon and the sun and the stars and the deepest part of the ocean. Her hips thrust of their own volition, without invitation, without consequences. But there was a consequence. Brandy met each heady thrust with one of her own, igniting something she couldn't name inside her center. Fluid, the unnamed consumed her rising, unrelenting passion.

"Oh, my god, Lacey. Look what you're doing to me. I'm losing my mind," Brandy mumbled into the soft space just above Lacey's collar bone. She trailed one of her hands downward, over Lacey's shoulder to rest on her breast.

Lacey groaned. She couldn't help herself. It had been so long, months, maybe years, since anyone had touched her like this. Nobody should ever suffer this way. It wasn't fair!

As Lacey arched her back, thrusting her breast deeper into Brandy's palm, Brandy moved her hand away, eliciting an even deeper moan. The hand reappeared beneath Lacey's top, stroking and kneading the flesh over her rib cage.

And then higher...

The world came crashing down. The frantic beating of her heart no longer reflected long-abused passion. No longer sought to engage and propel her to that secret place where so few are allowed to go. The passion turned instantly to panic. She scrambled to safety, pulling herself away from Brandy. Pushing her hand away.

"What's wrong? Did I hurt you?" Brandy sat upright, her brows furrowed into gull's wings.

Lacey tried to speak but the words died in her throat. Only a simple, weak whimper emerged.

"Lacey?" Brandy just sat on the sofa as though nothing were wrong; as though the entirety of her existence hadn't just collapsed.

It had for Lacey. She would never again be able to love anyone, or let anyone love her. A sob choked the back of her throat and she rolled off the sofa onto her feet. When had she kicked off her shoes? What had made her think she could ever make love to anyone again? *Stupid, stupid rat creatures!*

She picked up her shoes and grabbed her purse from

the living room chair. She had to get out. Had to get away.

Trapped.

"Damn it, Lacey! What just happened here?" Brandy was just about to get up, but Lacey raised her hand to stop her.

"Don't. Please don't. It's not your fault. It's me. It's me." Lacey turned and raced out of the condo.

As Lacey passed through the doorway, Chandra appeared in her place. "Was it something I said?"

"No. I think it was something I did." Brandy regained her feet and tried to adjust her jeans without cluing Chandra in on what she'd almost interrupted. "Did you have any trouble getting past the concierge?"

"Nope." Chandra placed her oversized, designer purse on the counter and opened the refrigerator. She pulled out a can of Mountain Dew, popped it open and drank at least half the contents in just a few gulps. Then she released a belch that would make any red-neck proud. "Sorry. That was good." She smacked her lips. "So, how does it feel to be Las Vegas' most wanted?"

"Cute," Brandy replied with a smirk. "You're just adorable, aren't you?"

"Can't help it. I've never represented someone as... popular... as you before. I have to advise you to turn yourself in. You know this, right? You're a fugitive, as of 10:25 this morning."

Fugitive. That was one ugly word, and one she never thought would be applied to her in a million years. She nodded.

"We'll need to stop by your place to pick up your passport."

Brandy closed her eyes and groaned. The passport wasn't at her place. It was still at what had been Cynthia's house. In her old home office in Mission Hills.

"When you bail out, the judge will insist that you relinquish it, so having it handy will save some time. It will also show that you're cooperating and have no intention of fleeing."

Fleeing? That option was beginning to look better every second. The delinquent thought left as soon as it arrived. She wouldn't run from this. She didn't run from anything. Still...

"Can't get in. Still a crime scene from what I gather."

"Oh, it's there, huh? It's okay. Channel Nine broadcasted from in front of your place this morning and the tape's gone. If you have a key, we can get in."

When Brandy didn't answer, Chandra continued, "I can go by later to pick it up. I don't mind."

"Thanks. But no. We might as well get it over with, right? What if they catch us, though? Jethro Martin is already out gunning for me."

"I've called Sal Crenshaw and arranged everything. They're letting you go to them."

When they arrived at Cynthia's house, the remnants of yellow crime-scene tape still fluttered from the trunks of several trees in the front yard. Ghostly shadows moved across a manicured lawn in need of mowing as the tape caught the warm afternoon breeze. Chandra parked in the driveway. When she'd moved back to the ranch, Cynthia had insisted she leave her garage door opener behind. She still had a key to the front door, only because Cynthia had forgotten they kept extra keys in their glove boxes for emergencies. But she'd never used it; not once since she'd moved out. The only time she'd been in the house since then was the day they'd found her body.

After pulling down the remains of the crime scene tape, something she'd never thought she'd have to do in her entire career as a person, she crossed the threshold into the house.

It was silent. Not just quiet. But completely and utterly silent, like the very molecules that made up the air had ceased to move. A stagnant, offensive odor hung on the air, reinforcing her theory. She went into the kitchen and found an empty trashcan in the center of the floor. Not even a liner remained. "What the hell?"

Chandra, standing on the far side of the island, spun in her direction. "What?"

"The cops took Cynthia's trash. What in the world?" She frowned, retrieved a new bag from the pantry, shoved it into the can and then tossed in the yellow tape.

"You'd be surprised what you can find in the garbage. There have been cases where criminals have actually ditched the murder weapon at the scene of the crime."

"Leave the gun. Take the cannoli, right?"

"What?" Chandra laughed.

"You've never seen The Godfather? You leave the gun at the scene of the crime, fingerprint free of course, so that you won't be caught with it. If you're caught with it, you might as well just check into cell block nine. If the cops find the gun at the scene, they have no way to link it to you."

"Ah. Not sure how I feel about you knowing that."

"It was a bestseller made into a blockbuster. I'm not sure how I feel that you didn't."

Chandra stuck her tongue out. "They didn't take all the trash. This place is a wreck."

"The housekeeper quit after I moved out. She said she didn't want to clean up after the wild parties and was actually afraid of getting stuck with a needle."

"Can't blame her there."

Chandra was right. The interior looked like a tornado had blown through, ripping and shredding everything in sight, just as it had that day. Apparently, the garbage strewn throughout the living room hadn't interested the cops as much as the trash that had managed to find its way into the can. She'd have to hire a professional crew to get the place ready to sell. Replace the carpet and repaint the towering walls in the great room.

Her passport should still be in her office. She made her way to the back of the house, walked around the pool which was badly in need of a cleaning, and into the pool house. The pool house was too small, according to Cynthia, to serve its purpose, so Brandy had taken it over as a home office and freed the room off the kitchen to serve as a dressing room for guests.

There was a time she'd been willing to do anything to make Cynthia happy. None of it had mattered.

She located her passport in the top drawer of her desk where she'd left it. She checked the picture and glanced at the most recent stamps she'd collected. Paris, France, less than a year ago. It had been her last-ditch attempt to save her marriage. She and Cynthia had taken a Mediterranean cruise that departed from the south of France after renting a car and driving through the countryside from Paris. They hadn't had such a leisurely time on the way back. As had become the norm, by the time they'd spent three days together, they couldn't wait to be apart. Cynthia had spent the entire two-week cruise in the bar and the casino while Brandy had taken in the sites at each port of call and become friends with the ship's captain. It had been either that, or spend the entire time alone in her stateroom.

She tucked the passport into her back pocket and slammed the desk closed. Did she have any other personal belongings here? Other than cleaning out the last of her records from the office, she had no intention of ever setting foot inside the house again. Hell, if the cops had their way, she wouldn't have much choice in the matter.

Like a tourist packing up a hotel room, she went through a checklist in her mind. Then, like that same tourist, she decided a final pass would ensure she left nothing of value. She would have to go upstairs to see what she may have forgotten when she moved out so hastily just after Easter.

She made it to the bottom of the stairs and gripped the railing until her knuckles turned white. She never wanted to come back here. Ever.

Sucking in a breath, she steeled herself against useless emotions, and then took the steps two at a time.

Chandra followed more slowly. "What's your rush. You do know you're getting arrested next, right?"

"I want to get this over with!" Brandy approached the bedroom door just as Chandra made it to the hallway.

"Is this where it happened?" Chandra pursed her full, shimmering lips and creased her brow. "Girl, I don't even want to go in there." She shook her head slowly, her dark brown eyes wide.

"You can wait out here." Brandy pushed on the door and it slid easily over the thick carpeting.

Instead of finding an enormous blood stain on her carpet where she'd seen one last time, she found an enormous hole where the carpeting should have been. They had removed it, slicing at odd angles in what might be considered a circle from the foot of the bed to the opposite wall. The padding had also been removed, leaving naked sub-flooring. There was no blood.

Thank God. Had there been blood, the cops probably would have left a gaping hole in the middle of the room.

The dress that had been balled up on the foot of the bed was gone, as were the bed clothes. The mattresses were bare, the top one slightly off kilter as it hung a few inches over the box spring.

She skirted it, careful not to touch it, as she went to what had been her closet. She frowned at the huge, empty space where her clothes had been. Her wife's side of the closet was still filled to capacity with sparkling evening gowns, designer suits and jeans, and rows upon rows of insensible shoes. She pulled open the narrow drawers that stacked neatly against one wall. The velvet-lined interiors were empty. All of her wife's jewelry was gone. Platinum. Gold. Diamonds.

All gone.

A robbery? Had it all been a simple robbery? Why wouldn't the cops mention that so much had been missing? Why would they still believe it was Brandy, when it was obviously a robbery?

Anger heated her blood as she slammed the drawers.

Realization dawned slowly over the rough terrain in her mind. The simplest explanation was usually the right one. The jewelry probably hadn't been stolen. It had probably been sold.

She grabbed Cynthia's suitcase from the top shelf on her side of the space and laid it on the dressing table that separated one side of the walk-in closet from the other. She pulled stacks of underthings and bras she'd left behind when she'd moved out from the top drawer, and then filled the suitcase with jeans and shirts with no particular order or reason. She hadn't taken the items earlier because she hadn't believed there to be much of a rush. She'd taken enough to get by and hadn't given it much thought since.

She slammed the suitcase closed, struggled with the zipper and then she and Chandra hurried out of the house. After she threw the case into the back seat of her truck, she dug for her keys in her front pocket.

It took almost an hour to get to the jail. When they arrived, the entire parking lot was filled with news vans and on-lookers. Everyone seemed to be standing on quicksand until they realized that Brandy was in Chandra's Lexus. Then they looked less like humans and more like a school of piranha in a blood-induced feeding frenzy. Except for one. One reporter didn't rush the car or shout questions.

Brandy focused her attention on that one reporter with soft blonde hair and lips that tasted like rosewater. Lacey looked back at her, her blue eyes clear and her lips curved in a reassuring half-grin that seemed to let Brandy know that everything was going to be okay.

Brandy ignored the questions thrown at her from every side and allowed Chandra to lead her into the building. Inside, the prosecutor met them with a deputy in a crisp uniform. The booking area was empty. Somehow, Brandy didn't believe that was normal. She'd never seen the inside of the jail in person, although she'd watched the reality television program set there enough times to know that they were always busy.

The prosecutor was a robust woman, standing with her feet slightly apart in almost a military fashion. When they reached her, Chandra extended her hand and the other woman took it in a gentle grip. "Sal Crenshaw, I'd like you to meet my client, Brandy Kincaid. Brandy, this is Sal Crenshaw."

"Mrs. Kincaid," she said, nodding slightly. "I'm sorry about that crowd outside. Somehow, it got out that you were turning yourself in this afternoon and everyone got wind of it."

"I guess I kind of expected it." Brandy shrugged.

"But, we've made some arrangements that should make this about as painless as possible."

"Thank you, Sal. I appreciate you helping out with this whole thing." Chandra leaned forward and nudged the prosecutor.

"No problem. Now, let's get you taken care of so you

can get out of this nuthouse. If you'll follow me."

"What happens now?" Brandy tried to sound strong, but her bravery, if she'd ever had any, faltered at the prospect of being placed in a cage. "How long do you think I'll be here?"

"Not too long. I've already talked to a judge, and with the help of your attorney, we've been able to work out a bond agreement."

"I can't access any of my funds. Someone froze my assets."

"Yeah, sorry about that. That was me. It wasn't my idea, but since you're pretty solvent from a financial standpoint, we couldn't risk you running before we could bring you in. Just in case. We'll be releasing the hold once you're booked and surrender your passport."

"How much?"

"Five million," Chandra offered.

Brandy nearly choked. "Five million? Dollars? I don't have five million dollars lying around. Holy shit!"

"Don't worry." Sal insisted. "First, the bond portion of the bail is one-tenth that amount, and secondly, it's already been paid."

"I'm sorry? Did you say it's been paid?" Brandy struggled to think how that would even be possible. "By whom?"

"I'm not sure, actually. I just know that Lynda Fairchild Bail Bonds was here about twenty minutes ago and posted you out. You won't even see the inside of a cell while you're here."

The large black SUV made Lacey's blood run cold. Emblazoned with a white decal that ran the length of one side, it announced the arrival of Lynda Fairchild Bail Bonds. It approached from a side street and crawled to a stop about three feet from where Lacey stood across the street from the jail. When the word got out that Brandy was going to turn herself in, about an hour after she'd raced out of the condo, her producer had called and relayed the message that Addison expected Lacey to be there.

By then, she'd already made her decision.

Brandy was not going to spend a single night in jail for something she didn't do. Not if Lacey could do anything about it. She'd called Michelle and received the name of the bondsman Michelle used for her celebrity clients when they partied a little too hard in Vegas. Discreet and efficient. That was exactly what she needed.

She'd been surprised to learn that it was the same company that Brandy had used to keep an eye on her late wife.

Now, she stood outside the jail, far from the throng of reporters who all hoped that Brandy would make a public statement when she came out. Of course, she wouldn't. Lacey knew that. She was there for only two reasons. To make sure Brandy did come out of the building, and to see her again. She'd accomplished the second goal when Brandy had arrived.

The deeply tinted window of the SUV slid open and a woman with ash-blonde hair who looked to be in her mid-forties pulled back a pair of designer sunglasses, securing her longish bangs to the top of her head.

"Lacey Williams?" she asked.

"Yes. You must be Lynda Fairchild."

"The one and only."

"Did everything go okay? No problems?"

"Nary a one. She should be coming out in a half hour or so."

"How did she look? Was she nervous? Scared?"

"No idea. I didn't see her, myself. You really care about Brandy, don't you?"

"I suppose."

"You just put up a half-million bucks that you'll never see again, not to mention your sister's ranch and other assets, for someone you suppose you care about? Oh, honey. I've seen this before. Most of the folks I bail out are guilty as hell. I have four bounty hunters working full-time for me just to keep my client base where I can see them."

"Brandy isn't going to run. And she isn't guilty. She's your client, for crying out loud."

"You think she's innocent because she hired us to tail her wife for a few months?" Linda grinned and shook her head as though to say she pitied Lacey for thinking it. "I'm in business to make money, hon. I learned a long time ago that everyone is guilty of something. So, she hired us. So, what? The fact that her wife is now dead doesn't bother me nearly as much as the fact she might have used the information we provided to push her over the edge. That's why we have a section in our contract where a new client affirms they will not use any of the information we collect to harm or damage any other person. If they do, it's on them. My conscience is clear."

"She's not guilty of anything."

"Whatever you say," Lynda mumbled with a shrug. "I got paid."

"I appreciate you keeping my identity close to the vest."

Lynda shook her head again with the same piteous attitude. "I'll never understand how so many people fall into the same old traps. But hey, it's your money. Your secret is safe with me."

"Thanks."

"Oh, by the way. I wasn't the only one in there looking to bail out your girlfriend. Kenny the Fish was in there, too."

"Who?"

"Kenny Maretti. We call him Kenny the Fish because he's connected, and all that that implies, and he looks like Abe Vigoda, you know? Anyway, he was trying to throw her bail, too. Apparently, your girlfriend is of some interest to the Maretti crime family."

"Why would they throw her bail? I mean, you don't suppose—"

Lynda smirked as she interrupted. "Listen, there are only two things it could possibly mean. Either they want her dead, in which case, you're lucky you got to her first. Or, and this is the way I'm leaning... She's working with them. She's family. They take care of their own."

CHAPTER EIGHT

"Michelle, what the hell aren't you telling me?"

"God, Lacey. What's wrong? Oh my god, did they not let Brandy out of jail?"

"No. I mean, yes. They're going to release her after they book her. She's still inside. No, I'm talking about the fact that the mob sent a freakin' emissary to bail her out. What the hell is that all about? I went out on a limb with that interview. How could you let me do that?"

"Whoa, whoa. Slow down. What do you mean an emissary?"

"I mean the Maretti family sent their attorney-slash-enforcer person to bail Brandy out. Why is the mob hanging out? What is it you're not telling me?"

"Brandy is not involved with the mob. No way."

"Are you sure they're not, I don't know, like partners in the casino or something?"

"No, and if they were, why would they bail her out? They'd just take over the operation, wouldn't they?" Michelle paused. "What in the world am I saying? She's not involved with the mob!"

"I hope to God you're right, Mike, because if she is, and

it gets out, my career will be over before it starts. I vouched for her in that interview. I went all Barbara Walters and it came off like I was on her side."

"Calm down. I'm sure there is a perfectly reasonable explanation."

Why did people always say that when there probably wasn't. There was nothing reasonable about the mob wanting to get their hands on Brandy. How long had they been looking for her? Had they not been able to find her because she'd been staying at Kendra's place? Or did they know she was there already? Had they staked out the building?

The familiar panic started in the very cells of her flesh, raising her temperature until she couldn't breathe. "Mi... Michelle. What's going on?"

"Are you driving right now?"

Lacey nodded.

"Lacey? Are you driving?"

"Yes."

"Pull over. Right now. Get off the road. Where are you?"

"I'm on I-15. I can't breathe."

"Yes, you can. If you can talk, you can breathe. Take a deep breath and pull off the road."

"No exit."

"Pull onto the shoulder, then. As close to the edge as you can."

Lacey, already in the far-right lane, pulled to the side of the road and tapped the button to turn on her hazard lights. She sucked in a sharp breath, and then another.

"Are you off the road?"

"Yeah. Still... can't breathe."

"Inhale. Deep and slow."

Lacey obeyed. For the next several minutes, she breathed in when Michelle told her to. She exhaled when Michelle told her to. Finally, her heart rate slowed, and her skin began to cool. The world, which had been dreary, returned to full color and she looked up at a billboard advertising a life insurance company. A middle-aged woman with her hands on the shoulders of two little boys towered over her. They all looked so sad. Forlorn, even. The text hovering above them read, "When you least expect it, everything changes." At the bottom edge of the sign, it continued, "Trust Insurance... because we care."

"Lacey, are you okay?"

"Yeah. Yeah, I'm okay now, I think."

Trust.

"I'm going to head over to the courthouse and look up a few things. I'll call you when I know something more. Listen, don't mention this to Brandy. At least, not yet."

"You know... we could just ask her if she knows what's going on."

"No. If she's into something neither one of us knows about, I'd rather not tip her off."

"I don't like this. But okay. Let me know if you learn anything."

The Maretti family was into a wide range of activities, both legal and not-so-legal. Some of it was just plain not legal. They were smart and experienced after generations of pushing the envelopes of the law. It wasn't always easy to differentiate between illicit and legitimate activities.

She'd learned that much from her contact at the FBI; off the record, of course.

At the courthouse, she'd scanned all of the property records for each of Brandy's businesses, her home in Mission Hills and the ranch outside of town. All of it was owned either by Brandy, personally, or her corporation, Brandy Kincaid, Inc. There were no shell companies. There were no partners. Her attorney, Chandra Miles, was listed as the receiver for the corporation, but other than that, nothing.

By the time she got back to her place, it was well after dark. And she was still completely in the dark. Determined to figure out what was happening, she headed directly to Kendra's condo instead of her own.

Or maybe she just wanted to make sure Brandy had gotten home alright.

The condo was empty. When Brandy didn't answer, Lacey let herself in. She went immediately to the guest room, the same room her older brother Brent used when he was in town. Nothing was out of place. The bed had been neatly made. The door to the en suite stood open, revealing the clean surface of a single sink vanity. A pink toothbrush and a tube of Crest rested to one side and this was the only indication that Brandy was even staying there.

No briefcase. No portable files. Nothing that would hold incriminating documents. Of course, there wouldn't be, would there? Those types of records would be in her office at the casino, or more likely, at her home.

She had no idea what she was looking for, but she pulled open the dresser drawers anyway, only to find a few articles of her brother's clothing, including a pair of black boxers with, "How you doin'," scripted on the front. She cringed. Some things, you just could never unsee.

Slamming the dresser closed, she returned to the living room. She was still standing there, wondering if she should leave, when Brandy slid open the door.

"Lacey! Man, you are a sight for sore eyes."

"Am I?" Lacey asked, not certain if the fluttering in her belly was a good thing or a bad thing.

Brandy nodded and collapsed on the sofa. She tilted her head back and rubbed the heels of her palms over her eyes. "Well, I guess I'm glad that's over."

Claiming a seat for herself in an armchair, Lacey propped her elbows on her knees. One of her legs bounced rapidly with unchecked adrenaline. It was so confusing. She wanted to confront Brandy about her mob connection, but at the same time, her heart ached for what Brandy had just been through. Her heart won the small, internal battle. "Was it horrible?"

"Not as bad as I thought it would be, thanks to Chandra." Brandy lifted her head and focused on Lacey. "Did you know that you don't have to get ink on your fingers when they take your fingerprints anymore? On TV and in the movies, they always roll your fingers in black ink and then press them onto a card, right?" She relaxed her head ag ain. "Now, it's all on a touchscreen. I'm officially on the grid. My prints went into a huge database. They'll probably match them to the baseball card wrapper I left behind at the department store when I stole them. I was eight."

Lacey chuckled. "Doubtful."

"I left the wrapper because it was shiny. Like tin foil. I thought that was how the alarms at the doors got set off. I was such a little criminal, back in the day."

Back in the day? Or right now?

"Aren't your fingerprints already on file with the Gaming Commission?"

"Oh, yeah. I forgot about that." She sat up higher and rolled her head back and forth, stretching the muscles in her neck. "I guess I'm home free on the baseball card thing, then."

Lacey tried to form a smile, to acknowledge Brandy's self-deprecating humor, but she couldn't be certain it worked. Her leg continued to bounce, and she bit the inside of her cheek instead.

"What's wrong?" Brandy sat up and leaned her elbow on the armrest before canting her head to rest in her palm. "You look like something's bothering you."

Silence filled the space between them for more than a few seconds before Lacey finally spoke. "You owe me a half-million dollars."

"It was you?" Brandy whispered through a grin. "I should have known."

"Well, it was all of us. I put up the cash and Michelle and Kendra put up the ranch."

"Are you kidding me?"

"We couldn't leave you in there, and your assets were frozen." Lacey shrugged as though she'd just explained how to pour a glass of milk. Open the container, tip it and milk falls out. Simple.

"You could have. I'm really, really glad you didn't, but you could have."

"It's okay. Really." Lacey's fingers worked against each other where they met in the space between her jumping knees. The knuckles turned from white to red and back as she rubbed them together.

"Something else is wrong. What's the matter?"

"I'm just going to get this out there, because I have a lot riding on this. I wasn't even going to tell you that I posted your bail because I don't care about the money, really. But..."

"I'm listening?" Brandy sat up, mimicking Lacey's position, right down to her entwined fingers.

"Do you know a man named Kenneth Maretti?"

"Not personally, no. I know of the family. Everyone in the casino business knows of that particular family."

Most of the color left Lacey's complexion. The blue of her eyes seemed to deepen in contrast.

"What's going on? Why are you asking about the mafia?"

"Because Kenneth, the family attorney, tried to post your bail earlier today. I'm a little concerned about why he would want to do that."

It was very seldom that Brandy was at a complete loss for words. She couldn't think of a single thing to say. She just shook her head as her mouth fell open, searching for a syllable or two. One. One syllable would work. "I..."

"I've been over and over it. The only reason they would want to bail you out is if you were--"

"Hell, no!" Finally, she'd found both syllables she'd been looking for. She stood up and took several steps across the room before turning back around. "No. I know what you're thinking and you're wrong."

"What am I supposed to think, Brandy?"

"I haven't got a clue, but not that. I am not connected to organized crime. I run a clean operation. I pay my taxes and I do everything by the book. Everything. You can look it up, if you like. Talk to the Gaming Commission. I've been cited three times in ten years by the health department, and once last year for not having enough cash in the vault, but that's it. How could you think..." She ran a hand through her hair and turned away to face her reflection in the glass door.

Lacey sat behind her, still weaving her fingers together. She looked at the floor for a moment before raising her head to face Brandy's back. "There is one other possibility."

"What's that?"

"They think you have information that can hurt them. They may have been the ones who killed your wife."

Was it possible? What could they possibly have to gain?

"I mean, it makes sense, right? You said that Cynthia needed about a half-million? What if she owed that money to the Maretti family?"

"You mean, like she took a loan? Why would she do that?"

"A loan, or for drugs, or whatever. It could be anything, really."

Brandy crossed the room and stood near Lacey's chair. "I don't know why they tried to get to me. I don't know if Cynthia was involved with them or if she owed them money. I don't know anything."

Lacey looked up at her with shimmering, moist eyes. She ran her fingers through her hair, obviously being careful not to reveal the side of her face with the scar. The movements came so naturally to her, Brandy wondered if she even realized she did it anymore.

Inhaling a ragged breath that burned all the way down, Brandy continued, "I can only promise you that I haven't done anything to make you question my innocence or my honor."

"I want to believe you, Brandy—"

Dropping to one knee beside the chair, she took Lacey's hands and stared directly into those endless eyes. "Then do it. Believe me."

Silence stretched until Brandy thought Lacey would choose the lie. Lies were so much easier to believe, particularly when they served to protect one's heart. Finally, Lacey nodded and pushed out a determined sigh. "Okay. I believe you."

"Do you trust me?"

"Trust is a big word, and most people don't know what it means."

"I do. I know exactly what it means. If you can trust me, then I can promise you, I will never hurt you."

"I'll try. That's the best I can do right now, Brandy."

"I'd like you to stay the night."

What color remained in Lacey's cheeks drained, leaving her flesh the same color as fine porcelain. "Excuse me?"

"It's not what you're thinking. I'd just feel better if you weren't alone. I'll feel better if I'm not alone, either, when it comes right down to it. This whole thing just took a really frightening turn."

Lacey nodded. When she lifted Lacey's fingers to her lips and placed a resolute kiss on them, Lacey didn't fight it.

The clock on the fireplace mantel chimed, drawing Brandy's attention. It read eight o'clock. "It's late."

"It is. Where were you, anyway?"

"Chandra insisted on taking me back to her office to make an official statement for the cops. She's going to write it up and give it to them tomorrow. Then she wanted to take me out to dinner to make up for it."

"Oh."

"I wanted to come here. I wanted you to be waiting for me. And you were."

"I was."

"I'm glad."

"Me, too."

"Let's go to bed. I won't try anything. I promise."

"I trust you."

"Does this mean you really believe me? That I'm not a gangster or a mobster or whatever they're called these days?"

"I believe you. But you still owe me half-a-million dollars."

Wednesday morning, Addison was sitting at Lacey's desk when Lacey made her way into the newsroom at the station. Lacey approached the tight cubicle and then hitched her bag higher onto her shoulder as she cleared her throat. Addison started, turning around swiftly in the unsteady, rolling chair.

"You scared me!" Addison remarked as she tossed one of Lacey's files back on the desk.

It was a report she'd been working on for a series of shows about sex trafficking in the city. She hadn't proposed it yet, and she wasn't certain the station manager would go for it. "What can I do for you, Addison?"

Addison stood, smoothing the front of her short, tight skirt over her thighs, and offered Lacey her own chair. "Nothing, really. I'm just curious why you weren't at the jail yesterday when that woman was released?"

That woman? The biggest story the station had covered in a year, and Addison couldn't remember Brandy's name.

"I was there. When she went in. She wasn't going to make a statement, so I didn't feel like I needed to stick around." She spun the chair to face her and sat at her desk.

"But you were supposed to be there. That was your assignment. If you're not going to follow directions--"

"What's the big deal, Addison? We have exclusive access to Brandy. That's nothing to sneeze at, you know."

"The problem is, we were going live, expecting you to be on the line, and you weren't there. You made Marshall Brennon look like an amateur as he announced, repeatedly all morning, that he was going to you, live, as Brandy left the jail."

Lacey frowned. "Nobody told me that. Nobody said a goddamn word about calling it in." She tossed her bag on her desk and folded her arms over her chest.

"Really? You're going to sit there and claim that you didn't know."

"Yes, that's what I'm doing, Addison."

"You'd throw your producer under the bus like that? Make it look like her fault?"

"No. I'm telling you that nobody said we were going live."

Her boss's eyes narrowed to tiny slits and her jaw worked slightly before she said, "I don't like you, Lacey. You don't belong here. I know we were your second choice. I know you'd rather be on television and that when you lost your looks, you lost your chance. It wouldn't take much to yank this away from you, too. Next time, do exactly as you're told and stop thinking that you have any control over what you do around here." Addison sneered as she picked up the file she'd discarded a moment before. "And stop wasting your time on crap like this. Your story idea is completely worthless." She dropped the file back on the desk. Then, she executed a perfect turn on her four-inch Louboutin heels and stalked in the direction of the station manager's office.

Lacey felt like her entire body might cave in on itself. A week ago, those words might have broken her. Now, they just made her angry; fighting mad. She wanted to rip into her boss, scream at her for being a bitch and an ass. She couldn't do that. Addison only wanted a reason to fire her; she wouldn't give her one. She knew damn well that when Lacey's producer had called her, she hadn't said anything about a live feed.

What had changed? What made her angry about Addison spewing words that she had said to herself, over and over again, ever since the accident? It had to be more than the fact someone else had finally voiced them, right? Did she still believe it? Did she still believe that she was somehow 'less than' because of how she looked?

Brandy didn't seem to think so.

Last night had been amazing. She hadn't slept so well for longer than she could remember. No nightmares. No tossing and turning and struggling to rest. The only difference had been Brandy. True to her word, they hadn't been intimate; at least, not sexually. No, Brandy had simply held her while she slept. Lacey had cocooned herself inside the protective embrace and felt like nothing in the world could ever harm her again.

She'd felt safe.

She didn't know if that was a good thing or a bad thing, but it was there. She couldn't avoid it. She couldn't possibly be falling in love with Brandy, could she? The fact that she wanted nothing more than to cradle her in the same protective bubble that Brandy offered her was absurd. Her entire plan for her life included nothing of love. But then, her plans had changed before...

She sat down at her desk, picked up the phone, and then dialed the coroner's office.

The switchboard answered on the third ring. After being placed on hold four times, she found herself redirected to the public relations office. They would be holding a press conference "on Thursday morning at ten and until that time, the department has no comment."

Just as she hung up the phone, it rang. She didn't recognize the caller ID except that it was an out of state number. She picked it up, cleared her throat and said, "News desk."

"I'd like to speak with Lacey Williams, please."

"You got her."

"Hi, Lacey, this is Grace Phillips from the Carleen Carson show. How are you?"

Carleen Carson! The blood thickened in her veins and when she tried to speak she thought her tongue might have swelled to twice its normal size. "Um, I'm fine. How are you?"

"I'm fantastic, thanks for asking. Hey, we were just listening to a tape of your local broadcast, All That and More, from Monday morning. You got quite the scoop there. An exclusive interview with Brandy Kincaid? Carleen would love to have you on the show tonight, and if you could bring Mrs. Kincaid along for the ride that would be great. We'll live feed from the affiliate in Henderson."

"Wait, wait, no, you don't understand--"

"I'm sorry, was I going too fast? You didn't understand? Carleen Carson wants to interview Brandy Kincaid, and we've already contacted her people. They said she's pretty much exclusive and that we should talk to you about it."

"No, I understand perfectly. You want me to appear via satellite on your program tonight, preferably with Mrs. Kincaid." A live feed to the highest-ranked news channel on television in the entire world... a video link up, with her face split-screened with Carleen Carson... Lacey's heart throbbed, and her ears began to ring.

She stood slightly and peered over the partition. Addison was standing by the water cooler, one hand toying with the thin gold chain around her neck while she flirted with one of the sound tech guys. She sat back down and cleared her throat. "I'm afraid Mrs. Kincaid has made it very clear she won't be granting any more interviews. I'm happy to participate in an interview about my interaction with Mrs. Kincaid."

"Oh... well, okay. I guess we can work with that. I'll call you back in a few minutes. I'll need to clear it with Ms. Carson."

"I'll be here. Or on my cell." She gave Grace the number and hung up.

National TV. Lacey traced the scar on her cheek and winced. The question remained whether she could pull this off.

It was nearly dark on Wednesday evening when Brandy reached the condo. Earlier that afternoon, she'd driven out to the ranch and found that only a small handful of seriously dedicated paparazzi were still hanging around the gate. After braving her way through, she'd visited with Marko and Juanita for a while.

True to her word, Sal Crenshaw had released the hold on Brandy's accounts, so she'd transferred cash into the ranch's working account for Marko. Then she'd authorized a wire transfer from one of her investment accounts to Lacey's bank. Her broker had to liquidate some of her stocks to do it, but she'd managed to come up with the half-million in cash in a little under an hour. Finally, she arranged a meeting with Lynda Fairchild to put up her own holdings as her guarantee, freeing Kendra and Michelle's property. It didn't really matter, and they'd told her not to worry about it, but it made her feel better knowing that such things weren't hovering over their personal or professional relationships.

Marko and his mother had both wanted her to sleep at the ranch, considering she'd rested so well before. And there was no real reason for her not to. Except for last night. Except for Lacey.

If she stayed on the ranch, she wouldn't have the opportunity to see Lacey again. With everything else going on in her life, Lacey was the bright spot. The reason she didn't mind opening her eyes in the morning.

That morning, she'd opened her eyes to find the lovely wisps of golden hair spread across her chest with Lacey's slumbering body tucked neatly next to hers. She'd been hit with emotions so strong, they'd literally taken her breath away.

The rest of her world wasn't so relaxing. It was like she was in a holding pattern, waiting for the authorities to release Cynthia's body so they could have the funeral, waiting for the court hearing to determine the schedule of her trial. Waiting for the results of the postmortem. Waiting.

She hadn't wanted Lacey to go to work; hadn't wanted her to be out there, in the dangerous world where the Maretti family hovered in the shadows for some unknown, probably nefarious, reason. Lacey had almost buckled, but in the end, had decided she had to go. She was a reporter, she'd said. And reporters didn't cave to the mob.

The determination hadn't reached her eyes. There had been a certain amount of panic there, but she hadn't caved.

Back at the condo, she stepped into the great room, picked up the remote, turned on the news and sank into the plush sofa. She wasn't surprised when she saw a picture of herself in the tiny window near Carleen Carson's perfectly-coiffed head. The story had aired on Lacey's station this week and it hadn't taken more than a few hours for the national media to pick it up.

"...we have local Las Vegas investigative reporter Lacey Williams of KLVN joining us via satellite. Thank you for joining us Lacey."

Brandy sat up straight and focused on the TV screen. Her image disappeared as the screen shifted to a split screen. Carleen on the left, and Lacey on the right. She turned up the volume.

"Thank you for having me." Lacey's voice sounded full, rich and confident. Like hanging out on national television was something she did all the time. She looked amazing.
"What can you tell us about your impressions of Brandy Kincaid, since you're the only one who has managed to talk to the elusive millionaire about the murder of her wife since she went into hiding?"

Brandy slammed her fist on her knee. That bitch made it sound like it was a given she had killed her wife. What the hell was Lacey talking to her for?

"*I spent several hours with Mrs. Kincaid in the home of a friend where she's been staying. She's not hiding from anyone except the press, Carleen, just to make that clear. My overall impressions of her, so far, are that of a woman in shock, and a woman greatly concerned for what has happened to her wife.*"

Go, Lacey! Brandy's grin hurt her cheeks, but she couldn't stop smiling.

"*You say she's shocked. What, exactly, do you believe she's shocked about? Is it the fact her wife has been killed, or that the body turned up in her own home?*"

That was a little better. At least it left open the possibility she hadn't done it.

"*Both, I think. She's been completely forthcoming with me for any questions I've had about her relationship with her wife, and I think anyone would be in shock to discover their partner had been kidnapped and murdered.*"

"*Do the police know that the late Mrs. Kincaid was, in fact, kidnapped? Is there any possibility that she wasn't missing at all, but happened to return home, say, during a burglary or some other crime?*"

"Anything is possible and that is certainly one avenue that the local authorities will need to investigate. There is probably more to it than that, since the home is located in an affluent, gated community. You can't simply walk up to the property and break in. As for when she was murdered, we don't know. At the moment, I'm waiting for the coroner's report to determine a cause and time of death."

"The time of death. Right, right. That would indicate whether the surviving wife had the opportunity to commit this crime. We know she's got the motive, and the prosecutors were able to convince a grand jury to indict, so really we are just waiting for that confirmation from the coroner that Brandy Kincaid had the opportunity. We also know that she and the dead woman were going through a nasty divorce. She more than likely had the means, yes? A ranch owner in the Western US would most certainly own a number of guns. And Nevada doesn't require registration of firearms, so we would have no way of knowing, precisely, how many guns she owns or whether any of them are missing. Once the authorities know she had the time, they'll have everything they need to proceed with a trial. With that kind of evidence against her, are you hearing any rumblings about a plea deal?"

Lacey rolled her eyes. "That's a loaded question, Carleen. You're taking a few liberties, aren't you? There was nothing nasty about the divorce; in fact, it had barely started and Brandy Kincaid is fairly certain things would have been wrapped up amicably. As for assuming she owns guns, that's like saying every person with a car should be a suspect in the next hit-and-run on Las Vegas Boulevard."

Yes!

"She's already been arraigned, booked and released, and is awaiting a preliminary hearing. That's when we'll find out just how much evidence, or lack of evidence, there is in this case."

"Can you answer me this, Lacey. Does she have an attorney, yet?" Carleen Carson tossed her light wheat-colored hair in a way that seemed to say she was above the conversation she was having, as though she already knew all the answers to her own pointed questions.

"Yes, her regular attorney has filed an appearance with the court."

"Well, that, at least, tells us quite a bit, doesn't it? Thank you again for joining us, Lacey."

"Thank you for having me."

The screen returned to focus solely on Carleen Carson and Brandy's mugshot occupied the top right corner.

"I have to wonder why an innocent woman would secure the services of an attorney? And why wasn't she more concerned when her wife turned up missing? We've learned that several witnesses saw the two lesbian women arguing vehemen--"

Brandy turned off the television and stared at the ceiling. Inhaling deeply, she maintained a measure of control over her temper. Brandy hadn't hired counsel because she was guilty. She'd already had an attorney on retainer! She owned a casino. She was getting divorced. Of course, she had an attorney! Of course, the infamous, illusive they would believe hiring an attorney meant trying to hide guilt. Of course, the media would focus their unregulated attention on her as a suspect.

She hadn't expected to hear anything less, but that didn't remove any of the sting.

And what did the fact she was a lesbian have to do with anything? Brandy pushed herself off the sofa, turned on the CD player and browsed the CDs already loaded. Melissa Etheridge. Neon Trees. Carole King. Jim Croce. She settled on an old Carpenter's album before making her way into the kitchen. Food. She needed to eat something if for no other reason than to ground herself into something normal.

Normal people ate dinner right about now. She used to be normal. How long ago was that?

She glanced at the clock. She should be at the casino.

She'd taken more time off in the past week than she had in the past three years. But she couldn't bring herself to go in unless she absolutely had to. Not with an indictment hanging over her.

Nothing really caught her fancy in the nearly empty refrigerator. Kendra and Michelle had told her to eat as many of the leftovers as she liked, since they weren't planning to come back for at least a month. She'd taken them up on it and hadn't prepared anything new in a couple of days. The only items left now consisted of half a steak and mashed potatoes in a Styrofoam to-go box that she'd placed earlier in the week, a plastic storage box of Brussels sprouts in cream sauce, a half-pound of ground beef that should have been cooked two days ago, and a loaf of bread.

She closed the door with a sigh. Nothing.

Instead, she took a shower and got ready for bed. When she returned to the living room, Jim Croce was singing about calling his ex-girlfriend, who'd run off with his best old ex-friend. The doorbell chimed.

Nobody knew where she was staying. She'd been in contact with her business managers by phone, of course, but other than her in-laws, and her attorney, there was only one person who would seek her out.

She opened the door without peering through the security peep-hole. On the other side Lacey smiled, her eyes dancing a little in the dim light of the hall. In one hand, she held a grocery bag containing two large Styrofoam cartons and she cradled a bottle of wine in the crook of the opposite arm. "Did you eat yet?"

Stress seeped out of her body like water through a spout. Warmth replaced it, creeping up the back of her neck and ultimately pooling in her midsection with sanguine fluidity. "As a matter of fact, I haven't. What did you bring me?"

Lacey slid past her, the soft scent of lilacs in her wake. Was it her shampoo, perhaps, that carried the scent? It wasn't powerful enough to be perfume. Brandy frowned. Cynthia had always worn too much perfume. It was one of many things she now realized she'd overlooked for the chance to be in love; to be loved in return.

"Pasta from the Venetian. I'll have to reheat it. I picked it up on my way home. Guess what I just did?"

"Hmm," Brandy said. "I'm not a super good guesser, but I'll go out on a limb. You just did a live interview on the Carleen Carson news show."

"You saw it?" Lacey beamed. "They actually wanted you to go on live, too. I didn't think that was such a hot idea, and Michelle agreed." The rosy pink of her cheeks paled slightly as she paused in mid-step and swiveled to face her. "I hope that's okay? Carleen Carson can be positively brutal to her guests."

"No. I mean, yeah. Yeah, that's fine with me. I've watched her. If I'm going to meet up with her, I'd rather it be across a blackjack table and not on her turf." Brandy smiled as she escorted Lacey the rest of the way into the kitchen. "You looked fantastic, by the way."

"Yeah? I think it went pretty well, all considering."

"I don't know about that. You were fantastic. But she pretty much already thinks I'm guilty. It was pretty obvious."

"That's her schtick. If you go back and look at her coverage, she's right about forty percent of the time, which isn't saying much since she only brings on people she, and pretty much everyone else, believes are guilty."

"So, she's wrong about sixty percent? More than half of the people she highlights and smears across the airwaves are actually innocent?"

"Basically, yeah. But she never actually says they're guilty. She never actually accuses them. The word 'allegedly' is tattooed on the tip of her tongue, and then, of course, she frames her non-accusations in the form of questions. She did that to you tonight. Did you notice? She said something like, 'Why would she hire an attorney if she didn't do it?' I'm paraphrasing. And, of course, she didn't give me a chance to explain that you already had an attorney because you'd filed for divorce. They'd already cut my feed." Lacey rested the food packages on the counter and ran a hand through her hair, pushing the blonde locks away from her face and tucking them behind her ear. Then she turned away, biting her bottom lip. Her voice changed slightly. "Anyway, we didn't think it was a good idea for you to get caught up in that sort of thing directly. Like any good prosecutor--you know she used to be an assistant DA back in Mississippi, right? --she would have used everything you said to her advantage."

"No, I didn't know that."

"Yeah, she was a guest on loads of shows during the OJ Simpson trial; Court TV, CNN and lots of local stuff in the deep south. That's how she ended up with her own gig."

Lacey moved with efficiency through the kitchen. She withdrew two plates from the cupboard above the breadbox and unceremoniously dumped the contents of the take-out boxes onto them. Brandy would have been happy to eat out of the to-go boxes, but she remembered Kendra explaining how dinner time was supposed to be special. Lacey had been raised that way and somehow, Brandy suspected she would never dream of eating out of a box unless she had no other choice. She placed one dinner plate heaped with pasta in the microwave and pressed the automatic selection for reheat. After she pulled silverware from the drawer, she turned to face Brandy and sighed.

God, she was gorgeous. She wasn't just pretty in a girl-next-door kind of way, although she definitely had that going for her. No, she was truly magnificent. Her skin held just the right tone to be beautiful in any lighting. She didn't wear make-up beyond mascara, and her hair shimmered when the light hit just right, like now.

Even dressed in an obviously worn track suit, black with silver piping, she carried an air of elegance. The track suit, zipped up to her neck the same way she'd worn the other one the day they'd met, hugged every tempting curve and accentuated the lush ripeness of her breasts.

"What are you looking at?"

"You."

Lacey's mouth turned up at the corners into what couldn't actually be described as a smile. It was more of a smirk that wanted to be a frown but couldn't quite bring itself to fall.

While she cut into the remains of a loaf of Italian bread she'd found in the bread box, Lacey chewed lightly on her bottom lip. Her cell phone, resting at the end of the counter where she'd dumped it, suddenly played the theme song from The Monkees.

Brandy laughed. "The Monkees? Seriously?"

"Hey, I love The Monkees. Don't you? Hey, Hey, we're the Monkees..." she sang.

"Well, yeah, sure. I guess. You just don't strike me as a Day Dream Believer kind of girl, that's all."

"Well, I was homecoming queen." Lacey lifted one finger as she answered the call. Brandy waited quietly, picking a piece of broccoli off the plate of Alfredo.

"Why? What's up... okay... nine-thirty? Okay, I'll be there. I'm pretty sure I know what it's about." Lacey paused and rolled her eyes. "Fine. Fine. I'll be there." She disconnected the call and set the phone down. "Sorry. That was work. I have a meeting with the station manager in the morning."

"Were you really?"

Lacey rested a steaming plate of pasta in a red meat sauce on the bar in front of her. She grabbed the plate of Alfredo and placed it in the microwave. Pressing the reheat button a second time, she asked, "Was I really what?"

"Homecoming queen."

"Oh. Well, yeah. And I was Miss Randall County, too. But that was a long time ago." Lacey moved the dinner plate to the dining room table and pulled silver flatware from the top drawer of the hutch to set the table.

"Rodeo queen?"

"No," she laughed. It was a nice laugh. It was the first time Brandy had heard it and she instantly wanted to hear it again. "Why would you think I was a rodeo queen?"

"I've heard about the ranch. Cows. Horses. Cowboys. Cowgirls. The works. So, I figured, maybe."

"My brothers were big into rodeo same as our folks, but I was mostly a spectator. A lot of my friends competed in barrel racing, and Kendra always wanted to ride bulls. I think that may have been part of the reason she taught Brad how to do it. He was kind of her last chance. Casey, he's my twin brother, was never into the whole cowboy thing, and Brent rides saddle bronc like Dad, so Kendra pretty much insisted Brad was going to master the bulls. And he did, too. He was High School Rodeo Bull Riding Champion in Utah his senior year, and he even qualified for his PRCA card. That summer, he probably would have taken the regional championship before going pro full time." Lacey's brow furrowed, and she hesitated a moment before pulling the second dinner plate out of the microwave, as though she were working up the nerve not to run away.

She was like that, Brandy realized. One moment she could be perfectly chatty and amiable and then something would happen to change it. An errant thought? A bad memory? Whatever it was, it stole the light from her eyes and sent a tangible chill through the air. She absently smoothed her hair back over her cheek.

"Is something wrong? You okay?"

That beautiful smile reappeared as Lacey apparently sucked back what might have been tears. "Yeah. I'm fine. It's just I was crazy in love with that kid, and then he had to up and die on me. On all of us. It's not fair, really." She took the plate to the table and nodded for Brandy to join her there.

"No, it's not." Brandy at the table, then dug into her pasta.

Lacey sat, playing with her food rather than eating it. "They killed him for no reason. It was stupid really. He got caught in the crossfire and he was just gone. His wife, too, only Harold Mason straight-up murdered her. Point blank."

They ate in silence for several moments. Michelle had told Brandy about the events leading up to Brad's death and that of his wife.

Lacey was obviously still upset at the loss of her brother and Brandy couldn't blame her. What concerned her is that Brandy felt very little grief at the loss of her own wife. Cynthia had been murdered. She'd been stolen from this world as succinctly as Lacey's brother had.

Suddenly, Lacey bolted off her chair. "The wine! Gads. You know, there is a reason Michelle is the hostess in our family. Would you like some?" She opened the bottle of Merlot with a corkscrew she found in a drawer and then poured herself a tall glass. Brandy nodded, and Lacey poured her a glass as well. "I suppose you should really have white wine to go with your chicken, but I didn't have any. Sorry about that."

Brandy shrugged. "That's it. You're fired."

Lacey laughed again. "We'll see." She stuck her tongue

out at Brandy as she handed her the glass, half full of the rich red wine.

"So, tell me more about the real Lacey Williams," Brandy urged before taking a sip.

CHAPTER NINE

"I'm sure there are far more interesting things to talk about than me," Lacey replied, placing her glass of wine on the table. She'd left her purse and her medication in her apartment, three floors below, and suddenly wished she hadn't. Brandy had a way of looking directly through her. It made her feel naked; exposed. She wasn't sure if she liked it at the same time that it made her feel... wanted? Special? Two things she hadn't believed about herself. Two things she wished could be true. Especially if they came from Brandy. When Brandy held her, she felt like she could fly. Like she could do anything.

"I can't think of a single thing. I sure as hell don't want to talk about my life right now. Your life sounds much more amiable."

"You think? Any minute now I'm going to get a call from my sister and her wife about when I'm supposed to travel back home to testify against a man I've known my entire life for the murder of his daughter and my brother. Amiable isn't really the word I would use to describe it." Her words sounded bitter in her own ears. "Sorry. I didn't mean to sound snarky."

"You didn't." Brandy took another bite of pasta and

washed it down with another sip of the wrong wine.

Lacey took a couple more bites and then pushed her plate away, leaving the lion's share of the dinner behind. She'd lost her appetite. She excused herself from the table and sat on the sofa. Out of habit, she pulled the throw blanket off the back. Pulling her feet onto the cushions, she curled into it slightly.

"So," Brandy continued as she finished her dinner and refilled her wine glass. "What do you think they'll ask you at the trial? I mean, what kind of questions are you worried about?"

"I'm not really worried. I don't know anything about Mac's involvement. I was still here in Vegas most of the time. Until Kendra got it into her head that I'd be safer in Utah, where she could keep an eye on me. Fat lot of good that did for Brad and Lenise, right? Or for me." Lacey cleared the emotion that had formed in the back of her throat. She wouldn't cry. She'd cried enough. No more tears. Resettling herself deeper into the sofa cushions, she added, "Mostly, I can testify to the accident. That damn accident."

"The one you won't talk about."

"Yeah. That one."

"And that worries you, because, well, you know, you won't talk about it."

It was a statement, not a question. It made Lacey's stomach collapse into a knot. Brandy shrugged and sat down on the center of the sofa with one arm propped on the back. She was so close – only inches away from Lacey's foot – that Lacey could feel her body heat through the thin throw blanket.

"Sounds legit," Brandy muttered into her glass as she took another sip of wine.

"No. It's not legit."

"Okay."

"I mean, sure, I don't like to talk about it much. It's not a happy memory. But I can. If I want to. Which I don't."

"It's okay. You don't have to talk about it now, but you will have to talk about it in a couple of weeks. And that worries you."

Why was Brandy grilling her about this? What business was it of hers, anyway? Lacey glanced at the door and her legs itched to carry her through it. Her throat grew tight and she swallowed against the swelling. It had been a mistake to come here.

"Lacey, it's okay. Really. Let's change the subject. What made you want to be a reporter?"

Lame.

Still, she sighed in an attempt to release her sudden case of nerves. After a pause during which Brandy quietly sipped her wine, Lacey answered, "I like... I like to solve puzzles." It was true. She'd fed her love for mysteries by reading true crime novels. When the other girls were reading stories about sparkly vampires, she was devouring old Agatha Christie novels and forensic science textbooks. She had even once considered becoming a forensic scientist, but she didn't actually have the grades to make a go of it, and she was fairly certain that her job would be nothing like CSI on TV.

"Well, then, it looks like Michelle hooked me up with

exactly the right person. So, you didn't just want to be a reporter. You wanted to be an investigative reporter. You're lucky. You're doing just what you set out to do."

"Mostly."

Brandy settled back in her seat and finished her wine, resting the empty glass on the sofa table. She really was an attractive woman. Lacey couldn't help but admire the way she held herself, partly cocky and completely confident.

She didn't go out of her way to mask her emotions, but rather to school them in such a way that when a person encountered them, they knew she was under control. It was that harness that made her seem just slightly dangerous; like she could release the reins at any moment and all of the pent-up energy would unleash a barely held passion.

"What's different?"

"What?" Lacey shook herself out of the palpable distraction that was Brandy.

"What's different about what you're doing now than what you set out to accomplish? Seems to me, you've taken the world by the horns."

"I had planned to do investigations, sure, but I ultimately planned on tackling politics. I majored in broadcasting, with an emphasis on political science. I considered law school at one point to get a full understanding of law as it pertained to politics." She'd forgotten about that summer three years ago when she'd seriously considered going to a law school back east with zero intentions of actually practicing law.

Funny she'd think of it now.

"A pundit? Helping to form the thoughts and desires of the American people. Pretty ambitious. But I have no doubt you'll get there someday."

"I'd planned to do it on television."

"You keep talking in the past tense, like your career is over. You're young. You'll get there. And with any luck, your coverage of my situation will help you."

"That's a pretty generous attitude for someone who just got blasted on national TV. Thanks."

"Well, I majored in hospitality services and business management in college. I live to serve, right?" Brandy chuckled, and a hint of pink suffused her strong, angled cheeks. Was it the wine? Or something more.

"But no. I don't have a chance of moving from radio to television."

"Why not? Have you tried?"

"I had a great internship set up for the summer after graduation, actually. I had to give it up, though."

"You turned it down? Why on earth would you do that?"

Lacey tossed the blanket aside as her blood flow sped up, racing through her veins like a super-charged bullet train. She stood, turning her back on Brandy as she tried desperately to make the panic go away. This is why she didn't like talking about herself. This. The fact that it always came back around to what she lacked.

She lacked bravery.

She lacked consistency.

She lacked the ability to adapt and overcome.

And she lacked the looks necessary to make it in a modern,

twenty-four-hour news cycle of cable network reporting.

She hugged herself tightly, keeping her back to Brandy so she couldn't see the panic in her face. "It was pretty obvious I wasn't going to go on the air, so what was the point? The only reason to intern at a TV affiliate is to work your way onto the small screen. I refocused on radio. Radio is a totally legit market share. It's not a second choice." No matter what Addison had said.

"Well, sure. For people who want to be on the radio. I can see that, but you wanted TV. You don't seem like the kind of girl who would just give up. Something had to have happened to make you adjust course in midstream."

The heat of her blood reached the base of her brain and Lacey threw her arms to her side as she turned back to Brandy. "Why are you doing this? Did Michelle put you up to this?"

The frown that appeared on Brandy's features reached from her lips to her forehead, her dark eyes squinting in apparent confusion. Either she was a consummate actress, or she really had no idea what Lacey was talking about. Lacey reached one trembling hand to her face and pulled her hair away from her cheek. With the other hand she pointed. "This, Brandy. This happened!"

"The accident? The scar? Is that what you're talking about?"

"Yes," Lacey practically screamed before she took hold of her rising panic and whispered. "Yes. The scar."

Brandy stood slowly, gently placing the crystal wine glass on the side table before shoving her hands in the front pockets of her jeans. "I don't get it. Why would you think that could stop you?"

"Because nobody wants to see an ugly woman delivering the news."

Brandy actually laughed as she placed both of her hands loosely on her hips. "You can't be serious. Ugly? You?"

Lacey's throat burned. Moisture formed behind her eyelids and threatened to escape like steam from a kettle. "You couldn't possibly understand. I was… I was homecoming queen. I was Miss Randall County. A bona fide pageant queen complete with a tiara and a dozen dying roses."

"What about tonight? You were on TV and you looked fantastic. You were smart and articulate." Brandy stepped closer and Lacey answered with a step in reverse.

The back of her calf hit the armchair and she danced around it. "Don't."

"What?"

"Don't try to make me feel better. Tonight was a fluke. I was only a guest. I have this handled. I'm doing just fine and I can make it through some stupid trial for some stupid accident that changed my entire stupid life." The sobs building in her chest defeated her, escaping with a hoarse cough.

"But it wasn't an accident, was it, Lacey? Someone did this to you."

Lacey couldn't stop the dam from giving way. All of the pain, all of the hatred, and all of the emptiness came crashing out. She sobbed.

Before she could move, Brandy was at her side pulling her into a warm embrace, comforting at the same time every connection of their bodies sizzled with electricity.

"Let it out, babe. I've got you."

Lacey's throat burned. Finally, after a few moments, she found that she had very little energy left to cry. Her body melded into Brandy's and she just stood there, as naked as one could be fully dressed.

Brandy whispered into the top of her head, "You have every right to be angry about it. I just didn't think you were the kind of girl who would let it define her. But if your looks have something, anything to do with that definition, I think it's really important for you to know one thing. You're absolutely gorgeous."

Lacey sniffed her derision.

"You really don't believe me. You don't see it, do you?"

What would Brandy do if Lacey were to take off her shirt? What if Lacey exposed the thick, welted scar that slithered from her shoulder to her elbow like some wretched serpent? Or the surgical scars from the emergency procedure she'd had two months after the accident when the doctors discovered a tear in her heart valve. The scar on her face would keep her off television, but that was only the tip of the iceberg.

Beautiful?

Not on her life.

Brandy couldn't stop thinking about that kiss the other day. It had been heated. And wholly inappropriate. Her lips tingled with remembrance, and holding Lacey the way she was, she wanted to do it again. It was obvious Lacey was as skittish a new colt. Could that also be due to the accident and the self-perception that she was no longer worthy? "You really can't see it."

"I have to go." Lacey broke the embrace and took several hurried steps backward.

"Do you really? Or are you running away?"

Lacey frowned. Her eyebrows drew together above the wrinkled bridge of her delicate nose.

"Please don't run away from me."

Lacey leaned her backside against the wall that led to the hallway and lowered her head. As if it were deliberate, and maybe it was, her hair fell into place to hide the scar. Earlier, in the kitchen, she'd forgotten to hide it, absentmindedly pushing her hair away from her face while she'd reheated their dinner.

But now, that hair didn't just hide the scar, it hid Lacey. Not just her face, but her. Who she was. It muddled her dreams and placed a gossamer veil over everything that defined her as a person. Brandy's fingers itched to move the silky strands out of the way; to reveal the whole person.

Brandy stepped closer. This time, Lacey had nowhere to go with her back, quite literally, against the wall. "Let me see you, Lacey."

"There's nothing to see," she whispered. "I really should be going. The coroner's office has called a press conference at the courthouse for ten a.m. I'm thinking there's a really good chance we'll get a glimpse at the prelim coroner's report. The station has blocked out the time for a live feed, so I need to be on my toes, you know?"

"I have no doubt you'll be fine."

"And I have that meeting with the station manager in the morning at nine."

"Then let's go to bed." An unexplained heat that started in her feet crawled over Brandy's entire body until it settled somewhere in the region of her heart.

At the same time it thrilled her, it disturbed her that she was developing feelings for a reporter, of all people. She'd already been used by one woman, and the thought that Lacey was involved in her life only for the story made her wary. Still, the temptation the younger woman posed was like a force of nature; as impossible to deny as a raging summer storm.

As the heat in her belly grew, she allowed the trembling muscles of her legs to draw her back into Lacey's personal bubble. Where their first kiss had been full of vigor and not-a-small amount of anger, the second time they'd crossed the line had nearly passed the point of no return. That had been all passion and hormones and sex.

Right now, Brandy wanted nothing more than to kiss away any doubts Lacey had that her physical scars made her any less desirable. She wanted to make sure Lacey knew, for a fact, that she was worthy of being wanted; that she was a desirable woman.

Did that make Brandy noble? Her heart skipped a beat. No. It didn't. Sure, she wanted Lacey to know she was beautiful, but that wasn't the only reason why she wanted to kiss her right now. There was something else struggling to make itself known in the back of her heart. It was more selfish. Needier. Greedier. Brandy simply wanted.

Lacey's eyes, filled with fear that poured out those

amazing blue depths, fastened on Brandy's. She seemed so much like a frightened rabbit that Brandy forced herself to move even more slowly. Gently, she raised her hand and ran the backs of her fingers over Lacey's cheek.

A combination of a sigh and a moan escaped perfectly shaped lips the color of soft pink roses, slightly parted in… what? Could it be anticipation? Lacey raised one hand and placed it lightly on Brandy's wrist to stop the movement. It lingered there for more than a moment until Brandy lowered her mouth to capture Lacey's full lips.

For a few blessed seconds, Brandy relished the absence of Lacey's fear. It was as though Lacey had vanquished her anxiety just long enough to enjoy something as sweet and innocent as a kiss.

But only for a few seconds. Then every pliant part of her body tensed. Lacey released another sound. This time, it was a sound filled with fear and she turned her face before ducking away.

The moment dissipated. Like the swirling massive tornado suddenly collapses on itself, it was gone. Once again, Lacey was all business, her emotions and her fears tucked neatly away behind a solid steel mask. Something inside Brandy suffered for it, marked by a wisp of pain that pierced her as surely as any blade.

She cleared her throat and sat on the arm of the antique overstuffed chair.

Lacey skirted the arm chair and stood trembling slightly in the center of the great room. "I can't do this."

It was apparent she wasn't talking about covering

Brandy's situation. She was talking about getting close to someone; to anyone who might care about her. "I'm sorry. I shouldn't have done that."

"If the press got a hold of something like this, they'd crucify us both because of my appearance on the news tonight and the interview. They'll think I'm helping you cover something up."

Brandy smiled to herself. Lacey was trying to act like the only reason she couldn't be involved with Brandy was her job. Cute. But altogether ineffective.

Brandy had no doubt that was part of it, but the rest came from her misguided belief that she wasn't strong enough or good enough to deserve the love of another person. "I see. I mean, I get it. You don't have to leave on my account. It won't happen again." Brandy nearly choked on the words as the tightness in the air lessened by a tiny fraction. It was probably a lie.

Lacey seemed slightly more relaxed, but she didn't move from where she leaned once more against the wall, her arms wrapped around herself like an iron shield. "We should concentrate on what is going to come from the coroner's report."

If that's what it took to make Lacey more comfortable, then Brandy could talk about it until her last breath. She could play the game as well as anyone, but she would give anything for just one chance to prove to Lacey how beautiful and wanted she really was. "What do you think it'll say that we don't already know? It's pretty obvious how she died, right? I'm not sure I want to know the details."

"That depends. What did you see, exactly, when you were in the house?"

She'd been pretty upset that day. If there were ever a time she wasn't thinking clearly, it was in the immediate moments – hours really – following the news that they'd found Cynthia's body. Searching her recollection, she tried to focus on the visual snippets playing in her mind.

"I thought there would've been more blood. I mean, don't get me wrong, there was a good amount. It's just, I had heard about head wounds bleeding a lot. She was face down on the carpet at the foot of the bed. Well, not face down exactly, but on her belly. Her face was turned away from the door, so what really got to me was that most of the back of her head was missing." A sudden wave of nausea rose into her throat. She took a steadying breath and slid into the chair. "Obviously, that would have been enough to kill her. Her mother didn't even want an autopsy. Did I tell you that? I don't think I did. Tell you, I mean. But that day at the funeral home, she was trying to come up with any reason she could to make them release Cyn's body right away. To avoid hurting her little girl anymore, she'd said."

"It's pretty common for parents to feel that way. But anytime there's suspicion of foul play, and a gunshot to the head would certainly qualify, the state insists on a postmortem."

"Yeah, I know that. But she was incredibly upset about it. I wonder why it would bother her so much."

"Like she said, she just doesn't like the idea of anyone cutting into her daughter like she's nothing, you know?

Marion isn't one of my favorite people, and the feeling is mutual, but she's not a bad person."

After picking up her previously abandoned glass of wine, Lacey moved to sit back on the sofa. She settled in place and pulled the blanket to snuggle. "How do you feel about it?"

Brandy shrugged, scoffing a bit at the thought that she had any feelings one way or another. Did it make her a monster to not mourn for Cynthia? She asked Lacey that question and held her breath as she waited for an answer.

"I don't think so, Bran. You may have been married to her, but your marriage had been over for quite some time, really. You weren't even living together anymore. How long before you moved out had you really been a couple? I mean, really, really been together."

Brandy shook her head. "We hadn't slept together in months, and we hadn't made love for months before that. Probably more than a year now, actually."

"So, if you think about it, it's not so odd that you're not a wreck over the whole thing. At least, I don't hold it against you. We just have to be careful of the picture you present to the world."

"You and Michelle want me to lie." Like she'd just lied to Lacey about not wanting to kiss her again. Right here. Right now.

"Not lie, exactly. But when you talk about Cynthia, you need to acknowledge that she was your wife, that you loved her, and that you didn't want any harm to come to her. We talked about the divorce on the air, so it's no secret.

But lots of people get divorced and lots of people know that it has little or nothing to do with love. Divorce filings are a matter of public record and many of my colleagues have already bought copies at the courthouse, I'm sure. We just need to make certain that you were perfectly okay with your relationship and bore her no ill will."

"I didn't. Not really."

"Good. And someday, perhaps you'll find some lucky woman you can really care about."

"That would be really nice, I think." After a brief pause, Brandy smiled. "Do you really want to talk about this?"

Lacey frowned. "Not really."

"Thanks for dinner, by the way."

"No problem. I wasn't sure how you'd react to being on the national news. Dinner may have been a preemptive apology." Lacey laughed, and it sounded like tiny bells tinkling through her borrowed condo's still air.

Lacey's cubicle at KLVN consisted of a worn, laminate top spanning the short distance between two filing cabinets, cushioned, tweed walls in a sickly gray that had been fashionable in 1986, and a rolling office chair that only had two working wheels. Such was the existence of a publicly-funded radio venture. She clicked on the shut-down button on her computer and began to gather her purse and recorder. She had her meeting with the station manager in a few minutes and then would have to race to the courthouse for the coroner's press conference. To be certain, she'd already cleared with the morning news anchor that they had planned for a live feed.

"Lacey, can I see you for a minute?" Addison poked her head over the top of the wall between their work stations. She smiled, sending warning signals up and down Lacey's spine.

"Can it wait? I'm late for a meeting with Lionel."

"Oh, I didn't realize he'd called you. That's what I needed you for. Lionel's office, then."

Addison didn't wait for Lacey to respond. Instead, she turned away and marched to the station manager's office on the edge of the huge, open floor where all of the station's talent, researchers and interns communed in organized chaos.

When Lionel's secretary had called her yesterday to set up the meeting for this morning, she hadn't said anything about Addison being involved. A frown pulled at the edges of Lacey's mouth as she followed her boss down the narrow hallway between the cubicles. Whatever Lionel wanted, the idea that it could be good news was quickly evaporating. Tossing her bag over her shoulder, she hurried to catch up. "What's going on? Did something happen?"

"Yeah. Something happened, Lacey. In the office."

Lacey preceded Addison into the poorly-lit space holding a single large, metal desk that looked like a cast-off of an old Soviet regime. She found Lionel Schindler and Nick Bauman waiting for her. Lionel, she'd expected. It was his office, after all. Nick surprised her. The much older man was the station's most generous living contributor, but he seldom came to the station in person. He looked out of place in his black and white satin windbreaker and

Elvis-style, gold-rimmed sunglasses. His dyed-black hair lifted in a dated pompadour that seemed even more out of place on a man of his advanced years.

"Good morning, Mr. Johnson," she said, faking a smile that made her cheeks burn.

"Ms. Williams," he replied. No fake smile. No smile at all.

"What's going on?" Lacey asked. "Is something wrong?"

"Lacey, we're a little concerned about how close you've become to the Kincaid story," Lionel stated deliberately, as though he'd carefully chosen and rehearsed the words so many times they'd lost all meaning.

"How close I've become? I'm not sure I follow you." They couldn't possibly know... or had someone seen Brandy kissing her on the street that day? Her heart flummoxed.

"Why don't you take a seat," Nick suggested before he pulled off his glasses and took his own advice.

"I'm fine standing, thanks. Why don't you tell me what's going on here?"

Addison released a heavy, sudden breath. "Oh, for God's sake, Lacey. You have to know what you did was out of line."

"It wasn't my fault!"

"Really? That's your defense? Blaming someone else? Again? You went behind my back and--"

"Addison, shut up!" Lionel interrupted what was the beginning of a full-on tirade. He turned his attention back to Lacey. "About your visit with Carleen Carson last night..."

"Is that what this is about? You're pissed that I went on CNN? What was I supposed to do? Turn down a personal invitation to appear on the highest-ranking news show on television?"

"No, you should have forwarded the call to me. All That and More is my show."

"But it's my story."

"Because I handed it to you!"

"I got the exclusive. I did the leg work. It's mine. This is ridiculous." Lacey dismissed Addison with an eye roll and turned her attention back to the station manager. "Lionel? You're not going to take this seriously, are you? Did I say or do anything out of line? Did I embarrass the station?" She hiked her purse higher on her shoulder and folded her arms over her chest. "Of course, I didn't. I killed that interview."

"That doesn't matter. The fact is that I'm the anchor and I should have been the one to appear on CNN. Nobody wants to look at someone like you. It reflects badly on us."

Lacey's heart pounded her chest, each beat heavier than the one before, as the weight of those words fell over her. Tears burned behind her eyes.

"Addison, that was unnecessary and patently untrue." Lionel's voice carried a low baritone riddled with disappointment.

"Ladies, ladies," Nick interjected. "I'm sure there is some way to work this out. There is no need to get personal."

Personal? So Nick thought she was too ugly for prime time, too.

Lacey bit her bottom lip and lowered her head slightly as heat suffused her cheeks. When she had gathered what little composure she had left, she raised her head again. "I don't understand what the big deal is. The Kincaid story is mine. I have exclusive access to the principal and I had every right to accept that invitation."

Addison threw her perfectly-manicured hands in the air. "I can't work with her anymore. I want her gone. It's her, or me, and considering that my show is the top ratings earner around here, and keeps more advertising dollars coming in every quarter than the next three shows combined, I don't think you have a choice." Addison hurled the ultimatum at the two men behind the desk with all of the hatred a single Prima Dona could possibly muster.

"Let's not get vengeful, Addison," Lionel retorted. "There's no need to—"

"Uncle Nick? What do you think about all this?"

Uncle Nick? Seriously?

Lacey braced herself for the blow she knew was coming.

With both hands flat on the surface of the desk, Nick looked directly at his niece. There was a moment of obvious but silent communication between the two of them. Addison preened, her shoulders back and her nose high enough to leave a chem trail if she sneezed. Nick frowned and shot daggers at her. After a moment, Nick turned to Lionel and said, "Do what we talked about. There will be no reasoning with her about this."

Lionel pushed himself to standing as though his own body weighed too much to lift. "I'm sorry, Lacey. I'm going to have to ask for your credentials. I was hoping that we could come up with another solution."

"We haven't even discussed other solutions, for crying out loud. Are you serious?"

Addison folded her hands over her chest and released a sigh. "We've been discussing this all morning. No matter how you slice it, you were out of line. On top of screwing up your assignment the other day? You are just fooling yourself if you think you have even a tiny future here. You're done."

Numb from the shoulders down, Lacey opened her purse and withdrew her press pass and security badge. She tried, unsuccessfully, to keep her fingers steady as she handed them to Lionel. He took them, refusing to meet her eyes.

"I didn't do anything wrong," she whispered. "I was doing my job."

"Oh, really!" Addison spat. "You think you're so inno--"

"Addison!" Uncle Nick interrupted. "Shut the hell up. You need to remember what we talked about, too."

Addison fell into an unquiet silence, her very presence screaming even if she wasn't.

Five minutes later, Lacey stood on the sidewalk in front of the station holding a cardboard file-storage box with the personal effects from her desk. It was like a bad movie. She sat down on a park bench next to the water feature that Nick had contracted for the station. It had been completed the month Lacey had started working for KLVN. The water sprays, reminiscent of the dancing fountains in front of the Bellagio but on a much smaller scale, would continue to do their job every day.

What the hell was Lacey supposed to do?

Her cell phone chimed with a ring tone that sounded

like huge, cathedral bells. It was the sound she'd set for her important reminders. She flicked her finger across the screen to silence the deliberately obnoxious noise.

Press Conference. Courthouse.

She had forty-five minutes to drive across town if she wanted to get to the coroner's press conference in time. She no longer had a job. She was no longer on assignment. She had no press pass and no credentials.

But nobody knew that.

She stood, picking up her box of belongings, and marched in the direction of her car. Once she reached it, she pressed the button on her key fob and loaded everything into the largely empty trunk. She liked this car. She'd bought it mostly because of the space. For a midsize, it had a huge trunk. What was it Casey had said? That he could easily fit three bodies in here; four if he broke their legs?

A body in a trunk.

Lacey slammed the trunk lid and looked up a phone number as she headed for the driver's side door. She selected the number from the Google results and waited for the recipient to pick up. "Come on... come on..."

"West Shore Marina."

"Hi, there. Is this that cute young man who helped me out the other day on the missing person's case?"

"Yeah, it's me. What's up?"

"Can you tell me if John Miller has a car?"

The boy laughed. "I guess you could call it that. It's a Ford POS about three hundred years old."

"Do you think you could get me the license plate number?" she asked, more out of habit than anything else.

"Yeah; hold on." The kid obviously took the phone with him to look outside. The atmosphere of the call changed from interior to obviously outdoors. A horn honked.

"Yeah, yeah, whatever," the boy responded to the driver, most likely. "Well, that's funny."

"What's funny?"

"His car's gone. I mean, if he's out on his boat, where the heck is his car?"

CHAPTER TEN

Brandy pulled her ball cap lower over her eyes and shucked her biker jacket higher up her neck. She'd never worried about being recognized in her life. She wasn't sure why she was so inclined to attend the press conference. She already knew how Cynthia had died, but some macabre curiosity had made her come anyway.

Or maybe it was because she knew Lacey would be there. She'd already called Lacey twice this morning and she hadn't picked up either time.

Leaning against the trunk of one of several palm trees that dotted the abstract courthouse steps, Brandy folded her arms. The last time she'd been here, she'd been testifying against a man who had tried to rob the restaurant in her casino. She'd always assumed that her next visit would have been a hearing in her divorce. She'd never dreamed in a million years that she'd be here to discover how, exactly, her wife had been murdered.

The news crews had already started to gather, even though the medical examiner and Sal Crenshaw weren't going to appear for another ten minutes. She recognized several of the vans along the curb as those she'd seen in front of her neighborhood and at the gates of her ranch. Kevin What's-His-Name, from one of the TV stations, stood preening into a small mirror about fifteen feet away from her. He flipped his hair out of his eyes and opened his mouth wide a few times before he settled in to wait with everyone else.

Lacey hurried around the corner of the building and Brandy's pulse quickened. Taking a position near the edge of the crowd, Lacey spoke to a couple of the reporters as she inched her way toward the center of the throng, smiling hello and nodding in greeting.

Smooth. Her peers didn't even realize she was manipulating herself into the best possible position, directly in front of the podium that had been placed at the top of the cement steps. When she reached her ideal place on the third step from the top, she pulled her small digital recorder from her pocket and flipped it on.

When the glass doors that led to the courthouse lobby opened, a ripple of tension ran roughshod over the gathering. Silence followed closely on its heels. Sal Crenshaw carried a file in one hand and slipped on her sunglasses with the other. She was one tough-looking woman. If that attitude parlayed into her abilities as a criminal trial attorney, Chandra had her work cut out for her.

The medical examiner was a woman with a rich, olive complexion that spoke of Mediterranean ancestry, most likely middle eastern. They stopped in front of the podium and the prosecutor turned on the mic.

"We'd like to welcome you and thank you for coming today. We will each make a brief statement and then we'll open it up for questions. I'd like to caution all of you, however, that we won't be answering all of your questions. This is still an open and ongoing investigation."

She took a moment to introduce Lydia Jensen, the medical examiner, and then the doctor took a position at the mic. "Thank you, Madame Prosecutor," she stated with a monotone and stilted accent. "The preliminary results of my examination into the cause of death for Mrs. Cynthia Kincaid has revealed two interesting facts that were heretofore unknown. The first point of interest is that the victim was most likely not alive when the body was placed in her living quarters in the home located in Mission Hills in Las Vegas."

Cameras flashed in quick succession and several of the reporters began shouting questions. It was impossible to understand any of the jumble of words. Sal raised both of her hands and shouted, "If you want us to answer any questions when we're done here, ladies and gentlemen, you'll need to mind your manners!"

The reporters quieted, and the medical examiner looked at the crowd over incredibly small granny-style glasses before continuing. "Based upon the lividity of the blood and the lack of brain matter found on items surrounding the victim's body, it is the conclusion of this office that the victim had been deceased for at least twenty-four hours prior to being relocated to the Mission Hills residence.

"The second item of note is that Mrs. Kincaid was

approximately twenty-nine weeks pregnant at the time of her death. The fetus was undersized but otherwise healthy. The official cause of death pending toxicology results is a gunshot to the head."

Brandy nearly choked aloud at the revelation. Still concerned that no-one recognize her, she hid her surprise in as bland an expression as she could muster. Cynthia had been pregnant? Sure, the last time she'd seen her, that night in the casino, Brandy had noticed she'd put on a little weight. Not much; just enough that Brandy had thought for a moment she was simply eating better. Taking better care of herself.

It had never dawned on her that her wife might actually be pregnant. How in the world did she think she was going to get away with something like that? It would have been too easy to prove her infidelity in the divorce proceedings and if Chandra were successful in having the pre-nup thrown out, Cynthia would have easily lost everything. At twenty-nine weeks, she was well past the point where abortion would have been an option. Brandy frowned and shook her head.

Pregnant.

She'd asked Cynthia years ago if she'd wanted children. Initially, the answer had been a resounding yes, but the longer they were married, the less likely that option had become.

She and the boyfriend were going to have a family, instead, apparently.

The prosecutor cleared her throat when she took over the podium, causing ear-splitting feedback from the speakers. The sound sent a shiver over Brandy's entire body, ripping her back into the present. "Sorry about that, folks. I have one item to add, before you ask. Because I know you're going to ask. Because of the apparent viability of the fetus, the decision has been made to modify the charges being filed against Brandy Kincaid in the murder of her wife to include the murder of Mrs. Cynthia Kincaid's unborn offspring. We will now take your questions."

The press corps exploded.

A slow, steady dread formed in Brandy's stomach. She didn't need a law degree to understand that something like this would greatly influence a jury. Somewhere in the back of her mind she could hear the voices of the reporters asking question after question, but she couldn't focus on the words. She suddenly didn't care about the answers. A few minutes later the attorney and the medical examiner went back inside the building while the reporters scattered to either record their stories or leap into their vans and race back to their stations. She closed her eyes, willing her feet to move. She couldn't. It was like her feet had rooted to the step.

"Brandy? Are you out of your mind? What are you doing here?" Lacey whispered.

The inherent light of Lacey's voice shattered the darkness that had engulfed Brandy. She opened her eyes to find Lacey staring at her.

"We need to get you out of here. Come with me." Lacey took her by the hand and led her discreetly away from the courthouse steps until they could turn the corner. Once they were out of view of the few remaining reporters, she stopped, but didn't release her hand. Instead, she stroked the back of Brandy's hand with her thumb in an intimate gesture that cast a ray of heat to the four corners of her body. "Are you okay?"

Brandy nodded, but it was a lie. She'd been doing a lot of that lately, hadn't she? She wasn't okay. Her body ached, and her heart was breaking. "Yes," she released with a sob. "I'm fine." Her body shook, her shoulders taking on the brunt of the agony that escaped with a sudden, deliberate force she could no longer control.

Lacey pulled her into an embrace, cradling her head on her shoulder and tenderly stroking her back. "Everything is going to be okay, remember?"

"How? How is everything going to be okay? She was pregnant. They're going to hang me from the god damned Stratosphere Hotel."

"No, they're not. Didn't you hear what they said? Cynthia was killed somewhere else, and I have a pretty good idea where it happened. We have a new mission, Brandy. We have got to find Miller and that boat."

Brandy released a quiet cry, sniffing as she straightened her back and then inhaled deeply. She wiped her nose on a fast-food napkin she found in her pocket. "You think he killed her on his boat?"

"I think it's likely, don't you? He's been gone, not coming in for more than a week now. I've got some free time. What do you say we go sailing?" Lacey smiled, canting her head slightly to one side. Her hair fell away from her cheek and for the second time since Brandy had met the charming young woman, she didn't try to cover it up.

Lacey waited silently for Brandy to respond. Finally, Brandy stiffened her shoulders and released a hard breath. "Let's go get the son of a bitch."

"I'm parked just up the street. I got here later than I'd planned. Hell, I almost didn't make it at all."

Brandy fell into step beside her. "How did your meeting with the station manager go? You getting a promotion?"

"In a manner of speaking, I guess."

"That sounds cryptic."

"I got fired. So, if by 'promotion' you mean going freelance, then yes, I got a promotion."

Brandy stopped, dead in her tracks. "What are you talking about? Fired? What the hell for?"

"For outshining my boss, I imagine." Lacey stopped and pivoted on her heel. "You coming, or what?"

Brandy started walking again, matching her longer strides to Lacey's shorter ones. "You're going to fight this, right? They can't just up and fire you. You have a contract, don't you?"

"Nope. I'm, I mean, I was, an at-will employee serving at the pleasure of Addison Parker. She wanted me gone, and I'm gone. That's all there is to it. But it means that I can now do whatever the heck I want to when it comes to covering the story. I don't have to play into any professional ideas of what is acceptable and what isn't. I'm officially freelancing this thing. And I still have exclusive access, yes?"

"Of course."

"And the book rights?"

Finally, Brandy cracked a smile. "Okay."

"And I'm still on the story. Don't you worry about that."

"You're still going to cover it? How?"

"Hey, I can blog with the best of them, right? Michelle will help me set up the website. And I don't have to hide how closely we're working together. We can spin this thing like nobody's business."

They arrived at Lacey's car and she unlocked all of the doors with her key fob. Brandy pulled open the driver's side door for Lacey and settled her into the seat before she hurried to the other side and climbed in. "Well, alright then. Lead on!"

When they arrived at the marina, they arranged to rent a small ski boat. It was a little fancier than they needed, but it was the only boat left that wasn't purely wind-powered. It was light and fast, and it didn't smell like day-old large-mouth bass.

"You ladies didn't exactly plan for a day on the lake, did you?" The clerk shook his head. Neither of the boys she'd met on her first visit were there. "You're both going to bake out there."

"He's right, you know. We should change clothes. I've got a little cash with me," Brandy said as she eyed the sportswear hanging on several manikins near the entrance to the tourist shop.

"I'm fine."

"You're going to cook out there in that outfit. There is zero shade."

"We'll put up the Bimini top if it gets too hot. I'm fine. Really." Lacey folded her arms over her breast and planted her feet. She was not putting on a bathing suit or a t-shirt, no matter how hot it got out on the water. She'd be fine.

Reaching into the ice-chest cooler by the rental desk, Lacey pulled out two extra-large bottles of water and placed them on the counter. "We'll take a couple of these for good measure."

Brandy frowned as she reached around Lacey and pulled out two more bottles. "I have a feeling we're going to need it."

Once they were on the lake, Lacey realized that Brandy and the clerk had been right. The sun sent more heat down on her head and shoulders than she'd ever experienced in her entire life. It wouldn't be so bad once they left the no wake zone of the marina itself.

"Are you sure you're going to be okay? It's like over a hundred degrees out here."

"Yup."

Brandy had taken off her jacket the second they'd climbed onto the craft, slinging it haphazardly over one of the captain's chairs. Lacey adjusted her collar slightly to allow some of the gentle breeze to reach the sides of her neck.

The water danced in the sunlight, the choppy surface sending the heat back in the direction it had come. The boat, caught in the middle, offered little relief. Finally, Brandy floated past the buoy that marked the marina's border. She laid on the accelerator and the bow of the vessel lifted several feet out of the water.

Gorgeous, cooling wind rushed past Lacey's face and she closed her eyes against it, relishing the effect on her heated flesh. Even with the suddenly cool air, the heat on her cheeks remained, but it was pleasant now instead of torturous.

It was all a matter of perspective, wasn't it?

"I figure we'll make a full circle of the perimeter first, and then maybe check out a couple of the coves. What do you think?" Brandy shouted over the engine and the air rushing past Lacey's ears.

"Sounds like a plan!"

There wasn't much point in talking over the noise after that. Instead, Brandy watched the horizon, and Lacey tried not to watch Brandy.

They were looking for a huge luxury yacht. There was little chance they would miss it should they come upon it, so it seemed like there wasn't much to do but enjoy the day and the view. The lake, surrounded on most sides with tall, red-rock walls, was really a reservoir formed as a product of the Hoover Dam hydro-electrical plant. The water level had decreased over the years, but it still served as a huge outdoorsmen's paradise. They passed a great number of boats as they made their circle. Some were filled with fishermen. Some served as platforms for swimmers. Some boaters were just plain partying and raised cans of beer high into the air in salute as Brandy jetted past.

After nearly a full circle of the outside edge, more than two hours on the lake, they hadn't seen a single yacht.

As Brandy slowed down near the entrance to an alcove on the Arizona side of the lake, she craned her neck. "Do you see a boat in there?" she asked.

Lacey stood next to her at the front windshield and narrowed her eyes against the glare. She pointed in the direction of a rocky outcropping. "Just there, behind that rock, you mean? Yeah. I think that could be the back end of a boat."

Brandy edged the accelerator forward and increased speed slightly. "We should check it out."

Slowing down significantly, they entered the alcove, more of a lagoon, really, and as they navigated around the outcropping, they found not just any boat, but the very boat they'd been looking for.

It was moored to an outcropping, although there was no pier. The surrounding area was desolate and in any other circumstances would make a fantastic place to camp. Or dock. Or whatever it was that someone did on a big boat on a lake.

There was nobody on the deck.

A red flag with a diagonal stripe hung from a short pole mounted on the aft railing. An American flag moved slowly in response to the gentle lapping of the waves on the boat's hull. Other than the creaking of the boat itself, there was no sound from the vessel.

"So, now what?" Lacey bit her bottom lip and placed her hands on her hips. "Isn't it illegal to board a ship without permission?"

"What? I'm a pirate now? I have no idea." After a moment, she cupped her hands around her mouth and yelled, "Ahoy, there!" Brandy looked at Lacey and shrugged.

Lacey laughed. "Seriously? 'Ahoy, there?'"

"What? Would you have preferred, 'Yo! Asshole!'"

"I suppose not."

There was no response from the yacht. Brandy called again and there was still no reply.

"I guess we should check it out." Brandy moved the ski boat closer to the yacht. For someone who didn't own a boat and had never actually operated one before, she did a great job of lining them up with a ladder that hung over the side. "You okay with this?"

"I'm all in." Lacey hoped she sounded more confident than she felt. She was pretty sure that boarding a boat without permission was some kind of nautical capital crime.

Brandy climbed the ladder while holding to a mooring line. When she reached the top, she tied it off and then waited for Lacey to join her on the deck.

"Mr. Miller?" Lacey called as she made her way to the bow.

"Look at this." Brandy stood in front of a picnic style table that was secured to the deck with metal rings. The remnants of a meal sat neglected. Two plates. Two wine glasses. White bird droppings covered the table and the plates. What food may have remained at the end of the meal had been picked clean. A single steak bone sat discarded on the tabletop.

"Unless he's a total slob, I'd say he hasn't been around for a minute or two." Brandy scrunched her nose.

Lacey made her way through an open doorway. The

door itself was off its runner and the bottom corner was cracked a few inches from the base and side, as though someone had kicked it. Hard.

Inside, the living area was elegant, but unkempt. The style was dated – it looked like a set from an episode of Miami Vice – but had obviously been rather nice at some point in the 80s. An overturned coffee table had sprayed its contents all over the worn carpeting on the floor.

"Is this blood?"

Lacey found Brandy squatting near the entrance to the galley. She was scrutinizing a few smears of something dark on the carpeting. The stains could have been anything as far as Lacey could tell. But blood wasn't out of the question. "Maybe," she answered, bending to take a closer look. "Could also be chocolate."

"Let's check the bedroom."

When they entered the hallway that led away from the main living quarters, they found three additional rooms. All of them were probably bedrooms at some point, but someone had converted them into other spaces. Most likely, Miller had made the changes since he lived on the boat alone.

The first space was an office, complete with a full-sized desk, computer work station and cabinets. One wall held a fax machine attached to the wall. The wires had been disconnected and hung limply to one side. It looked as though Miller spent a great deal of time in this room. A pair of boat shoes had been dropped at the side of the desk and the computer screen displayed a rotating collection of photographs.

Beautiful images of the surrounding desert flashed on the screen for several seconds before the image changed to a woman in a wedding dress. The woman's eyes danced and sparkled as she stood in a line with three other women in full length scarlet dresses. The bride wore white, of course, with more lace than any one person should ever be forced to wear. The image changed to a close-up in profile and Lacey gasped.

"Brandy?"

"Yeah," Brandy answered, her voice muffled. Lacey turned to find her rummaging in a cabinet.

"What are you looking for?"

"Anything. Nothing. I don't know." She regained her full height and pivoted in the tight space to face Lacey. Her gaze fell immediately on the computer screen. "Are you serious?"

"Right?" Lacey asked, turning to face the screen again. "Is... is that Cynthia?"

The picture moved. This time the groom was in the picture. Lacey immediately recognized John Miller from the private detective's photographs. The newly married couple looked into each other's eyes with obvious love and supposed devotion. The picture moved again to reveal a candid shot from their wedding reception. With her skirt hiked up to her thigh, Cynthia was obviously laughing wildly as her groom made a show of pulling down a soft blue satin garter.

"No tattoo."

Lacey tore her attention from the screen and focused on Brandy. "What?"

"These were taken before we started dating. I mean, she obviously looks a little younger here. I don't think I ever saw her look quite so relaxed in comparison to the woman I married, but she doesn't have a tattoo on her leg. We got them within a couple of weeks of our first date."

"Oh." Lacey paused. "So, John Miller isn't... wasn't... her boyfriend. He was her ex-husband?"

"Looks that way." Brandy's voice had grown choppy and tight. She pulled open a filing cabinet drawer and rifled through the folders. "Before you ask, I'm looking for a divorce decree."

"Well, they had to be divorced, right? I mean, you don't think she married you while she was still married to him, do you?"

"She was obviously still seeing him. I have the artwork to prove that. Who does that? Who has an affair with their ex-husband?"

"Lots of women, probably." Lacey shrugged. "Don't jump to conclusions."

Brandy pulled open another drawer and shuffled through the contents before slamming it back into place.

"I'm going to keep looking around. We need to hurry. When he comes back, we need to be long gone."

Suddenly, their visit to the boat seemed far less authentic and much more criminal. It was one thing to come on board to look for him. She could, in a pinch, claim to have been worried about him. He obviously wasn't on board and they probably should have turned right around. Unease crawled over her flesh like a prowler and she shivered.

The next room was a game room, filled with an old, all-but worn-out air hockey table and a small shuffleboard table. A dart board hung on the far wall with tiny pin holes forming a wide arc in the paneling beside it. Apparently, hitting the target was even more difficult on a swaying boat. In one corner, a poker table covered in maroon felt bore the name of Brandy's casino in crisp, white lettering. A gift from the ex-misses?

Without bothering to do more than peer into the game room, Lacey made her way to the final door. She pushed on it and it opened silently. The bedroom was fairly plain, considering that the yacht had once been pretty luxurious as yachts go. Not that she'd been on any personally. The bed was a typical captain's design, with cabinets underneath that sported brass hardware. The headboard was also made from a series of cabinets broken up with slivers of narrow mirror tile.

The worn bedclothes hung in disarray, falling off the opposite side of the bed. It seemed more than the result of simply tossing them off in the morning. Rather, like the main living area, this room looked as though it had seen a significant struggle.

Lacey took a step into the room and glanced to the far side of the bed where the blankets pooled in an untidy heap.

"Oh, God! Brandy? Come in here!" Lacey called, backing out of the room as quickly as she could.

Brandy slammed the last of the drawers in the office. She hadn't found anything that remotely looked like a divorce decree, but she did find a marriage license. Cynthia and John Miller had been married in 2007, just two years before Cynthia and Brandy had eloped in Canada.

Two years.

Did that mean that they had realized their mistake early on and ended their marriage that quickly? Or, as Brandy suspected, did it mean that they had never bothered to get divorced at all?

She focused on the images rotating on the computer and one struck her as particularly incriminating and confusing. Cynthia sat on top of a horse, her face stricken with panic, while Miller held the lead rope and laughed. Cynthia had a white-knuckled grip on the pommel and her feet hung outside the stirrups. She looked like she'd never sat on a horse in her entire life.

She had long suspected that her marriage, at least from Cynthia's point of view, had been a marriage of convenience. If she was right and Cynthia had never been divorced from Miller, her marriage wasn't only loveless, it was a total sham. If her story about riding the rodeo circuit were a lie as well, the marriage had been a deliberate sham.

Brandy's stomach turned.

"Brandy! Hurry!"

"I'm coming. What is it?" Brandy picked up her pace down the narrow hall to the third door where Lacey stood waiting with her back pressed against the wall.

"In the bedroom."

"Stateroom."

"Whatever. Go look on the far side of the bed."

Brandy entered the room and wrinkled her nose. The honeymoon suite, perhaps? Not a lover's nest. No, that would imply something illicit was going on. If they were married, then all of the bumping and grinding that went on here was completely legit. It was Brandy's bed where all the betrayal had happened.

She reached the far side of the bed and froze. "Now, that's blood."

Lacey appeared behind her, close enough that the heat coming from their bodies melded. "I think so. That's a lot of blood, right?" Lacey whispered.

"Yeah." Brandy backed up a step and caught herself as she pressed against Lacey.

Lacey was trembling.

Brandy escorted her back into the hallway. "I think we need to get out of here."

"Right," she agreed. Her voice trembled, too.

They made their way back to their rented ski boat and climbed down the latter. After pushing back from the hull of the larger vessel, Brandy maneuvered the boat slowly away before accelerating in the direction of the marina. They had spent nearly two hours looking for the yacht, but they made it back to the marina in under ten minutes.

They turned in the boat, reclaimed the security deposit Lacey had paid, and climbed back into Lacey's sedan.

"What do you make of it?" Her voice sounded more under control, but her tone was still one of disbelief.

"I have no idea. He hasn't been back to his slip in almost a week, maybe longer. I don't know if that was his blood, or if it was…"

"Cynthia's. I know. I was thinking the same thing. What if she was playing him more than she was playing you? What if he found out that you and she were married and-"

"We weren't married." Brandy's throat burned as her stomach roiled beneath her diaphragm, which refused to work properly.

"What?"

"If she was married to him in 2007, according to this," she said, pulling the certificate she'd stolen from the boat from her back pocket, "then we were never married. And if we were never married, then the pre-nup would mean nothing. She didn't stand to lose half of my portfolio when we divorced. She would have lost everything. That's why she didn't want to divorce. That's why she was stalling."

"You would have thought that with the baby, she'd be in a hurry to get it over with." Lacey took the folded paper from Brandy's fingers and opened it. She read the document and then placed it inside the folder with the private detective's report. "You shouldn't have taken this off the boat. How are you going to explain that you have it?"

Brandy shrugged. "I didn't think that far ahead. I guess I'll just say I found it in her things at the house." She turned to look out the window in the direction of the boat slips.

"We have more work to do," Lacey announced, placing her car into reverse and backing out of the parking stall.

"Naturally. But what, specifically, are you talking about?" Brandy tucked the PI file between the console and the passenger seat she occupied, and then fastened her seat belt.

"If that is Cynthia's blood on the boat, if Miller killed her for whatever reason, he had to take her body back to her house and dump her right? I doubt seriously that he would have carried her body to his car right here on the pier, and I don't think he took a cab, do you?"

"What's your point?"

"I think he had help."

Brandy followed the direction of Lacey's gaze to land on a young, Asian woman carrying a bag of groceries along the dock. "Who's that?"

"Her name is Marcia Johnson. She lives in the slip next to Miller's."

"And that means... what?"

"Maybe nothing. Right now, we need to find Miller's car." Lacey's eyes danced as the wheels in her mind churned. She shoved the transmission into drive. As she pulled out of the parking lot, she grinned so broadly that the interior of the car seemed brighter.

"And where are we going to find it?"

"Look in the file. Did Lynda include the information on his car?"

Brandy opened the file, scanning the contents as she turned the page. "There's a little bit of information, but the license number is blocked out."

"She probably didn't want you following him on your own. Hang on a sec." Lacey retrieved her cell phone from her pocket and handed it to Brandy. "Find the number for Paul Smithfield."

"Okay..." Brandy scanned the contacts until she found the name. "Shall I dial?"

"Please." Lacey pulled the car onto the main road. "Put it on speaker."

When a man answered, he did so with a smile in his voice. "Well, if it ain't little miss famous reporter! I saw you on CNN. Nice job, babe. What can I do you for?"

"Hey, Paul. I need you to run something for me real quick, if you can? Off the record?"

"Anything for you, sweetheart. Shoot."

Lacey gave her contact Miller's name and birthdate. Within a few minutes, Paul had his entire driving record. "Awesome. Now, can you tell me what vehicles are registered in his name?"

"Sure thing. Let's see here... there's a boat registered jointly with a Cynthia Rachel Miller, a camp trailer that hasn't changed ownership but hasn't been licensed in," he paused for a moment before continuing, "about nine years, and a 1982 Lincoln Town Car. White. Nevada license number Oscar Charlie Bravo, three-niner-five."

"You are my hero, Paul. I don't care what they say about you!" Lacey laughed. "That's all I needed, buddy."

"When are you going to go skinny dipping with me, hot stuff?"

"Every night, doll face, in your dreams."

Paul laughed. "Right. So, we're good here?"

"We're great. I'll talk to you later." Lacey nodded at Brandy to disconnect the call.

"Is that your boyfriend?" Brandy asked, only half-kidding.

"Paul? Oh, hell no. His boyfriend would take serious issue with that." She rolled her eyes. "We just flirt. It's harmless. And since he works for the DMV, he is a huge help pretty much whenever I need him. You know, like now?"

"So, we're looking for a white Lincoln Town Car."

"Exactly. It'll probably be dumped somewhere, out of sight."

"If we're heading off road, we should have brought my SUV."

"True, but we're looking for a car, so we should be able to reach any places he did."

Lacey turned off the main road onto a relatively easy-to-navigate dirt road that led in the direction of the lake. She slowed to a crawl in a few areas that were covered in hard, washboarded soil. The rough ride and excessive noise from the drive kept conversation at bay.

Brandy half-heartedly scanned the desert for any signs of a white car. The sun's glare proved a difficult mask to break, but would help if the car's metallic surfaces reflected the light.

After an hour, with the prospect of losing light and running out of gas, they gave up and headed back to town.

"I have some contacts at the county courthouse. That's a Nevada marriage certificate. If they were married here, and still lived here, there should be a public record of any divorce. I wouldn't mind taking a look at their tax records, but those would be confidential."

"You really get into this stuff, don't you?" Brandy leaned back against the seat and stretched her legs as far as she could. "You're practically glowing."

CHAPTER ELEVEN

Brandy stood in front of the mirror in the guestroom of Kendra and Michelle's condo. She studied her reflection in the clear glass and frowned. Why was she even going to the funeral? She was an interloper at this point. Lacey had confirmed her suspicions about Cynthia's marriage to Miller the previous afternoon with a single phone call. As far as the State of Nevada was concerned, Cynthia Rachel Miller was the blissfully wedded wife of John Miller right up to the day she died.

She had considered not going to the funeral dozens of times since that phone call. What right did she have? What reason did she have to even show up? Michelle had immediately brought up the charges and the suspicions that were being cast ever in her direction as reason enough to attend. For the cameras. For the reporters. The wily blonde's mind worked like an intricate gear box, one thought spinning another, spinning another. By the time they'd gone to bed last night, fully-clothed and holding each other, Michelle had figured out a way to use this new information to build sympathy for Brandy.

She wasn't sure whether she liked the idea of disparaging the reputation of a dead woman to save her own skin. She had gone back and forth on that particular issue even more than the question of whether to attend the funeral.

She sighed, gathering her keys and her wallet from the smooth surface of the dresser and slipping them into the pocket of her black blazer. A knock sounded on the front door and a moment later Lacey called from the living room. "Brandy?"

"In the guest room!"

A moment later, Lacey appeared in the doorway. She folded her arms over her breasts and leaned on the jamb. Her hair, normally straight with a slight wave, curled wildly around her delicate features. She'd put on a little makeup this morning, as well, and the natural tones highlighted her already large eyes. "You look really great," she said.

"Funny. I was just thinking the same thing." Brandy tried to smile, but it felt wrong.

"Everything is going to be okay."

"You keep saying that. I sure hope you're right."

"I'm right. I talked to the Fairchild Agency this morning and Lynda is putting her best investigator on finding the Town Car. Once we can establish that Cynthia's body was in the trunk, you're in the clear. Game over."

"It can't be that simple. There's more. What about the Maretti family?"

"I have no idea. Let's jump off that bridge when we get there."

Brandy laughed as some of the stress poured off her shoulders.

Lacey grabbed her hand and squeezed gently. "Come on. I'll drive."

When they arrived at the chapel, Brandy got out of the car and then circled it to open Lacey's door. They sat together in the front row of the sanctuary. Cynthia's mother, father and two brothers sat in the front row across the aisle.

The alter was covered in soft pink roses and stark white lilies. The casket, pure white with gold accents, took up the center of the altar. Inside, it was lined in crimson satin, though nobody knew that except her parents and Brandy. Even before the service began, as Cynthia's casket had been displayed in the viewing parlor, it had been closed. A photograph taken just a few years ago in Madrid sat on top.

Brandy's stomach jolted. It should have been her wedding picture. Not the snapshots taken in Canada, though. She should have found prints of her real wedding, to Miller, and used one of those. She glared at her in-laws.

They had to have known. How could they not know their daughter was committing such a blatant crime? She nearly snorted aloud. Of course, her mother would have only cared that she had enough money to support her habit. She must be doing fairly well lately, Brandy realized. She was wearing a diamond broach and matching diamond solitaire earrings.

Brandy frowned. Had they all been in on it? Was it some kind of huge conspiracy?

By the time the service ended, Brandy had had all she could take of pretending to be anything but angry. The longer she sat, the deeper she stewed and the angrier she became. The pall-bearers escorted the casket down the aisle and Brandy, obligated to keep up appearances, walked stoically behind them. Guests fell into step behind Cynthia's parents as everyone made their way out of the building and into the blinding Nevada sunlight. Brandy stopped next to a palm tree, deliberately separating herself from her in-laws, or whatever she should call them now, as the pall-bearers loaded the casket into the back of a shining white hearse with pink chiffon curtains gathered in the windows.

"I'm not riding in the family car," Brandy announced once they parted from the main group.

Lacey folded her arms over her slender belly. "Okay. I can understand that."

"In fact, I'm not going to the graveside service at all. I'm done. I can't do this anymore."

"Alrighty, then. Where would you like to go?"

"Home. To the Rocking T."

"We can do that."

"We should."

"Let's go."

"Alright."

Brandy's feet felt like they were anchored to the earth. Her stomach turned over a couple of times and then landed in her throat.

Lacey just stood there, not making a sound. She looked into Brandy's eyes with a kind of trust that doubled as reassurance. Reassurance that everything would be okay. That she'd stay right where she was until everything was, actually, okay. She didn't smile, but she didn't frown, either. She blinked against the heat and the sunshine, but never once removed her gaze.

Brandy sighed. "I can't do that, can I?" It didn't really feel like a question. It was more of a statement looking for confirmation. Confirmation she didn't really need. Or want.

"I think it would be better if we gut through it. That is, if you're looking for my opinion. I'll still be here. I'll hold you up, if I have to."

Was it completely twisted that Brandy found herself unable to keep her heart in check at her supposed wife's funeral? All she could think of was the luxury of Lacey's lips and how tasting them right now would give her the strength she needed to soar above all of horrible things happening in her life. One little kiss would give her the power she needed to make it through the rest of this miserable day. Of course, she wouldn't stop at just one kiss, would she? The next time she kissed Lacey, she was fairly confident she wouldn't be able to stop. "If you're there with me, I think I can do it."

Lacey grinned. "You got it, babe."

They made their way to Lacey's car and fell inside, enjoying the air conditioning for a few minutes as the procession got ready to move out of the chapel parking lot.

By the time they reached the cemetery, the news crews had set up their cameras to catch an image of anyone who walked through the gates. She tried to ignore them, but it wasn't easy. A couple of the pushier reporters shouted questions at her as she walked by. The same ones they had already thrown at her. Had she killed her wife. Had she known that her wife was pregnant. Jethro Martin stood with two uniformed officers a few yards away from the grave. When their eyes met, the old cop nodded and tipped his cowboy hat at her.

The graveside internment only took a few minutes once everyone settled into place. Brandy stood next to Lacey at the edge of the row of cheap, plastic chairs that lined the edge of the grave. Cynthia's parents sat in the middle with a few close friends flanking them on either side. As Cynthia's wife, she should be seated in the center, but it didn't matter anymore, did it? She hadn't been Cynthia's wife. Not legally. Not really in any way.

Did it matter that she had thought she was? Or was it relief that it had all been some kind of weird mixture of nightmare and reality?

Finally, the priest finished his remarks and invited the family to place single pink roses on the casket as they left. Cynthia's mother did, with a final sob that sounded like a cannon shot. Her father tossed his flower next to his wife's before placing his arms around her shoulders to keep her from falling. The pall-bearers looked at Brandy and she realized they were waiting for her to add to the bouquet.

"I don't have a flower," she whispered to Lacey.

"It's okay, we can just go, and they'll get the hint."

Lacey placed her hand gently on Brandy's upper arm and they turned together to leave the graveside.

Standing at the back of the crowd, slightly separate from the rest of the group, a young man with short, black hair and a dark complexion that spoke of many hours in the sun, stood motionless. His hands were pressed firmly into the front pockets of his black dress slacks, his starched, white dress shirt almost glowing.

He was standing at the foot of a grave, but there was something about his demeanor that called out the lie. He wasn't there by coincidence. He was there for Cynthia. Maybe it was the way he cast furtive glances in their direction from behind sunglasses so dark they looked like blinders. Or maybe it had something to do with the obvious pain and grief that fell off him like a waterfall of putrid emotion, even though the grave at which he stood wasn't even remotely recent.

"Who is that?" Lacey asked. "Have I seen him somewhere before?"

"You don't recognize him? That's Carlos Maretti."

"Maretti?" She gulped. "As in Kenny-the-Fish-tried-to-bail-you-out Maretti? As in, they-own-every-illegal-gaming-site-within-a-hundred-miles Maretti?"

"You're thinking of his father, but yes. That would be the Maretti I'm talking about. Junior over there is being groomed to take over the family farm."

Lacey paused, pulling gently on Brandy's arm. Brandy turned her gaze away from Carlos Maretti's still form and put it on Lacey's stern features. "What?"

"How do you know so much about what's going on in the Maretti household?"

Brandy slipped her sunglasses over her eyes, which burned from the sunlight and not from tears as they probably should have. "It's fairly common knowledge in certain circles."

By the time they reached Lacey's car, the crowd had thinned considerably. Even Cynthia's parents had left the grounds in the family limo. There was a gathering scheduled for that afternoon, of course. A luncheon to begin the life-goes-on aspect of the great American funeral experience. They'd wanted to have it at the house. Her house.

Brandy had refused. She'd used the excuse that it was simply in poor taste to have a funeral luncheon in the same building where Cynthia's body had been discovered, but in truth, she simply didn't want those people in her house. Now that Cynthia was gone, and in light of the fact that they were most-likely never married, it was her house. Hers to do with as she wished. She'd made arrangements to use one of the private rooms at the hotel closest to her casino for the luncheon instead. She'd arranged for everything because Cynthia's mother had been so distraught. Not too distraught to gamble, of course, but distraught nonetheless.

"Brandy?"

"What?"

"Were you listening?"

"I'm sorry. My mind was wondering a bit. What did you say?"

"I said that Maretti guy is still there. He's moved over to Cynthia's grave now and he's... he's crying. Like, a lot. Look."

Brandy watched as Carlos Maretti fell to his knees at the side of Cynthia's casket. There were a couple of cemetery employees waiting to one side, obviously wanting to lower the casket and get out of the midday heat. Maretti just laid there, looking every bit the grieving lover...

"We aren't going to the luncheon, right?" Brandy asked.

"I'm fine if you want to skip it."

"Good. I'd like to take a little detour."

Lacey moved her car around the corner and parked in such a way that she could watch the exit gates of the cemetery. Eventually, Maretti would have to leave. She wasn't entirely sure what Brandy thought they might learn by following him when he did, but it wasn't as though she had anything better to do.

Her career was in the toilet. Her reputation was on life support now that every news crew in two counties had seen her and Brandy walking arm-in-arm through the cemetery. It was only a matter of time before all the work she'd done to spin Brandy's story came crashing down around them.

She simply hadn't been able to force her to go through the funeral alone. Of course, she'd only insisted that Brandy attend in an effort to continue the spin machine. She'd been going for a rinse cycle, and what she'd ended up with was full-on agitation.

Sighing, she forced herself to keep her eyes on her subject. At least she could control that, if she couldn't control her thoughts. Or her body for that matter. Even now, just thinking about Brandy, made her insides tremble like fresh Jell-o.

Finally, after what seemed like hours, Carlos Maretti walked through the cemetery gates as though he were walking toward his own execution. Shoulder's slumped, his features swollen from tears, he kept his eyes on the ground in front of him as he shuffled to his car. The bright red Ferrari looked out of place in the midst of such sadness.

The engine roared to life and Maretti made an immediate U-turn out of the parallel parking space next to the grounds. He drove away and, after a couple of seconds, Lacey pulled out and followed.

"Hey, at least he'll be easy to spot, right?" Brandy quipped. "And I thought my truck was conspicuous."

"It's Vegas. Your truck is practically invisible. But that little Italian job? Ferraris are never inconspicuous."

Fifteen minutes later, the little sports car pulled into an old parking lot next to a strip mall. Weeds grew through the cracked blacktop and if there had ever been parking lines, they'd long since melted away under the desert sun. The building itself was just as beaten; the weathered cedar siding boasting of a hay-day sometime in the 70s. There was only one business that seemed to still exist in a long line of soaped windows and boarded doors.

Carlos Maretti climbed out of his car, slammed the door and marched up to the windowless exterior of the Kitty Cat Grille. Once he disappeared inside, Lacey said, "If we go in, we're blown. No way will he not recognize us from the funeral."

"I don't care. You should probably wait here, but I'm going in to have a few words with him."

"To find out why he was at the funeral? Obviously, but what good will confronting him do? The Maretti family is dangerous, Brandy. When they say that these guys work in the garment industry, they're talking about cement shoes, not sequined tops."

"I'll be perfectly safe. Don't worry. I've met him before. He won't be even a little surprised to see me."

Brandy's features were pulled into a grim line of

determination and wounded pride. Her eyes transfixed on the door through which the young, good-looking man had vanished. "Wait here."

"Oh, no. I don't even want you to go in there, and if… if I can't stop you, you sure as hell aren't going in alone."

Another car pulled up in front of the business, long and black and sleek. The chauffer exited, jogged around the front end and then opened the back door. Two men appeared from the back seat. One of them looked just like Abe Vagoda, only more heavy-set – Kenny the Fish, obviously. He was hard to miss. The second man was enormous, with no neck to speak of and short, curling hair that greyed at the temples.

"Wait," Lacey announced, tugging on Brandy's arm to keep her in the car. "Do those guys look like they're here for the entertainment?"

"Not even a little." Brandy settled back in her seat and sighed. "We're officially outnumbered."

"They must be here to meet with Carlos about something. Carlos has some kind of link to Cynthia." She bit her cheek and focused on the front of the strip club. "Now what?"

A hotel van pulled into the parking lot and slowed gently to a stop in front of the club, the brakes squeaking. One after the other, a succession of women piled out onto the broken and bleeding pavement. One of the women wore a black t-shirt with the image of a tuxedo that had originally read, "Groom," in bright white lettering. The word had been crossed out and superimposed with iron-on letters that said, "BRIDE," in bright pink.

The other women circled around her, pulling her in the

direction of the club door, as she pretended to fight them off.

"What if you don't confront him? What if we just blend in and keep an eye on him?" Lacey suggested.

Brandy smiled. "Under the circumstances, that's not a bad idea at all, actually."

They got out of the car just in time to file into the club with the wedding party. The girls had obviously been drinking quite a bit already and they scarcely noticed they'd been hijacked. When one of the last women in the procession did notice them, she beamed wildly and threw herself into Brandy's arms. "I'm so glad you could come," she slurred before planting a sloppy kiss on Brandy's cheek.

Brandy grinned. "Wouldn't miss it for the world."

Once inside, it took a moment for their eyes to adjust to the darkness. There were a few lights near a small, cheaply built stage, and a few more over the bar, but the rest of the interior was lit only by single artificial candles in red votive holders on each table. It was the kind of place that didn't need light, where the men who came in didn't necessarily want to be recognized should someone they know slink through the door.

A fully naked woman danced on the stage. Danced, of course, was a definite matter of opinion. She writhed and shook and almost kept time with the deep bass beat of an old rap song. Some might call it exotic, others might call it dancing. Lacey called it exploitation, and she felt nothing but pity for the young woman on the stage.

She followed Brandy to a table near where the bridal party had ended up. Rather than sitting with them, Brandy swept her to a booth near the rear exit. As the music faded,

Lacey realized they were sitting very near, but out of sight, of Carlos Maretti.

He was huddled in an identical booth directly behind them. A tall, scrolled wooden panel separated the high-backed booths. It seemed odd that a performance venue would have such a design, but then, those particular tables probably existed more for privacy than viewing pleasure.

A topless waitress, who was barely twenty-one if she were even legal, came over and asked them for their drink orders. Brandy ordered a beer for herself and a glass of wine for Lacey before she settled back against the cushions.

Carlos voice slithered over the top of the divider as the current, blaring song faded into silence. "I don't care what my father thinks, Uncle Kenny. She was important to me. She was mine, god damn it. She loved me for who I am, not my family or my connections. That bastard killed her and I want justice. I deserve it. And so does Cynthia."

"That isn't disputed by anybody. But then you weep like a child where anyone can see you. You know the cops was at the funeral, watching everything. Now they might look at us, you know, for what happened. You bring shame on your family. What happened wasn't authorized. He put us all at risk. But so do you. You bring attention to what should be handled within the family. These rules we follow have a purpose. You need to let the family handle things and make sure you remember who you are."

There was a pause; the type of silence that steamed with heavy thoughts and disdain. Finally, Carlos replied, "She was mine. He had no right to take her from me. If I failed to protect her, it is my honor and my right to avenge her."

Brandy hadn't moved, her ears poised to overhear as much as possible of the mostly low, growling tones of the conversation next door. Lacey slid closer to Brandy on the worn and torn, red vinyl seats. Their thighs touched under the table and Brandy shifted her weight slightly. The sudden friction sent a wave of desire coursing through Lacey's entire body. She sucked in a breath and tamped down the feeling.

"You will have the opportunity, but not now. Now is the time to concentrate on the family and where we go from here. Your father isn't well. Someone, either you or one of your brothers is going to need to take over. If we don't establish that now, one of the other families will think they can come in and push us out."

"Not... him. Never him."

"Damn it, kid. You need to get over it. You'd sacrifice your whole family, everybody, not just the guys, mind you. But the whole family, including your little cousin, Marisa, and your sister's kids? You'd do that? You'd sacrifice everybody just to get even for some grifter who don't amount to nothin' compared to family?"

"Watch what you say, Uncle Kenny. We have been friends for a long time. I've known you since I was born, and I couldn't love my own father more, but that won't mean nothing if you insult her again. She wasn't a grifter. She was like a child caught between the misguided love of warring parents. She did only what they told her, trying to stay far enough out of their way that she wouldn't get hurt."

"Whatever you say, Carlos. If you say she was an angel with the gossamer wings of your own sainted mother, then who am I to disagree? But there is that other matter to contend with. The fact remains that her mother owes us a half-million dollars, and we will get paid. One way or another. You capish?"

"Hands off the old lady. You'll get your money. I have a plan. Capish?"

The elevator chimed as it reached the top floor of Lacey's building. It opened, and they stepped into the hall in front of Brandy's borrowed condo.

"I'm sorry about everything." Brandy unlocked the door and held it open for Lacey.

"You don't really have anything to be sorry about, honey. None of this is your fault."

"I feel like I've dragged you into some lost episode of the Twilight Zone. I can actually hear Rod Sterling asking whether Cynthia was married to a man or a woman; was she boinking a local gangster; was she really a lesbian, or had she just entered... well, you know."

"Why don't you go relax and I'll mix us up some grub."

Brandy poured herself a drink and then tossed her blazer on the back of a dining room chair. She crossed to the thermostat and read the digital display. "It's almost eighty degrees in here. You must be broiling in that get up."

Lacey came around the kitchen island with the store-bought tray of vegetables and dip they'd picked up on their way home. She was still wearing a high-necked shirt, not quite a turtleneck, and a black suit coat. It suddenly dawned on Brandy that she'd never seen her wear anything that didn't have a high collar, no matter how hot it was outside. She always wore sleeves. She practically dressed like a nun. "Aren't you hot?"

"I'm fine," Lacey replied with a forced smile. "The question is, are you fine?"

"I'll live, I guess." She sat down and picked up a sprig of broccoli, dipping it in ranch dressing before popping it in her mouth.

Lacey sat next to her and did the same. Her musky scent rose gently in the warm air and invaded every sensibility Brandy had left.

"What are you thinking about?" Lacey asked.

That was a loaded question. What was she thinking about? She was thinking about how she'd love to watch the pulse beat in the soft flesh at the base of Lacey's slender throat. About how she'd love to measure the cadence with the tip of her tongue. That she needed intimate contact to prove she was still alive, and that there was something, anything, redeemable about her as a woman and a human being.

"About how I know now what Cynthia needed that money for. She asked me for a half-million the night she went missing, remember? Obviously, she needed to pay off her mother's gambling debts to the Maretti family."

"And yet, you don't seem the least bit surprised by that fact."

Brandy pushed herself off the bar stool and paced from

one side of the living room to the other, her arms wrapped around her midsection in a tight hug. "Let's just say that I had some suspicions I didn't bother mentioning earlier. It was just too fantastic."

"Like what?"

"When we were on the boat, I saw a picture of Cynthia that looked a lot like she was just learning how to ride. Miller was in the picture, too. It was taken at a public riding stable that I recognized because I've sold them my older stock. It's over in the Prim Valley."

"But you said she was a barrel racer..." Lacey poured herself a Dr. Pepper.

"Right. So, I met her at the Rocking T. We sell saddle horses to all sorts of people – riding outfits, outfitters, individuals, rodeo stock contractors, and of course, people who ride in the circuit. One day, Cynthia shows up out there looking for a new barrel horse. Marko had trained several good possibilities earlier that year, so he offered to let her ride them for a while and try them out. She did, supposedly, and when she came back a few days later, I was there." Brandy tried to remember the feelings she'd developed that day, but the only thing she could muster bordered on nausea. "That was all she wrote. She never did buy a horse, and she told me she had decided to quit riding and settle down. We started dating almost from that first day I met her, and six months later, we were married. Just like that."

"What are you saying?"

"I'm saying that there is no way Miller killed her because

of me; at least not for marrying me. I'm saying he was in on the scam to marry me. You heard Kenny Maretti. She was a grifter. A con artist. Never once, in the entire time I knew her, loved her, and was kind-of married to her did I ever see her sit on a horse. It was all a ploy to get to me."

Brandy turned her attention away from the nothing she'd been looking at and stared directly at Lacey. "That kind of makes me the King of Fools, doesn't it?"

"No. It makes you human." Sliding to her knees, Lacey scooted to kneel in front of Brandy. She placed her hands on Brandy's knees and said, "We are going to get you out of this. I promise."

Brandy inhaled a huge breath in attempt to calm the swirling emotions that wracked the deepest parts of her soul. She released it in a heavy sigh. It worked, a little, to soothe. "So, if Miller didn't kill her because he was jealous; I mean, if he knew all about the set up and was in on the whole thing, then why did he kill her?"

"Jealousy is jealousy. I think we only have to look to Carlos Maretti for an answer. Obviously, you didn't knock up your wife."

Cynthia was having an affair with Carlos Maretti, the younger. The how or why that relationship had developed escaped Lacey, but it was there, nonetheless. Brandy sat quietly, the implications of that information more than likely leaping from one side of her mind to the other.

Pushing off her knees, doing her best to ignore the pain in her joints, she stood before releasing Brandy's hands.

"If Carlos was the father of Cynthia's baby, and somehow Miller found out about it, that would be a pretty damning reason for murder, don't you think?"

"Sure. And if we can prove that, then maybe we can get past this whole thing. Maybe I have a chance. But how? How do we prove something like that? I can't exactly walk up the Carlos and say, 'Excuse me, but can I have a little DNA, so I can give it to the coroner for a post-mortem paternity test? Thanks.'"

"Of course not. And none of this explains why they tried to get their hands on you, right?"

"Unless they thought since Cynthia couldn't pay off Mommy Dearest's debts, I could."

Lacey felt the color drain from her face as her cheeks grew cold. They would still be after Brandy, wouldn't they? It was an echoing accusation more than a question in the far, terrified part of her mind. Of course, they would be. Carlos had told his uncle that they should leave the old woman alone; that he had a plan to get the money. Carlos was going to come after Brandy!

Clammy palms.

Shortness of breath.

Her chest ached, pressure like an elephant sitting on her built over her ribs. The tightness in Lacey's lungs pushed all of the air out. She sucked in a deep, useless breath and rushed to her purse. The contents of the bag found their way onto the counter as she searched for her medication.

Everything was going to be alright.

Everything was going to be alright.

Nobody wanted to kill her anymore.

Nobody had any reason to hurt her anymore.

Except the mob. Except the god damned Las Vegas mob!

She finally found her medication, wrestled off the lid and poured three tablets into her palm. She slammed them into her mouth, swallowing them dry before grabbing her glass of wine and taking a huge swig.

It was just like before. When those assholes ran her off the road, when they nearly killed her, they weren't after her. They'd been after Kendra. It didn't matter that the mob had no reason to come for her directly. She could get caught in the crossfire again.

And the crossfire can kill you.

Brad's pale, lifeless face stared back at her from the darkness of a grave. She squeezed her eyes closed, but the image seared itself to the backs of her eyelids.

Brandy grabbed her shoulder and swung her around. "What did you just take?"

Forcing her eyes open, she replied, "My medicine. Panic. Panic attack. I'll be fine in a minute."

"Jesus. How many did you take?"

"I'm fine. Let go of me!" Lacey shrugged out of Brandy's grip and took long, determined strides to the sofa. She sat in her corner and pulled the throw blanket over her curled legs.

Nobody had any reason to harm her anymore. Nobody could ever do more damage to her than had already been done. Not without killing her. And nobody had any reason to kill her.

Except, they do.

Except it didn't matter if they did.

She closed her eyes and placed her palms over her ears. Her mantra attacked her. Again and again the sound deafened her reason.

"Lacey!"

Brandy's voice cut through the nightmare. Like a light to a dark shore, it forced Lacey to focus on a way out of the panic. When she opened her eyes, Brandy was crouching above her, her face just inches from Lacey's. So close that their breaths mingled.

"Lacey, I will never let anyone hurt you. I will do anything I have to, but nobody is ever going to hurt you again."

"But, how can you-"

"I promise you this. I promise that if someone wants to get to you, they have to get through me, and I'm not easy to kill."

Lacey's entire body thrummed with a desire she'd never known before. Suddenly, she didn't want or need protection. She just wanted and needed. She needed to belong to someone so fiercely that she could trust them to care what happened to her. She wanted a mark on her soul that announced to time and all eternity that she belonged to someone else; that she had a guardian over her heart and her soul. Over her very existence.

"Can you promise me that? Can you really?" Lacey had never hoped for anything so much in her life as she did in that moment.

"Yes. Oh, God, yes, I can promise you that and so much more."

Lacey took Brandy's face in her hands and pulled her

down to meet her lips. The kiss was urgent and soothing and raw and filled with all of those unspoken promises. Brandy tasted like scotch whiskey and spice and forever. Her body unfurled beneath the blanket as it slipped away to land silently on the floor next to the couch.

Brandy lowered her body to blend with Lacey's. Her hands touched Lacey everywhere at once, with heat and passion that seemed to leap from her fingertips directly into Lacey's flesh. They scorched her and left a trail of fire in their wake.

When Brandy found her way under Lacey's skirt, Lacey's hips arched with anticipation and a basic need. Brandy pulled her mouth away from Lacey's throat and pierced her with an anxious gleam in her shimmering, almost-black eyes. "Are you sure?"

"Yes, please. Don't stop," Lacey pleaded. If Brandy stopped now, she would implode. She would die instantly, and Brandy had promised that nobody would ever harm her again. Surely, she included herself in that promise. Brandy would never harm her. "Please, please," she panted, placing kisses like exclamation points in the hollow at the base of Brandy's throat.

"Yes!" she panted. Instantly, she pushed the soft cotton barrier of fabric away from Lacey's center and pressed two fingers inside the swollen folds. They found their target immediately and with practiced elegance began to dance there.

The rising tide beat against the rhythm of a caress so intimate that Lacey could see forever in the darkness of her own eyelids. Images of fear displaced by shimmering hope. She forced herself to leave that infinity behind as she opened her eyes to stare deeply into Brandy's dark orbs.

Passion resided there. As she worked against the flesh of Lacey's finite interior, Brandy's hips pushed against the exterior with forceful, needy strokes. Lacey met every thrust, willing Brandy deeper; into her body and into her soul.

When the crest broke and the salty sweet wave of passion crashed into the shore, Brandy's scream blended with Lacey's ethereal cry. Lacey pressed her thighs together, trapping Brandy's hand as her lover milked her dry with each bold stroke. When the pleasure turned to the beginnings of a sweet, torturous agony, Lacey froze, and the enormity of her orgasm swept her to that safe place Brandy had created for her.

She landed, weeping and utterly spent, on the soft bed of roses Brandy had prepared for her without even trying. Or perhaps she had tried. Perhaps that had been the difference. Brandy had been willful and mindful of what Lacey had needed.

She needed to feel safe.

She wasn't safe, but at least for those few minutes, she had been able to feel completely protected from everyone and everything outside of that single instant.

Brandy collapsed, her head resting on Lacey's breast. "Are you alright?" she asked, her voice slightly muffled by the fabric of Lacey's shirt.

"Wonderful…"

"Good. I say we go to bed now and we don't sleep until dawn."

CHAPTER TWELVE

Brandy sat upright, her heart thumping wildly. She listened intently for whatever had woken her. Only silence filled the bedroom she'd begun to think of as her own. Maybe she'd been dreaming? After a few seconds, she began to relax, glancing at the clock.

4:17 a.m.

She had only been asleep for a couple of hours at the most. Her entire body ached with that pleasant, overworked feeling that came from making love, over and over again, until sleep had waged a war on them and won.

The bundle of sated woman next to her wiggled beneath the light coverlet. The room was freezing, and Lacey still wore her top; high collar, long sleeves and all. She'd refused to take it off, admitting after they'd made love twice more that she wasn't comfortable with her body. Brandy didn't care what her body looked like. She'd realized during that conversation that she hadn't even noticed the scar on Lacey's face for quite some time. It was a part of her; part of all the things that had happened to create the woman she was falling in love with.

Brandy reclined back onto her pillow, propping herself

on one arm as she trailed her fingers through the long, wavy blonde strands that spread like a fan over the pillow. Lacey stirred at the touch, but didn't awaken. Instead, she curled toward Brandy and reached for her with delicate fingertips that brushed against Brandy's naked breast.

Their lovemaking had lasted for hours, at times hurried and ravenous. Other times, it had been slow and seemed almost reverent as they nurtured each other from a place of total abandon to a point of triumph and power. She could do this for the rest of her life. She could never discover all of the intricate, inner places of this woman who had taken her heart from the gutters of her own disappointment.

All that had changed when Lacey had loved her.

A sudden crash came from the living room. It snapped her attention away from Lacey's still form. She leaped from the bed, grabbing and then pulling on a t-shirt over her bare breasts, she searched her immediate surroundings for anything she could use as a weapon.

Her frantic gaze fell on a baseball bat propped in the corner. She snatched it and held it in one hand as she listened behind her closed door.

"Fuck!" The male voice echoed in the stillness. Whoever he was, he wasn't even trying to be quiet.

She frowned. Did he think nobody was home? How the hell had he gotten in?

Lacey stirred, propping herself half-upright. "What's the matter?"

"Someone's out there," Brandy whispered. "Don't move."

Lacey sat upright and wiped sleep from her eyes. "What

are you talking about?"

Another crash.

Lacey was instantly awake. "What was that?" She threw her shapely legs over the side of the bed and pulled on her skirt from the night before.

Biting her lip, Brandy looked at her bedside table for her cell phone. It wasn't there. She'd developed the habit of leaving it on the kitchen bar deliberately to avoid the temptation to check the news feeds. There was no land line. She swallowed hard. Should she wait and hope the intruder wouldn't find them? Or confront him?

Carlos Maretti's face formed in her mind. What if this wasn't a coincidence? What if he'd seen them earlier? What if he suspected that they knew something about what had happened? He could have followed them here.

How could he have bypassed security? How did he have the code for the elevator? Her stomach somersaulted.

Unwilling to leave their fate in the hands of patience, she turned the doorknob as quietly as she could. She had surprise on her side and if she played her cards right, she might be able to ambush him, knock him senseless with one swing. Then she could get Lacey out of the condo before the shock wore off. Thankful for twelve years of organized softball leagues, she pulled open the door.

The hallway was dark, but the muted light from the living room beckoned her forward. She crept along the wall, the bat held aloft in both hands as though she were crowding home plate. When she reached the end of the hall, she peered stealthily around the corner.

A huge man in a black leather jacket and jeans stood at the kitchen island with his back facing her. His head was bent slightly, checking his phone like he hadn't just broken into a private residence. Just as she was about to rush him, the cell phone rang. The stranger answered it.

"Hey, sis," he said, turning around. His eyes grew wide as he saw her.

Brandy screamed and lunged at him, swinging the bat. The man had reflexes like a cat and she only managed to graze one heavily muscled arm.

"Christ!" he bellowed, nearly dropping the cell phone. With agility that belied his size, he skirted to the kitchen side of the bar and held up both hands, one of which still held the cell phone. "Put down the bat, lady. I don't know who you are, but this is my place."

"The hell it is, you son of a bitch. How did you get in here!"

A muffled voice screeched from the cell phone. Brandy was too far away to make out the words, but a second later the stranger pressed the speaker-phone option.

"...and we forgot to tell you before you left. She's staying in the spare bedroom for a while."

"Kendra?" Brandy asked, shouting at the cell phone as she lowered the bat slightly and stood straighter.

The man sprang at her, pinning her arms to her side as he knocked the bat out of her hand. It clattered as it hit the naked tiles. "Who are you?" he demanded, spinning her away from him and kicking the bat out of reach before he tossed her onto the couch.

"Casey! Listen to me," Kendra shouted. "Brandy Kincaid

is staying at the condo. She's supposed to be there. We forgot to tell you about it before you left, and she doesn't know you're coming."

"Casey?" Brandy asked. "You're Lacey's brother?"

Casey took the phone off speaker and pressed it to the side of his head. With his free hand, he wiped his face from his eyes to his chin. "Yeah," he stated flatly. "I just met her. Thanks for the heads-up." After a few parting words, he disconnected the phone call and picked up the bat.

"You've got a pretty good swing, lady. Maybe you should go pro. In the meantime, you want to put on some pants?"

Lacey raced into the living room. Brandy was sitting on the sofa, shaking her head. Casey stood next to the kitchen bar, tucking his phone into a leather holster attached to his hip.

"Casey! What are you doing here?" She leaped in his arms. He rewarded her with a tight bear hug that all but squeezed her breathless. "Why didn't you tell me you were coming?"

"Hey, little sis. I didn't know myself until last night." He kissed the top of her head.

"Are you okay? Brandy didn't hurt you, did she?"

He canted his head slightly and drilled her with an accusing stare. "Who are you talkin' to? Her? Hurt me? I don't think so."

"Hey, I did have a bat. I mean, I could have…"

Lacey had almost forgotten Brandy was still in the room.

She hadn't seen her brother in nearly a year. The last time the family had made a trip to Vegas, he'd been working out of state and couldn't come with them. And she hadn't been home since... since Michelle and Kendra had insisted she stand on her own two feet. How long ago was that? Over a year ago?

"Are you alright, babe? He didn't hurt you? Casey, if you put so much as a bruise on her, I swear-"

"She came at me with a Louisville Slugger, Lace! What was I supposed to do?"

"I'm fine. I think my ego is more damaged than anything. If it's okay with you two, I'm going to take Casey's suggestion and put on some pants."

Brandy stood, and the moonlight reflected on her bare legs. Just beneath the hem of a Hard Rock Cafe t-shirt, the edges of her boy-short boxers caught her attention. Her insides clenched with ghost-like waves of remembered passion. Her body was amazing. Taut. Perfect.

After Brandy vanished into the hall, Lacey turned her attention back to her older twin brother. "So, what are you doing here? You needed some time off in the playground?"

"Not exactly." He frowned as he shucked his jacket and sat heavily on the sofa.

"Not exactly?" Lacey folded her arms. "Sounds ominous."

"C'mon, Lace. You know why I'm here, right?"

"No, I don't." Or maybe she did. Fear replaced the lingering passion and her breath hitched.

"The girls were afraid that you wouldn't come back

home when they called, so they sent you an escort. Me."

"I would have come on my own. You didn't have to drive all night to get here."

"Yeah, well, the Virgin Gorge is a pretty spectacular place at midnight from the back of a Harley. I didn't mind."

"When?" Lacey sat in the armchair and hugged her knees to her chest.

"Sometime this week."

"That soon?"

Her brother nodded.

"I thought I'd have more time. I mean, I knew it was coming, but I... I just thought I had more time."

"We'll all be there. You're not going to go through this alone." He reached across the coffee table and took her hand.

Brandy reappeared and knelt at the side of the chair. "You're talking about the trial, aren't you?" She placed a kiss on the back of Lacey's hand and held it to her cheek.

"Yeah. Apparently, they're ready for me. I have to go home for a while. I'm not sure how long. A couple of days, maybe."

"Could be longer. I'd plan on at least a week. The trial is moving pretty slowly."

"A week, then."

"I'll go with you."

Lacey's heart found purchase in the back of her throat. "You don't have to do that. You have so much going on here."

Brandy laughed. "Like what? I can't work. Hell, I'm not even supposed to go into the casino until this whole thing is over and done. I have nothing to keep me here, except you. If you're not here, I have no desire to be."

Lacey's cheeks warmed and the panic rising in her chest wavered.

"Am I missing something?" Casey asked, sitting slightly forward. "Lacey? Why aren't you at your place?" He paused, glancing at their clasped hands. "Oh. Oh! Okay, never mind. I don't need to know. Fine, yeah, sure. Brandy can come with us. You'll need to bring your own car, though. Like I said, I'm on the bike."

"Of course. Are you coming back right away, too, or are you going to hang out for a while?"

"I'm dead heading. I testify right after you." Casey picked up the TV remote and turned on the screen. "Ya'll go do whatever it was you were doing… quietly, please, and I'll just catch up on the world for a few hours. If we leave after breakfast, we'll get to the Heartland by dinnertime."

Lacey flipped her brother off as she got to her feet. "We were sleeping, smart ass."

"Yeah. That's what you're calling it these days? Cool."

Brandy snickered. "I'm not tired anymore," she quipped with a wink.

"You're insatiable, that's what you are." Lacey giggled and skipped down the hall to the bedroom.

As much as they played around to irritate her brother, it was obvious when they reached the room that Brandy had packing on her mind. She pulled her suitcase from the top of the closet.

"I'll have to go down to my place to pack." Lacey chewed on the side of her mouth for a second as Brandy dug her limited wardrobe out of a dresser drawer. "You're sure you don't mind coming with me?"

"Of course not." She kept packing.

"Because, I'm really glad that you are. I mean, I am not going to lie about this. I'm a little freaked out by the whole thing. With you there, I think I can actually do it."

Brandy stopped packing, dropping the handful of socks into the case before circling the bed to take Lacey into a soft embrace. She pushed the hair away from Lacey's cheek and tucked it behind her ear. For the first time she could remember, Lacey didn't flinch. She wasn't driven with the overbearing need to cover her scar. When she looked at Brandy, she felt like who she used to be; the pretty girl with the tiara collection and a picture on the courthouse wall with all the other pageant winners. She felt whole. She felt beautiful.

Almost beautiful.

She frowned as the real world pounded on the exterior of her tiny little fantasy.

She felt... not as ugly.

Casey's face peered around the slightly opened bedroom door. "You girls may want to step it up. The sooner we get out of here, the better."

"What's going on?" Lacey asked, clearing her throat.

"You might want to take a look at the news. Come on."

The scene on the television was almost too dark to make out and the "LIVE" label flashed on a red stripe across the bottom of the screen. Kevin Conrad was on screen, reporting something from Lake Mead. He moved slightly to his left and the camera followed him, revealing his location as the marina where Lacey and Brandy had rented the speed boat.

As the camera angle zoomed past him, John Miller's enormous boat was being towed to the marina where his slip had been waiting, empty, for nearly two weeks.

"Kevin, can you tell us what they know, so far?"

"Right now, all the authorities are telling us is that the body of a local playboy, John Miller, was found in the freezer of his yacht by Arizona sheriff's deputies in the Search and Rescue squad after a call came in to do a welfare check on the vessel. It had apparently been anchored in the same place with a dive flag on display for quite some time when a group of kids from Tempe University, who had been partying on a houseboat in the same cove, realized the diver had never surfaced."

"Are there any leads?"

"Yes, actually. Authorities are looking for Brandy Kincaid and former KLVN news reporter Lacey Williams as persons-of-interest in the ongoing investigation. Apparently, this image..." the screen changed to a still photograph of a speed boat leaving the yacht, "...was captured by a boat of tourists just a couple of days prior to the discovery of the body. It was rented from the marina by Lacey Williams and when the desk clerk was shown a photograph, he identified Brandy Kincaid. If you'll recall, Melanie, Mrs. Kincaid is currently under indictment for the murder of her wife, Cynthia Kincaid, in Las Vegas."

"Turn it off." Brandy ran both hands through her hair, scrubbing her scalp with her fingertips. "Just... turn it off!"

"Miller is dead? How can he be dead? He wasn't even on the boat when we were there!" Lacey pulled Brandy into an embrace, the other woman's frame trembling like a small earthquake.

"So, you guys were there?"

"Yeah. We were there. But he wasn't dead!" Brandy nearly shouted.

"We didn't look in the freezer," Lacey whispered.

"What?" Casey asked.

"I said, 'We didn't look in the freezer.' Why in the name of all that is holy would we look in the freezer?"

"Why were you there at all?" Casey cut the TV signal and chucked the remote onto the sofa. He placed both hands on his narrow hips.

"Because my dead, ex-wife who wasn't really my wife was having an affair with her ex-husband who wasn't her ex-husband."

Brandy stood by the door as Lacey hurried through her bedroom and collected everything she might need for a week, or longer as it may turn out, in Utah. When she finished, she slammed her suitcase closed and pulled the zipper around, catching her finger in the teeth. "Ow!" she cried, sucking on her fingertip and stamping one foot.

"Are you about done?" Casey called from the other room.

Brandy hurried to the bedroom door and shouted back. "In a minute! Christ!"

A heavy groan replied.

"He's a bit on the touchy side, isn't he?"

"You did hit him with a bat," Lacey mumbled around the tip of her finger.

Brandy slid next to her and took Lacey's injured hand in both of hers. Then she placed a short kiss on her finger with a wry grin. "I can still taste you."

Lacey blushed the color of spring roses as she pulled her finger away. "I think I've got everything. He's right. We should go now."

"Yeah. I know."

"Like, right now." Lacey picked up her suitcase and set it on its wheels.

"Yeah. I get it. We should leave. Now." Brandy moved closer to Lacey, eliminating even the air between them.

"Brandy!"

Brandy allowed her shoulders to slump and she dropped her hands to her sides in an exaggerated expression of defeat. "Alright. You win," she teased. Then she took the suitcase, extended the handle and pulled it behind her out the door. Lacey followed.

Brandy didn't have to turn around to know that her cheeks still held the soft pink of her blush.

Leaving town hadn't been in her plans. She'd thought about calling Marko to let him know where she'd be, but thought better of it before she'd dialed the number. The less he knew, the better. She didn't want him to even consider lying on her behalf. The same thing applied to her managers at the casino. They could handle things.

She'd call Chandra once they arrived at Kendra's ranch. By then, it would be well into normal business hours. Not that it mattered. She could all Chandra at home, but something told her she shouldn't inform her attorney that she was going on the lam.

It's not like there was yet another warrant for her arrest. She and Lacey were "persons-of-interest," not suspects. Right?

The cops just wanted to talk to them to see what they knew. But if the cops had searched the boat, which they most certainly had by now, it was only a matter of time before they realized the connection between Cynthia and Miller. That would up the ante on their reasons for wanting to have a conversation with her.

On the way down to the parking garage, in the silent, tense atmosphere of the elevator, Brandy thought hard about what she might be forgetting. It wasn't like she had to worry about leaving the garage door open, but she couldn't escape the niggling feeling that she was leaving something behind.

The weekly deposit in her office safe.

She'd forgotten all about it with all the changes in her routine the past few days. Yesterday was Friday. That meant that her casino manager would have placed fifteen thousand dollars in petty cash in her office safe.

"I have to make a detour," she announced.

There was a soft pause before Casey asked, "What kind of detour?"

"I have to get something out of the safe in my office. It's important."

The large man sighed and rubbed the bridge of his

nose. "Alright. We can stop by on the way out of town, but that's it. After that, we're on the road and we're not stopping until we hit the Heartland."

"Understood, Heir Commandant."

"Not funny."

"Lighten up."

Lacey shook her head. "This is going to be dreamy, isn't it? Thank God we're not riding in the same car."

"You got that right," Brandy and Casey answered at once.

After the short drive to the casino, Brandy hurried up the back entrance to her office. The sun hadn't yet risen and the casino was nearly empty. She was able to slide through the upper deck and into her office without encountering a single employee.

She entered her office and her eyes fell immediately on the slightly open safe door. She had to remember to get that fixed as soon as this whole thing was over.

In just a few long strides, she arrived at the safe and pulled it open, so she could reach inside. The envelope was there, near the back of the two-foot cube. She pulled it out and flipped it over to open the seal. Smears of something dark dotted the outside of the manila-colored paper. She frowned. It looked like...

Flipping on the desk lamp she peered into the solid steel cube.

Sitting directly in the center of the safe, in front of the velvet box that held her mother's pearls, was a handgun. Not just any handgun. Her handgun. A Glock 19, Gen 4, 9-millimeter that she'd kept in her bedside table at her house. Rather, at Cynthia's house. She hadn't actually seen it in months, she realized. She frowned, backing away from the safe. The last time she had seen it, it was definitely not here in the casino office. It had been in her bedroom in Mission Hills. She was certain of it.

How had it gotten here?

She pulled the gun out of the safe and stared at it in the full light. The barrel was stained. Her stomach hit her knees and she choked back the threat of nausea. Was that really blood?

Was there blood on the barrel?

Christ!

She dropped the gun on the desk and it made a loud crack as the metal casing hit the surface.

She pulled the cash out of its stained envelope, stuffed it into a new envelope she'd pulled from the desk drawer, and then wrapped the envelope into a tube around the cash. She shoved it into the back of her waistband.

The gun was another matter. Should she leave it where she'd found it? Should she take it with her and get rid of it? What if they were stopped on the way out of town? What if they were arrested and the cops searched the truck?

She hadn't put the gun in the safe. That's just about the only thing she knew for certain. Someone had snuck into her office and planted it there. But who? Only her immediate staff had the keys and the combination...

The safe was broken. If it had fallen open, anyone could have put the gun inside. But how did they get into her office in the first place?

She swallowed against the searing burn in her throat. Her stomach roiled.

Leave the gun. Take the cannoli.

Better to not be caught with it in hand. If the cops searched her office, there would be a video record of anyone who had gone in or out of the door. Unfortunately, that now included her for the first time in more than a week.

She slammed the safe out of habit and hurried back to the parking garage. When she leaped into the driver's seat of her Range Rover, which they'd decided to take to Utah for purely mercenary and legroom reasons, she threw it into gear. With a quick wave to Casey, who was sitting on his motorcycle a few feet away, she took off.

"What took so long? Everything okay?" Lacey asked.

"Just had to wrap up a couple of things." Brandy drove to the interstate. Once she'd merged into the North-bound traffic on I-15, she set her cruise control at precisely one mile per hour under the speed limit. Checking her rear view, she watched as Casey drew his motorcycle into line behind her. She shifted in her seat and finally removed the bulky package from the waistband of her jeans and tossed it into the back seat.

"What was that? What did you grab?"

"Just some traveling cash. My weekly deposit at the casino."

"You get paid in cash? That's not shady or anything," Lacey laughed.

"It's the petty cash deposit. If the cops search my office, I didn't want them to confiscate it and screw over my staff.

They might not need it but I figure I can always wire it to them if anything comes up, right?"

"Sure." Lacey paused as her gaze burned a hole in the side of Brandy's face. "There's something else going on though. I can see it written all over you. What happened? Did you run into someone while you were in the office?"

"No, I didn't run into anyone."

"What's got you so flustered then?"

Brandy forced a smile. Turning to face Lacey, she said, "I'm just worried a little about the whole Miller thing, that's all. Really. Aren't you?" She picked up Lacey's hand, entwined their fingers and then brought it to her lips. She placed a kiss on the back of her hand and then lowered it to the center console box.

"Brandy, you're hurting me."

CHAPTER THIRTEEN

"There are my favorite fugitives!" Kendra yelled from the front porch of what must be the family home at the Heartland Ranch. Brandy waved in her direction and then moved to the back of the truck to unload the luggage.

The house was large compared to many of those they'd passed along the way. Ranch houses built over a century ago, despite what fans of Bonanza had been led to believe during an earlier generation, weren't often mansions. Generally, they were only big enough to allow for one or two private bedrooms and the bulk of the children slept in a loft. This house, in a simple Victorian style covered with white clapboard, black shutters and flower boxes under the windows, looked like something out of a story book. It would be considered large even by today's standards.

The sound of metal-on-metal drew her attention to a weather vane on the highest peak of an enormous, three-story barn. The vane depicted an old nursery rhyme. A dish and a spoon spun on one side of the crossbar and a dog jumped over a full moon on the other.

"That was horrible!" Michelle appeared on the porch

and gently slapped Kendra on the shoulder.

"What? Too soon?"

Lacey offered to help with the bags, but Brandy declined and told her to go inside. "I'll only be a minute, sweetheart. Go hug your sister."

As she approached the porch, Lacey limped just enough that Brandy frowned. They should have taken more breaks along the way. They'd both been hell bent to get here as quickly as possible, but it had only been a couple of hours before it was obvious Lacey was in some amount of pain. She'd finally confessed that she hadn't ever completely healed from the accident and her muscles were still sore if she sat for too long. She'd offered to stop several times, but Lacey had insisted they keep moving. Adamant that she wasn't in a rush to get home for any reason other than they weren't necessarily safe on the roads should they get pulled over. Had it not been for that small fact, she would have preferred not to go home at all.

"I'm guessing you've heard the latest, then?" Lacey asked, slowly climbing the wooden stairs onto the porch. She hugged Kendra.

Kendra squeezed her tightly and Brandy could almost feel it herself. The love Kendra poured out to her younger sister was practically tangible. The soft sound of Lacey's voice carried the distance to where Brandy had parked next to Casey's bike like dandelion snow on a summer breeze. It warmed her to the very center of her existence.

"Casey came in about a half-hour ago and he filled us in," Kendra stated.

"Huh. I figured he would just head to his place. He roared past us as soon as we turned off Highway 10."

"That man drives like a crazy person," Brandy yelled from the rear of the SUV. "He should be arrested!"

"Yeah, we know. But... he is a crazy person, so there isn't much anyone can do!" Kendra hollered back."

Michelle glared at Kendra, turning the conversation back on track. "The national news picked up the story, linking the whole thing to Cynthia's murder."

"I'm surprised it took them this long," Lacey announced.

With one bag hoisted over her shoulder and the other on its rollers, Brandy manhandled the bags onto the porch. Kendra immediately took the smaller one off her hands and invited her inside. "We're putting you in my Grandma's old room, if that's okay."

Brandy looked at Lacey who smiled. "It's okay. I'll stay there too, since my room only has a twin bed." She winked.

Kendra and Michelle froze on the bottom steps of the staircase they'd already begun to climb. Kendra turned slowly. "Excuse me?"

"I'll be staying in Grandma's room while we're here, too. With Brandy."

"Is that so?" Kendra sounded like a perturbed father.

Lacey laughed. "Don't get your nose out of joint, Kennie. I'm a big girl."

A tall, dark-haired cowboy strolled down the corridor rubbing a shining, red apple on the breast of his artfully-pressed shirtfront. He inspected his handiwork and took a chunk out of the fruit with a loud crunch. He said, with an enormous grin around the apple, "So, ya'll are going to be big ol' lesbians together, is that it?"

Lacey laughed again as she scurried to meet the man with the wide smile and dark, friendly eyes. "Brent!" She squeezed him as hard as Kendra had squeezed her as she looked up at him with adoration. It made her features glow even more brilliantly. Brandy hadn't thought that was possible.

"Brandy," she announced, leading the cowboy by his free hand. "This is my big brother, Brent. He's just teasing, you know. Brent, this is my... my friend, Brandy Kincaid."

"Very nice to meet you, Brandy. And don't let Kendra scare you off or anything. She's a little protective and likes to think she's in charge around here. We've found it's easier to let her think it than try to fight, so we just nod then do whatever we want."

"I get no respect," Kendra muttered as she hauled the suitcase up the stairs. "No respect, at all."

The way the family interacted with one another was at once charming and a little awkward. They were all so close, and she was an outsider. She didn't belong there and for a moment, despite the bantering and obvious sarcasm, she couldn't help but feel like an interloper. An intruder into this cohesive unit.

"Come on, Brandy. I'll show you the room," Michelle said, nodding up the stairs.

"Thanks. It was nice to meet you, Brent," she offered as she started up the stairs.

"I'll be right behind you, hon," Lacey added.

"She seems nice," Brent said as he and Lacey moved

into a room off the foyer that looked like something out of an antique catalog.

"Don't let them get to you. I know what you're feeling. I felt the same way when I first got here. The biggest difference is that I wasn't really welcome. At least, not by everyone." Michelle looked down the hall in the direction Kendra had gone.

"Yeah?"

"True story. Kendra didn't want me here at all. It may take her a little while to get used to the idea of her little sister sharing a room with someone here at home, but it's not like she is under some delusion that Lacey is a virgin or anything. This just removes all plausible deniability. That's all. If it's awkward for her, she'll get over it."

"I understand."

"Good, then here's where you'll be staying. Isn't it just gorgeous?"

Brandy crossed the threshold into a room that seemed to step out of the past. An enormous antique bed in dark, shining wood took up most of one wall. Small tables on either side held metal lamps with Tiffany-style stained glass shades. A matching dresser with an elegant, arched beveled mirror that nearly reached the ceiling stood guard on another wall. The surface had three sections, two of them higher than the center and each of them covered in marble. On one raised side, a bowl and matching water pitcher sat ready for some old cowboy to wash up before bed. Kendra had placed Lacey's suitcase on the antique chenille coverlet. The modern design seemed completely out of place. Out of time.

Setting the second suitcase near the first, she noticed a black and white photograph in an elaborate silver frame on the bedside stand. "Who's this?"

"That's Lacey's grandmother. This was her room until she died." Michelle was quick to add, "But she didn't actually die in here."

Brandy laughed. "That wouldn't really bother me, but thanks."

"Good. Well, then, okay. Welcome to the Heartland, Brandy. When you get settled, we'll be having supper in the dining room in about thirty minutes or so. I hope you're hungry. It's Brent's turn to cook, and when Brent cooks, we have steak."

"Thanks."

Michelle turned to leave, and then paused by the door. She placed one small hand on the frame and turned partly back into the room. "Brandy?"

"Yeah?" she answered, unzipping her bag.

"Thanks."

At the meaningful tone of Michelle's voice, Brandy turned to focus all of her attention on her friend. "For what?"

"For being nice to Lacey. She's been so alone the last couple of years, you know, since I barely get to the city anymore. She really needed someone, and I'm glad that someone is you."

Lacey ducked into the bathroom near the top of the stairs as Michelle walked past and headed back downstairs.

Once Michelle reached the bottom of the stairs, Lacey left the bathroom and crossed the hall into her Grandmother's old room.

Thanks for being nice to Lacey?

Seriously?

Of course, Michelle would think that being nice to Lacey, to care about Lacey, would require some monumental achievement by some outstanding and honorable person. A person who had a heart big enough to look past the ugly exterior to see the fabled beauty within.

She ignored the burn of tears behind her eyelids and smoothed her hair before entering the bedroom. "Did you pick a drawer?" Her voice cracked despite her attempt to keep it steady.

"Yup. I'm on the bottom. I didn't want you to have to bend over quite so far. How are your hips?"

"Much better, thanks. It doesn't take too long for them to loosen up again. You don't have to do anything special for me." Lacey turned her attention to her suitcase and pulled out her underthings to shove them into the top drawer of the old dresser. "I'm not crippled."

"Okay," Brandy replied, the word drawn out with a bewildered tone. "That's not what I meant?" It was more a question than a statement.

Lacey sensed more than saw Brandy's bristled posture. She glanced into the mirror and caught her reflection. She stood ramrod straight, wearing a frown and a halo made of confusion. Lacey turned back to grab another handful of items from her suitcase.

"I'm just saying that my problems are my problems and you don't have to go to any heroic lengths to babysit me. If I don't use my legs routinely, I'll lose them. So, bending to put away my panties isn't that big a deal."

"Whoa, baby. What's wrong? Did I do something?"

A sudden wisp of something like shame fell over Lacey's body, standing at the side of Grandma's bed in a place that should always feel safe, even if that was only a dream. She swallowed hard, placed the items she'd pulled from the suitcase back and turned to look at Brandy.

She still wore a mask of incomprehension that turned down the corners of her delicious lips.

It broke her heart.

"I'm sorry, Brandy. I don't know what got into me just now. I... I guess..." She released a pent-up breath. She didn't know what to say, so she said nothing.

"I didn't mean to patronize you, if that's what you thought. Maybe I'm just selfish. It hurts me when you hurt. It pains me to see you limp after driving here, and I just didn't want to cause you any more pain."

"I know. It was thoughtful." It was thoughtful, and she'd let her own insecurities turn her into a passive-aggressive monster. She could easily make excuses.

She was home when she didn't want to be home.

She was here for a reason she didn't want to face.

She was trapped in a body she hated, with visible reminders of a time in her life that had found her completely out of control of herself and her future.

She was frightened of what had happened to her and her brother.

She was frightened of the coming trial.

She was frightened of the investigation in Las Vegas and what that meant to her future; and Brandy's.

And she was terrified of what her future might hold both personally and professionally.

She was frightened.

It suddenly occurred to her that she was absolutely frightened of all of those things, and more, and yet...

She wasn't panicking. She wasn't reaching for her purse where she had placed her entire month of Xanax tablets. She wasn't curling into herself to disappear into the corner of her mind that served as her private hiding place from the world.

Instead, she was standing strong and tall, taking responsibility and admitting her own weaknesses.

Brandy approached her, one slow step at a time. "I can see the gears in your mind grinding... what are you thinking about?"

Lacey smiled. "They aren't grinding. For the first time in a long time, they're turning rather smoothly."

Lacey placed her arms around Brandy's waist and offered her lips for a kiss.

Brandy immediately obliged, intending to simply give her a quick peck. The moment their lips met, however, that intention flew directly out the window. Or into her jeans. She couldn't tell which, nor did she care.

She pressed her lips hard against Lacey's and then trailed the tip of her tongue against them, begging for entrance. Lacey obliged without further prompting and their mouths danced as the rhythm of the kiss spiraled heat throughout her entire, rigid frame. When they parted, each of them breathless, Brandy suddenly realized that it didn't matter if she belonged to the Heartland. She belonged to Lacey and that's all that mattered.

"Dinner! Come and get it!" Brent called up the stairs.

"We better go. Apparently, it's steak night," Brandy whispered, but not releasing her hold on Lacey's waist.

"Oh, goodie. I love me some dead cow."

Reluctantly, Brandy dropped her arms and they hurried down the stairs. They settled into two of the high-backed chairs that surrounded a massive table set with china and crystal. A platter covered with a dozen choice cuts of beef, dripping with juices, took up the center of the long table. Potatoes, asparagus, salad and even a basket of steaming, apparently homemade, dinner rolls filled every open space on the surface.

Kendra sat at one end of the table and Michelle sat at the other. Two precious little girls, twins so completely identical that Brandy was sure she'd never be able to tell them apart, sat on the opposite side. The twins had brilliant blue eyes that danced as they stared at Brandy. "And who are these little darlings?" she asked.

"This is Trina and Lyssa."

"I'm Trina," said the one on the right. "You're Miss Brandy, I think. Am I right, Mama K? Is that Miss Brandy?"

"Yes, it is. But we don't talk about people like they aren't here, do we?" Kendra admonished so gently that it didn't even sound like a scolding at all.

"No, ma'am. Sorry, Miss Brandy. Are you going to be staying here? If you're staying here, I can show you my horse. Her name is Prancer, because I got her for Christmas last year, and I really wanted a reindeer, but Mama M said they didn't like living where it was so hot in the summertime. So, we got a horse instead and we named her Prancer because I wanted a reindeer."

Her sister poked at her dinner roll with the tip of her fork as she added, "We are putting antler horns on him on Christmas, though, so he can pretend he's a reindeer."

Brandy took the platter of steak from Michelle and placed one of the cuts on her plate, grinning as she listened to the little girl prattle on. "I'd love to meet her," she responded. "What about you, Lyssa. Do you have a horse?"

"Yes, but my horse didn't want to be a reindeer. She likes being a horse."

It was easy for Brandy to forget that she had so little to smile about when she was faced with such precocious and adorable children. It was easy to forget that she was neck-deep in a pile of fertilizer when she sat around a table with friends, old and new, next to a woman who made her feel so invincible.

The sudden understanding that it wouldn't last forever, that she would have to return to the scene of the crime, literally, to fight for her very life, stole the joy for a moment. Lacey brushed her arm as she reached for a small plate of butter pats. The contact sent a deliberate shiver through her flesh.

If Lacey could face something like testifying in court about what had happened to her and to her brother, then

Brandy could certainly fight something as innocuous as a murder charge, right? She'd just borrow from Lacey's courage and determination. And for now, she'd refocus her attention on the more immediate problem. She couldn't reach the steak sauce.

Lacey handed her the bottle of A-1 before Brandy could ask for it.

Brandy grinned. "How did you know?"

Speaking around a bite of steak, Lacey replied. "I saw a bottle in your office that day Michelle and I came over."

"You mean the day we met?"

"Yeah," she said after she swallowed. "You were practically living there, I guess. I mean, who keeps A-1 steak sauce in their office?"

Brent pushed through the swinging door from the kitchen with a second platter of steaks and said, "I would totally do that."

"You're right, Brent. You totally would." Lacey laughed, and the girls joined her, even though they probably had no idea what the grown-ups were laughing at.

"Is everything okay at the condo, Brandy? Is there anything we can do for you while you're there?" Kendra reached forward and moved Trina's glass of milk away from the edge of the table before cutting herself another bite of her perfectly rare steak.

"It's wonderful. I really appreciate it, but you've done more than enough. I'll try not to be there much longer."

"Nonsense. Stay as long as you need or want to. There's plenty of room," Michelle added.

"Chell's right. Stay as long as you like."

"Thanks. You know, this is a really beautiful home you have here, too. It's so... so... homey."

"Thanks. We like it."

"I like it too, and me and sister get to live here forever. Did you know that, Miss Brandy? Mama K and Mama M are going to be our forever family."

"I did hear something about that. I think that's wonderful!"

"Adoption should be final next week, actually. Thanks to what those two women in town went through a few months ago, we shouldn't run into any snags."

"What two women?" Lacey asked.

"I don't think you know them, but they were fostering a little girl, and even though the birth mom and the foster care workers had no problem with the fosters adopting the kid, the judge ordered that she be placed in a 'normal' home with a mother and a father." Kendra's voice was the closest thing to bitter that Brandy had heard since she'd met her.

Michelle continued, "He said that research showed kids do better in hetero homes than with people 'like us.' Can you believe that?" She huffed. "I couldn't believe he would say such a thing, but he did. On the record!" Michelle shook her head and rolled her eyes.

"That's terrible. I'm guessing it all worked out?"

"Yes, fortunately. So much pressure came down, from the equality folks upstate and from the national press, that he changed his order even before it went into effect. Took himself right off the case, too. He's not our judge, thank goodness, but even if he were, I doubt he'd pull the same stunt a second time." Kendra placed her silverware on her plate and took a sip of her wine. "I guess it's true that activism can really make a difference. Michelle taught me that."

A knock on the front door reverberated through the entire house and Michelle pushed her chair away from the table in response. Just then, Brent appeared again from the swinging door. He said, "Don't get up, Michelle. I've got it."

He returned a couple of minutes later with a folded sheaf of papers in one hand.

When he handed them to Lacey, her complexion turned a ghostly white. All of the natural blush drained from her cheeks and her mouth fell open slightly, as though she wanted to say something but couldn't find the words. Finally, she took the papers and held them in both hands without opening them. She only stared, her eyes wide.

"Is that the summons?" Kendra asked.

Lacey nodded.

Michelle said, "Lacey, are you okay? Do you want me to open it for you?"

"No," Lacey squeaked before she cleared her throat. "No, it's okay. I've got it." She opened the folded sheet and after scanning the contents announced, "Wednesday. Three days from now. I have to be in court to testify against Mac in just three days."

CHAPTER FOURTEEN

"This is nice." Lacey pulled on the reins and brought Bethany to a halt next to a spring hidden in a copse of trees.

"It's beautiful," Brandy replied, mimicking Lacey's movements as she dismounted. "We're still on your property?"

"Yup. Pretty much as far as the eye can see. We're still on the Heartland Ranch, but most of the land out here is owned by the BLM. We just have forest service grazing rights up in the mountains, too. That's where the herd is now, actually. Kendra and the boys run them up there because it's cooler this time of year. In the fall, they'll drive them back."

"Drive, as in: cattle drive?"

Lacey nodded and pulled the picnic basket from behind Kendra's saddle.

"Here," Brandy announced. "Let me get that."

Lacey almost bristled, then reminded herself that Brandy was only being kind. There were so many little things Brandy did for her that could only be described as "gentlemanly." She opened doors. She held out her chair before she sat at the table. It didn't mean she thought Lacey was incapable. Lacey knew this, but sometimes needed to remind herself because she hated being weaker.

Swallowing against a small thrust of anxiety, she said, "Thanks."

Brandy pulled the basket down, gripped the handle with one hand and reached for Lacey's hand with the other. Lacey took it and relished the burst of energy that moved between them. "There's a path, just over here." She led Brandy through the trees and into a clearing.

"Wow."

"It's nice, right? And perfectly fresh, too. You can drink it, but if you do, you'll want to take the water from there." She pointed to the four-inch pipe that spouted a miniature fall of shimmering white water into the pool. "You never know what's been living in the pool, but the water from that pipe comes directly from the underground spring. Clean as the driven snow."

"I may own a horse breeding operation, but that was pretty much an investment and a desire to live outside of the city. I'll stick to Evian, if that's okay." Brandy laughed.

She had an amazing laugh, one that reminded Lacey of a summer breeze or a gentle rain. It wasn't the sound. It was the comfort. If Brandy was laughing, then everything must be right with the world, and that made Lacey feel safe.

After spreading a tablecloth in the driest part of the clearing they could find, they shared a lunch of roast beef sandwiches and macaroni salad. For dessert, Brent had packed them two slices of the apple pie he'd been baking when they'd arrived the day before.

Bellies full and separated as they were from the rest of the world, they laid back and watched the clouds pass overhead in the shapes of dragons, elephants and various video game characters.

Lacey snuggled against Brandy's side and lifted her head so she could see her face. She was so beautiful, the way the dappled rays of light dotted her features. "I wish we could stay here forever."

"Me, too."

"Do you think it would be horrible if I didn't go to court Wednesday, and we just... you know... made a run for the border?"

"No. But we wouldn't get very far. A certain judge in Vegas owns my passport at the moment."

And just like that, a pall fell over the day. Lacey had been so wrapped up in the nothingness of being, the serenity of simply existing at the edge of the spring, like she had when she was a little girl, that she'd nearly forgotten about everything hanging over them. A murder investigation. An indictment.

Brandy wasn't truly free. She might never be free again if Sal Crenshaw had her way. The sun peeked from behind a cloud and targeted them with bright, white light. Lacey squinted against the pain in her eyes until it receded again, leaving her in near twilight darkness.

No matter how beautiful or romantic a picnic was, it didn't remove what was coming. And before they even went back to Las Vegas, Lacey had to face her fears.

She had to face Mac, the only man standing trial for

killing Brad and Lenise, even though he hadn't pulled the trigger. The trigger man was dead. The three henchmen who had been arrested had all pleaded guilty and were already in prison. But the conspiracy charges extended to the old Randall County Sheriff. He'd covered up too many illegal maneuvers to count. Mac, who had failed to properly investigate the cattle rustling and other intimidation tactics Harold Mason had used in his attempt to steal the Heartland, because he'd been on the Mason payroll. Harold Mason had killed himself, but Mac had been arrested. Pulled away from the bloody corpse of his own daughter after Mason had shot her, point blank, in the head.

The old, familiar and terrifying panic formed in Lacey's chest, strangling her breath. She closed her eyes and willed it away, but it didn't listen to her. Images of her brother's face flashed in her mind's eyes. Lenise in her wedding dress standing in the corral, surrounded by the cowboys as she'd married Brad. Lenise in her wedding dress, lying in a pale pink coffin, a brand new bridal veil covering the hole in the side of her head that the mortician couldn't hide. The snapshot of an ultrasound tucked into the bridal bouquet her mother had insisted she carry into the afterlife.

The images changed, returning her to the wreckage of an old pickup truck. Glass shattered on the roadway, blood soaking the asphalt. A voice calling her name, over and over and over again.

"Lacey!" Brandy's voice penetrated the darkness.

Lacey was lying in a glade of soft grasses, surrounded by the shade of the trees and warmed by the spotted sunlight. The trickle of the cool spring gurgled against the stillness of the air. She curled into Brandy's arms and wept.

The most horrible sound she'd ever heard knifed through her brain. Brandy lifted her head off the pillow and forced her eyes open. "I will never get used to that!" It was the third time she'd awakened to the obnoxious metal triangle on the front porch that let the ranch hands know they could come around back to pick up their breakfast.

"Dawn comes early on a ranch." Lacey mumbled into her pillow.

It was the third time Brandy had heard that, too. "Good Lord. Did you wake up to that your entire childhood?"

"Nope." Lacey rolled over, straightening the long-sleeved t-shirt she'd slept in as she rose to sit with her back against the headboard. "Michelle started this little practice after she moved in. She said the least we could do was feed the hands a good, solid breakfast before they left to work the fence lines every day."

"Romanticize, much?" Brandy replied. "On the Rocking T, Juanita makes breakfast for everyone, too, but they set their goddamn cell phone alarms and get their asses to the table on their own. Someone should slap Michelle back to reality."

"Right?" Lacey laughed. "She'd seen too many westerns; that's the problem."

A knock sounded softly on the bedroom door. A second later, a tiny blonde head poked around the edge.

"I see you, Lyssa," Brandy chided gently. "If you want to come in, you can."

"I'm Trina." The little girl shoved open the door and ran to the bed, and then threw herself onto the mattress. She landed in Brandy's arms and squeezed her in a hug so enormous, she thought she might choke. If she did, it would be on her own heart. She kissed the top of Trina's head and smiled.

"I'll get it right one of these days."

"It's okay. Everybody messes it up. I missed you."

"You did? I missed you, too."

"I think I might have to be jealous," Lacey interjected, although her tone took away any sting. "I've been replaced already."

Brandy leaned over to place a kiss on Lacey's slightly parted lips. "Never," she whispered.

"Mama M says we're going into town today. I have to get dressed to go to the jester's house." Trina leapt from the bed and landed with a two-footed thud on the hardwood floor. She steadied herself with both hands, like she was on a high-wire, before she took off like a sprinter into the hall.

Brandy shook her head. "The jester's house?" She laid back on her pillow and turned to face Lacey.

Lacey's expression had closed. She wasn't smiling anymore. Instead, she bit her bottom lip and worried her fingers on the coverlet. "Court. That's where jester's live, remember? Someone must have mentioned that we're going to court."

For the past two days, Brandy had made it her life's

purpose to distract Lacey from what was coming. They went riding around the ranch in the evening, either on horseback or in the old Jeep Wrangler that Kendra, apparently, refused to replace no matter how banged and bruised it was. They spent several long hours playing chess in the parlor. They'd even helped move hay in the barn for a while before taking the girls into town for ice cream the previous morning. It had worked, too. There were a couple of times when Brandy could almost see the woman Lacey had been before. Not once since they arrived had she made a deliberate effort to hide her scar. In fact, for a couple hours yesterday, she'd worn her hair pulled back in a cloth-covered band. An actual ponytail had fallen from the back of her head to the nape of her neck, like a shimmering bundle of silk.

Monday afternoon, by the spring, Lacey had finally let out some of the pain she'd been hoarding like solid gold. Brandy had held Lacey while she'd cried for nearly an hour. So much anger, so much hurt had poured out of her it had been tangible. Her heart had ached – still ached – for her inability to make it better, to take away the sting of realization. Lacey was incredibly good at packing away her emotions and hiding them in tiny boxes in her mind. When those boxes opened, all of Pandora's evils came pouring out. Not one at a time, which would be easier to deal with, but all at once in a torrent wilder than a raging river.

Lacey had screamed at the man she was set to testify against today. She'd screamed at her sister for not protecting her. She'd screamed at her brother for dying. She'd screamed at herself for not being careful enough and ignoring her sister's orders to not leave the ranch by herself that day. She'd railed at her parents for dying in a plane crash and leaving her alone.

It didn't have to make sense. When she'd finished crying, when the tears had slowed, she had laughed through the final droplets. "I'm not sure where that came from. I honestly didn't feel alone back then. Kennie was a really great mom, you know, for a big sister."

Brandy understood where it had come from. It had come from the unrealistic but perfectly authentic wounds of a childhood she couldn't understand. It came from loss and it came from being unable to adequately cope with that loss.

But now?

Now, the Lacey she'd met in Las Vegas was back. She'd met with the prosecutor the previous afternoon. When she'd come back to the house, her entire demeanor had returned to the guarded, almost sullen, cloak she'd worn that first day.

"It's going to be okay, baby. We'll all be there for you."

"No. I... I'd rather you stay here."

"What?" Brandy sat up again, shifting her body so she could look directly at Lacey's narrowed eyes. "Of course, I should be there. I don't want you to go through this alone."

"I won't be alone. You said it yourself. 'We' will be there... Kennie and Michelle will be there. And Brent and Casey."

"You said that if I was there, you could get through this. You said that, back in Vegas. What's changed? Why don't you want me to go?"

"I don't know. I just don't." Lacey tossed the coverlet off

her legs and climbed from the bed. She yanked her purse from the rocking chair stationed in the near corner and pulled a medication bottle from inside. After twisting off the cap, she poured a couple of small, yellow tablets into her palm and threw them into her mouth. She swallowed without a drink, making a face that reminded Brandy of a little girl forcing down asparagus.

"Not good enough. I think I've earned the right to know why you think you don't need me."

"That's it. You got it. I don't need you. So, you can stay here and just hang out and we'll be back in a few hours."

"I don't buy that. Come on. At the very least, you owe me some kind of an explanation."

Lacey pulled on a pair of sweats. Her voice cracked as she said, "Please, don't do this. I'm sorry." A single tear formed on her curling lower eyelashes and then tumbled onto her cheek. "I do need you, but not there. Please, just wait for me here? I can't explain it. I don't even understand it, but I just... I don't know that I can do what I need to do if you're watching me do it."

Brandy sighed. "I don't like it. This is going to be really difficult for you. What kind of girlfriend would I be if I let you do it all alone?" She paused. What kind of girlfriend would she be if she forced herself into parts of Lacey's life that she wasn't yet ready to share?

Those damn boxes. Don't put me in one of those damn boxes!

"I don't like it. But I'll wait here."

Lacey's shoulders squared and she lifted her chin, her lips spreading into a meek smile. "Thank you," she offered in a trembling voice. "Just knowing you'll be here when I get back really means a lot to me."

"I still don't like it."

Lacey couldn't remember the last time she'd been so frightened. It was as though she were back in the old truck, lying on the asphalt, trapped between the jagged, broken windshield and the uncertainty of death all over again. She closed her eyes against the image, but she couldn't do a damn thing about the remembered scents of blood and gasoline.

Of fear.

She wished she were stronger. Brandy had been right, of course. Now that she sat on a bench in the narrow hallway behind the courtroom, she wished Brandy were sitting next to her. Holding her hand. Being her rock.

There were three other witnesses in the hall with her. They weren't testifying in the same trial and sat in a group near the entrance to a different courtroom. They held hands and every so often the woman in the middle sniffed back tears.

Lacey was alone. She didn't want to be. Not anymore.

But she knew what was going to happen inside her courtroom. Her meeting with the county attorney had prepared her for the questions he would ask. She'd given him her answers and he'd helped her form them into the best possible structure to help the state's case. He'd grilled her with the questions that Mac's lawyer was most likely to ask. Together, they'd covered the best ways to answer and come up with contingencies for possible traps.

She was ready to testify.

That wasn't the problem. No, the problem was the pictures. She didn't know if she had the strength to sit next to enormous, larger-than-life-sized images of her face that day in the ER. Pictures of her wounds, healed now, but still raw. Still painful. Still ugly.

That's why she'd insisted that Brandy not come to court with her. She didn't want Brandy to see her the same way that Lacey saw herself. Damaged.

Damaged and ugly.

"Lacey Williams." A bailiff in a starched gray uniform adorned with a half-dozen patches called her name. He stood an intimidating six feet or more, his bulk made even more threatening from the bullet proof vest he wore under his shirt.

"Here," she responded, gathering her purse and rising to stand on shaking knees. "I'm here."

"They're ready for you."

She took a deep breath and followed the officer into the bright courtroom.

It was packed. There had to be at least forty people crammed like sardines into rows of benches. It looked almost like a church meeting, everyone seated shoulder-to-shoulder in the pews, but nobody was happy to be there. Some of the faces, she recognized. Her high school math teacher was in the back row. He smiled at her, winked, and nodded his encouragement. She'd always liked Mr. Z.

Michelle and Kendra sat in the front row, directly

behind the prosecutor. He'd placed them there on purpose and had instructed her, if she had any problems at all, to look at her sister instead of him as she answered his questions. She didn't understand how that would make anything easier, since Kendra blamed herself more than anyone for what had happened. It was supposed to have been her driving the truck that day.

An easel holding several sheets of two-by-three-foot foam boards had been erected near the witness box. She avoided it with her eyes as she took her place in a hard, wooden chair behind a microphone.

As soon as she sat down, the same bailiff demanded that she rise. He administered the oath and Lacey answered with a nod.

"Ms. Williams, you'll have to answer verbally," the judge insisted. "For the record."

"Yes," she answered again.

"You may sit down, now, Ms. Williams."

She sat, her legs fairly vanishing beneath her.

"Ms. Williams, were you driving on Highway 6 on the day after your late brother's wedding, two years ago?"

"Yes."

"And were you involved in an automobile accident during that trip?"

"No, sir. I was not."

"Could you please elaborate?"

"My sister's truck, the one I was driving, was deliberately run off the road. It was not an accident."

"Do you know who ran you off the road?"

"Not at the time, but I learned their names later. They were hired by Harold Mason, and their intention had been to kill my sister. They didn't know I was in the truck, instead."

"Objection." Mac's attorney, a woman Lacey had known most of her life, stood and addressed the judge. Peggy McDonald was a shark in heels. She'd built a reputation in Randall County as an attorney who would sue her own mother so long as she got forty percent of the take and another notch on her mahogany desk. Lacey had worked closely with her during her reign as Miss Randall County because Peggy had been the president of the Chamber of Commerce that same year. "Speaks to information not in evidence, Your Honor. She's answering questions she hasn't been asked."

"Sustained," replied the judge. He looked down from his lofty perch and said, "Please answer only the questions you are asked, Ms. Williams."

The attorney asked her questions which allowed her to provide exactly the same information she'd just given. This time, opposing counsel seemed to accept the answers. Lacey's stomach burned. She just wanted to go home.

For the next hour, she explained every aspect of her injuries. A broken arm. A facial laceration. She'd nearly lost one eye.

She focused on Kennie and Michelle's faces. One moment, they looked at her with strength as they willed their own power into her. Other times, they could barely keep from crying themselves, much less keep a stiff upper lip on her behalf. When the attorney asked for permission to approach the bench and enter several exhibits into the record, Lacey thought her entire body would come apart. The world slowed to a crawl as the large man strode directly at her. When he finally reached her side, he said, "I'm going to show a few pictures to the jury now, Ms. Williams, to emphasize the pain and suffering that you endured at the hands of this horrible conspiracy to take over your family's ranch. Will you be able to identify the injuries and explain to the jury what they are looking at; how each injury came to be?"

Her mouth was too dry to answer, so she nodded quickly. The judge's comments from earlier sprang into her mind and she hastily added, "Yes."

The prosecutor moved immediately to the table he'd recently left, filled a plastic, disposable cup with ice water and handed it to her. She took a few short sips. In her current state, she didn't trust she could keep even small amounts of water down.

"Are you ready?"

"Yes."

He pulled away a single, blank piece of foam board to expose a close-up image of her face. It was the most gruesome of all the images he'd shown her when they'd met on Monday. He'd done it deliberately for the greatest emotional impact on the jury.

It worked. Three of the women jurors in the front row gasped. Mrs. Hall from the city library, sitting stoically and erect in the second row of the jury box, started to cry. Lacey had never seen her cry before. She always seemed as though she were made of cast iron; never smiling, never frowning. Just... there. Like a rock. Lording over every child in the small town with the threat of late fees and suspended borrowing privileges.

Seeing her cry at a photograph of Lacey's torn and bloodied features seemed wrong. Surreal.

Proof of just how ugly she really was.

"Ms. Williams, you have a scar on your cheek. Is that scar the result of the injuries depicted in this photograph?"

She nodded. "Yes. The laceration began here," she said pointing to a spot just above her temple, "and extended to my eye, and then traveled over my cheek, to my chin." In the image, the width and depth of the cut was obvious to anyone. It didn't take a doctor to understand that it was responsible for her scar. "I've undergone several cosmetic surgery procedures to reduce the effects, but they can't erase it. The scar on my face now will be there for the rest of my life."

He moved the image aside, but rested it on the floor, leaning it against the legs of the easel, so the jury could still see it. The angle made it appear as though her own distorted image was staring directly at her. She shivered.

The next image reflected the scar on her arm.

"And this image? What are we looking at in this picture?"

She pointed to her arm. "Just here."

The prosecutor looked to the judge and said, "Let the record reflect that the witness is indicating her upper, left arm." Then he continued to Lacey directly, "Can you raise your sleeve, so the jury can see the aftermath of that injury?"

She obeyed, her fingers trembling as she pulled up the loose sleeve of her blouse. Her stomach flipped as she did it, but she managed to tug the fabric to her shoulder. The scar was puckered and raised a half inch from her skin. It looked like a silver snake, complete with scales.

"Have you had any reconstructive surgery on this part of your body?"

"No, sir. This is what the scar on my face looked like originally. My therapist insisted on facial reconstruction, but I haven't inquired about having my arm fixed. I just cover it up." It wouldn't matter if she changed her arm. They couldn't make the scar vanish there any more than they could the scar on her face. She'd still be damaged goods.

Several more pictures revealed her lying in the hospital emergency room. She frowned, just as she had on Monday. She hadn't recalled, and still couldn't remember, anyone taking the horrid images at the time. Kendra explained that she'd been medicated heavily, and her lack of memory was normal. The sheriff's department, under the control of the very man sitting at the defendant's table, had insisted on the pictures for the case file. Had Mac ordered them to do it, knowing his own involvement in the conspiracy, or had the deputies just been following procedure? If he had suspected that these pictures would be used in a case against him, would he have destroyed them?

Probably. He probably would have destroyed the film or ordered his deputies not to take them in the first place.

The prosecutor revealed the final picture, taken months later. Whoever had prepared the images for court had been kind enough, at least, to cover Lacey's bare breasts with post-it notes. They looked like flapping, yellow pasties.

"Were the injuries in this photograph the result of the same event?"

"Yes, but it happened later." She closed her eyes, unable to look at herself, at her body, with such a vicious wound. That had been the final blow; it had removed what was left of her heart. Not literally, of course, but it had removed her ability to care anymore.

"Can you please elaborate?"

"It was about two months after I was run off the road. I thought I was having a panic attack, but my brother thought it was more serious. I'd been having chest pains all morning; trouble breathing. That sort of thing. I finally allowed him to take me to the ER and the doctor there discovered that I'd torn a part of the sack that surrounds my heart. The tear had been getting bigger and had developed an infection. That's why I was having pain. They had to do emergency surgery to fix the tear. Basically, I had open-heart surgery to save my life."

"What effect has this entire event had on your life, Lacey? Can you tell the jury what the impact has been?"

"Objection, Your Honor." The defense attorney stood up again. "The prosecutor is asking for a victim impact statement, which as this court knows very well, occurs during the sentencing phase. He's trying to unduly influence the jury."

"I can't sleep most nights, Peggy! I have trouble breathing at times. Panic attacks. Every time I drive on the interstate near a merge lane, I shake. Sometimes so hard I have to pull my damn car over. I fear things; people. I was trapped in the wreckage for more than an hour, awake the whole time. Do you have any idea how long an hour is when you think you're going to die? Have you ever been trapped like that? I've developed claustrophobia because of it, so I hate elevators. I hate stairwells, but sometimes they are easier than the elevator, so I force myself to gut through one or the other, even though climbing stairs makes it feel like a red-hot branding iron is burning through my thigh bone."

"Your Honor?" the defense attorney asked. "May I have a ruling on my objection? As well as an instruction for the jury to disregard the witness's answer in its entirety?"

Lacey bit her lip and turned her gaze to the ceiling in an attempt to hold back her tears. She wouldn't cry. She was too angry to cry. She wasn't weak, damn it!

"Overruled. The witness may finish her answer. Ms. Williams? You were saying…"

The tears came anyway. "I had landed my dream job for that fall. I was going to work for an affiliate station of a national network in Las Vegas. It wasn't on-air work, but it would lead to it. I had spent the previous five years studying broadcasting, communication and journalism at UNLV, and everything was going perfectly until that day. Because of the scarring left from that day, I can no longer be on-air talent for any TV station. My earning potential is down; my career options are limited. But that's not the worst part. No, the worst part is that it's entirely possible I will never be able to safely carry a child because of the stress it would place on my heart."

Never carry a child. Never know the simple, exhilarating brilliance of suckling her infant at her breast. Never.

She could no longer hold back the sting of the tears behind her eyelids. She wiped at them with the backs of her hands before the county attorney handed her a box of tissues.

"Lacey," he said, "Do you see in this courtroom one of the people responsible for what happened to you that day?"

She nodded. She didn't want to. She couldn't bring herself to say the words. Mac had been sitting next to his attorney the entire time, but only now did Lacey seek him out. He was staring at the surface of the table, as still as a post. If she answered out loud, it would make it all true. She didn't want it to be true. She didn't want Mac to be guilty of anything. She loved him. He'd helped her grow into the very woman she had been before.

And then he'd taken it away, just as profoundly.

She looked at Mac, sitting with bent shoulders as he stared at the tabletop. Fury burned her lungs. Burned her throat. Her limbs trembled and she clenched her fists. "Why!" she screamed. "Why, Mac? How could you do this!"

A single tear slid down his cheek.

CHAPTER FIFTEEN

Brandy sat in the lobby of the courthouse in the small town of Randall, Utah, watching the girls run in circles around a large, bronze statue of a coal miner. She'd told Lacey that she wouldn't go into the courtroom, but she'd been simply unable to stay at the ranch. As it turned out, Kendra and Michelle hadn't intended to take the girls to court, after all, and that had provided her the excuse she'd needed to come into town.

Lyssa had overheard a conversation between the adults and become so excited about seeing where a court jester lived that Brandy had leaped on the opportunity to be there, at least somewhat, for Lacey. She'd decided to bring the girls into town for more ice cream.

She glanced at the clock. It had been more than three hours. She and the little ones had already walked down Main Street and visited the local museum, bought the ice cream, and walked back. If the trial didn't break soon, she'd be forced to take the restless children outside again.

"Miss Brandy! Come look at this!" Trina called from around a corner.

Brandy stood more to corral the girls back into the foyer than to see what they'd found. When she turned the corner, both girls were staring up at a portrait. It was surrounded by other portraits, but this one image seemed to have garnered their interest more than the others. Brandy stopped directly behind them and stood eye level with a portrait of Lacey. Her wide, confident smile raised the hair on the back of Brandy's neck. Her flawless skin radiated warmth and her hair shimmered under the photographer's lights. A large, elaborate crown reflected that same lighting, covered in rhinestones as crystalline and pure as any diamond. A brass plate attached to the wide, wooden frame read, "Lacey Williams – Miss Randall County – 2006."

The photograph hadn't been taken straight-on, but at a slight angle, as most portraits were. Her gaze looked not into the camera but at a future full of hopes and dreams. The girl in the picture didn't have a scar on her cheek. She didn't wear a vest of fear or diluted ambition.

There were subtle differences in the shape of her face, as well. The eye, nearest to where the scar was now, was just a little higher at the corner, almost cat-like. Brandy hadn't noticed it before; that the shape of Lacey's eyes weren't absolutely identical.

Did Lacey believe she wasn't as beautiful as the girl in the portrait? Just because of a few physical changes?

"Miss Brandy?" Lyssa's voice brought Brandy back from wherever she'd gone; back from that place where Lacey used to live. "You look really sad. Did something bad happen?"

"I'm not sad, sweetheart. I'm just worried about your Aunt Lacey."

"When she comes back, you should give her a great big hug. Hugs help a lot of things."

Brandy led the girls back to the chairs in the lobby. "Your moms should be back soon. Let's wait for them here, okay?" They were great kids. She'd always thought she'd have children of her own someday. She wasn't necessarily interested in carrying a child herself, but she wasn't completely against the idea, either. When she and Cynthia had discussed it, in the beginning, they'd planned for Cynthia to be the one to carry a baby. Later, Cynthia had pushed away the idea more and more. By the time a few years had passed, Brandy had changed her mind, too.

It was decidedly good they hadn't had a child together. The fact Cynthia had been pregnant when she died had to be the result of a mistake on her part. The woman she knew would never get pregnant on purpose.

Of course, as it happened, she hadn't really known Cynthia at all, had she? If her suspicions were correct, Brandy had been nothing more than a mark for a long con. A good, old-fashioned target. She had been wealthy and lonely. Her so-called wife and her partner-husband had probably watched her for months. The thought sent a cold shiver over Brandy's back and made the hair on her arms stand on end.

But there must have been something more going on with Cynthia; something that had nothing to do with Brandy.

She'd been sleeping with two men – that they knew of. John Miller, her husband, and Carlos Maretti, her lover. Which of the two had fathered the child was anyone's guess. Had the medical examiner run any tests to determine whether Miller was the father, yet?

She pulled out her cell phone and dialed her attorney.

After the secretary put her call through, Chandra came on the line. "Where the hell are you?"

"Hello to you, too. Sorry. I meant to call when we got here."

"Nevermind that. Where are you? Nevermind. Wait. Wait. Don't answer that. Did you know the cops are looking for you? Somebody saw you leaving the scene of another murder. You want to tell me what the hell is going on?"

She took a few minutes to recount her and Lacey's visit to the yacht, emphasizing the fact that they had not encountered Miller at all, alive or dead. "What we did discover is that he and my wife had been married at one time. Lacey called a friend at the courthouse and apparently, they were still married. At least, they hadn't been divorced in Nevada. So, she wasn't really my wife, after all."

"That is interesting, isn't it?"

"We also found out that she was having an affair with Carlos Maretti. That's why I'm calling. Is there any way to find out who fathered her child? Is it possible that one or the other killed her in some kind of jealous rage?"

"Anything is possible, Brandy. I'll see what I can find out. How long are you planning to stay away?"

"For a while, I think. There really isn't anything in

Vegas I want or need to get back to right now. I mean, my next court date isn't for another month, right?"

"Just be back here by then. And call me once a week to check in." Brandy disconnected the call and slipped the phone back into her pocket.

Nearly an hour later, the courtroom doors slid open and a line of people exited, quickly filling the lobby. Brandy called the girls over to stand near her as they waited for Kendra, Michelle and the boys to come out.

She saw Lacey first. Lacey's eyes met hers and Brandy half-expected her to be angry she was there. The wide eyes and sudden tears told her differently. Despite obviously harried emotions, she seemed more relieved than angry.

It took only a couple of seconds before Lacey reached her, throwing herself into Brandy's arms. "I'm sorry. I'm sorry," she cried. "I'm so sorry."

"Shh. What are you sorry about, sweetheart? I'm here, aren't I?"

Lacey nodded, her face still buried in Brandy's shoulder as she held on for what seemed like dear-life.

"I'm not letting you go," Brandy whispered. When Kendra and Michelle approached, Brandy stroked the back of Lacey's head gently and asked, "Was it really bad?"

Kendra's lips formed a half smile as she shook her head. "Lacey was great. She really held it together."

"So, it was bad."

"Yeah. It wasn't fun," Casey interjected. "That's for damn sure. She did really well on direct. That bitch of a lawyer though, on cross-examination, really put the screws to her."

The blood in the back of Brandy's neck sizzled. "I thought it was open and shut. What kind of things did she ask her?"

"She asked her if she'd been drinking the day before, at Brad and Lennie's wedding, trying to make it sound like she might have still been drunk or something. Can you believe that? It had been almost twenty-four hours since the wedding. And then she kept trying to make it sound like the wreck was Lacey's fault and that the guy who confessed to running her off the road had been coerced into saying it. That he was just some innocent victim in the whole thing. He testified a couple of days ago, actually, with immunity on the murder and attempted murder aspects of the case, I might add, and so she brought up the whole plea-deal he's getting in exchange for talking."

"I don't want to talk about it," sniffed Lacey, finally pulling herself upright. "Can we not talk about it?" She found a tissue in her pocket and wiped her nose before running a hand through her hair. "I don't know about the rest of you, but I'm ready to go home. Can we go home, please?"

"Sure thing." Brandy took her hand and led her in the direction of the parking lot. Brandy's phone rang, and she answered it. "Yeah? That was fast."

Lacey listened to the one-sided conversation as they walked to Brandy's truck. Brandy started the engine and turned on the air conditioner full blast to fight the soaring, desert heat. Once Lacey climbed inside, she waved to Kendra, Michelle and the girls and told them she and Brandy would meet them at the ranch. Then she waited in the cab of the SUV while Brandy paced in the parking lot, her head bent as she listened intently. Every so often, she would talk, but Lacey couldn't hear her anymore. Whatever it was, it was serious.

Finally, after more than five minutes, she touched the screen and stared at it for long, slow seconds before sliding it back into her pocket. When she turned back to the truck, she was smiling. Well, not exactly smiling. More like, trying to smile even though she had no reason to.

Brandy opened the door and slid into the driver's seat. "That was Chandra. She tried to find out if the medical examiner is going to run tests to determine whether Miller was the father of Cynthia's baby. They've made the connection between the two of them, but they aren't really talking."

"That makes sense. And we knew they'd make that connection the same way we did, sooner rather than later. It'll be okay."

"In other news, Cynthia's parents have filed a wrongful death lawsuit against me, as of about ten minutes ago, and they're putting a hold on the probate. She thinks they are going to try to inherit whatever Cynthia would have gained from the divorce or better yet, win the wrongful death and take anything and everything I have."

"Wow. That didn't take long, did it? They buried her less than a week ago."

"Marion needs the money, right? To pay off Carlos Maretti."

"So, should we assume that they believed you were really married? Or are they just grasping at straws, hoping nobody will figure out that their lovely daughter would have received precisely nothing in the divorce? Gads, the whole thing gives me a headache."

Brandy backed slowly out of the parking stall. "I don't think God Himself knows what those people are thinking."

By the time they reached the highway, Brandy had settled back against the seat and taken Lacey's hand. "You're not mad at me for being at the courthouse?"

Lacey smiled, her heart swelling at the relief she'd felt when she'd seen Brandy waiting for her. She hadn't realized until that moment how much her very presence would mean to her. She must have been out of her mind to have asked her to stay behind. "No. I'm not mad at all." She paused and inhaled deeply. "It's not that I didn't want you there. It's just... I didn't want you to see the pictures," she finally announced.

Lacey stared at the floorboards between her feet, but she could feel Brandy's eyes on her for the moment she'd taken them off the road. When she sensed that Brandy had turned her gaze back to the traffic lanes, Lacey ventured a peek at her profile. Unable to read the expression, she continued. "The county attorney blew up the emergency room pictures and a few others to show the jury. They're so ugly. It's disgusting. I didn't want you to see the horrible scars all over... all over my body." Lacey couldn't stop the burning sensation in her throat from changing her voice slightly, but she managed to suck back the sob that threatened to escape.

"Is that what this is all about?" Brandy shook her head, easing the SUV from the surface streets onto Highway 6.

"You don't understand. If you saw them, you'd probably... I don't even know what."

"You must not think very highly of me."

"What? No, that's not true. It's just that, well, the scar on my face is pretty mild compared to the rest of them."

"Is that why you won't take off your shirt? Because you think I won't like you anymore? You think I'll leave?"

Lacey's conscious self, hearing the words fall from Brandy's perfectly soft lips, knew the concept was ridiculous. But there was another part of her, hidden somewhere in the cavernous rooms of her subconscious, who believed it. It was the place where the scared child inside Lacey lived in a dark corner, afraid of the world.

They rode in near silence for the last twenty miles to the Heartland turnoff. No sound, other than the whining of the tires on the old highway, filled the truck. Brandy still hadn't let go of her hand, but there was a palpable tension floating between them that seemed to grow with each passing mile.

Three miles shy of the turn that would take them to the ranch, Lacey almost yelled, "Pull over. Here. Pull over for a second."

Frowning, Brandy obeyed and stopped the car on the rocky shoulder of the narrow, two-lane highway bordered with an acceleration lane.

Lacey pushed open her door and climbed down from

the truck. Brandy followed and the two of them stood in the midst of a vast, empty desert landscape. The brush on each side of the road stretched for miles until it reached the base of the orange sandstone that formed the Bookcliff Mountains. "This is where it happened."

Brandy sucked in breath. "Here?"

Lacey nodded. "Right here. I was driving into town from the ranch to pick up some pictures I'd ordered from Wal-Mart. It was a simple errand, right? What could go wrong? One of them was this huge portrait on canvas I'd had blown up from Lenise's bridals. It was supposed to be my wedding gift to Brad and Lennie. Anyway, these two guys started tailgating me. They eventually pulled alongside me, in the oncoming traffic lane. One of them smiled at me." Her throat grew tight at the memory. "He smiled, that sonofabitch. He knew what they were going to do, and he was smiling about it!"

"You don't have to do this, Lace."

"Yes, I do." She steadied the panic forming in her chest. "They rammed into Kennie's pickup. I kept control the first time, scared out of my wits. But I managed to stay on the road. Then they fell behind me again, backing off a little. I think they thought I would be stupid enough to pull over. You know, to make a police report or whatever. Like it was a normal accident. But I knew better."

"Uh-huh."

"Well, yeah, because of everything that had been happening with Harold Mason trying to steal our land. Things had already turned violent. There'd been vandalism at the ranch and he'd been rustling our livestock; just killing them outright most of the time. He even started a stampede that killed a friend of ours."

"Yeah, Michelle told me."

"So, I didn't stop. I drove faster and faster. I just wanted to get through Cat Canyon, so when I got to Wellsville, that little town between here and Randall? There'd be witnesses there. They'd have to back off, right? They knew that too, I think. That's when they finally pitted me. You know? Like on the cop shows? But hard! They didn't just barely nudge my rear quarter panel. No, they rammed it and that was it. I was airborne. I'd been going so fast that the collision sent me into a spin and flipped the truck three or four times. Nobody really knows, but that's what the Highway Patrol concluded based on the wreckage. The car that hit me just took off. Sometimes, when I close my eyes, I can still see the upside-down tail lights leaving me there to die."

"Who found you?"

"Just a guy passing through. He came up not long after, thankfully. It's not a terribly busy road, but it is the only way to get to Salt Lake from Moab and Grand Junction without going another few hundred miles to I-15." She shrugged and then a chill suddenly washed over her. What if nobody had come by? That thought had haunted her ever since that day. She would have died. "He called the UHP and it took them about an hour to get me out. I was bleeding, broken. Near dead by the time they pulled me free. The fire department had to use those Jaws of Life things to peel the truck apart like an orange in order to get to me."

"I am so sorry. You must have been terrified."

"I was, but it could have been worse, I guess. I knew just about everyone helping me. People I'd gone to school with. People who I'd known my whole life."

"They saved you. I owe them everything."

Lacey turned to face Brandy, who looked down at her with eyes glistening with tears. "You're saving me too, Brandy," she whispered. "I didn't realize how much until I saw you there, at the courthouse. I'd told you to stay away and you didn't listen."

"Hell, no, I didn't listen. Wild horses couldn't keep me away. Not when I knew you needed me, even if you didn't know it yourself."

"I think I'm falling in love with you."

Brandy's eyes finally released a single glistening tear and a small laugh tempered by a quiet cry. "Well, good. Because, I'm already a goner."

Finally, they arrived in front of the house, the tires crunching over the gravel drive as they slowed to a stop. She turned to face Lacey with a piercing gaze. "The next time we make love I want to feel nothing but you. I want to feel the heat of your skin on mine. I want to slide along your body and worship you the way you deserve. There is nothing about you that I don't want to touch. No crevice, no crest, no scar that I don't want to consume. You are a beautiful woman, and it has nothing to do with titles or tiaras. It has to do with the amazing, wonderful, talented, intelligent, beautiful woman that you are now; that you've always been. That's the woman I've fallen in love with. And that's who I want to love me back."

Lacey couldn't breathe. At once exhilarated and terrified, she could only nod.

"You called the coroner's office today," Sal offered as she entered Chandra's office, well past business hours.

Chandra schooled her expression into one that she often employed in the courtroom when someone surprised her. As bland as toast. "I did. Why am I not surprised that you knew that?"

Chuckling, Sal sat in the chair opposite Chandra's desk and crossed her legs. "I have my sources. What I'd like to know is why. What's your angle?"

"Do I have to have an angle? I'm working on a murder defense. Obviously, my client isn't the father." She leaned back in her chair, reclining slightly on the springs, and tossed her pen to the surface of the desk.

"Why would anyone but her boyfriend be the father?"

"Her boyfriend. Is that what you're calling him?"

"Do you know something I don't?"

Shaking her head, Chandra grinned. "This is the part I hate about my job. All the pussy-footing around."

"Off the record?"

"You're an assistant DA. You're prosecuting my client. There is no such thing as off the record."

Sal's expression lost all pretense of the game. Her eyes grew dark, like a forest at midnight when the witching hour brought out anything and everything that slithered or crawled.

Deadly serious. "I mean it. I'm going to share something with you, off the record, and if it leaves this room I will lie on you like a cheap rug. You got it?"

The air in the office seemed to drop several degrees under the weight of Sal's stare. Chandra swallowed, her throat suddenly dry, as she nodded.

"I don't think she did it. I don't think Brandy Kincaid had anything to do with Cynthia's murder, or Miller's murder. But I do think she was on that boat and that's why you asked the coroner if she was planning to run a paternity test on the fetus."

"Go on."

"This isn't a lecture, Chandra. You're turn."

Chandra sat up and leaned her elbows on the desk. She had always been good at sizing people up. That's part of what made her such a great lawyer. She wasn't immodest, but she knew she was good at her job – no, great at her job – and her skills hadn't failed her yet. There was nothing in Sal's demeanor or attitude that made her think she was being anything less than honest. She canted her head. "Is it the lesbian thing? You just don't want to think that we can murder each other? I hate to break it to you, but we can be just as ruthless as straight people." She forced a laugh.

"Don't be obtuse. No, it's not the lesbian thing. If she was guilty, I'd throw the book at her that much harder for giving the assholes ammunition. I just don't think she did it, for... reasons."

Inhaling a deep breath, Chandra straightened her

posture even more. Nothing ventured, nothing gained. "My client was on the boat."

"I knew it. She figured out that Miller and her wife were married. She thinks he might have killed Cynthia if he found out she was cheating." Sal slapped her raised knee and shook her head. "I don't mind telling you, that's kinda what I'm thinking, too."

"So, let's just go with that. If Miller killed Cynthia Kincaid, then who killed him? I know you don't think my client did it."

Sal reached into her briefcase and withdrew a letter-sized manila envelope. She slid it across the desk with a slick grin that said she held more than one ace.

Chandra picked it up and read the exterior label: Paternity Test Results.

Sal leaned forward and whispered, "Maybe the baby's father did."

CHAPTER SIXTEEN

After dinner, Lacey disappeared. They'd all been sitting in the living room for a while, listening to Michelle play old Ragtime hits on the antique, upright piano when Lacey stood, kissed the top of Brandy's head and went up the staircase. After another thirty minutes, Michelle quit playing to read stories to the girls. When Lacey still hadn't returned, Brandy went looking for her.

The old house creaked and settled in the nighttime quiet. The sound of running water came from a bedroom at the end of the hall, quickly drowning the giggles that had followed her up the stairs. Moving beyond the guestroom, she followed the sound until she reached what must be Kendra and Michelle's bedroom. A sliver of golden light came from a slightly cracked door. Lacey's shadow crossed it before the running water turned off. The sloshing sound of the bath water seemed louder than it should have as Lacey reclined in the tub again, sending another shadow over the doorway.

"Lacey?" she called.

"Yeah?"

"Are you alright?"

Only silence followed.

"Lacey?"

"Yeah. I'm fine. You can come in, if you want."

Brandy crossed the master bedroom on legs that suddenly felt too weak to hold her. She pushed gently on the door and peered inside. In a room lit only by candlelight, Lacey relaxed in a large soaker tub filled with soft, white bubbles. Lavender filled the air. Brandy couldn't tell if the scent came from the candles or perhaps the bubble bath, but she allowed it to wrap her in a quiet embrace. Lacey looked like a vintage pin-up girl with her hair piled loosely on top of her head and her pert cheeks rosy with the steam.

"Are you sure?"

"About what?"

"That you're fine."

She nodded. "Do you know what I didn't have to do after court?"

Brandy shook her head as she leaned back against the counter between twin sinks in a dated, dusty rose color.

"I didn't have to take one of those pills."

"Really?"

"You were there."

"You're right. I don't remember you taking one."

Lacey grinned. "No, silly. I mean, I didn't have to take one because you were there."

"So, you're saying, I'm like a drug?" Despite her joke, Brandy's chest filled with something powerful; something she didn't have a name for. It was like a tide had pulled her in and filled her with all the strength of the moon. If she was having even a slight impact on Lacey compared to the way the smart, beautiful young woman had impacted her...

Lacey laughed. "Well, that's not exactly what I meant, but yeah, I guess so."

"Am I addictive?" Brandy's mouth had gone dry and she licked her lips.

"I'm beginning to think so, yes."

"Good. Anytime you need a fix, hon, just let me know." She punctuated the statement with a grin and a risqué raise of her eyebrows.

"I could use a fix right now, actually." Lacey held out her hand. "Help me out of the tub?"

Brandy could barely breathe. There was something in Lacey's eyes that made her think of promises and long walks on the beach and sunrises over the desert. There was that little bit of fear, too. And a fair measure of trust. And there was something else there that didn't have a name. It reminded Brandy of a timid little bird on the verge of flying away even though the thing it was most afraid of was holding out a morsel of something wonderful.

"I didn't mean to pressure you before. If you're not ready, I can wait." She didn't want to wait. Not even one more minute, but this particular bridge belonged to Lacey, and Lacey alone.

"No pressure."

Taking Lacey's hand, Brandy steadied her as she rose. Thick, white bubbles clung to her chest, arms and belly for a second before they began the sensual and awe-inspiring descent over her full, luscious curves.

As the bubbles slipped away in shimmering rivulets, Lacey's flesh came out of hiding. From just between her collar bones, where that tiny hollow of her throat lived, a rigid scar extended down and between her breasts. It ended a couple of inches above her navel.

Lacey sucked in her breath, her chest rising suddenly. Brandy refocused her gaze on Lacey's wide eyes, the blue depths misted with gathering tears. Her bottom lip quivered, and she bit it gently.

"Is this what you've been so afraid for me to see?"

Nodding, Lacey's eyes could no longer hold back her obvious fear.

"Come on. Let's get you dried off." Brandy helped Lacey out of the tub and then wrapped her in a thick, cotton bath sheet before holding her close. "Shh, baby. You don't have to cry."

"I've never let anyone see it before. It's... it's so ugly. Uglier than most because they couldn't be careful. It was an emergency, so they just ripped... ripped me open and they didn't even care about it. They didn't care that I'd be so ugly after."

"You know," Brandy whispered into the top of Lacey's head, pausing long enough to plant a firm kiss there, "I've heard a lot of crazy things in my life. I'm a little bit older than you, you know, and I've been around the block a time or two. Anyway, I think that has to be just about the craziest thing I've ever heard."

Lacey's frame grew stock still in Brandy's embrace. She sniffed quietly, and her body seemed to melt a little more into Brandy's.

"They didn't care about the scar because they were saving your life. But then, you know that as well as I do. Better than anyone, really. So, to me, it's not ugly at all. It's beautiful. It's the result of something that brought you into my arms; into my life. Without that scar, I never would have met you. Without that scar, you wouldn't be standing here, dripping on my shoes and making my entire body ring with feelings I thought I'd never have again."

Lacey couldn't move. Her body had rooted itself to the bathroom floor. Had it not been for the support of Brandy's arms around her, she might very well have collapsed into the cold, hard tiles. Finally, Lacey pulled away enough to focus on her lover's face. A soft smile formed on Brandy's rugged features. Her eyes crinkled slightly in the corners and the dark orbs sparkled in the dim candlelight.

Lacey had wanted the evening to be so romantic. In her mind, she'd overcome all of her anxiety and allowed Brandy to love her completely. To love her with the naked passion that human beings craved. When the moment had come, she'd reneged on her own plan and all the hurt and self-loathing had come back. She didn't even know what had caused it, precisely. It hadn't been the way Brandy had looked at her. The look on Brandy's face hadn't been anything near disgust, even though Lacey had prepared herself for it... expected it. It hadn't been shock. It hadn't been pity.

There was only...

Awe.

If she had to name the expression, Brandy had looked at her with wonder.

How could she have mistaken it for anything else?

Lacey licked her lips and closed her eyes for a little more than a blink, gathering strength to overcome those last hurdles of doubt lingering in her heart. "You said you were falling in love with me, Brandy. Did you mean it?"

"No, you said you were falling in love with me. I already love you; there's no more falling to be done."

"Do you mean that?"

"Yes. Every word."

Lacey's heart snagged like a piece of fabric torn on a bramble.

"I fell in love with the woman you were and the woman you are. With all of your flaws – you're too stubborn sometimes – and all of your beautiful scars, and all of your wit, and charm, and grace. Every piece of you. Right here. Right now."

"I wish I were as brave as you are, Bran."

Brandy frowned. "What do you mean?"

Lacey gathered every ounce of courage she had and whispered, "You've been strong enough to protect yourself, but I'm weak. I've already fallen in love with you, too. And I have no idea how to get my heart back if you change your mind."

Brandy attempted to roll over, but the tangled sheets massed around her legs prevented the movement. She lifted her head slightly to gain a line of sight before she carefully adjusted the covers to free herself without waking Lacey.

Morning sunlight sneaked through a separation in the dark curtains that covered the window beside the headboard. It reflected off the dresser mirror and cast a golden glow onto Lacey's hair. Lacey snuggled deeper into the pillow as the bright line moved across her closed eyelids.

Brandy wasn't young anymore. She had celebrated her forty-fourth birthday three months earlier, alone in her office as she'd gone over the previous month's proceeds and finalized her ledgers for the week. She'd cracked open a bottle of wine, but had only sipped part of one glass before she'd wrapped up her solitary evening and headed home. Cynthia had gone out with friends.

That's when she'd finally worked up the nerve to file the paperwork for the divorce. She'd finalized the forms the week before, but had insisted that Chandra not file them right away. She'd foolishly held out that last bit of hope that maybe... just maybe, Cynthia would do something to show she cared.

She hadn't.

Brandy's birthday had come and gone without any notice at all.

And now, she knew why.

It wasn't just because Cynthia hadn't loved her anymore, and from all the evidence she'd seen lately, never had. No, it was deeper than that.

Brandy had never really loved Cynthia. If she had, perhaps she would have fought harder to keep her, even if it would have been ultimately useless.

Oh, she'd thought she'd loved her. She had honestly believed that Cynthia was the one, but she'd felt that way before. Many times, in fact. She'd dated women her entire adult life. She'd crushed on girls in high school, had a wild fling in college where she'd discovered the truth of her sexuality and embraced it. She'd even lived with a woman, Rebekah, her senior year at UNLV. So, she'd been pretty sure that the feelings she'd had for Cynthia ranked right up there at the top.

But now?

Now she compared all those feelings with the sensations that came from just looking at Lacey. They faded away like so much fairy dust.

She was old enough, experienced enough, to know exactly what love wasn't. And that gave her a cheat to completely embrace what love was.

This.

This was love.

She knew it as certainly as she knew the world was round and the sky was blue and the ocean was wet. She knew it by the palpitations in her heart when that invisible sigh formed deep inside her chest to choke off her air and send tiny, dancing shadows into her brain.

She knew it because she'd never felt like this before in her entire life.

Not once.

"Too early," Lacey muttered, pulling the sheet over her face, not to hide her scar, but to dispel the sunlight.

That invisible sigh shook Brandy to her very core again. "At least there's no triangle bell thingy this morning," Brandy offered.

"Wait for it..."

The horrifying ring broke the morning silence. "Your family is evil." Brandy, no longer fettered with fear of waking her sleeping lover, pulled her legs free of the sheet and pushed herself higher to lean against the headboard.

"Yeah, well. You can't choose your family, right?" Lacey mimicked Brandy's posture and rubbed her eyes with the heels of both hands. The sheet slipped off her alabaster skin to reveal breasts with taught nipples, still swollen from the ravenous attention Brandy had paid them the night before.

Unable to resist the urge, she leaned forward and gently suckled the one closest to her before moaning aloud. She held the tip between her teeth as she mumbled, "You taste so good."

Lacey giggled and wrapped her arms around Brandy's head, arching herself away from the attention. "You are truly insatiable, aren't you!"

"So I've been told."

Lacey slid downward with Brandy's insistence to lie prone as Brandy half-covered her with her own naked form. Brandy lowered her mouth to capture Lacey's bottom lip and pulled gently as she committed the feel of her skin to memory. Pulling away, she mumbled, "I could live in this moment forever. Right here. Just like this."

A knock sounded on the bedroom door. "You girls awake yet? We've got visitors." Brent's deep baritone crashed into the room despite his obvious attempt to gentle it.

"Who?" Lacey asked, untangling herself from Brandy's embrace.

Brandy could actually feel a part of herself being removed, as though their souls were as connected as their bodies had been only a few hours earlier. It physically hurt.

"Not sure, exactly. But they're asking for Brandy."

"Who knows you're here?" Lacey pulled her hair away from her face as she turned to glance at Brandy.

"I don't know. Nobody. Chandra didn't even want to know."

"Well, obviously, someone does." Lacey crawled out of the bed and then threw on a pair of jeans and an old tee-shirt. The fact she didn't put on panties wasn't lost on Brandy and she nearly moaned aloud. She'd have to think about that little tidbit all damn day.

"Must be important." Louder, she replied to Brent. "We'll be down in a sec."

"So much for lazy mornings, right?"

Brandy dressed quickly and then joined Lacey where she stood in front of the mirror pulling her hair back into a bright red band. She dipped her head to place a hot kiss on Lacey's exposed neck and left her with a tiny, gentle bite. "I'll take a rain check."

When they arrived downstairs there were three men in the parlor. Two of them were strangers. A tall man in a dark blue suit stood next to the front window apparently admiring the collection of antique spurs displayed on glass shelves. The second stranger wore a sport coat and khaki slacks with a red polo shirt that made him look like a sports newscaster.

The third man was more than familiar to Brandy and her entire body tensed at the sight of him. There was only one reason she could think of that would bring Detective Jethro Martin all the way to the middle of nowhere, Utah.

"So," she announced. "I'm guessing you found the murder weapon."

CHAPTER SEVENTEEN

"Wait. What?" Lacey tried to bring her suddenly swirling confusion into some semblance of order.

"As a matter of fact, we did, Ms. Kincaid. What I can't figure out is why you would leave it in plain sight like that? It's almost like you want to get caught."

"What is he talking about, Brandy?" Lacey ignored the detective and his goons and turned to face Brandy directly.

Brandy looked at her with a stark frown, her eyebrows forming a solid, stern line. "I didn't want you to worry about it. It's not like it had anything to do with why we left town."

"Don't say another word, Brandy," Kendra barked from the foyer. She looked every bit the mother tiger that Lacey remembered from her childhood. As tough as any man on the ranch, she wasn't physically as large as they were, but she'd always commanded a room with her larger-than-life presence. She marched into the space, her spurs jingling as her boots landed with determined strikes, to stand between Jethro and his friends and her family. "I don't know who you are, Mister, but you're in my house. You have anything to say, say it to me."

"Listen mister, these two women are fugitives. If you want a heap of trouble, I can serve it up anytime. You're harboring criminals."

Kendra turned to look at Lacey with an exaggerated expression of astonishment. "Who is this guy?"

"The detective in charge of the investigation," Lacey whispered, "from Las Vegas."

"Oh," Kendra expelled, nodding as she placed her hands on her hips. "And these other guys?"

The shorter man who looked like a sports announcer offered her a hand. "Kyle Briggs, ma'am. I'm with the FBI. It seems that the alleged criminal activity has crossed state lines, with one of the deceased being found in Arizona. So, we've set up a task force. Just a formality, though. This is my partner, Kendall Jensen."

"Kendra Williams, owner and operator of the Heartland Ranch." Kendra had emphasized her first name as she tossed a glare at the detective.

Lacey shook her head. The FBI agent sounded like he was ordering a pizza and couldn't decide between anchovies or pineapple. Just a formality? Brandy wasn't a serial killer, for crying out loud! "This is nuts. It's crazy! Brandy? What is going on?"

Brandy shook her head. "I am so sorry you got involved in this. I didn't mean for this to happen." To Kenda, she continued, "Kennie, I appreciate your help but I--"

"No problem, Brandy. You're my guest and I take care

of my guests." Kendra put one hand on Lacey's shoulder, squeezing gently as she said, "And you may actually wind up more than that from what I'm seeing."

Detective Martin handed Kendra a folded sheet of paper that looked very much like the summons Lacey had received a few days ago. Kendra unfolded it, frowned, and then handed it to Brandy.

Lacey couldn't bring herself to look at the paper herself, although Brandy wasn't trying to hide the text it contained. She just didn't want to see it. They'd found the murder weapon and they'd immediately come for Brandy.

The world started to close in. Steady pain started in her chest and worked its way into her jaw. Not a heart attack. She knew herself and her traitorous body that well, at least.

"Can I pack up a few things?" Brandy asked, crumpling the paper in trembling fingers.

"That won't be necessary," Detective Martin replied, his lips turned into a wicked sneer at both corners of his mouth.

"What's going on!" Lacey felt like she was swimming in slime, slipping further away from reality as the panic found purchase with a cold, whispering vengeance.

"It's a warrant. For my arrest on new charges of murder." Brandy let the paper fall from her fingertips to land silently on the rug.

"Miller," Lacey whispered. She glanced at Jethro, thankful he apparently hadn't heard her.

Michelle appeared at the edge of the living room, standing in the arch that connected it to the foyer. "I'll call Lynda. We'll work something out and have you out before you even get there."

"You can try, but I wouldn't hold my breath. Judges don't really take to multiple murderers walking around town like they own the damn place."

Brandy hurried to pull Lacey into a tight embrace. "I didn't do it. You know I didn't do it right? When I stopped by the office on the way out of town, the gun was just... there. It was in my safe, but I didn't put it there. I swear to God, I did not put it there."

"It's your gun, Ms. Kincaid. We would have picked you up two days ago when we found it, but we traced it first, to give you the benefit of the doubt." One of the FBI agents stated. "It's yours and ballistics says it's a definite murder weapon. Why would you leave it in plain sight like that if you used it to kill your wife and her former husband?"

"You mean her current husband," sneered Brandy, her voice more venomous than anything Lacey had heard from her until that moment. "That bitch was married to him the whole time!"

"Brandy, shut up!" Kendra yelled. She turned back to Jethro. "Listen, Detective, there must be some way to work this out without having to drag Ms. Kincaid all the way back to Vegas. You know as well as I do that she'll just post again, right? Her attorney will talk to some people and those people will talk to some people. How about we just make a few calls and get it all worked out here."

"Not gonna happen." Jethro pulled a set of shining silver handcuffs from a leather holder on his belt and approached Brandy with heavy strides. "You're under arrest for the murder of John Miller." He began to recite the Miranda warning as he pulled her arms roughly behind her.

Lacey had never actually seen someone slapped into handcuffs before. Brandy's slender wrists immediately turned red as the handcuffs tightened around them. "Those are too tight! You have to loosen them! Oh God, Brandy!"

As Jethro pushed Brandy toward the front door, he laughed. "Don't worry, Ms. Williams. We're fairly convinced you had nothing to do with it. Hell, you probably didn't even know she killed Miller that day on the lake. You might get away with only having to testify."

The thought made her nauseated. Her throat burned. Never. Not ever. She'd marry Brandy tomorrow, right there in the jailhouse, to avoid testifying against her for anything. Not only had she had her fill of the witness box, thanks, but she couldn't bring herself to even consider doing anything that would help put Brandy away for life.

As the feds led Brandy through the foyer, Lacey's cell phone rang. Day Dream Believer seemed incongruous with what was happening. She glanced at the screen out of habit. Lynda Fairchild was calling her. Did she know they were coming for Brandy?

"Hello?" she said, her patience and her wits at an end.

"Hey, Lacey. It's Georgie Beck from the Lynda Fairchild Agency. So, we found Miller's car."

"You did? Oh my god. Where?" She pulled the phone away from her lips slightly as she followed Brandy onto the front porch. "Brandy! They found the car!"

Brandy yelled from the side of the police cruiser, "Tell

them to call the cops. I can promise you, I never touched that car and if Cynthia's blood is anywhere on it..."

"There's a problem," the deep voice continued.

"What kind of problem?" Lacey froze in place at the top step of the porch. One of the agents placed his hand on Brandy's head to guide her into the back seat of an unmarked, white sedan.

"After we found it, at an auto shop that fronts a chop shop, they crushed it."

"Who is they?"

"That's the best part. They would be the Maretti family."

The cell wasn't as dark as she'd imagined it would be. Having never actually been in jail before, she hadn't been entirely certain what to expect. Still, her imagination had run rampant during the long drive back to Las Vegas. Images of dark, slimy walls had been superimposed periodically with institutional green. What she found once she'd been processed into the holding facility was a square room with six metal-frame beds – three lower and three upper bunks – with three desks built against the walls. Two of the desks were on the side of the room with only one bunk bed while the other one was positioned between the two bed units on the opposite wall. The walls themselves were painted a cheery yellow and the single window boasted a pink and yellow curtain with ruffles along the bottom edge. Pictures of children and families hung with scotch tape on the glossy cinder blocks above two of the beds and over one of the desks.

A large woman with dark skin and tightly-braided hair lounged on the top bunk furthest from the door, ignoring Brandy as she entered. Two other woman, a tiny blonde girl who couldn't have been more than twenty years old and an older woman who was probably younger than the fifty or so years she appeared to be, sat at a small table beneath the window. The table held an apartment sized microwave, a jar of creamy peanut butter, and a stack of ramen noodle packages.

"You ladies have a new celly. Be nice to her. Kincaid, this is Royale, Beth, and Janet. One of your cellmates is in Ad Seg for another couple of weeks, that's Marty, and the last one is in the infirmary. She just had a daughter, so she'll be gone for another three or four days. No fighting. No stealing. Not so much as an argument. I don't want to have to come back here today."

The guard left, and Brandy stood in the door way of the cell, not sure what she should do next. Not sure what to expect, but from the admonition, it couldn't be good.

"Ain't you that millionaire lady that offed her wife?" asked the older woman with a voice roughened by smoking and too much bourbon.

The woman on the top bunk suddenly shifted and glanced down from her perch. "Yeah? We got ourselves a regular celebrity, don't we?"

"I'm no celebrity. And I didn't kill my wife."

"That's what they all say, honey. So, come on in and make

yourself at home. I'm Janet," the older woman announced, rising and making at least some effort to greet Brandy. There's only one top bunk left. You can have it." She indicated the top bunk nearest the window, opposite the smart-ass.

"Thanks. Works for me." She climbed onto the edge and spread the sheets and blanket over the two-inch thin foam mattress. When she finished, she settled onto it and propped the pillow behind her back. "So, what do you do for fun around here?"

Smart-ass slipped her legs over the side of the bunk and faced Brandy. "Not much. But then, girls like you and me, well, we have more fun than some others, if you know what I mean. I'm Roy."

"Nice to meet you, Roy. I'm good though."

"Suit yourself, but after a few weeks, you're going to be singing a different tune. There's a whole lot of prime young pussy around here. Might as well get a taste before the screws cut your balls off."

A buzzer sounded, and Roy jumped off the top bunk to land with a hard thud. She was surprisingly limber, even nimble, for a woman pushing two-fifty of what appeared to be mostly muscle. The other two women also headed for the door. Janet turned back to Brandy and smiled. "You coming? It's visiting hour."

"Nobody's coming to see me. I just got here."

"Not even your lawyer? I mean, you do got a lawyer right? Come on. Worst thing that can happen is you take a little walk around the yard."

What did she have to lose?

Brandy followed the others out of the cell. Falling into step behind them, they moved with a crowd of women to the main floor of the unit. Once they'd all gathered, they were herded into the yard where picnic tables in neat rows filled a cement slab that might have been a patio if it hadn't been a thousand degrees.

To her surprise, seated at a table at the edge of the platform, Chandra was waiting. To her right was the one face she hadn't dared to believe she might see again so quickly. It had been nearly a week of holding cells and interrogations, but now her entire body flushed with want and need.

Lacey noticed her and smiled widely.

Brandy hurried, without shoving, through the crowd until she reached the table. She moved immediately to hug Lacey, needing physical contact to prove she was real. Needing that contact to make sure she was still alive.

"No touching," a guard called from the corner of the patio.

The blood drained from Brandy's heart for a second before she forced a smile. The same physical pain she'd experienced when she'd pulled away from Lacey in bed returned; an emptiness that felt like she'd never be whole again until they touched.

What would happen to her if she couldn't prove she hadn't killed Cynthia or Miller? What if she actually wound up in prison for the rest of her life? How could she live like that? How could she exist without Lacey with her, if not in person, then at the very least in her heart?

She certainly couldn't ask her to... to what? Wait for her? If she were convicted, she might never be free again.

That certainly wasn't realistic.

"I couldn't stay away. I had to see you, so Chandra added me to your visitor's list."

Brandy sat across the table and reached for Lacey's hand. Part of her waited for the guard to chastise her again, but as she looked at the other tables, she surmised that holding hands must be okay. "It's okay. It's selfish, I know, but I'm glad you're here."

"Alright ladies, enough mush. We've got business to discuss." Chandra opened her briefcase and explained exactly what the charges and evidence were against Brandy, as well as confirming that Lacey would be a witness to place Brandy at the scene of the Miller murder.

"And there's more. Carlos Maretti was found dead in the kitchen of the strip club he owned with his half-brother, Roman. Notice, I did not say 'executed.' There hasn't been an official determination, but I'm thinking he committed suicide."

"Wow," Brandy mused. "Of course, they'll probably try to pin it on me, anyway, right?"

Chandra was silent as she folded her hands together over her notepad.

"You're kidding me, right? What the hell?" Brandy was beyond fear. Anger swelled, filling every muscle in her body until she thought she might burst.

"They don't have any proof," Lacey interjected.

"Ballistics says the same gun that killed Miller and Cynthia was used to kill Carlos."

Brandy lowered her head to rest on her hands, flattened on the not-so-clean surface of the metal picnic table. "It's like the Sisterhood of God Damned Traveling Semi-Auto." She raised her head as a thought ignited in the back of her mind. "Wait. Does that mean they know about the connection between Cynthia and Carlos?"

"They do."

"What about the paternity test? Are they doing one?"

"Don't get so excited," Chandra warned. "Right now, they are focusing on you, and only you. Regardless of the result of a paternity test, if they even do one, they'll still try to make it look like you killed both guys for screwing the woman you thought was your wife."

"But you think Carlos killed them, and then offed himself, right?"

"It's a working theory, and one I think we might be able to use."

Brandy's sudden balloon of hope popped. She didn't need theories. She needed proof.

After about ten minutes, during which she explained the state's case, Chandra leaned back slightly and said, "There is no plea deal on the table. They plan to take every bit of this to trial if they don't get guilty pleas across the board."

"Well, I guess that's that, then. We go with the whole reasonable-doubt thing." Brandy wasn't filled with confidence. The prosecutor had a gun and ballistics and plenty of circumstantial evidence to link all the cases together into one massive conspiracy that painted Brandy as the quintessential jilted lover cum mass murderer.

"We have to make them think someone else had the motive and opportunity. We only need one juror to have enough reasonable doubt, right?" Lacey squeezed Brandy's fingers as she spoke to Chandra, her voice filled with childlike faith. "What about Miller's car? If he transported Cynthia's body, there must be blood all over the damn thing."

"You told me they crushed it already." Chandra pulled her lips into a curious frown.

"Well, sure, but the blood would still be there. Why can't we tell the DA about it? She can get a search warrant and they can test it."

"It's not that simple, Lacey. They have to have probably cause, and someone witnessing a junk yard doing what junk yards do is not probable cause."

"Someone killed Cynthia," Brandy insisted. "And the only thing I know for sure is that it isn't me."

"The one-armed man defense is only going to get you so far. We need some real evidence that can place someone else in a position to not only benefit from the murders, but who could have actually pulled it all off."

"Oh, my God, Lacey. Are you okay? Your face is all over the news. Did you know that? Of course, you know that. How could you not know that? Where are you?"

"I just got back into town yesterday. Right now, I'm on the strip." Lacey cradled her cell phone in the holder mounted to the dashboard of Michelle's Ford Mustang and waited for it to connect to the Bluetooth. When her old producer's breaths sounded through the car's speaker system, she asked, "What are they saying?"

"That you were running away with Brandy Kincaid."

"We weren't running away, for crying out loud. I had to testify in a trial back home. If we were running away from something, don't you think we would have picked someplace other than my hometown, hanging out with the county attorneys, no less, in a district courthouse?"

"Brandy Kincaid is back in jail."

"I know. They arrested her at my house." Lacey sighed. She didn't want to talk about any of this, but Mary was a friend and it's not like she had many of those to spare. "I just don't know how they figured out where to look."

"Oh, that's easy."

"Yeah, you're right. My name was a matter of court records for the trial or something. Not exactly a mystery."

"Actually, Addison told them. She called them. She told Jethro Martin and the FBI that if you weren't here in Vegas, you'd be there. And then, she provided them with the address from your employment file. You know, so they wouldn't have to be troubled to look it up or something." The derision in Mary's voice was practically physical.

"Seriously? That's good to know. What's her beef?"

"She just wants the story, I think. Did you know she took all those files you'd been working on? She's running with your sex trafficking story next week. I really, really don't like her."

"It's okay. You can say it."

"I hate her. There. I said it. Someone should hit her with

a car. Did you know that if you hit someone with your car, and they don't die, it's like a misdemeanor or something? It's true. I looked it up once. Oh, by the way, Roger has been trying to reach you."

Lacey looked at the face of her cell phone and noticed she'd received several voice mail messages. "What does he want?"

"He says he has something to show you. Do you want me to call him?"

"Actually, I was just on my way to see him. Is he at work?"

"Yeah."

"Good. Will you call him and ask him to meet me at the Rio?"

"Consider it done. Be careful!"

Roger had been looking for her. It was Roger who had supplied her with the security footage of Brandy and Cynthia's argument the night Cynthia had vanished. Mary and Roger had been dating pretty steadily for a couple of years and Lacey had believed Mary when she'd said she could trust him to keep quiet about it until the story broke. That had been her first big break in the story, of course, and it seemed strange that it was only a couple weeks ago.

She chewed on her bottom lip as she swung off Las Vegas Blvd and headed for the Rio. Only about two blocks from the Touchdown, with any luck Roger would already be there when she arrived.

What did he have to show her? It had to be security video, and if it was the footage she was looking for, she might have more answers than questions in short order.

Finally, she arrived at the hotel and turned her car over to the valet. She pulled her satchel from the passenger seat and hiked it over one shoulder. Inside the casino, the cacophony of sharp sounds and brightly-colored lights made her head swim. Suddenly, she missed the peace of the ranch, even with that damn triangle alarm. The days she'd spent with Brandy there had made her hunger for something quiet and calm. A pain of wanting sliced her heart.

After a quick scan of the interior as her eyes adjusted to the light, Lacey found Roger sitting at a slot machine near the reception desk. Both hands buried in the pockets of his forest-green uniform jacket, his upper body jostled as one knee jack-hammered in place.

"Let's get out of here," she stated flatly when she reached his side.

He hadn't seen her approach and he jumped at the sound of her voice. "God, Lacey. You scared the shit out of me."

"Not here. Let's take a cab ride."

They waited silently at the cab stand for less than five minutes before climbing into a bright yellow van. Opting to sit in the very back row of the ten-seater, she called the driver, "Take us on a tour."

"You got it," he mumbled, pulling away from the curb.

"What did you call me for?"

"This," Roger whispered, pulling a thumb drive from the pocket of his jacket. "It's a copy. I left the main file on the hard drive, of course. I only recorded it because you asked me to keep track of anyone going in and out of Brandy's office. The thing is, a couple of days after I recorded this, the DA serves a subpoena, right? I go to make copies of everything and that entire section is nothing but snow. No recording left on the hard drive."

"Show me." Lacey pulled her tablet out of her bag and handed it to Roger. He inserted the drive. When the file loaded, he tilted the tablet screen, so she could make out the black-and-white image clearly.

The image was fairly clear, though small, with three angles split across the four quadrants of the screen. The fourth section remained black.

A slender man wearing a plaid, button down shirt, jeans and boots entered the screen from the right side and moved in a lazy course through the slot machines on the deck outside Brandy's office. He kept one hand in his front pocket and secured a paper grocery sack in the crook of the same elbow. After a couple of minutes, during which time he didn't play any of the games, he reached the edge of the catwalk. Glancing around as though he was checking to see if anyone watched him, he jetted across the catwalk, stopped at the door long enough to unlock it with a key card, and disappeared inside.

"Scroll that back a little. Can we zoom in on his face?"

"There's a better image of his face when he comes back out," Roger replied. "I sped it up a little on the copy. He was inside for exactly three minutes and forty-two seconds. You can see the time lapse here." He pointed to a digital clock in the bottom corner of the quadrant. As he'd mentioned, the seconds ticked away at warp speed.

When the door opened, and as Roger had indicated, the man looked up; almost directly into the lens of the eye-in-the-sky camera hidden behind the rather noticeable black globes that dotted just about every casino ceiling in town.

His eyes grew wide and his mouth fell slack for a moment. Lacey froze the screen. He was an older man with silver hair and slightly hunched shoulders. "There. Zoom in there."

Roger obliged. "Any idea who it is?"

"I know exactly who that is."

CHAPTER EIGHTEEN

Lacey tapped her fingers on the steering wheel of her sister-in-law's car. She'd left Brandy's SUV in Utah and driven the 2015 Mustang Shelby back to Utah, for fear that the Range Rover might be confiscated for some reason. It turned out to be a good idea for more than one reason. She couldn't take a chance that they would recognize her, although she wasn't sure they'd ever seen her before. Had she only had her own vehicle or Brandy's to choose from, she would have rented a car. Driving Michelle's Shelby had saved her the trouble.

Night had fallen over the strip. Neon lights sparkled and flashed in a strobe of color, lighting just about every corner of Las Vegas Boulevard. Many of the tourists who found daytime in Las Vegas far too hot now left the confines of casinos and hotel rooms to enjoy the cooler evening air. They crossed the street in front of her, some using the crosswalk and others ignoring it as they sidestepped around slower moving foot traffic to walk directly on the main drag.

She was parked. Waiting for one glimpse of Brandy's

would-be in-laws. Earlier that afternoon, she'd driven to their house only to find it empty. A handful of newspapers had collected on the front porch of the bungalow style home just outside of town, and their car was gone. There wasn't much mail in the mailbox, but then, they didn't live in Vegas full time. Still, it was obvious they hadn't been there in a while.

A call to Lynda Fairchild had resulted in a hit on their credit card. Lacey didn't know how Lynda's skip tracer had found the information so quickly, and she didn't want to know. All she knew is that Cynthia's parents had checked into a motel on the strip last week, the day after the funeral. It was the kind of hotel where guests could expect to clean blood off the walls, but it was cheap. With their ATM dead and buried, it was probably all they could afford.

She'd found their car in the parking lot a few hours earlier. They'd left for a while during the afternoon, making stops at a grocery store and the city government building. When they came out, Frank carried a small cardboard box and Marion had been crying.

They'd returned to the hotel an hour ago. She hadn't moved since.

Her stomach growled. She reached into her satchel on the passenger seat and withdrew an energy bar. It tasted like cardboard with chocolate chips, but she couldn't leave to find any real food. If she did, she risked losing them. If her hunch was right, Cynthia's parents were preparing to leave their little tourist trap for good.

Cynthia's mother owed a large debt to Maretti family.

That much was crystal clear now. Cynthia had wanted Brandy to pay that debt for her, but Brandy had refused. Would she have paid it if she'd known what it was about? If Cynthia had told her what the money was for? It was probably a good thing that wasn't really an issue. On the one hand, Brandy had every right not to pay off someone else's debts, family or not family. On the other, when debts are owed to people like the Maretti family there were generally only two options. Pay up or check out. Lacey liked to think that Brandy would have paid up.

The next question on her mind centered around who had actually killed Cynthia, and whether that really mattered now that Brandy was facing prosecution. She suspected John Miller as most likely. But that wouldn't explain his murder or the untimely death of Carlos Maretti. "What if Miller killed his wife when he realized she was having an affair with Carlos, and Carlos killed Miller for killing Cynthia?" she asked the dashboard.

The dash didn't answer.

She frowned. That might explain why Carlos had killed himself, right? He couldn't live without Cynthia? Or, if he had actually been murdered, who did it? One of the parents? It made a little bit of sense, since Frank had been the man in the video, planting Brandy's gun in her safe. If they could frame her for the murder of their daughter successfully, they'd not only get rid of Brandy, but almost certainly ensure a huge judgement in their wrongful death lawsuit. They could pay off the Maretti family and have enough money to last... well, to last for as long as it took

Marion to gamble it all away.

Lacey ran her fingers through her hair until she fisted the strands at the back of her head. It was like a movie-of-the-week. Completely implausible, yet based on a true story.

And completely out in left field. Cynthia's parents were not career criminals. They were just an old couple with their own problems and they most certainly didn't have the criminal IQ to pull off something like this...

Releasing the strands of hair, she stifled a yawn.

When she stretched, she grimaced against a pain that shot through her hips and down her legs. The clock read ten after ten.

At some point she'd need a bathroom.

A solid knock came from the back of the car and she screamed. Immediately, she reached for the key to ignite the engine, and then checked her side view mirror. A shape appeared at the passenger window. It was dark. And it was enormous. The shape of a man so large that it blocked all light from that side of the car just stood there. Not moving; not doing anything. Another shape appeared at her driver's side window.

"Go away! Leave me alone!" she yelled. Her breath caught in her throat and panic seemed the only logical next step.

The form on the far side of the car shifted and her twin's face appeared in the window. "Christ, Lacey. Nervous much?" he called through the glass.

She released a heavy breath, gripped the steering wheel with both hands, and leaned her forehead on her knuckles.

After a moment, she looked out the driver's side window to find Brent looking back at her. His lips parted into a sheepish grin and he shrugged. "Sorry about that. We didn't mean to scare you. Casey tripped. You know how clumsy he is."

"Bite me, dickhead." Casey's retort sounded more like a teenager with an attitude than a highly-trained covert military operative.

Flipping the unlock mechanism on the driver's door, she chuckled. Her cover clearly blown, she climbed out the car to stretch her legs. "Well, you did. What the hell are you guys doing here?"

"You didn't think we were going to let you take this on alone, did you? You'll get yourself into a world of shit and then we'd have to come rescue you anyway. Or bail you out of jail." Casey grinned.

"Okay. So... how did you find me?"

It was Casey's turn to look sheepish.

"Seriously, Case? You lo-jacked my car?"

"Well, no, not exactly. Technically, we lo-jacked Michelle's car, but not because of this. We lo-jacked it last year when she had to drive to Sedona on business. Kendra was worried about her making the trip alone and--"

"Okay, okay. I get it. You figured why not use it to track me down and scare me half to death. Awesome!"

"And where do we find you? Hanging out in a dark alley staking out... what? The hotel?"

She nodded. "Yeah. Turns out Cynthia's father, Frank, planted that gun in her office safe. He had a key. What I can't figure out is how they got it. Is it possible they killed their own daughter for some reason? She might have had a key to the office on her, right? Or would she? With the divorce and everything, would Brandy have allowed her to keep a key to the casino office? It doesn't really make sense."

"None of it makes sense. I'm hungry." Brent leaned his backside against the fender.

"I'm not leaving here until they poke their law-breaking little heads out of their hotel room. I want to know exactly what they're up to."

"You mean them?" Casey pointed across the street.

The older couple dragged one suitcase each to their car and loaded them in the trunk. After settling his wife into the car, Frank lowered his tall frame into the driver's seat.

"Get in the car," Lacey demanded.

"I'm driving." Casey hurried around the front end.

Normally, she would have argued with him, but he was much better defensively behind the wheel. She wasn't going to relegate herself to the back seat either. "Shotgun!" she shouted.

Brent groaned. "Do you have any idea how small that back seat is?"

"You'll be fine. Now, get in."

After squeezing his immense frame into the backseat of the two-door sports car, he tossed his legs over the seat. "I feel like a five-year-old," he grumbled.

"A five-year-old would fit back there. Quit bitching," Casey stated over his shoulder.

Lacey planted herself in the passenger seat, adjusting

it forward to give Brent a little more room. "Follow them. And don't lose them. And don't let them see you."

"Have they ever seen this car before?"

"No. I tailed them this afternoon, but I doubt they noticed me."

"Have they ever seen you in this car before?"

"No."

"Are you going to let me take care of the espionage shit?"

She paused before answering, glaring at Casey from beneath her narrowed eyelids. "Yes."

"Good girl."

After reaching a main intersection, Cynthia's parents turned toward the outskirts of the strip. They passed the Touchdown Club, and then the Rio until the resort areas fell behind them.

"I thought they'd be heading for the highway. It looked like they were packed to go home. Where did you say they were from?" Brent had managed to lean himself forward to a position between the front seats.

"I didn't. Out of state, I think. Oregon, maybe?"

"This isn't the way to Oregon," Casey stated, flipping on his blinker as he changed lanes. "And the first rule of black ops is to never believe your eyes. It may have looked like they were packed for home, but it may have only looked that way. All we know is they hauled out a couple of suitcases. There could have been anything in them. Cash. Drugs. A body."

"There were two suitcases," Lacey observed. "Where's the other body, then, huh?"

Casey glanced at her with his eyebrows raised slightly.

"Oh. Oh! Eww. You would think that, wouldn't you?" She repositioned herself in the seat as the unwanted image of a body, sawed clean through and stuffed in two suitcases, swam in her mind.

A few blocks later, Cynthia's parents changed lanes to merge directly in front of them, slowing down before taking a left. Lacey frowned. "They can't be..."

"Can't be what?"

"Hang on. I think I know where they're going now."

About five minutes later, the elderly couple pulled their Lincoln into a large, circular driveway that arched around an enormous manicured lawn. They stopped in front of a massive iron gate as a private security guard approached them. They spoke for a couple of seconds and Cynthia's father handed him a keycard.

A second later, the guard returned the keycard and the gate opened.

"We don't have one of those card things, do we?" Casey asked.

"No," Lacey said with a heavy sigh.

"Where do you think they're going?"

"They're moving into Brandy's house."

Chandra had never been to Sal Crenshaw's house before. It wasn't large; probably only a two bedroom; built in the 30s. The small Craftsman style bungalow had obviously been renovated, although if Sal were the woman responsible for the design, Chandra had misjudged her tastes as running to the plain and simple. The house was nothing less than elegant, and perfect for a woman living alone.

She sat on a leather sectional with throw pillows decorated with elephants. Two matching ceremonial masks, imitations carved from wood, stood guard on an oversized, square coffee tables. A trinket box covered in a fairly generic African motif rested on one corner. Unable to withstand her own curiosity, Chandra opened it and found two remotes. One was obviously for the television with Vizio engraved on one end. The other was probably for the satellite system, based solely on the many and myriad buttons. Chandra had a dish at her place, but she couldn't remember the last time it had been set to anything other than CNN.

"Sorry about that. It was my mother. She's planning my sister's wedding and apparently the fact I won't wear some incredibly tacky prom dress has gotten me booted from the wedding party." Sal put her cell phone on the coffee table and shrugged as she sat down. "So, where were we?"

"You were just telling me that you have precisely zero authorization for what you're planning."

"Oh. Right. Yeah, so I talked to my boss about my gut feelings on this whole thing and his reaction was to basically do my job or get lost."

"That's not ambiguous, you know. They want you to successfully prosecute my client; no pleas, just prison, thanks."

"That about sums it up. So, we're on our own."

"We're going to need reinforcements. We can't do what you're planning without help." A frown pulled at Chandra's lips. "What about the FBI?"

"I'm working on it. It's likely they'll pitch in a little, but they really aren't keen on it. Not to mention, there's no guarantee Brandy will be in jail after the hearing tomorrow. Even with you agreeing to remand, that shady son of a bitch will probably let her out. We can only hope she won't get in the way."

Chandra leaned back against the soft folds of the sofa and crossed her legs. Her skirt, split on the side nearly to her hip, fell away and revealed her thigh. Sal shifted in her seat and sipped her wine. "I think I know someone who can help."

"Do you think it's possible they killed their own daughter?" Brandy sat in the front seat of the late model Mustang she'd seen at the Heartland Ranch and struggled to make out Lacey's eyes behind a pair of dark glasses embellished with rhinestones. Frank had planted the gun. She still couldn't wrap her head around it. Her mother-in-law? Ex-mother-in-law, she reminded herself, would stoop to anything, but Frank had always seemed well above it all. The gambling. The money. His own daughters lack of morals.

The thought of living in the Mission Hills house made her stomach turn. Even if she liked the house, which she didn't, she couldn't live in a place where someone she'd loved had been so brutally murdered. And she was their daughter!

Where the hell were they sleeping?

"I don't know. I think anything is possible at this point," Lacey responded. Her hair was pulled back in a ponytail, slightly askew from the center of her head, and when she pulled her sunglasses away, she revealed dark circles beneath her eyes. "Cynthia's mother obviously owed a huge amount of money to the Maretti family. When you wouldn't bail her out, they might have been just desperate enough to kill their way out. Someone once told me that money is a powerful motivator, and I've personally seen it turn the staunchest citizen into something horrible."

"You're talking about the Sheriff, aren't you? Mac?"

Lacey nodded. "He got caught up in something he couldn't control, and it cost lives. His own daughter's, for one. And my brother's for another."

"But he didn't actually kill them, right? I mean, he didn't physically, personally commit the act. You're suggesting that Marion and Frank pulled the trigger, literally, to kill their own daughter for money. Why? Why wouldn't they have simply killed me so their daughter could inherit everything?"

"I don't know. I'm just saying we can't put blinders on. We have to look at all the options. Maybe they couldn't get to you? Or maybe there was some other, more personal, problem between them." Lacey sighed, tilting her head back until it landed on the headrest. "I'm probably not thinking clearly. I just want to find a way out of this for you. For us. It is possible that Frank and Marion killed her; that's all I'm saying."

"I don't buy it. There has to be something more going

on here. When was the last time you slept, baby?" Brandy stroked Lacey's cheek, still mesmerized by the soft flesh and crooked smile that formed on her sweet lips every time she touched her.

"We were watching the house, well, the neighborhood, all night." Lacey yawned. "The boys are still there, just hanging out at the bus stop across the street."

"Was it worth it? I mean, did they leave or anything?"

"No. Not a sign of them anywhere. There's only one way in or out of Mission Hills, so if they had gone anywhere, we'd have seen them."

"How long have they been there?"

"Three days." Lacey put the car into gear and headed to the main road that ran alongside the jail. "I'm sorry you had to be in there for so long. Was it horrible?"

"Not really. I mean, I've been in worse places, I guess." Brandy rubbed her eyes. "No, no, I don't actually think I have. It was awful." She laughed at the absurdity of it.

"I can only imagine. I've never worn a pair of handcuffs I didn't want to." Lacey shrugged with a wink.

"Really... that sounds promising." Brandy paused, relishing the quiet and the simple fact that she existed in the same world as a woman like Lacey. She frowned. "There was one thing that was odd, though."

"Just one?"

"Yeah. In court this morning, Chandra acted like she didn't care if I got out of jail or not. I mean, she was going through the motions, but pretty much everything she did reinforced what Sal Crenshaw wanted. At one point, she even said that if the judge was going to set the bail as high as the prosecutor was asking – ten million this go round – that he should just not set any at all. Who would put that in the judge's head like that?"

"She must have been trying to get him to lower it."

"That's just it. Sal was asking for ten million. The judge didn't add any bail at all in the end. He just applied the bail I'd already posted. He wanted me out of there, no thanks to my so-called lawyer."

"No, he took her advice and didn't set a new bail. She did good, right?"

"You weren't there. Something was more than a little hinky."

Lacey's phone chimed before she could respond.

"Hi Brent. I got her and we're on our way back to you..."

Lacey was probably right. She hadn't slept well while she'd been a guest of the county. And the daylight hours had been filled with her new best friend's attempts to be her new best friend. Roy didn't leave her alone for longer than it took to shower the entire time she'd been on the inside. Was it still called the inside? Or was it the mix?

What did it matter how she'd gotten out? She was out. Thank God.

"Crap! Okay. We'll be right there." Lacey tucked the phone back into the center console and frowned. "They're moving. They just left Mission Hills, heading in the direction of the strip."

"That's no good. We'll have to wait for them to come back before we can get eyes on them again, right? You should have sent a cab for me at the jail."

"No way! When my girl gets out of jail, she gets picked up in style. It's a rule I have."

Brandy laughed. "Let's try not to make a habit out of picking me up from jail at all. And... did you just call me your girl?"

"I did."

"I like it."

"Me, too."

A comfortable silence fell over the interior of the car. Brandy reached across the console and took one of Lacey's hands in hers, brought it to her lips and kissed the soft folds of her palm. "Can I keep you?"

Lacey smiled. "Of course."

That quiet sigh wrapped around Brandy's heart and she fell in love all over again. She swallowed it and breathed deeply the leather-scented air. They didn't speak anymore as they hurried through Las Vegas traffic. When they approached Mission Hills, Brandy noticed Casey and Brent lounging on an enclosed bench on the corner. As bus stops went, it was rather nice. It only existed here because the housemaids and caddies who worked inside the surrounding neighborhood and golf club needed it to get to work. The people who lived in Mission Hills had insisted the city put up a bus stop that wouldn't detract from their aesthetics.

She'd never wanted to live in Mission Hills, and even if Cynthia hadn't been killed there, she couldn't wait to sell the house. Shaking off the suddenly dark realization that her life would never be the same, she asked, "So, what do we do now that we've lost our prime suspects?"

"We haven't lost them. We're just picking up the boys first." Lacey pulled into the loading zone and hopped out of the car. "Get in," she ordered.

Brandy stepped out of the car and tilted the seat forward for Casey.

He smiled. "Welcome back, gorgeous. You'll need to ride in the back."

"Seriously?"

"It's nothing personal or anything, but I'll need to see the road." Casey waved his smart phone casually.

Brent climbed into the back seat and slid to the driver's side. "Let's go!"

Brandy slid into the back seat next to Brent. "It is ridiculously small back here."

Lacey and Casey plopped down in the front seat simultaneously and both doors slammed shut. Brandy was in a cave accentuated by the tiny windows on either side surrounded by black interior. Like all convertibles, the interior ceiling was made of metal bars and canvas, adding an industrial feel to an otherwise luxurious vehicle. "Can we put the top down?"

"Only if you want them to see us," Casey replied.

Brandy leaned around the back of his seat. He was bent over his smart phone screen, tapping a series of small icons. "We lost them, in case you forgot."

"No, we didn't," he mumbled. "There! Got 'em. Take the next left."

"What the hell is going on? Can someone please tell the

jailbird what we're doing?"

Brent laughed. "You haven't known Casey very long. Despite the fact that you got the drop on him last week – yes, we heard all about your bat skills – he's a pretty darn good secret agent."

"Combatant," Casey corrected. "James Bond is a pussy."

"He's a pretty darn good – combatant. Two nights ago, under the very nose of one part-time rent-a-cop, Casey here managed to lo-jack the subject's car."

"We're following them digitally. That way we can hang back a little bit, keep our profile low, and still show up wherever they end up soon enough to see what's going on. Take a right at the light."

Brandy leaned back and kept her eyes on Lacey. She appeared to be focusing on the road and the traffic. There was something different about her. It was a good difference. She hesitated to call it an improvement because that would imply that she'd been lacking before the change, but it was definitely good. Her confidence seemed to be higher. She no longer worried about covering the slight scar on her cheek. When Brandy had asked her that silly, romantic question about keeping her, Lacey's answer had been immediate and sure.

If either of them survived whatever this was, if their love survived, Brandy intended to hold her to that answer for the rest of their lives.

"We're here."

It didn't surprise Brandy that they were parked in front of a local casino. What did surprise her was which casino it was. "This is a Maretti operation," she announced like she'd just found a bug in her soft drink.

"Are you sure?" Lacey asked.

"Yeah, pretty sure. That guy with the black ball cap standing by the door?"

"Yeah?" Brent asked.

"That's Roman Maretti, Carlos' older brother."

"Pull up the street aways and stop on that side street." Casey pointed to the end of the block. When they arrived, he said, "Stay in the car. Drive around the block a couple of times and come back to pick me up in five minutes right here." He pushed the door open and set one foot in the gutter. "Five minutes. Got it?"

Lacey placed a hand on his arm. "What are you doing? What if they recognize you from the bus stop?"

"Don't worry. Just give me five minutes."

Brent leaned back in his seat. "Let him go, Lace. He knows what he's doing."

"I don't like this," Lacey huffed in that way she had that said she was behaving against her better judgment.

Brandy rubbed the bridge of her nose. "If it weren't for the fact Carlos was killed with Brandy's gun and Cynthia's dad had access to it, I'd say her mother was just gambling. But something is going on, and chances are good they won't recognize Casey, so let him check it out. What could happen in five minutes?"

After exiting the car, Casey leaned back inside. "Actually, quite a bit can happen in five minutes. But not today."

CHAPTER NINETEEN

Lacey circled the block. It seemed strange to have two passengers in the back seat and nobody at her side, which just amplified the overall strangeness of the circumstances. Her heart told her that Brandy was innocent. The evidence told her that Cynthia's parents were ass-deep in the whole sordid business, but Lynda Fairchild's insistence that Brandy was up to something made her just a little uneasy.

She loved Brandy. That much was certain, and it was just about the only fact she could hold onto. She wasn't even entirely sure that Brandy loved her back in the same life-altering, life-confirming way. It was certainly possible Lacey was only imagining that she did; that her need to be loved was so strong, she had turned hope into her own version of reality. Was it possible that her love for Brandy was clouding her judgment? Sure, it was possible. But she couldn't stop feeling as though without her, Brandy would be lost.

She liked that feeling. She liked belonging to something or someone with an indelible connection. A connection that if broken would cause some catastrophic space-time continuum breakdown of epic proportions. Okay, so that might be a little dramatic. She only knew that if she lost Brandy now, epic destruction wasn't entirely out of the question.

She circled the block and they passed in front of the casino again. When the traffic slowed, she touched the brake slightly and found her brother in the crowd. "Who is Casey talking to? He looks familiar…"

"Oh, my God!" Brandy exclaimed. "He's talking to Roman Maretti! Your brother is absolutely insane! What the hell is he doing?"

Lacey swerved around a car that stopped suddenly in front of them. "Are you kidding me? Brent? Brent, what is our brother thinking!" Her heart skipped a beat as she slowly merged back into her own traffic lane.

The quick motion must have caught Casey's eye because he glared directly at the car before turning his attention back to the eldest Maretti heir. Other than that glare, he didn't give any indication that he knew them. He took what looked like a business card from Roman.

Brent leaned between the seats and looked out the passenger window for a half-second before he turned to face Lacey. "Our brother? I can't say, really. I can tell you what he's doing. He's talking to Roman Maretti. Just keep circling a couple more times and then park on the corner like he said."

Lacey followed the traffic and then turned the corner again.

"You're awfully calm about this," Brandy suggested. "You know something we don't?"

"It's possible," he said with a shrug. "I mean, I'm a

pretty smart guy. I watch a lot of documentaries on TV. Did you know that there is a river in Burma – well, it's not called Burma anymore – but there is a river there with a 60-ton golden bell on the bottom?"

"What?" Lacey asked, her brain nearly melting at the absurdity.

"It's true. Worth millions! It was a religious bell that the Buddhists used and some Portuguese explorer stole it, but it was so heavy it sank his boat."

"What the hell are you rambling about?" The exasperation in Brandy's voice was almost comical. If Lacey weren't wondering the same thing, she might have laughed. "What is Casey doing talking to the goddamn mob?"

On their second pass in front of the casino, Lacey announced, "He's leaving." The traffic moved at a steady, snail-like pace and Lacey crawled to the corner. She turned and slid as close to the curb as she could in a no-parking zone.

Casey slipped inside and slammed the door behind him. "I'm hungry. Is anyone else hungry?"

"What was that all about? I thought you were going inside to find Cynthia's folks." Brandy barked from the back seat. "What are you doing talking to Roman Maretti?"

"I could really go for a steak," Brent announced.

"You can always go for a steak!" Lacey shouted.

"Steak sounds good to me. How about the Hard Rock? They have a great steak there."

In the back seat, Brandy's brows formed a V and she narrowed her eyes. Her upper lip curled slightly. She was obviously just as confused as Lacey. "They aren't going to tell us anything until we feed them."

Leaning back into the folds of the backseat, Brandy shrugged. "Whatever. I give up. The Hard Rock it is, then."

Twenty minutes later, they were sitting in a booth inside the Hard Rock Cafe. Casey ordered a beer for himself and Brent and Lacey ordered a soft drink. "Do you want something a bit stronger?" she asked Brandy, who still wore a crease in her brow.

"No. Dr. Pepper is fine."

When the waitress left, Lacey turned her attention to her twin. "Now. Do you want to tell us what the hell is going on?"

"Do you remember when Brent and I came to Vegas to find the guys that ran you off the road?"

Lacey's chest suddenly felt like it carried a thousand-pound weight. The crushing sensation took her breath away for only a second before she swallowed against the expectation of panic and nodded. "Yeah. I remember."

"Well, we didn't find him all by ourselves. I mean, we're good, but we're not that good." Casey's eyes sparkled with a grin. "No, we called up an old Black Ops buddy of mine who had a few connections, and all that that implies."

"Roman?" Brandy asked.

"Roman," Brent confirmed.

"Are you telling me that Roman Maretti is an old Army friend?" Lacey shook her head.

"That's exactly what I'm telling you." Casey grabbed a Keno card from a pocket attached to the wall and started circling random numbers.

"And?" Lacey urged.

"What?" Casey looked up from the card.

"What did you talk to him about! Jesus, Casey. You're killing me!"

"Oh, that. I just mentioned I was in town having a little fun and thought I'd say hello and shit. He was waiting for his girlfriend to get off work, so I didn't want to keep him."

"That's it?" Brandy ran a hand through her hair. "That's all?"

"We made plans to get together at his place later tonight. He's having a little party and we're all invited."

"I seriously doubt that. The Maretti family and I have never gotten along."

"Oh, he doesn't know who I'm here with. He just said to bring my friends. So technically, we're all invited."

"There is no way I'm going to a party at the Maretti mansion. You're out of your skull."

"Suit yourself," Casey quipped. "Oh, and I forgot to mention it, but I also slipped inside the casino, found the parental units playing Blackjack, and tucked a mic into the old broad's handbag."

"Now what?" Brandy asked.

"We pay a visit to your house."

Brandy stepped out of the shower, drying herself with a plush, lavender towel before wrapping up in her favorite terry robe. In the corner of her room, Lacey sat in the old overstuffed chair beneath the window and looked at something, or nothing, outside. The waning twilight made her profile glow with a golden hue that complimented her complexion. She was already dressed in a stunning, shimmering red gown, ready for the party at the Maretti house on the outskirts of Las Vegas.

After they'd left the restaurant, they'd gone directly to Mission Hills. Parked down the street, across from the sixteenth tee, they'd waited for Casey. It had taken him forty-three minutes to sneak into the gated neighborhood, in broad daylight no less, place wireless cameras in key areas of the house, and return to the car. He'd tapped an app on his smart phone and a second later the screen revealed images of Cynthia's kitchen, bedroom, master bath, garage, and the great room. He'd been sitting in front of a laptop and a miniature satellite receiver in the dining room of the Rocking T from the moment they'd arrived. Juanita had practically had a fit when he didn't bother with a tablecloth and placed his equipment on the antique wood surface. She'd bustled around finding doilies, which made his rather manly set-up look like something out of a cozy mystery novel.

Brandy and Lacey had spent two hours of the time since arguing about whether Lacey should go to the party. Lacey insisted it was an opportunity to discover the connection between Cynthia's parents and the Maretti family, other than the debt, of course. Brandy insisted it was a good way to get killed.

She'd gotten her way, as Brandy suspected she often did. Brandy still didn't think it was a good idea to show up at the home of a crime family with an ax to grind, but she wasn't letting Lacey walk into the bear cave without her.

"It's so beautiful here," Lacey whispered.

It was the first time Lacey had seen the ranch.

Brent had collapsed in a guest room and, as far as she knew, was still sleeping.

When they arrived, Lacey had wandered directly to the corral by the barn and leaned against the fence. Two of the horses had joined her there and nudged her with their snouts until she'd pet them gently on their foreheads.

Standing in the middle of her bedroom, just drinking in everything about the woman she loved, Brandy replied, "You're beautiful here."

Lacey smiled. "I didn't realize how much I missed home until we got there. And I had no idea that this place would feel so much like..."

"Like what?"

"Like home." Lacey turned to look at Brandy. The stain on her cheeks was endearing and authentic and lovely.

"It's yours. If it makes you look like that, makes you look at me like that, then it's all yours."

"Don't talk like that. You're going to get out of this mess. I just know it, and--"

"That's not what I meant. I didn't mean that if I go away, you can have the ranch. I mean, I want you to be here with me. I want you to look like you look right now for the rest of our lives."

Lacey turned back to the view and the peaceful calm that filled Brandy was both visible and palpable. But they had to get through tonight to get to the peace on the other side.

"You're still sure about this?" Brandy asked.

Without turning her gaze away from the desert landscape, Lacey nodded.

"Alright then. We're all in."

She reached into her closet and withdrew a pair of black slacks and a white tuxedo shirt. From one of the built-in drawers, she pulled out a pair of boxers and a fresh bra.

"You're coming with us?"

"I'm not letting you go in there alone."

"My brothers will be there. If you're worried--"

"I'm worried about you. I'm going because I can't stand the thought of letting you go in there without me to protect you."

"That's very chivalrous of you, Sir Brandy, but I can take care of myself."

"I know that. You've proven it to me, but this time, I'm going with you. You don't have anything to hide from me, and I sure as hell don't have anything to hide from you. We're in this together, now. And I will always be there for you."

Lacey pulled at the high collar of her cocktail dress. She'd picked it up downtown right after they'd left Mission Hills because even if she'd felt like stopping by her condo, which she hadn't, she didn't have anything suitable for an evening get-together with the mob. She balanced on her four-inch patent leather heels as she descended the stairs into the dining room. Casey had already dressed in the Armani suit he'd purchased at the same outlet where she'd bought her dress. Brent sat beside him at the table in a black, western style suit with a cutaway waistline on the jacket and black jeans.

The last time she'd seen him so decked out had been at Brad's wedding. She hid a shiver.

"What are they doing?" she asked, nodding at the computer screen.

"Not much. They're back at the house now. Apparently, they'd tried to get a meeting with Maretti Sr. at the casino, but nobody would let them in. The old lady lost a few hundred dollars at the tables and they went home. It's a live feed now, but they're just watching television."

"Sound like Must-See-TV, to me."

Lacey turned at the sound of Brandy's voice. She stood in the entrance to the dining room looking every bit the elegant woman of means in a slender, black tuxedo, a diamond necklace and makeup so subtle it was barely there. Diamond studs in her earlobes caught the light from the chandelier and sparkled. She carried a small, black leather clutch under one arm and a single rose in her other hand.

"For you," she whispered, handing the rose to Lacey. "You look amazing."

"So do you," Lacey replied.

Lacey had often struggled with what it meant to be a lesbian, mostly because she didn't look like one, whatever that meant. She liked bling. She liked dresses and high heels and she used to like makeup, before the accident. She liked flowers and chick flicks and perfume. She had always been attracted to butch women who carried themselves with a certain confidence. That confidence she'd always equated with the male side of the binary code that delineated the world into the femme and the masculine. The society in which she'd been raised had been defined by that split. Her own sister was more like a father figure to her, at least in her own tiny mind. At one point, she'd even asked herself whether she really was a lesbian if she was attracted to the maleness of butch women.

All of those doubts fell out of her mind at that moment. Looking at Brandy through the eyes of a woman who loved women and realizing that Brandy was all woman crushed every one of those doubts. It disintegrated every stereotype she'd ever known. Brandy might be butch. She might ride a Harley and wear clothes that spoke as much to her masculinity as they did to her androgyny, but she was a woman under it all. And Lacey loved her.

Casey stood and cleared his throat.

Lacey took the flower and held it to her nose, inhaling the fresh scent as she turned to face her brother.

He placed a small device into his ear and adjusted something on the laptop before closing the main window. The window behind it revealed the surveillance footage of Frank, just before he went into Brandy's office to plant the gun. She'd given it to Casey to analyze as soon as he'd set up his makeshift HQ. "Did you find anything on that recording?"

"Nothing much. I wanted to dig a little deeper, though. Like.... Right here..." he said as he rewound the video slightly. "He's looking at something over the edge of the catwalk. He's not glancing, he's really looking hard at something. Hang on a second."

Lacey tried to follow where Frank may have placed his attention in that moment, but the camera didn't pick up the lower angle. She looked into the huge, wall-sized mirror behind him. That image picked up the reflections in the mirror over the main doors, which reflected more of the casino floor. "Right there!" she yelled when she saw it. It was like one of those stupid memes on Facebook where there's something odd and obvious at the same time. A snake in leaves or an animal just-barely different in color than the rest of a big blue box. "Do you see it?" She pointed to a reflection of a reflection in the one-way glass of Brandy's office.

"Right here?"

"No. That's Marion. There is no mistaking that hair color or that polyester suit. I'm talking about this guy, right here. That's your friend Roman, isn't it? Why is he hanging around the Touchdown? And why would he be there at exactly the same time Frank is planting the damn gun?"

Casey zoomed more closely using first the mouse, and then the arrow buttons on the keyboard. "It's not a coincidence. See that newspaper?"

Brandy slid beside Lacey, her warmth almost overshadowing the chill running over her flesh. "Yeah? It's a newspaper." Brandy asked, squinting as she bent closer to the image.

"Oh, young Padawan, you have much to learn. That, my dear, is covering a gun."

CHAPTER TWENTY

"What are they doing now?" Brandy sipped a glass of wine as she stood next to Casey at the buffet.

Casey refilled his small, china dish with lobster and shrimp before spooning bright red cocktail sauce on the side. "Still home. Are you going to ask me that every five minutes all night?"

Outside the party, in a driveway that led from the street to the rear of the house by the kitchen, Brent sat in an unmarked van that belonged to Marko's brother. It blended nicely with others that belonged to caterers and the wait-staff. He continued surveillance on Marion and Frank through the wireless equipment. Casey kept tabs on what they were doing as Brent relayed their activities through the flesh-colored earpiece Casey wore. On the way to the party, Casey had outfitted his Armani with a few hidden tricks. He'd quickly sewn handcuff eyes into the hem and waistband of his slacks. He'd placed two hundred-dollar bills wrapped in thin plastic into the soles of his right shoe, and a razor blade in the collar of his shirt. "You frighten me, Casey. You really do."

He'd shrugged. "It's a living."

Lacey approached, having returned from the ladies' room. "They have a bathroom made entirely of mosaic glass tiles. The floor, the ceiling. The works. It's like peeing in Pompeii."

Brandy grinned. "When in Rome."

Lacey rolled her eyes. "How are you doing? Feeling any more comfortable. I mean, our hosts must know you're here by now."

"Maybe. I've only seen one of the brothers so far. Luca, the youngest, is over there with that singer whose face is all over the strip." She pointed to the handsome young man with the gorgeous brunette on his arm.

"Oh, I saw her once. She's really amazing! I didn't know she was dating a mob guy. Who else is here?"

"Taking notes for future freelance work?" Casey quipped around a mouthful of caviar.

"No. Just curious," Lacey answered with a raised eyebrow.

"So far, I've seen the judge who granted my bail, which doesn't exactly fill me with confidence. I ran into my old doctor a few minutes ago, and I've seen a couple of call girls I've rousted from the Touchdown on more than one occasion."

"No, I mean celebrities."

"You do understand that we're in the home of a mass murderer, drug dealer, pimp, and all-around-racketeer, right?" Brandy craned her neck to study the faces of the other guests. Casey walked away, heading for the front door. "Where are you going?"

"Nowhere. I'll be back in a second. It's too noisy in here and I think something is going on at the house."

"Like what?"

"I don't know. I'll be back in a minute."

After he left, Brandy continued to scan the faces in the crowd. She didn't recognize anyone new for several moments. Then, she pulled a sudden frown as she nudged Lacey with her elbow. "Well, that's not someone I expected to see."

Lacey followed Brandy's gaze. "Chandra? What's your lawyer doing here?"

As though their combined vision reached out and tapped Chandra on the shoulder, the attorney turned her head in their direction. Her eyes widened as Brandy lifted her glass in a mock salute and nodded. Chandra's full lips parted into a nervous grin as she held up a single index finger as an indication that she'd be with them in a second. The dim lighting reflected of the golden highlights of her corkscrew curls as she nodded at her date.

"She seems a little nervous, doesn't she? I wonder why? I mean, if there's a judge here, then why would she be worried about being seen?"

"I have no ide... wait a minute. Is she standing next to Sal Crenshaw?"

"Would you look at that..."

Sal Crenshaw looked over her shoulder and spotted Brandy. Brows pulled together, she leaned over to whisper something in Chandra's ear. A moment later, Chandra made her way around several party-goers to the buffet table.

"I didn't expect to see you here, Brandy," she stated in a

flat voice that Brandy had never heard before. Or perhaps she had, earlier that day in the courtroom. Steady as a rock. As impassive as a steam engine. Then she nodded at Lacey. "Lacey. It's good to see you again."

"Likewise," Lacey answered.

"I didn't expect to see you here, either, Chandra. Are you on a date with the woman who is trying to send me to prison for the rest of my life? Not that it's any of my business, but I think it's pretty much my business."

"It's not what it looks like. Just don't make a big deal about it and I'll explain everything tomorrow."

"It's not what it looks like, but it needs explaining. Hmm. I'm intrigued."

"It's nothing. Really. But you need to leave, like right now."

"I don't think so." Heat scaled Brandy's entire body as if she were a burning building engulfed in angry flames. The muscles in her legs stiffened and her feet rooted to the floor. "I'm not going anywhere until I get some answers."

"Answers? What the hell are you talking about, Brandy. You have no idea what's going on here. You don't need answers until you know what questions to even ask me. Now, go home. I'll call you tomorrow morning."

Lacey shifted her weight in Chandra's direction. "Is it ethical for you to date opposing counsel? Isn't that like some massive conflict of interest?"

Chandra bristled. "Actually, no, it's not. I have to get back now."

"To your date. Right. No problem. Enjoy the festivities."

"Brandy, don't be like that. I would never do anything

to put you in jeopardy. She called me and needed someone to come to this thing with her. I just happened to be available. It's okay. Trust me."

"I thought I could trust you. I've always trusted you, but then I see you here, with her? I don't know."

"I know it looks bad. I'll talk to you tomorrow, okay?"

"Sure."

Chandra's brow furrowed as she returned to Sal in the center of the room. They spoke for a moment, their heads bent as the exchange grew slightly heated. In a huff, Chandra pushed Sal's hand from her shoulder and stormed away. Sal glared at Brandy and Lacey before following her.

"Is Casey going to talk to Roman or what?"

"He's not here, apparently. At least, we haven't seen him."

"It's his daughter's eighteenth birthday. You'd think he'd show up. And I have to wonder if it's tacky to have a big birthday party like this the day after your brother's funeral?"

"I need some air. Join me for a stroll around the pool?" Brandy put down her wine glass and offered Lacey her elbow.

"I'd love to."

They left the room through a large opening nearly fifteen feet wide that led to a multilevel patio. On the bottom level, a natural pool collected water from an impressive man-made waterfall surrounded with layers of rocks and ferns. Behind the pool, a portico covered a four-piece steel drum band that hammered out a tinkling and fast-paced island tune. The backyard held as many people as the interior, but they were spread into small conversation groups that didn't come close to filling the grounds.

"I'm glad you came tonight. Even if it wasn't the smartest thing in the world, I'm glad you're here." Lacey squeezed Brandy's arm as she spoke.

Bolts of passion jolted Brandy. "I'm not exactly sure what we're doing here. We know Roman was there when Frank planted the gun. We know he did it under duress."

"He's just looking for a few answers, that's all. Cynthia's parents don't exactly strike me as criminal masterminds. Are you glad to know they may not have had a choice? About framing you with the gun, I mean."

Was she? Brandy wasn't sure. She'd never been close to Marion, and Frank was a hard nut to crack. She didn't dislike him, but they weren't exactly loving relations, either. "For Cynthia's sake, I am. But the end result is the same. That video doesn't show him planting the gun. It just shows him going into and out of my office, with a key provided by his dead daughter. He didn't even break in."

Casey hurried toward them from the side of the house, his jaw set in a grimace. A line of consternation had formed on his forehead. When he reached them, he whispered, "It's time to go."

"What? I thought you were going to meet with Roman and try to figure out what's been going on." Lacey must have had the same sense of dread as Brandy as she held Brandy's arm in a death-like grip.

"No time for questions. We're leaving. Now."

He took each of them by an elbow and lead them in the direction of the van. As soon as they boarded, Brent pulled away from the curb and exited the grounds as though nothing were wrong. No screeching tires. No squealing brakes.

When they reached the main road, he laid on the gas, throwing Lacey back into Brandy's chest where they sat on the floor of the cargo compartment. "What the hell, Brent?"

Casey stood, half bent, in front of them and pulled off his jacket. "Your in-laws are dead."

Brandy couldn't breathe. Dead? "What the hell happened?"

"A couple of goons broke into the house, and without so much as a by-your-leave, shot them both. Two hits each, head and chest. They weren't taking any chances."

If her anger had turned her into a towering inferno, this news turned her into an ice pillar. Cold like she'd never experienced froze her spine and sent tendrils of panic into her legs. She wrapped Lacey tight against her. "What's going on?"

The van made a sharp right before fishtailing wildly. Brandy guarded Lacey from impacting the sides of the van by holding her tightly to her chest. The van turned again and finally began to slow down.

"Hold on, girls. It's about to get real," Brent called from the cab.

The van came to a quick, jolting stop on the side of the road.

"Why are we stopping?" Lacey pressed herself into Brandy's embrace. She stamped down her rising fear. Fear wouldn't do her much good now, she reasoned. She could break down later. For now, Brandy needed her.

"We've got company." Casey focused his attention out the back window as the interior of the van captured the rays of approaching headlights. Light poured in from the front of the van, as well.

"That's bad, right?" she asked.

"Could be. Might not be. Wait here." He escaped the van through the passenger door, slamming it behind him like a hammer on an anvil.

Muffled voices came from outside. Too far away to make out. A second later, the side of the van slid open. Casey reappeared. "You can come out now."

Lacey, Brandy, and Brent joined Casey on the side of the road and followed him to the rear of the van. Chandra and Sal Crenshaw stood in front of a luxury sedan. The sequins on Chandra's formal gown created a halo of star-like reflections in the dark. Overhead, open sky, far from the light pollution of the resort strip, revealed millions of twinkling, dancing lights.

"Chandra?" Brandy stopped a few paces shy of her attorney.

"You weren't supposed to get out of jail, Brandy." Chandra's head canted to one side and her shoulders slumped slightly. "We did everything we could keep you inside, but the judge wouldn't listen. I've never before been to a bail hearing where both the prosecutor and the defense agreed to keep an accused locked up and the judge insisted that bail be granted. I realized why when I saw him at the party tonight."

"I... I don't understand." Movement in the corner of

her eye caused Lacey to turn. Three figures in silhouette approached from the front end of the van. Lacey couldn't think. She wanted to rail and scream and punch something as hard as she could. Chandra had been working with the other side the whole time? What was it about people who turned their backs on goodness, turning their entire countenance to the dark side of the goddamn force? This couldn't be happening.

And why was Casey so completely okay with it?

"Roman is cleaning house." Sal Crenshaw took a step forward, as though she were taking center stage. "We ran a paternity test on Cynthia's fetus. We got a hit on a DNA profile already in the system."

"Carlos, right?" Lacey asked, her whole body jumping at the conclusion she'd been right all along. "Miller killed his wife because she was having an affair and risking their long-con with Brandy. Then Carlos killed Miller."

"No." Chandra straightened. "Not Carlos."

"The hit was only a partial. It showed a paternal link to Maretti, Sr. He's the proud grandfather, but further investigation revealed something we didn't expect. The post-mortem revealed that Carlos Maretti was transgender, female to male, pre-op. He couldn't have fathered a child."

Casey shook his head. "That's why he didn't join the service with his brother. I always wondered about that. When we graduated from advanced training, Carlos said he'd wished he could be right there with us. When I asked him why he didn't, he just shrugged. That was years ago. He couldn't have been more than twenty years old at the time."

"So, who was the father?" Brandy asked, her voice flat and hollow like she'd just discovered every lie ever told.

"Roman." A voice came from behind her and Lacey turned. Lynda Fairchild shifted long bangs out of her eyes as she spoke. "That's our best guess. We'll know a little more tomorrow when the test results come back. While you ladies were sipping champagne with every would-be mobster in three counties, we managed to collect a little DNA sample from Roman's private bathroom. No warrant, of course, but it's something." To Sal, she nodded and said, "Hey, Counselor, look what I found in plain sight in a public place. Roman Maretti's DNA." She nodded at the woman to her right.

The woman standing beside her handed a bulging envelope to Sal. Sal took it and nodded her thanks. "Imagine that."

"Roy?" Brandy interjected as she leaned against the back of the van. "Am I missing something?"

"Hey babe. Nice to see you outta stripes."

"Roy works for us," Sal explained. "She was inside as a kind of protection detail for you. If Roman is cleaning house, then anyone who has any information, or even an inkling of what he's been up to, is fair game as far as he's concerned."

Lacey shook her head. "Wait. So, Cynthia was having an affair with Roman? Not Carlos?"

Sal answered, "No. We have a witness all locked up in a safe-house. That was the tipping for all of this. According to her, she was forced to help Roman transport Cynthia's body to the Mission Hills house the night she was murdered.

Miller was killed at the same time, but his body was left on the boat. We're not sure why, and neither is she."

"I'm confused. My head hurts." Lacey leaned against Brandy.

"You and me both," Brandy whispered in her ear.

"The witness says that Roman raped Cynthia. Not only when she was murdered, but months earlier. He'd claimed to be curing her; you know how it goes.

"Anyway, she only became acquainted with the family when she was trying to get her mother out of trouble with them. Maretti, Sr. wouldn't budge on the debt, so given her past in the confidence game, she focused on Carlos in an attempt to gain sway with the old man. She didn't love Carlos any more than she loved Brandy." Sal paused before she continued, "Sorry, Brandy."

"It's okay," Brandy replied, squeezing Lacey's shoulders. "I'm over it."

Sal took a breath, her broad shoulders rising as she stretched out some unseen ache. "We think Roman killed Cynthia when he discovered the fact she was pregnant. No greater evidence in the world than implanted DNA, right? Miller just happened to be in the wrong place at the wrong time."

"Right," offered Lynda. "And then, Roman offered Marion and Frank a way out of their debt if they helped to frame, you, Brandy. When they filed the wrongful death suit, Roman realized they were greedier than he'd thought. The idea of a long, drawn-out trial and investigation wasn't something he'd be willing to risk. He took care of them tonight. They won't be testifying against him, or anybody else."

Brent asked, "How do you know about that? I mean...

um... did something happen to Marion and Frank?"

"Jesus, Brent. Don't ever go into black ops," Casey said, shaking his head. "They wired the place, too. Yes?"

"Not long before you did." Lynda ran her gaze over Casey's tall, slender build and said, "You look amazing on TV."

"Thanks," Casey replied, looking suddenly sheepish, as though he should have known the place had already been worked over. "Your people did a great job. The only thing I noticed was in-house security. Or so I thought."

Brandy stood to her full height. "Can we please try to stay on task here? Some of our futures depend on it. What about Carlos? Was it suicide?"

"It's hard to tell. He had a couple of strikes against him," Georgie Beck, who'd arrived with Lynda, spoke in a deep tenor.

Brandy shifted her weight. "Lacey and I overheard him talking to his uncle about something a family member had done. He was threatening to take care of the matter himself, and if that didn't work, he'd go to the cops. That wasn't long at all before he supposedly killed himself."

Chandra and Sal exchanged a pointed look. Sal stated, "Carlos was turning. He called the FBI and was going to sing like the proverbial canary on the whole family. He was that pissed that Roman had killed the love of his life."

Chandra said, "That's why we had you arrested as soon as we realized where you were. Our witness came in within hours of Carlos' death. She's going to testify against Roman and the entire family. That's why the FBI was there." She stepped forward to stand directly in front of Brandy and

Lacey. "I'm sorry I couldn't tell you. We didn't want to put you in any more danger than you already were."

"You thought I'd be better off in jail? Doesn't the mob have people on the inside?"

Roy patted Brandy on the back. "I wouldn't have let anything happen to you."

Brandy nodded.

"Name's Special Agent Royale Smithfield. I had your back the whole time."

A chuckle rumbled in Brandy's chest and tickled Lacey's back. "Brilliant. I never would have guessed."

"So, what do we do now?"

Brent, who had leaned silently on the grill of the van until now, stood to his full height. "We nail that son of a bitch to the wall."

"I don't like the idea of being bait. I'm not too proud to admit that much. But if this is the only way to flush him out, then I guess I'm in." Brandy sat on a beat-up couch in a tiny trailer house in the Prim Valley.

When they'd arrived in the early hours of the morning, three days ago, she had harbored doubts about the safety of the so-called safe house. She would have thought the bad guys would need more than a can opener to get inside in order for a house to be truly safe. Once Casey explained that two trailers on either side were actually government-owned and housed an FBI security team, that Fairchild's Enforcers had taken up residence in the house across the street, and that he would personally be watching their every move, she felt a little better.

The girl from the marina, Marcia, sat at a card table near the kitchen, picking at a breakfast of runny eggs and burned toast. "You're already a target, you know," she whispered. "Using you as bait is just a matter of geography. You'll be in danger out there, instead of in here." She tossed her plastic fork down and dropped her forehead into her hands. "You can't stop him. He's going to kill every one of us."

"Aren't you just ray of sunshine covered in candy glitter?" Casey replied.

"You don't know him like I do. He's sadistic. Evil. The way he treated Carlos, his whole life? It was horrifying. Used to call him faggot all the time. Refused to call him by male pronouns, too. Just to be mean."

"Homophobia isn't a crime." Casey shrugged. "It makes him an asshole. Killing people makes him a criminal."

"Fuck you!" Marcia stood so quickly her folding chair collapsed onto itself. "Carlos wasn't gay! He was trans. There's a huge difference, you asshole."

"Fine. Sorry," Casey replied, holding both of his hands up in a gesture of surrender that Brandy suspected wouldn't begin to stop the dervish brewing in the small woman's muscles. After a few seconds, she shoved the table out of the way and tried to march out the front door.

Lynda stood in her way and pointed to the sofa. Without a word, Marcia turned, stalked to the couch, and heaved herself into the corner.

Casey turned back to Brandy. "We'll have eyes on you

the whole time. Ears, too. All you have to do is show up. We'll take care of the rest."

"What makes you think he's going to track me down? If we're so safe here, how will he know where to find me?" Her throat closed and the words sounded like they were coming from someone else's mouth. Could she really do this?

"I'm going to tell him," Marcia answered, her voice tight as though she might cry at any moment.

"Well, that's one way to do it. And how are we going to manage that?" Lacey came out of the kitchen wearing a pair of jeans she'd borrowed from Marcia. Everything about her screamed, "Professional." Her perfect hair, even after three days without her curling iron. Her perfect nails. Her perfect posture. To see her in a pair of ripped levis covered in anarchy-themed patches and tattoo-style artwork drawn in black Sharpie marker was... intoxicating. The black, ribbed t-shirt accentuated every curve of her upper torso like a second skin.

She licked her fingers before she spoke again. "Of course, we'll know when he decides to move, right? Lynda was in his house. In his bathroom. I'm pretty sure they're listening to everything Roman is doing in one of the other trailers."

Casey grinned. "I made a trip upstairs, too. After the gifts I left in that house, they're listening to the Maretti family on the moon."

A resigned sigh formed in Brandy's lungs and she blew it out with the last of her reservations. "Alright then. When?"

Lynda checked her iPhone and grinned. "How about right now?" She pulled a small, black flip phone from her back pocket and handed it to Marcia. "Just got the go ahead from Sal."

CHAPTER TWENTY-ONE

Brandy paced in her living room. Back and forth in front of the large bay window. She expected to die at any moment and her blood surged through her veins in a fraudulent attempt to keep her alive.

She must be insane.

She'd sent Juanita away. Juanita had complained at first, and then finally accepted a few days in Laughlin as a bonus for all her hard work. Marko had figured out something big was going to happen and insisted that he stay to be a part of it. At this moment, he and a few of the ranch hands were keeping an eye on the Western edge of the property where a road passed through the federal lands.

Lynda and her Enforcers, the nickname taken by the four bounty hunters in her employ, watched the South gate. Casey and Brent were in the house, hidden in the interior, where no-one looking in from the outside would know they were there.

When Roman Maretti and his goons made it onto the property to take care of the last witnesses to his crimes, he would have no reason to believe that she and Lacey weren't completely alone. According to Casey's surveillance, he was on his way.

Stopping gradually, Brandy focused on Lacey. She sat on the edge of the long, leather sofa, her knees dancing in a staccato rhythm. "Are you okay?"

"So far, so good. I mean, what's the worst thing that could happen?" She paused. "Don't answer that."

"They won't let it get that far. You heard Sal, right? Just because her own bosses weren't willing to look past the obvious, doesn't mean that she isn't on our side. The Feds, too."

A crash rang through the front windows as a hail of bullets shattered the glass. They imbedded in the wall behind them. Wood flew in every direction. "Get down!" Brandy grabbed Lacey, throwing her to the floor before they crawled into the interior hallway. They leaned against the opposing wall, hidden behind several thicknesses of wood Casey and Brent had installed from the barn. The boards shook as more bullets came through the interior wall, stopping only when they reached the second planks.

Lacey stuttered, "I guess... I think... I mean, it w-worked, right?"

"One more item off the bucket list. Human bait." Brandy didn't feel like laughing. Every part of her body screamed to run.

She fingered the gun in her waistband. She'd nearly forgotten it was there. Pulling it free, she checked the chamber and pulled back the slider. She'd never shot at anything but a target. She didn't hunt. She had never been in the military.

The barrage ceased and heavy foot falls echoed on the porch. Someone kicked at the front door. It wouldn't hold for long given that it probably hung with about a thousand holes in it.

Casey and Brent crawled in from the kitchen where they had been hiding in the butler's pantry. "You started without us? How rude." Casey whispered. "Wait here. I'm going to introduce myself to our guests."

"He's such a gentleman," Brent interjected with a wink.

Brandy could only nod. She'd always believed she could handle something like this. That she was courageous. Strong. Lacey gripped her arm with fingers that felt like steel bands.

"Don't leave me," she begged. "Please don't leave me alone."

"I'm here, baby. I'm not going anywhere."

There it was. That single reason she needed to be strong. To be courageous. The love she'd found with Lacey was worth more than a house full of bullet holes. It was worth more than her own life. Fear turned to something good; something that would keep her vigilant. Something that would protect her rather than steal from her spirit.

She shifted her legs as Brent followed Casey in the direction of the living room. The front door crashed open just as the boys reached the arched opening, stood, and opened fire.

She turned quickly as she ducked out of pure instinct from the battery of bullets coming from the living room. Even though she knew they couldn't get through the wall.

Everything seemed to happen at once. Shots fired.

Boards vibrating with the impact. Smoke filled the air and burned her lungs as she took shallow, painful breaths. Without warning, something heavy pulled on her arm.

"Lacey!" she screamed as someone came up from behind and pulled Lacey away.

He was an enormous man with thick, black hair and eyes that seemed to bore through her. He grimaced as he placed the barrel of a gun to Lacey's head. "We're walking out of here, me and her. Call 'em off."

Brandy couldn't breathe.

"Call 'em off!" the man repeated, his voice bellowing across time and space.

A heavy thump shook the floorboards. Brandy couldn't be sure if it was a body hitting the floor in the living room, or her gun hitting the floor beside her leg. She raised both hands in an effort to calm the attacker and to show him she was now unarmed. "Don't do this. Please, don't do this."

"I told Roman it was a fuckin' trap. He don't listen to nobody."

Casey turned the corner, his gun pointed directly at the man's head. At Lacey's head. "Let her go."

"Forget about it. She's my ticket outta here."

The thunder of hoof beats approached from the back of the house. Marko and his men were back. Soon, Lynda and the girls would be here, too.

"You're outnumbered," Brandy insisted. "You'll never get away."

"You're gonna make sure I get away." He licked his thick lips as beads of sweat dotted his overgrown brow. Slowly, he stood, taking Lacey with him. Her legs scrambled for purchase.

Brandy followed, rising to stand on equal footing.

He was not taking her out of here; not so long as there was still air in her lungs.

"Where's Roman now?" she asked, stalling for time while she struggled desperately for any hint of a plan.

"What? You thought he'd come here personal like?" He took a step backward, toward the kitchen door.

"Sure. He likes to get his hands dirty, right? A regular hit man."

Lacey whimpered as the gunman increased the pressure of the barrel against her forehead.

"Not this time."

"But he did kill Cynthia, right? And her husband?"

The man nodded.

"And her parents?"

"No. He sent us in for that. He stayed in the fuckin' car."

"What about Carlos, Jr.?"

The man fell silent. "That was something else. That was business."

The Monkees theme song rang through the nearly-stagnant air. The mobster frowned, distracted just enough.

Brandy watched herself, as though she were in a movie, dive to the floor and grab her handgun. She rolled onto her back, aimed, and pulled the trigger.

Lacey's retinas burned as a flash of light blinded her.

She squeezed her eyes closed, too late, and braced herself for the impact of a bullet. It didn't come.

In an instant, the gun to her temple vanished and a second shot exploded through the tiny space. Her ears rang with a deafening, high-pitched tone as she dove forward. She landed on Brandy's crumpled form just as that horrible man fell to the floor behind her.

Casey leapt over them, kicked the mobster's gun out of reach and then knelt to take his pulse. He looked over his shoulder and said something Lacey couldn't hear. She couldn't hear anything but that infernal squeal.

Brandy moved beneath her, almost pushing Lacey out of the way. She vanished into the living room, leaving Lacey stunned with her back against the wall.

"Go..... shot... Go, ...ow!" Casey's voice sounded like it was under water. Lacey rubbed her ears to dispel the ringing. When she pulled her fingers away, the fingers of her left hand were covered in blood.

She'd burst an eardrum. Frowning, she shook her head.

Brandy reappeared, her shirt bloody and her eyes as wide as one of Kendra's china dinner plates. They were moist, too. She was crying. She was screaming and crying.

Lacey crawled to the living room, searching the debris that littered the floor. The tall lamp that had stood near the window was on the sofa where Lacey had been sitting only a few minutes earlier. Two of the cushions were on the floor, feathers protruding like soft quills from a malformed porcupine. Brandy knelt in the center of the room.

Brent lay on the floor in front her.

"NO!" Lacey screamed. Her throat burned. As though one word, one thought, were the catalyst for the very rotation of the earth, sound returned to her good ear.

"I can't stop the bleeding!" Brandy panted.

Lynda and two of her bounty hunters rushed into the room. Georgie, the one who had accompanied her that night on the side of the road, opened a huge first aid kit. It opened like a tackle box and she withdrew two individually wrapped gauze pads the size of footballs.

Brandy applied pressure as Georgie placed first one, and then the other, over Brent's injuries.

Brent turned his head to face her. Until that moment, Lacey hadn't realized he was conscious. He smiled; that silly, crooked grin that he wore when he was about to say something stupid funny. "Does this mean I have become a monk?"

Lacey laughed through the tears heating her cheeks.

Lynda took over applying pressure to Brent's arm, allowing Brandy to spin immediately to Lacey. "Are you alright? Oh, God. I thought I was going to lose you." She squeezed Lacey's arms first, then her legs, and then finally pulled her into an embrace that threatened to break her ribs.

"I'm okay. I think I'm okay. What about you?" Lacey broke the embrace and made her own cursory inspection.

"Not a scratch."

That wasn't entirely true. A few droplets of blood had formed above Brandy's left eye where she'd been hit by a piece of shrapnel. Probably wood from the reinforced wall in the hallway. Other than that, she seemed okay.

They were okay.

Casey stomped into the living room with Marko. "Christ Almighty, Bro. I mean it. Never go into black ops."

EPILOGUE

Lacey shifted closer to Brandy where they lay in Lacey's bed in her condo in Las Vegas. After the local police had arrived at the Rocking T, they'd taken reports from everyone, including Sal Crenshaw who arrived on the scene moments before they had. Of course, she'd been on the property the whole time, sitting in a nearby surveillance van with members of the task force assigned to Roman Maretti's investigation. The local cops didn't need to know that though.

A Life Flight helicopter had taken Brent to the hospital where he'd been kept overnight. When she'd spoken to him by phone, he'd insisted that she not visit him. He'd be going home soon and, in the meantime, he was enjoying all of the attention from the nursing staff.

Casey had called Kendra and Michelle, both of whom were livid with them for placing themselves at risk. But thankful everyone was fine.

Lacey lifted her head, looked up at Brandy's sleeping face, and frowned. She wouldn't exactly say that everyone was fine. Brandy had killed a man. Casey had fired too, but he was fairly certain that Brandy's aim had hit its mark.

She'd shot him almost directly between the eyes.

As though she could hear Lacey thinking about her, Brandy stirred. Cracking open one eye, she met Lacey's gaze and a smile curled those beautiful, soft lips. "Hi there, Mrs. Kincaid."

"Hi back, Mrs. Kincaid."

"What are you thinking about?"

"Our wedding night," she laughed.

"Liar." Brandy shifted and pushed herself higher onto her pillows, drawing Lacey with her to curl against her breast. "You're still worried about me."

"I'll always worry about you."

"But not about this. I'm fine. That asshole was going to kill you. I have no reservations about what I did. I'd do it again."

"I think I'll be okay, too."

"They'll catch up with Roman eventually. We don't have to walk around checking our cars before we start them, you know. According to Maretti, Sr., Roman is completely cut off. No money; no assets. When he found out that Roman killed Carlos, he all-but put a hit out on his own son. Roman may be gone, but he's a eunuch. No balls at all. Worse, no money."

The phone on the bedside table rang. Lacey had changed her ring tone to the wedding march yesterday when she and Brandy had married in the chapel at the Paris Hotel. Tomorrow, they were boarding a plane, with Brandy's recently-returned passport in hand, and flying to the actual Paris for a month of R&R. A honeymoon to beat all honeymoons.

Kendra's picture lit up the screen and Lacey accepted the call. "Hey, sis. What's up?"

"Guilty."

"Really?" Lacey closed her eyes and whispered a silent prayer.

"Guilty on all counts. The judge went directly to sentencing. Mac will be eligible for parole in twenty-six years."

"How do you feel about that?" Lacey asked.

A pause filled the line for a few seconds before Kendra replied, "I feel like... we're all going to be okay."

Excerpt

Looking for Trouble

Fairchild's Enforcers
Coming in 2018

Cait hadn't spoken that much about her childhood in a long time. Not that her childhood had been particularly bad, especially after Derek Bartholomew had exited, stage right. She'd grown up with good morals, plenty of food to eat, and a solid roof over her head. A foundation beneath her feet.

But something had always been missing. Something that most of her friends had taken for granted. She'd never even had the chance to be Daddy's Little Girl.

Her memories of her father were few, but those she could recall included a happy-go-lucky smile that never quite reached dark, smoke-grey eyes and a faith that everything would work out. It didn't matter what everything was; it would work out in the end and everything would be fine.

He'd been unrealistic and, even at five years old, she hadn't believed him.

She unlocked the trunk of her car and pulled out her riding jacket. The scent of heated leather wafted from the compartment as she tucked her chaps back into the netted compartment that kept them from sliding across the low-pile, black carpeting.

Slamming the lid closed, she turned to face the Virgin River Casino. Why had she exposed herself to Pam like that? She didn't need to get to know Pam better, and she sure as hell didn't need Pam getting to know her better. She kicked herself all the way back to the table.

"Here ya go," she announced as she handed the jacket to Pam and reclaimed her seat.

"Thanks." Pam slipped her arms into the leather sleeves and inhaled deeply. "I love the smell of leather. I'm assuming you ride, then?"

"Yeah." Pam picked up the dessert menu and pretended to peruse the offerings. That's all you're getting, little missy. Not one more word about me.

"So, Taylor called and I have a name and address for our suspect."

Cait jolted to attention as Pam related her phone call with her forensics guy. "We were half right. We're heading to the right town, but we're looking for a dude, not a chick. Got it."

"Is that your way of saying I was right?" Cait posited, refusing to lift her eyes from the menu. The refusal didn't keep her from catching the slow shake of Pam's head in her peripheral vision.

The server arrived with their breakfast. Cait grabbed

two plastic cups of strawberry jam from the cheap plastic holder and slathered it on her toast.

As she broke the yokes on two over-easy eggs and then cut her steak, Pam turned pensive. "That's what's bugging me."

"That I was right?" Cait bit into her toast.

"No," Pam answered with a half-grin. "No, that the prints came back to a guy. I can't wrap my head around the fact it's not a woman. I was so sure. And I'm not bragging or anything, but I'm not usually wrong about this sort of thing."

"Really?" Cait responded, not bothering to hide the sceptic tone in her voice. "And what makes you an expert in kidnapping?"

"Eight years working for the NCIS. That the Naval Criminal Investi--."

"I know that it means," Cait interrupted, waving a hand through the air to dismiss the explanation. "You were NCIS?"

Pam took a bite of her steak and washed it down with ice water, nodding her head as she swallowed. "Yeah. I cut my teeth on kidnapping, assaults, stalkers."

"Who were you sleeping with?" The words fell from Cait's lips before she could bring them back and she hid a cringe. "I mean, it would strike me as normal for a rookie agent to work petty theft and things like that. You went straight to the majors, it sounds like."

"We were short-handed. It was a couple of years post 9/11, so most of the experienced agents were swiped up by the newly formed Homeland Security Department, either on loan or transferring outright." She shrugged. "That left a veritable smorgasbord of cases assigned to newer agents."

"Lucky you." Impressed, Cait refused to admit it. She'd spent her first years on the force writing tickets to tourists and hookers who couldn't seem to get it their heads that prostitution wasn't legal in Las Vegas. "Where did you train?"

"Quantico. I was going to go in the FBI, but NCIS came up with a better offer."

"They came after you?"

"High test scores. What can I say?"

Cait pushed her remaining toast aside and stretched. "Well, it's a guy's fingerprints, but that doesn't mean you're wrong. Could be an accomplice."

"I suppose. All I know is our next stop is the residence of one Ralph Tucker. With any luck, we'll find Marcia and get this whole wretched business done." She took one last bite of her steak and pushed the plate to the edge of the table, resting her knife and fork on the plate together.

Pam's leg crossed under the table and tapped Cait's calf so gently she almost didn't feel it. Might not have felt it at all if it weren't the tremble that radiated from the spot.

Pam's eyes grew wide for a fraction of a second, but long enough for Cait to realize she had felt it – whatever it was – too. She'd heard plenty of people talk about chemistry; the kind of chemistry that existed between two people. She'd always believed that was a fantasy that people created to explain away their incessant need to share their lives with someone.

Cait didn't need that. Cait didn't need anyone.

You can't run in heels.

This was the first lesson Cait Bartholomew learned, raised on a farm in the buckle of the bible belt. The next lessons were more subtle - know how to hold your liquor and the house always wins.

A professional poker wiz has jumped bail. When Cait is assigned to track the girl down, she runs smack into Pam Roberts, a tough private eye from New York who has a more personal reason to find the missing gambler. She is convinced her ex-lover, Marcia Johnson, has been kidnapped. To get her back alive Pam is forced to work with a beautiful bounty hunder who proves to be more of a distraction than a partner. And when it comes to love, they're both just ... Looking for Trouble.

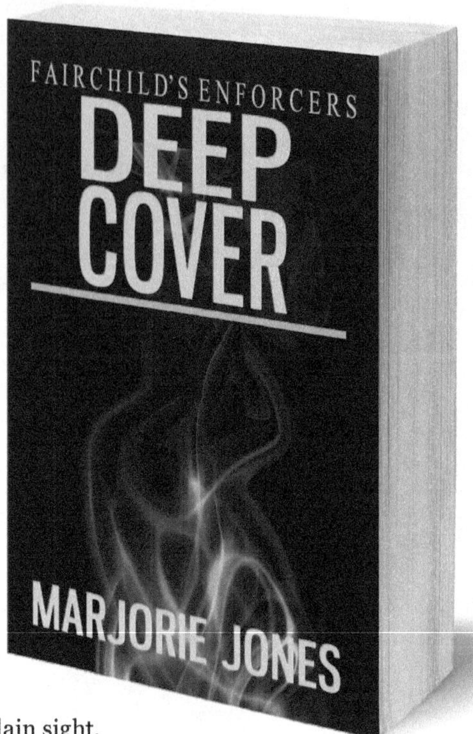

Hide in plain sight.

New Enforcer Mai Bian Chau has been hiding more of her life. First on the streets of San Francisco to avoid her abusive father and later on the streets of Las Vegas while her mother turned tricks to keep them alive. She learned early that being invisible is a good thing. After applying that school of thought to her card playing, she has earned her living at the poker table for years.

When her estranged-lover vanishes without a trace, Bian must blend into the high-stakes world of human trafficking to bring her home safely. Wounds that span more than a generation and a secret family history collide as two women, schooled at keeping themselves hidden, navigate the seedy underbelly of high society to discover that is no such thing as ... Deep Cover.

Looks can be deceiving.

Never think that a blonde in high heels can't roundhouse kick you straight into retirement. Alice Greene loves teaching this particular lesson to anyone who claims she is too pretty to be tough.

With the looks of an angel and a demeanor to match, she is often underestimated and uses that fact to her advantage every chance she gets. Her newest assignment is a little different. Instead of chasing the bad girls who make the mistake of jumping bail on Lynda Fairchild's dime, Alice has been asked to find a missing child.

Kimberly Tucker can't think of anyone other than her bail-enforcement-agent next door neighbor to help when her powerful and wealthy ex-husband steals their seven-year-old daughter from her own bedroom. Temperatures rise as two women who have misjudged each other for years focus their sites on Finding Elizabath.

Everyone is guilty of something.

Forget all the other rules. This is the only one that matters. If you believe that, nobody will ever get the drop on you. You'll be ready for anything. After all, it's worked for Georgie Beck for more than forty years. As second in command of the recovery team for Lynda Fairchild Bail Bonds, she has seen it all - from small-time crooks to celebrities behaving badly to major, underworld criminals. What she's never seen is a completely innocent person... until now.

Tilly McCormick is caught in the wrong place at the wrong time. With more to fear than the law, she makes a run for it almost as soon as her designer shoes hit the Las Vegas asphault.

Always ready to chase, Georgie follows, but even a world-hardened bounty hunter couldn't have expected what she discovers...

On the Hunt.

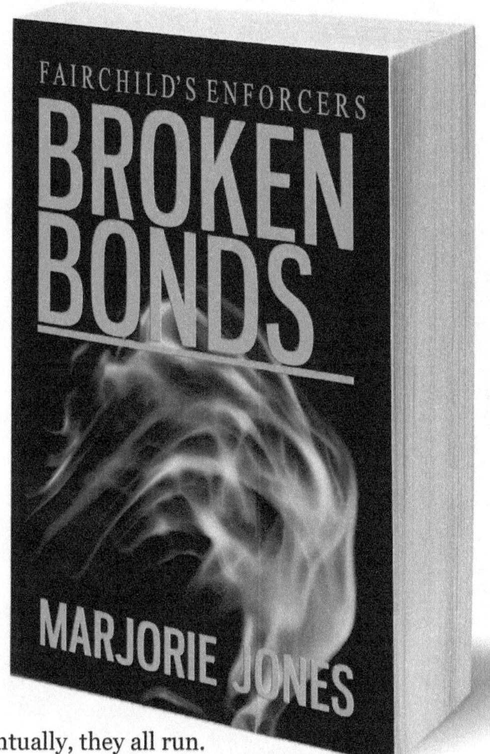

Eventually, they all run.

If there is one thing Bail Recovery Agent Lynda Fairchild has learned in more than twenty years in the industry, it is that simple fact. Raised by a loving father and a community of bikers, Lynda learned how to hold a gun before she learned how to drive a stick. She learned the difference between good and not-so-good. And she learned how to love a woman with all her heart and soul.

Twenty years ago, both were broken by the very girl she thought she'd spend the rest of her life with. When Carmen Bungay comes sliding back into town like hot sex on leather, Lynda is confronted with the sins of both their pasts.

With more than a quarter million dollars on the line, it's time to handle those Broken Bonds.

LGBT FICTION
VIOLENCE BEGETS...
A Gay Young Adult Novel
P. T. DENYS

LGBT FICTION
THE CYCLE
A Violence Begets... Novel
P. T. DENYS

Violence Begets...

After a tragic accident devastates his family, 16-year-old Rick St. James starts his junior year of high school without any friends in a suburb of Salt Lake City, Utah. When he meets Kevin Vincent, he's too distracted by the promise of new friends to see that Kevin has secrets of his own.

Having created an environment where he's feared and admired by his classmates, Kevin finds pleasure in using his good looks and violence to control and manipulate those around him. Secretly, he cruises the gay club scene, turning tricks to earn money so he can party and get high.

As Rick's dad becomes increasingly violent and abusive at home, the two form a surprising and volatile trust. In this battle of wills, their precarious friendship will either keep their lives from blowing up around them or possibly light the fuse that will cause the explosion.

Praise for Violence Begets...

"Without a single doubt, my best and most memorable read. Ever."
~ Nicola Haken - Author of Being Sawyer Knight

"I loved, and I mean absolutely LOVED this novel. I think the only way to run with any description is just... beautiful devastation." ~ Jack L. Pyke - Author of Don't

"Fantabulous! . . . I cringed. I cried. I wondered. Simply great."
~ Dr. Lisa O'Connor, MD Leading US doctor in psychotherapy and HRT for the TG community

"Gripping, tragically beautiful and honestly raw!"
~ Ramen noodle book reviews

"Brutal. Raw. Visceral. Pain. A lot of it. The in between. Oh God, that was like a symphony." ~ SheReadsALot

Indie Artist Press | Brackettville, Texas